1637
THE PACIFIC INITIATIVE

THE RING OF FIRE SERIES

1632 by Eric Flint
1633 by Eric Flint & David Weber
1634: The Baltic War by Eric Flint & David Weber
1634: The Galileo Affair by Eric Flint & Andrew Dennis
1634: The Bavarian Crisis by Eric Flint & Virginia DeMarce
1634: The Ram Rebellion by Eric Flint & Virginia DeMarce et al.
1635: The Cannon Law by Eric Flint & Andrew Dennis
1635: The Dreeson Incident by Eric Flint & Virginia DeMarce
1635: The Eastern Front by Eric Flint
1635: The Papal Stakes by Eric Flint & Charles E. Gannon
1636: The Saxon Uprising by Eric Flint
1636: The Kremlin Games by Eric Flint, Gorg Huff & Paula Goodlett
1636: The Devil's Opera by Eric Flint & David Carrico
1636: Commander Cantrell in the West Indies by Eric Flint & Charles E. Gannon
1636: The Viennese Waltz by Eric Flint, Gorg Huff & Paula Goodlett
1636: The Cardinal Virtues by Eric Flint & Walter Hunt
1635: A Parcel of Rogues by Eric Flint & Andrew Dennis
1636: The Ottoman Onslaught by Eric Flint
1636: Mission to the Mughals by Eric Flint & Griffin Barber
1636: The Vatican Sanction by Eric Flint & Charles E. Gannon
1637: The Volga Rules by Eric Flint, Gorg Huff & Paula Goodlett
1637: The Polish Maelstrom by Eric Flint
1636: The China Venture by Eric Flint & Iver P. Cooper
1636: The Atlantic Encounter by Eric Flint & Walter H. Hunt
1637: No Peace Beyond the Line by Eric Flint & Charles E. Gannon
1637: The Peacock Throne by Eric Flint & Griffin Barber
1637: The Coast of Chaos edited by Eric Flint & Bjorn Hasseler
1637: The Transylvanian Decision by Eric Flint & Robert E. Waters
1638: The Sovereign States by Eric Flint, Gorg Huff & Paula Goodlett
1635: The Weaver's Code by Eric Flint & Jody Lynn Nye
1637: The French Correction by Eric Flint & Walter H. Hunt
1637: The Pacific Initiative by Iver P. Cooper

1635: The Tangled Web by Virginia DeMarce
1635: The Wars for the Rhine by Anette Pedersen
1636: Seas of Fortune by Iver P. Cooper
1636: The Chronicles of Dr. Gribbleflotz by Kerryn Offord & Rick Boatright
1636: Flight of the Nightingale by David Carrico
1636: Calabar's War by Charles E. Gannon & Robert E. Waters
1637: Dr. Gribbleflotz and the Soul of Stoner by Kerryn Offord & Rick Boatright

Time Spike by Eric Flint & Marilyn Kosmatka
The Alexander Inheritance by Eric Flint, Gorg Huff & Paula Goodlett
The Macedonian Hazard by Eric Flint, Gorg Huff & Paula Goodlett
The Crossing by Kevin Ikenberry
An Angel Called Peterbilt by Eric Flint, Gorg Huff & Paula Goodlett

To purchase any of these titles in e-book form, please go to www.baen.com.

1637

THE PACIFIC INITIATIVE

IVER P. COOPER

BAEN

1637: The Pacific Initiative

This is a work of fiction. All the characters and events portrayed in this book are fictional, and any resemblance to real people or incidents is purely coincidental.

A Baen Books Original

Baen Publishing Enterprises
P.O. Box 1403
Riverdale, NY 10471
www.baen.com

ISBN: 978-1-6680-7248-6

Cover designed by Jennie Faries
Maps by Iver P. Cooper

First printing, March 2025

Distributed by Simon & Schuster
1230 Avenue of the Americas
New York, NY 10020

Library of Congress Cataloging-in-Publication Data

Names: Cooper, Iver P., author.
Title: 1637 : the pacific initiative / Iver P. Cooper.
Other titles: Pacific initiative
Description: Riverdale, NY : Baen, 2025. | Series: Ring of fire ; 39
Identifiers: LCCN 2024050626 (print) | LCCN 2024050627 (ebook) | ISBN 9781668072486 (trade paperback) | ISBN 9781964856049 (ebook)
Subjects: LCSH: Seventeenth century—Fiction. | LCGFT: Alternative histories (Fiction) | Science fiction. | Novels.
Classification: LCC PS3603.O582636 A615 2025 (print) | LCC PS3603.O582636 (ebook) | DDC 813/.6—dc23/eng/20241118
LC record available at https://lccn.loc.gov/2024050626
LC ebook record available at https://lccn.loc.gov/2024050627

Printed in the United States of America

10 9 8 7 6 5 4 3 2 1

To my family: my parents Morris and Lillie Cooper,
my wife Lee, and my children Jason and Louise.
I thank Eric Flint for giving me the opportunity to
participate in the development of the 1632 Universe.

Contents

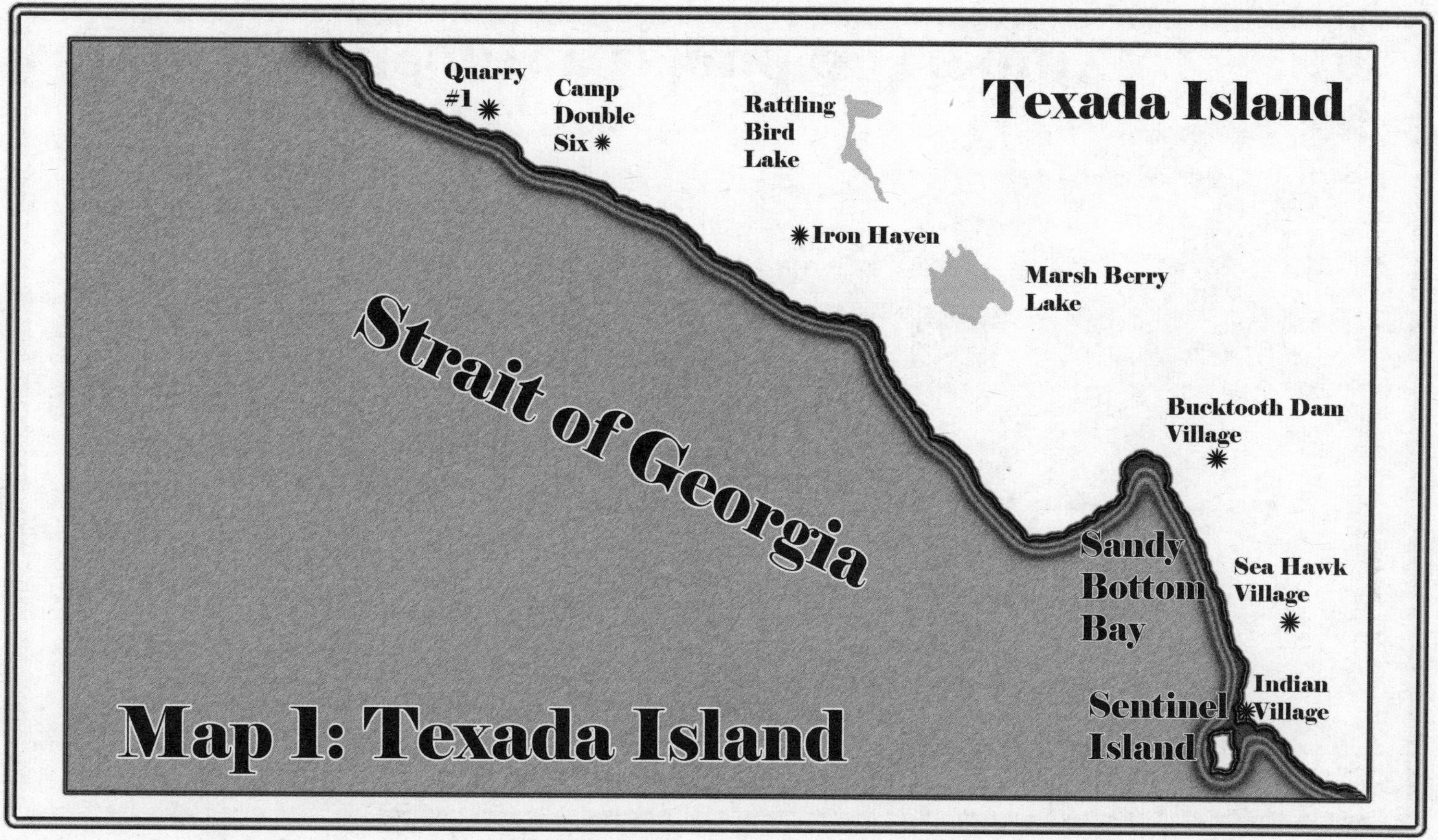
Texada Island
Quarry #1
Camp Double Six
Rattling Bird Lake
Iron Haven
Marsh Berry Lake
Strait of Georgia
Bucktooth Dam Village
Sandy Bottom Bay
Sea Hawk Village
Indian Village
Sentinel Island
Map 1: Texada Island

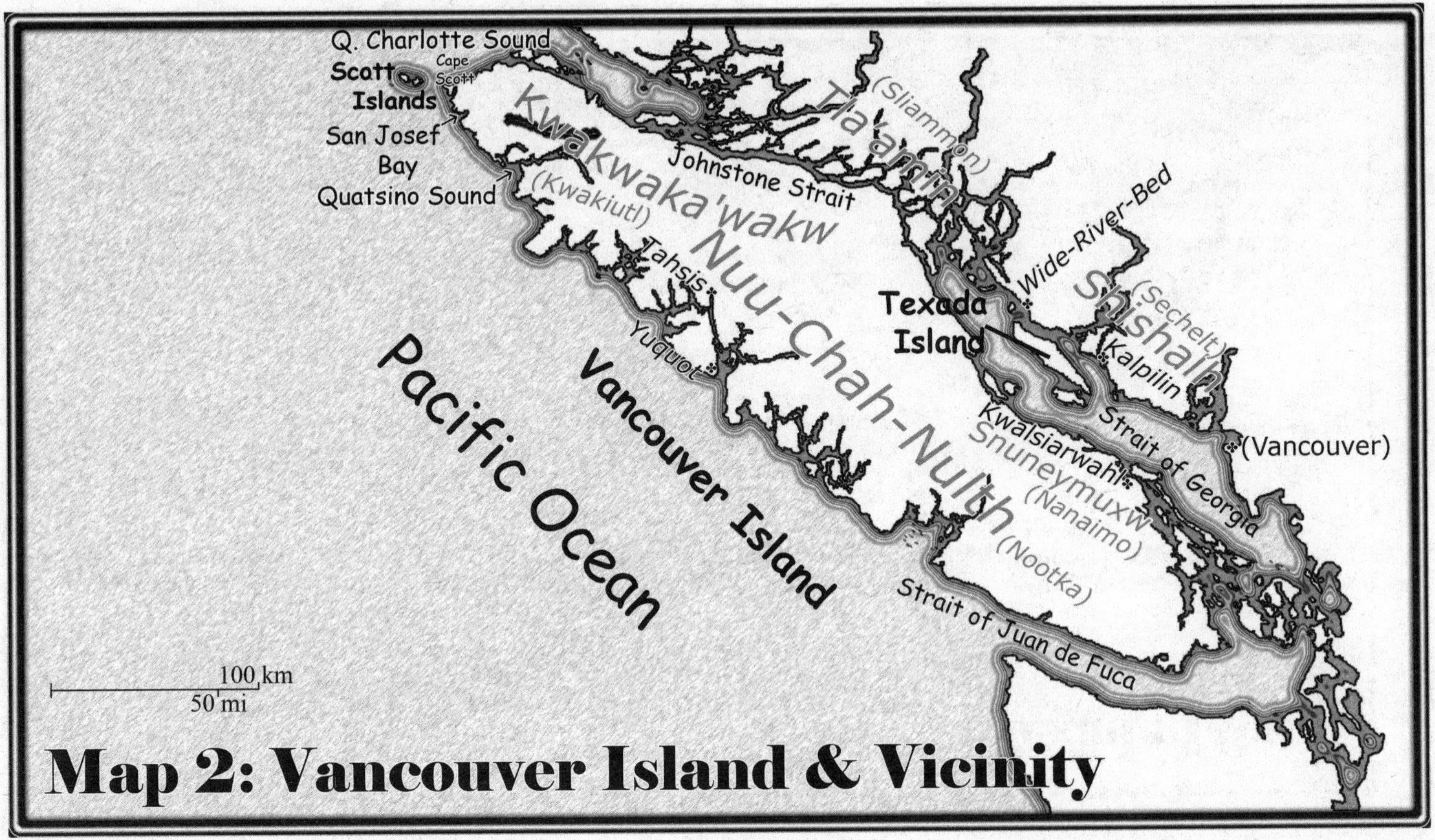
Q. Charlotte Sound
Scott Islands
Cape Scott
San Josef Bay
Quatsino Sound
Kwakwaka'wakw
(Kwakiutl)
Johnstone Strait
Tla'amin
(Sliammon)
Wide-River-Bed
Nuu-Chah-Nulth
Tahsis
Yuquot
Texada Island
Shishalh
(Sechelt)
Kalpilin
(Vancouver)
Strait of Georgia
Kwalsiarwahl
Snuneymuxw
(Nanaimo)
(Nootka)
Strait of Juan de Fuca
Vancouver Island
Pacific Ocean
100 km
50 mi

Map 2: Vancouver Island & Vicinity

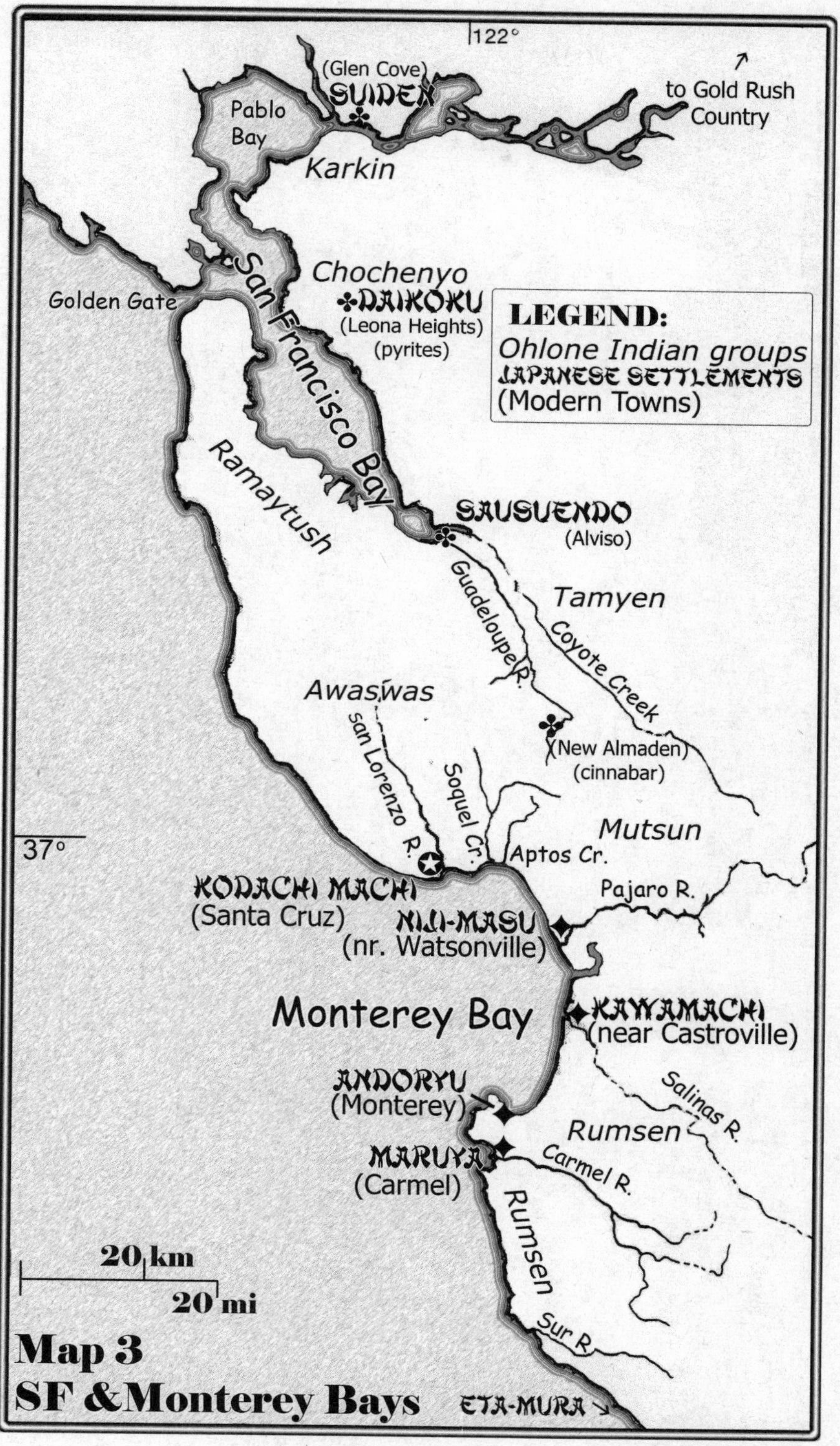
122°
(Glen Cove)
SUIDEN
to Gold Rush Country
Pablo Bay
Karkin
San Francisco Bay
Chochenyo
Golden Gate
DAIKOKU
(Leona Heights)
(pyrites)
LEGEND:
Ohlone Indian groups
JAPANESE SETTLEMENTS
(Modern Towns)
Ramaytush
SAUSUENDO
(Alviso)
Guadeloupe R.
Tamyen
Coyote Creek
Awaswas
San Lorenzo R.
Soquel Cr.
(New Almaden)
(cinnabar)
Mutsun
Aptos Cr.
37°
KODACHI MACHI
(Santa Cruz)
Pajaro R.
NIJI-MASU
(nr. Watsonville)
Monterey Bay
KAWAMACHI
(near Castroville)
ANDORYU
(Monterey)
Salinas R.
Rumsen
MARUYA
(Carmel)
Carmel R.
Rumsen
20 km
20 mi
Sur R.
ETA-MURA

Map 3
SF & Monterey Bays

Chapter 1

Sandy Bottom Bay, Texada Island
October 1634

Crabs scurried out of the way of the two samurai as they and their companions walked along the beach of Sandy Bottom Bay, the large bay near the middle of the southwest coast of Texada Island. They all wore straw raincoats and conical straw hats, as it had rained every day for the past week and the sky had been overcast when they left camp.

They now stood about two miles south and east of the head of the bay. "I should scout ahead," said Deguchi Masaru. He was ready for trouble, armed not only with the two swords that marked him as a samurai, but also with a half-bow that he held in one hand. There was a bamboo quiver on his back. His face was pockmarked, the relic of a childhood bout with smallpox.

Oyamada Isamu, the leader of the Japanese exploration party on Texada Island, motioned for him to proceed. Like Masaru, he bore the "big" and the "little"; the lacquered wooden scabbard of his *katana* pointed diagonally down and back, and that of the smaller *wakizashi* was almost horizontal. He had a white scar on the back of his *katana* hand.

As he watched Masaru walk south along the east side of the bay, the sand crunching under Masaru's feet despite his attempt at stealth, Isamu thought about the strange circumstances that had put him here, on an island in the Strait of Georgia between Vancouver Island and the Canadian mainland.

More than a year ago, the shogun had learned from up-time books given to him by the Dutch that in the far future Japan would be humiliated twice over by invaders from America. And he had also learned that the Japanese Christians, the *kirishitan*, of the Shimabara peninsula would rebel against the ban on Christianity in the very near future, 1637. He was persuaded that all of them should be sent into exile across the Pacific, to colonize California and there act as a buffer against European expansion. And the First Fleet, carrying the first group of *kirishitan* into exile, should have arrived at Monterey Bay by now. They were placed under the authority of Date Masamune, the powerful daimyo who the shogun had appointed grand governor of New Nippon.

Before the First Fleet lifted anchor, Date Masamune had sent an exploration vessel, the *Ieyasu Maru*, across the Pacific, and two months earlier, it had come to Texada Island. The Date clan had learned from up-time sources that the island had iron deposits. And when a large, telltale red stain was seen upon a hillside near Sandy Bottom Bay, Iwakashu, their mining engineer, insisted that they let him take a boat ashore.

Iwakashu had confirmed that there was iron ore on that hillside. Indeed, some of it was lying loose for the taking, and Iwakashu had brought back samples. The *Ieyasu Maru* had sailed for Monterey Bay, to report this discovery, with the firm expectation that the grand governor would send word home to dispatch new colony ships to Texada.

Isamu's party—sailors, miners, and interpreters—had been left behind, to begin mining, and to explore the island so that they could guide the expected colonists.

The Japanese expedition's present goal was to locate potential farmland near Sandy Bottom Bay, where the colonists were expected to land. Unfortunately, none of the expedition members were farmers, and so the best they could do, Isamu had decided, was to locate reasonably flat, vegetated land that was neither soggy wet nor bone dry.

Masaru returned with an alarming report. "There's an Indian village up ahead."

Isamu knew what that meant. First, they could not survey the Sandy Bottom Bay area on the colonists' behalf without revealing themselves to the Indians. And second, conflicts between the colonists and the natives were likely to occur soon after the colony was founded.

"So close to Sandy Bottom Bay! Why didn't the lookouts on the *Ieyasu Maru* see it?"

"Because the village was burnt down."

That was good news, up to a point; it meant that the villagers themselves would not be an issue. But it also raised several questions.

"What I want to know," said Isamu, "is why did the village burn down? Did a fire get out of control? Or was one set by an attacking tribe? Yells-at-Bears, what do you think?"

Yells-at-Bears was an Indian, of the Snuneymuxw of eastern Vancouver Island, near the up-time map's Nanaimo. She had been taken from her village by raiders, and then sold by her captors to another tribe, who sold her in turn to the Gwat'sinux on the western coast. They had kept her as a slave until four months ago, when Tokubei, the first mate of the *Ieyasu Maru*, had purchased her from the Gwat'sinux, and brought her into Japanese service.

When the Japanese had first met her, she had worn a fringed skirt of shredded cedar bark and had been naked from the waist up. She still wore the skirt, but had covered her upper body with an indigo blue-dyed quilted cotton jacket of the sort that some of the Japanese sailors favored. Her feet were bare, but she had tied deer sinews around her ankles.

Her black hair, parted in the center, grazed the top of her shoulders. It contrasted sharply with the Japanese men's coiffure; their foreheads were shaved, and the hair on top and back gathered into an oiled queue that curled forward, like the figurehead of a ship.

"Ever since Beaver stole fire," said Yells-at-Bears, "we have used it for many things. Not just for cooking at camp. Near my old home, there was an island covered with a camas prairie. We would come to the island each summer, after the camas had flowered, and the men would fish and we women would dig for camas bulbs. When we were done, we would burn off the island. That way, the camas crop would be good the next year.

"Here, there is much forest. We would set fires to clear undergrowth from the forest to make it easier for hunters to pursue game. It is possible that such a fire, mishandled, accidentally burnt this village."

This speech was only partially in Japanese. While Yells-at-Bears had come aboard the *Ieyasu Maru* in June, and had been learning Japanese both from lessons and by osmosis ever since, she was also making explanations in Kwak'wala, the language of her former captors. And this in turn was being translated by Dembei.

Dembei had been one of several Japanese castaways whose rudderless and dismasted junk had been carried by the North Pacific Gyre to the northwest coast of Vancouver Island about a decade earlier, where they had been enslaved by the Nakomgilasala. They had been freed by the *Ieyasu Maru*, and two—Dembei and Jusuke—had been assigned to Isamu's exploration party. Denbei's face was wide, and Jusuke's, narrow, but they were cousins.

"And do you use fire in warfare?" asked Isamu.

"I am not a warrior, but I have heard my father speak about this," said Yells-at-Bears. "It depends. Some raids are just to take slaves. But if there is much bad blood between the two sides, then you might burn the village so the band that lived there is broken up."

"The lookouts would have seen smoke," said Isamu, "if it were still burning when we came up the coast. Or while the *Ieyasu Maru* was anchored in Sandy Bottom Bay. So the fire, whatever its cause, must be from before our visit to Texada."

"If you're right," said Masaru, "then even if the fire was the result of an attack, it was not likely the attackers lingered for more than a week afterward. If the attackers' goal was to occupy, rather than destroy, they wouldn't have burnt the village in the first place."

"Are you sure that there are no unburnt buildings, Deguchi-san?" asked Yells-at-Bears.

"No, I am not. When I saw a row of buildings, I stopped and returned to warn the rest of you." He sounded annoyed.

"As well you should have," said Isamu in a placating tone. "Masaru and I will go forward. Dembei, Zensuke and Yells-at-Bears remain here. If we are not back in an hour, your mission is to return to camp and warn Fudenojo to avoid this area." Fudenojo commanded the sailors left on Texada by the *Ieyasu Maru*.

"What if we hear fighting from your direction? Four warriors are better than two," Zensuke protested. He was a sailor, and he and Dembei were armed with hatchets. Yells-at-Bears only carried a knife, and Zensuke obviously didn't count her as a warrior.

Isamu pondered the suggestion only briefly. The situation appeared to call for stealth and skill, and Isamu had never seen Dembei or Zensuke in action. And if a fight went awry, Yells-at-Bear's knowledge might be critical to the survival of the remaining Japanese.

"Masaru and I have guns, as well as bows, and chances are that even one gun will scare them away," said Isamu. "If you hear fighting, leave."

"*Hai.*"

That settled, Isamu motioned to Masaru, and they began walking, half-crouched, in the direction Masaru indicated. Isamu was not in fact as sanguine about the effect of a demonstration firing as he had led Zensuke to believe. From what Yells-at-Bears and Dembei had told him, the largest war canoes of the northwest coast of America could hold forty men, and even if some of those were merely slave rowers, the Indians would still overwhelm Isamu's fivesome. *Better for three to survive,* he thought, *than none.*

San Miguel District, Manila, Philippines
October 1634

The Jesuit Father Pedro Blanco twisted and turned in his sleep.

In his dream, he saw a giant demon walking across Manila Bay, making great splashes with each step. Pedro was in the bell tower of a church, pulling on the rope, and trying to warn the city, but for some reason, the clappers weren't working. The demon stomped on the Baluarte de San Diego, one of the bastions of the Intramuros, and—

Suddenly, he awoke to the realization that his host's son, Juan Kimura, was shaking him. "What's wrong?" Father Blanco asked groggily.

"My father needs to speak to you. Urgently."

"Give me a moment."

The basement hidey-hole that he had been living in the past seven months had no natural lighting, but Juan had brought down a lantern. It cast a harsh orange-red light on the bare walls of the hidey-hole. The latter did have one advantage, however: it was spacious, no doubt because it had been built to safeguard the entire Kimura family in a time of unrest.

Unfortunately, its ceiling was low enough that Father Blanco had to be cautious about standing up. But then, that had happened at some Spanish inns, too. Father Blanco was a giant even by Spanish, let alone Japanese, standards.

Father Blanco dressed hurriedly, wondering what could be the matter. He had been a missionary in Japan until 1614, when the shogun Tokugawa Ieyasu banned Christianity and ordered the expulsion of all European missionaries. He had returned to Manila and ministered to the Japanese Christians settled in the Dilao and San Miguel districts.

When a joint Dutch-Japanese task force captured Manila in March 1634, the Kimuras, a Japanese Christian family in San Miguel, had hidden him. Ironically, their hidey-hole was one constructed in case the Spanish launched a pogrom against the Japanese residents, as they had after the pagan Japanese living in Dilao revolted in 1606.

The Japanese had exiled or killed all of the Spanish residents of Manila that they had been able to find. They were particularly interested in finding government officials, soldiers and priests. The reward for turning in a priest like Father Blanco was substantial, but he had nonetheless been protected. Indeed, on several occasions, he had been shuttled to other Japanese Christian homes to hold secret services for the faithful.

That, too, was ironic. He had begged to be one of the priests who hid in Japan after the expulsion edict, but his superiors had denied the request. And yet he had ended up serving the Faith in post-invasion Manila in much the same way as he would have had he courted martyrdom by remaining in Japan.

"I am glad you are awake, Padre," said his host, Francisco Kimura. "We need to move you out of the city."

"What has changed?" asked Pedro bluntly.

"A servant betrayed one of the families who you held services for. They were arrested and held for questioning. It is only a matter of time before they reveal your presence in the area. Even if they can't specifically identify us, the Japanese will cordon off the area and conduct house-by-house searches."

"I understand. But I fear for what might happen to you."

"I am of samurai status myself. The authorities will be reluctant to torture me or my family. So, as long as they do not find you here"—he shrugged—"I think we will survive."

"I will leave at once then," said Father Blanco, "and leave my fate to the Lord."

"I'd rather give the Lord some assistance," said Francisco drily. "If you are captured, you will certainly be tortured, and will likely reveal our role. I have planned for this eventuality and it won't take long to finalize the arrangements to get you out of here safely. At least, more safely than if you try to make a run for it tonight, on your own."

"As you think best," said Father Blanco.

Francisco bit his lip. "One more thing. Your beard . . . it needs to be shaved off. I have a servant who has a deft hand with a razor."

"My beard? Why?"

"You will need to pass as a Filipino fisherman," said Francisco. "And how many of them have beards?"

Father Blanco sighed. "If I must."

"Better to cut off your beard now, than have your head cut off later."

Sandy Bottom Bay, Texada Island

Before long, as Masaru had warned, Isamu could see the burnt remains of a wooden structure through the trees. Isamu and Masaru exchanged hand signals; Masaru kneeled beside the trunk of a tree, and readied his bow. Isamu started crawling slowly toward the ruin.

Isamu found a place with good cover, took out his own bow, and signaled Masaru to come forward.

Now it was Masaru's turn again to kneel, and Isamu's to crawl. Isamu came at last to a point at which he had a much better view of the remains, while still enjoying, thanks to a barberry bush, some measure of concealment.

From this vantage point, he could see that the structure was the nearest of three, in a row paralleling the shore, all burnt down. The houses had been rectangular, each perhaps fifty feet long, and much shorter in width. Isamu noticed that the ruins were overgrown with vegetation. That helped explain why the *Ieyasu Maru* had not spotted the buildings. It also suggested that the fire had happened months ago, probably before the last rainy season.

He signaled Masaru to fetch the others.

Some minutes later, they made it to Isamu's position. "Masaru-san? Dembei? Zensuke? Yells-at-Bears? Doesn't this look long deserted to you?"

They all agreed with his assessment. With some trepidation—his armor had been left at camp—Isamu stood and walked alone into the more open area where the buildings had stood.

No arrows or spears came flying toward him.

He made the hand sign, "all join me!"

The deserted village was, he saw, just shy of the point that marked the southern extremity of Sandy Bottom Bay. Southwest of the point, there was a small island.

He directed Zensuke's attention to this. Zensuke expressed regret that they did not have a small boat with them to go check out the island; their raft had been left hidden near the mouth of Marsh Berry Creek.

As for the village, Isamu could see the remnants of the corner posts, and some long charred fallen timbers. There appeared to have been a central hearth running lengthwise in each building. Yells-at-Bears confirmed this, and told him that the front door would have faced the shore.

She studied the ruins for a time, and then said, pointing in the opposite direction, "Isn't that another building there?"

It was. In fact, they found two more rows of buildings. These were not burnt, but they were partially dismantled. All that was left of them was the framework: a row of tall posts in front, a row of shorter posts in back, and connecting beams.

"What are we looking at here?" asked Isamu.

"It is a house whose roof and wall planks have been removed. The roof would have sloped backward to carry away the rain."

"Is that normal? Does that mean the villagers aren't coming back?"

"Some families have both summer and winter homes. The winter homes are larger, because more families come together at that time. It is common to take the planks from summer house to winter house, and back again, leaving the frame behind. However . . . May I go closer?"

Isamu motioned her forward, and she walked onto the dirt floor of the house, and wandered around, her eyes cast downward.

"She looks like Saichi, hunting for iron ore," said Dembei. Saichi was the chief miner of the exploration party. He was back at their base, Camp Double Six.

"She is prettier than Saichi," said Zensuke.

"That isn't much of a compliment," Dembei retorted.

"Enough!" Isamu, accompanied by Dembei, walked over to join Yells-at-Bears. "Have you discovered anything?"

"It is what I haven't found that is interesting," she said. "I see no sign that this building was lived in over, say, the last year."

"So what do you think happened here?"

"It is unclear. It is possible that raiders ransacked and burnt the homes nearest the shore, and then were driven off. And afterward, the villagers decided to leave this place."

"It certainly has no natural defenses," Isamu observed.

"They could have built a stockade," said Dembei. "Some villages my former master took me to did. But perhaps the resources here didn't warrant the trouble."

Yells-at-Bears, via Dembei, aired some alternative theories. "There might have been an accidental fire, caused by a hearth fire let untended, or a lightning strike, and the inhabitants took it as a portent that they should move. Or the fire and the departure were unrelated; perhaps the game got wary or the fish swam away, so they left to find someplace better."

"Let us continue to explore," said Isamu, "and see if we can find anything useful that was left behind. Food, clothing, tools, even a boat if we're lucky?"

"You might as well wish for a stash of sake, while you're at it," muttered Masaru.

They didn't find anything that was movable, other than some slate arrowheads and a slate knife, but on the coast, at low tide, they found an intact fish weir. It was a set of hundreds of wooden stakes, arranged in the shape of a chevron, pointing away from shore. Yells-at-Bears explained that fish would enter the small gap at the base of the chevron, and be trapped in the wings when the tide reversed.

"We could do this at the beach at Sandy Bottom Bay!" exclaimed Zensuke.

"Why go to that effort, when this one is already built?" asked Masaru. "Let us settle the colonists here. In fact, let us move our camp here!"

Camp Double Six was so-called because it was a lucky dice throw in *ban-sugoroku*. The site was lucky because it was near their initial iron discovery. However, its nearest marine access, Iron Landing, was a dangerous place for boats to land or cast off. The abandoned village was much closer to Sandy Bottom Bay, the best anchorage on the southwest coast of Texada.

Isamu shook his head. "No. We don't know whether the village was abandoned, and, if so, why. We don't want to use this fish weir and attract unfriendly attention. At least, not until there are more *Nihonjin* here. Especially armed *Nihonjin*. Until the colonists come, we don't even want to occupy Sandy Bottom Bay."

"When they do, we can pull the stakes from here and move them to Sandy Bottom Bay," said Zensuke.

Masaru frowned at Isamu. "Didn't Yells-at-Bears tell you that this village has been abandoned for at least a year? The risk seems worth it. And if Sandy Bottom Bay would be just as good, then why did they build their village here, not there? In fact, we should move our camp here. I am sure the weir will make it easier to feed ourselves for the winter!"

"What do you think we should do, Yells-at-Bears?"

"There are only eighteen of us, Isamu, counting those left behind at Camp Double Six. We do not need this big fish weir to feed ourselves. And there aren't enough of us to fend off a big warband, especially if they were to surprise us with a dawn attack. We should not tempt fate; leave this village alone until your friends come back with their big ship and many guns."

Isamu sighed. "We do not have to make a decision this instant. Let us return to Sandy Bottom Bay and camp there for the night."

The following morning, at the beach of Sandy Bottom Bay, Isamu declared, "Yells-at-Bears is right. Forget the village and its fish weir for now. In the summer, when the colonists come, we can return and if it is still abandoned, it can be occupied."

Again, Masaru briefly tightened one side of his lip. "Are you sure your judgment is based on facts and logic alone? It isn't clouded by . . . other influences?" He didn't identify them verbally, but his eyes strayed briefly in Yells-at-Bears' direction. "Perhaps, after the rainy season arrives, and we are starving to death, you will reconsider."

There was little doubt in Isamu's mind that the separated references to clouds and rain were deliberate. In Japan, "making clouds and rain" was a euphemism for sexual intercourse. Masaru was implying that Isamu had favored Yells-at-Bears' advice over Masaru's, because Isamu and Yells-at-Bears were lovers. It was an outrageous position for Masaru to take. Even if they were in fact lovers. Which they weren't. Not that Isamu hadn't had some thoughts in that vein. Yells-at-Bears was attractive, in an exotic sort of way.

However, if Isamu took offense, it might lead to a duel. And even if Isamu won, he would lose; the expedition would be deprived of one of its two trained warriors, and he would ultimately have to report and justify the duel to his superiors. And they would only hear the words, not Masaru's tone and cadence.

"I am sure," Isamu said as evenly as he could manage. "Thank you for sitting before me on the white sand of Sandy Bottom Bay beach and telling me this." He hoped that Masaru would perceive the hidden meaning; the term "white sand"—*shirasu*—also referred to the area where a prisoner accused of a crime knelt before a magistrate and awaited judgment.

From the quick tensing of Masaru's brows, it was evident that he did.

San Miguel, Manila

Francisco Kimura had arranged for Father Blanco to be smuggled out of Manila aboard a fishing vessel that had come down the Pasig River from Laguna de Bay to sell its catch in the city market. Come morning, they expected a sea breeze, which would allow them to sail back upriver.

In the Hour of the Tiger, there was a knock at the back door of Francisco's home. Was it the fishermen, or Japanese soldiers from the occupation force? Francisco called out, "Who's there?"

"A flock of seagulls ready to fly away."

That was the agreed-upon recognition phrase. Sighing with relief, Francisco pulled open the door. Three Filipino fishermen stood before him. "Where is he?"

"We'll have him out in a moment," said Francisco. "I thought it best to keep him well hidden until you arrived." He turned to his son. "Juan, go fetch Father Blanco."

✣ ✣ ✣

Father Blanco had been given a red cotton *barong* shirt and a matching *patadyong* pleated skirt to wear. On his head was a plaid *putong* and over it, a straw *salakot*. The latter had a wide brim, which would help, Francisco hoped, to hide his face. Father Blanco had been ordered to leave his cassock and crucifix behind, in case he was searched. He kissed the latter before he handed it to Francisco.

The fishing boat captain looked him over closely. "Roll up your sleeves," he ordered, and Father Blanco complied.

"This is for you to carry," he added, handing Father Blanco a long-handled fishing net and a small container. "Put the handle over your right shoulder."

Father Blanco did so, and picked up the bait container in his other hand.

The Filipino shook his head. "No, hang it on the near end of the handle, by your right hand, to balance the weight of the net end."

After Father Blanco complied, he said, "I will take the lead, you walk directly behind me, with my friends on either side of you. That will help conceal you from unfriendly eyes. Walk as we walk. Do you speak Tagalog?"

"A little bit," Blanco said in that language.

"Hmph. Try not to say anything until we are on the boat and under way. Let's go!"

"*Ganbatte*!" said Francisco.

"God bless you," answered Father Blanco.

From Francisco's house, it was several blocks to where the fishing boat was moored. It was a small *guilalo*, with two lateen sails.

"Where do I hide?" whispered Father Blanco.

"In plain sight," said the captain. "You row when it is needed. Otherwise, act . . . nonchalant."

Father Blanco did his best to mimic the crew. As he was helping them raise the spars into position, he saw, out of the corner of his eye, a two-man Japanese patrol heading in their direction.

He mentally ran through the reasons why he should keep calm. *Primus*, they are walking, not running. *Secondus*, he was dressed just like the others on the boat. *Tertius*, if he did not keep calm, they would certainly notice. And *quartus*, he had to have faith in the Lord to protect him.

The sails were already bent onto the spars, so he didn't have to worry for long. The skipper put his hand on the tiller, and called out, "Cast off!"

And the boat started to move upriver.

On the Pasig River, Luzon, Philippines

"Thank you for helping me," said Father Blanco.

"We are good Christians," said the fishing boat captain. He shrugged. "And we were paid well."

The journey up the Pasig River to Laguna de Bay was about twenty miles. Thanks to the sea breeze, they didn't have to row much at all, giving Father Blanco the opportunity to study a part of Luzon that he had not visited before. The houses by the banks were *nipa* huts, rather than Spanish villas, and the Filipinos here wore less clothing than those in the city. *Bangka*, the Filipino double outrigger canoes, passed by the *guilalo*, the canoers calling out greetings. Around noon, he heard the "huh-huh-huh" call of the *kalaw*, the "clock of the mountains."

Laguna de Bay was a large freshwater lake, with the shape of a three-toed bird of prey. The boat had entered it from the northwest, but Father Blanco was being taken to the village of Bay, on the south shore, over twenty miles away.

Having successfully escaped Manila, Father Blanco was in good spirits, but this did not last. The sky darkened, and it started to rain heavily. The wind strengthened, and large waves formed. The captain ordered the crew to reduce sail.

The wind howled even more strongly. Father Blanco could see whole trees in motion on the shore.

"What can I do to help?" asked Father Blanco.

"Pray."

Father Blanco prayed to Saint Nicholas, the patron saint of seafarers. "Calm the wind and the waves, help us who are in the way of the storm to reach safety. . . ."

Chapter 2

Texada Island

Texada Island was long and narrow, running from northwest to southeast. Isamu's exploration party had, moving east from Camp Double Six, discovered two freshwater lakes, which they called Marsh Berry Lake and Rattling Bird Lake, and a creek that ran from Marsh Berry Lake to Sandy Bottom Bay.

Quarry One, above Iron Landing, was the site of the first iron discovery, and there was now a large pile of ore collected there by Saichi's miners. While nothing could be done with it now, Isamu was confident that it would be put to use. Japan was iron-poor; its iron was either laboriously extracted from iron sands in the province of Chugoku, or imported from China. Texada's iron ore could be shipped back to Japan on returning colony ships. Or, with the right craftsmen, it could be made into ironware here, saving the local *kirishitan* colonists and the Monterey Bay colony the expense and trouble of importing it from home.

Camp Double Six, a little east of Quarry One, was situated on a natural bastion, a broad ledge of stone. Before the *Ieyasu Maru* left Texada, its crew had helped Isamu's party put it into a reasonably habitable form. They had cleared away trees and brush, and built a defensive wall, part boulders, part logs, with some stakes facing outward.

Inside this enclosure were several wooden buildings. The main building was nothing like a traditional Japanese house. The floor was not covered with *tatami* mats, and the walls weren't sliding panels of wood or of translucent paper in a wooden frame. Under the direction of the ship's carpenter, the crew had erected structures more like the mountain huts used by hunters—simple wood frames covered with brush.

Spare sailcloth divided the inside of the main building into sections: a small headquarters for Isamu, a dining hall, sleeping quarters, and a storage room. The dining hall was only sparsely furnished, but there was a low table, made of local wood, cedar bark mats to sit on, and a fireplace in the center. Various provisions were hung over it, to be dried and preserved by the heat and smoke.

There were no fireplaces in the sleeping quarters, but they did have *anka*, small charcoal burners to heat the feet or the bedding.

The storage rooms held the supplies that the *Ieyasu Maru* could spare: some arrows and musket bullets, some tools and weapons, miscellaneous trade goods, and a starting supply of food and water. Fortunately, the party had been able to locate a spring nearby, and they had restocked their food stores with berries, smoked fish and other comestibles.

The kitchen was an outbuilding. But it wasn't much more than an enclosed firepit, with a smoke hole in the roof. There were several large rain cisterns nearby, built of native wood, so in case of siege, they would not be dependent on the spring. And there was a small bathhouse, too.

Between the main building and the gate in the defensive wall was a flat, cleared area, the "Assembly Field," where Isamu could address the entire exploration party.

After exploring the burnt Indian village near Sandy Bottom Bay, Isamu's party returned to Camp Double Six. That evening, Isamu was still unsettled by the dispute with Masaru. If only Commander Yoritaki, his immediate superior on the *Ieyasu Maru*, had assigned him a different second-in-command! There were over a dozen other samurai on board the *Ieyasu Maru*, any of whom Isamu would have preferred to Masaru. And one of them was Isamu's best friend, Terasaka Haru. But Isamu knew better than to protest.

Isamu came from a family that had been retainers to the Date family for decades. Isamu's most famous kinsman, Oyamada Yorisada, had been in the Date rear guard at the Battle of Nakaniida in 1588 against the Osaki clan, and had fought to the death.

In contrast, like most of the other samurai on the *Ieyasu Maru*, Masaru was a former *ronin*, a masterless warrior, taken into Date Masamune's service only a few months before the *Ieyasu Maru* left Sendai. Isamu did not hold this against Masaru—Isamu had many friends among the former *ronin*, and he knew that when the Tokugawa took power, they dispossessed many daimyo of their domains and thus turned their samurai into *ronin*—but he'd known from the beginning that Masaru was going to be a problem.

Despite Isamu's heritage, Masaru had been resentful of Isamu's appointment as leader of the exploration party. Isamu had heard from Fudenojo, the ship's officer assigned to Isamu's party, that after Isamu had publicly volunteered, Masaru had approached Tokubei and claimed to be a *kakure kirishitan*, a "hidden Christian." This, Masaru had pointed out, would mean that he would have better relations with the *kirishitan* colonists when they arrived, and he would thus be the better choice for local commander.

Tokubei was nominally the first mate of the *Ieyasu Maru*, but that fact did not adequately convey Tokubei's importance; he had traveled to China, Vietnam, Siam, and even, on a Dutch ship, to India, and hence had been Date Masamune's envoy to the Indians of Vancouver Island.

As proof of his assertion, Masaru had shown Tokubei that his sword guard had a hidden cross design. And he had explained that he was from the town of Iyo, once the center of Christian missionary activity on the island of Shikoku.

However, Tokubei was multilingual. He had encouraged the other Japanese to learn Kwak'wala—to reduce the mission's dependence on Jusuke and his fellow castaways—but Tokubei, Isamu and Saichi were among the few who made the effort while the ship was en route to Texada.

Whether because of Isamu's family connections to the Date clan, or his efforts during the passage to Texada to learn Kwak'wala, he had been chosen over Masaru.

Unfortunately, Masaru's arguments had been effective enough to put Masaru in a position to plague Isamu in the future. Hopefully, from now on he would accept his subordinate position with good grace. Hopefully.

There was no doubt that Isamu had taken a considerable economic risk by joining the samurai contingent on the *Ieyasu Maru*. When he was a child, as was customary, Isamu's family had arranged for him to marry a samurai woman of another clan. But when her family learned that he was going to New Nippon in Date Masamune's service, they had broken off the betrothal.

Now, his future marital prospects—and the benefits they would bring to his family and clan—would depend on how well he did in Date Masamune's service. And, of course, he would now need Date Masamune's approval, as well as that of his parents and clan elders, in order to marry. And with an ocean separating them, the negotiations were likely to be protracted and difficult.

Isamu decided that he needed a distraction from these dark thoughts. He turned to Yells-at-Bears, who was sitting with him and Dembei in the dining hall. They had been engrossed in a discussion of some translation issue, until Isamu interrupted them.

"So . . . you said earlier, 'since Beaver stole fire.' What did you mean by that?"

"It is an old tale of my people," said Yells-at-Bears. "It had rained for many days, and all the fires on earth were put out. The earth animals sent a messenger, Eagle, to the sky animals, to ask them for more fire, but they refused. So the earth animals decided to steal it. But Eagle could not steal it by himself because the sky animals watched him too closely when he came to visit.

"So the earth animals fired arrows at the moon. Once one stuck in the moon, they fired another, that stuck in the notch of the first one, and then a third, that stuck in the notch of the second, and so on, until there was a bridge of arrows, arched like a rainbow, from the earth to the moon. Beaver climbed up the bridge of arrows.

"Once Beaver was safely up the bridge, and hidden behind a cloud, Eagle went into action. He flew about the sky village in a strange way, and the sky animals came out to see what he was up to. He led them further and further away from the sky village, and Beaver crept into the village. He filled a clamshell with glowing coals from the sky village's campfire and ran toward the ladder of arrows. The sky people saw the glow from his clamshell and ran after him, but Eagle harried them, and Beaver made it to the ladder and slid down it. And then he swung his great tail and broke the ladder, so the sky people couldn't come after him."

Of course, in telling this to Isamu, Yells-at-Bears sometimes had to backtrack and say something more simply, or have Dembei explain her meaning in Japanese, but that was the gist of her story.

When she was done, Dembei added, "I heard a different version when I was a slave of the Nakomgilasala. That it was Deer that stole fire from the sky, and he did so by tying pinewood shavings to his tail, and then whisking it through the fire when he visited the Sky Village and danced around the campfire. They then realized what he was up to, but he gave a great leap and got away."

"I heard that, too, from the Gwat'sinux, but they are both wrong," Yells-at-Bears insisted.

"All right, but what I don't understand is how did the fire get passed from Beaver, or Deer, to people?" said Isamu.

Yells-at-Bears explained that long ago, animals could be transformed into people, people into animals, and for that matter, animals and people could marry and have children of either kind.

Relationships were easier then, thought Isamu. But he just said good night, as did Dembei, leaving Yells-at-Bears alone in the dining room.

Yells-at-Bears' thoughts turned to the unfortunate and mysterious residents of the burnt village. Were they the victims of raiders? Yells-at-Bears knew firsthand what that was like. As the raiders carried her off from her home, she could see the fires they had set where her own village had been.

At the time, the best she could hope for was that her parents had survived and would quickly ransom her. But they didn't, and she became a slave, traded from one tribe to another.

How fortunate she was to have been purchased by the Japanese, when all hope of a better future had long been lost! They, especially Isamu, were far kinder to her than the Gwat'sinux had been. Indeed, they had told her that they did not keep slaves themselves and hence she was free so far as they were concerned.

In theory, she could return to her own people when her service with the Japanese was complete. The catch was that they would surely realize that she had been a slave. And even though she was the daughter of a chief, and thus once of noble status, even an ex-slave had only slave status. Unless the taint of slavery were removed, a difficult and expensive ritual undertaking. In her present circumstances that didn't seem likely. At best, she could hope to be a concubine for a noble, or perhaps a secondary wife for a commoner.

Perhaps she would do better to live among the Japanese... permanently.

The next morning, Isamu called the entire party to the Assembly Field. Fallen leaves crunched under their feet as they formed a rough semicircle.

"Up to now, our focus has been on stocking up on food for the winter. But Indians may visit the island at any time. Maybe now, maybe not until spring. While we hope to avoid fighting, the Indians may have other ideas. I know that Masaru and I can fight, but I don't know what martial skills the rest of you have. I need to see that firsthand, and we need to start training regularly. We will use this area for weapons practice each day."

Masaru set up targets on one side of the assembly field, and the men who claimed to already know how to use a firearm were given the chance to prove their claims. Their firearms were all of Japanese make, and differed from the Portuguese arquebuses that the Japanese had initially copied. For one thing, they had waterproof covers to protect the matchlocks from rain. These were boxlike contraptions, made of waxed paper in a wood frame, which fitted around the touch hole. That was fortunate; this month had been wetter than the one before, and Yells-at-Bears had warned the Japanese that the next month would be even worse.

Fudenojo, the pointy-jawed ship's officer, proved to be a good shot, as did several of the other sailors. But Saichi, his miners, and the two castaways had never even held a firearm. Of course, neither had Yells-at-Bears.

Captain Haruno had given the expedition what he considered to be an ample supply of shot and powder. But it needed to be husbanded, as they couldn't expect resupply until the summer. Assuming either the *Ieyasu Maru* or the colonists actually showed up, that is.

"Masaru-san, please teach *teppojutsu* to our crew," ordered Isamu.

"Very well, but we can't afford to have novices waste our precious gunpowder. They will learn all thirty-two shooting positions, and just dry fire the guns, until I am absolutely satisfied."

"Proceed as you suggest."

⁂

The sailors and miners stood, muskets in hand. Masaru barked out one command after another. “Position Three! Kneel, resting the barrel on a stone. Separate your knees more . . .”

Bay, Luzon, Philippines

Father Blanco bowed his head as he entered the bamboo and *nipa* church of Bay. He gave thanks for the deliverance of the fishing boat from the storm, and prayed for the souls of his benefactors in San Miguel. Then he sought out the parish priest, an Augustinian.

“I am pleased to see you,” said Father Blanco. “I wasn’t sure whether the Japanese had made it this far into the interior.”

The Augustinian crossed himself. “Thank the Lord, they have not. But we are only a few hours’ sail from Fort Santiago, and I think it is only a matter of time. I will move into the mountains if they do.” He cocked his head. “What are your plans?”

“I will try to reach Cebu.”

“Not an easy journey, nor a safe one. I can find you a guide to take you to Tayabas, near the coast. Do you have money to pay for passage?”

“I do, thanks to the generosity of those who sheltered me after the fall of Manila.”

“It is well that you do, since the fare is likely to be high, to compensate for the risk. The Moro pirates have stepped up their raiding of the coastal *barrios* since the fall of Manila.”

Father Blanco fingered the stubble on his chin. “I will have to take my chances.”

Texada Island

At the general assembly in front of the main building, Isamu decreed that each day, those members of the party whose duties did not take them away from camp all day must spend an hour on weapons practice of some kind. And he chose to turn his attention to his men’s knowledge of *kyujutsu*—archery technique. Hardly any of the sailors were good archers. Fudenojo had told Isamu, apologetically, that it was much easier to teach a new sailor how to use a firearm than to use a bow, and so, once there were enough guns on board, little attention was given to archery. Indeed, while the *Ieyasu Maru* had given the exploration party enough guns and spears so everyone could have his own weapon, there were only enough bows for half the party.

"But we can't just rely on guns," Isamu had responded. "We can reuse arrows, or make new ones, and with Yells-at-Bears' help in finding the right wood, we can make bows, but we have only so much shot and powder."

Isamu chose to lead the lesson. While Masaru was the better archer of the two, he was not a good teacher. Isamu believed that it was because Masaru had learned archery so easily that he couldn't understand the mistakes of others and explain how to correct them.

Isamu tried to put the best face possible on this decision. "There is no point in wasting the time of an expert like you on a bunch of neophytes, Masaru. I will get them started, and you can show than what a master can do another day."

Masaru however, didn't seem convinced of Isamu's logic. Just for an instant, his lip tightened on one side of his face, indicating his displeasure.

Noting this, Isamu decided to divide the group in half, keeping one for himself for the archery lesson, and having Masaru take the other half to learn *yarijutsu*, the technique of the spear. Hopefully, keeping Masaru occupied would keep him from brooding on the slight to his *kyujutsu* teaching ability.

Both Isamu and Masaru had a *daikyu*, a "great bow," about eight feet long and made of pieces of bamboo glued together. However, it was not a practical weapon if you wanted to walk through forest, and it wasn't common equipment for a "red seal" ship, either. The men therefore had each been given the *hankyu*, the "half bow."

The *hankyu* was a piece of bamboo about four feet long, gently curved in the center but straightening at the tips. "Hold it here, where the leather is wrapped around the bow, not in the center." Isamu indicated the grip point to be about one-third of the bow length from the bottom.

"We string it like so." Isamu demonstrated.

He dropped to a peculiar position, half-kneel, half-squat. His left leg was forward, bent so the knee and toes were on the ground. His right leg was open, the knee pointing to the right, and sharply bent, but off the floor. He took several arrows out of the quiver that hung from his back, and set them so the feathered ends rested against the inside of his right thigh.

"Copy me," he said. "This is the first position, the kneel. It is one form of the stance, *ashibumi*. We use it in battle since you present a smaller target and have more stability." He patted his stomach. "Breathe from here, slow and deep."

He picked up his bow and planted the lower end beside his right leg, a few inches back of the knee. His bow hand was a little below his present shoulder level. "Pretend you have the bow in your left hand, like so." Isamu reached for an arrow with his right hand, brought it up to chest height, and notched it on the bow string. "Second position, *yugame*."

He pushed the bow hand forward as he raised it to level with the top of his forehead, arm straight. At the same time, he pulled the right hand a little back, and raised it, but not quite so much, so the arrow was inclined slightly upward. The elbow bent to a right angle, and pointed up and to the right. The arrow was drawn back half its length. "Third position, *uchiokoshi*.

He lowered both hands to mouth level, the bow hand moving in an arc with the arm still straight but relaxed, the right hand pulling the bow string back to a position a little further back than his ear, almost the full length of the arrow. "Fourth position, *hikiwake*.

"Sight on the target. If the target is close, as here, assume horizontal flight. Later we learn how to correct for distance.

"Now watch!" An instant later, Isamu released the arrow which flew toward the target, striking the center. "That was *hanare*, the separation of arrow and bow. That is the obvious part. But did you see what I did with my right hand?" Immediately after the release, he had flung his right arm straight back. "That was *zanshin*, the pause.

"Lastly . . . We complete the *kata* with *yudaoshi*, the 'lowering.'" He brought the bow back to the starting position.

Isamu had them repeat the *kata* several times with pretend bows and arrows before allowing them to hold the real thing.

After they had each, one at a time, shot several times from the kneeling position, with Isamu watching and correcting, he told them how to shoot standing up. He set out a *yadate* stand to hold the arrows. "Later, you will learn how to draw the arrow from a quiver."

Taking an arrow in his right hand, he spread his feet and looked over his left shoulder at the target. "Stand with your feet an arrow length apart, and turned out like so."

Otherwise, the technique was the same as for kneeling fire. Again he had his students practice with imagined weapons first, and then with the real thing.

As he expected, the arrows mostly missed the target altogether. It was disappointing, but Isamu reminded himself of how many hundreds, if not thousands, of hours he had spent practicing archery.

In the meantime, Masaru was drilling the men on spear fighting. As there wasn't room to do this on the assembly field when archery practice was also underway, he had taken them outside the enclosure to a convenient clearing. One well away from the trainee archers' line of fire.

Most of the men already had some notion of how to use the *yari*; the sailors were trained to use them to repel boarders. Of course, their spears were short, just three to six feet long. The *nagae yari* traditionally used by foot soldiers on the battlefield were twelve to eighteen foot long pikes.

Those foot soldiers fought in close formation, so that they presented a wall of steel points against an approaching foe. But given the size of the Japanese expedition, in any action against the Indians, the sailors would be fighting in open formation, much as they did against pirates. So the short spear was better for them.

Once Masaru saw that the men weren't novices, he let them use actual spears. The men first practiced their spear moves on a bag stuffed with leaves and hung from an overhanging tree. Then the blades were carefully removed from two of the spears and the men took turns sparring with each other.

After an hour, Isamu and Masaru swapped students, and each continued to teach the same weapons.

Yells-at-Bears did not participate in this day of weapon training, but she watched it carefully.

The next day, before the men were separated into groups, Yells-at-Bears whispered to Jusuke and, with him ready to translate if need be, went up to Isamu. "You need all the shooters you can get. Teach me, please."

Isamu was a little taken aback. "It is true that samurai women learn to fight, but their weapon is the *naginata*, not the bow," he told her.

"Why is that?"

"Because the *naginata* is a pole arm, it gives them greater reach."

"Doesn't the reach of the *hankyu* exceed that of the *naginata*?" asked Fudenojo, who was standing nearby. "And didn't Tomoe Gozen use a bow?" Tomoe Gozen was a legendary female warrior who fought for Minamoto no Yoshinaka in the Genpei War, four centuries ago.

The conversation, by then, had attracted Masaru's attention. "If her own people didn't teach her how to use a bow, why should we?"

Masaru's opposition provoked Isamu to decide in her favor.

"She's right, we need everyone to be able to bear arms, and it is better that she fight from a distance, behind cover, than hand-to-hand."

Once again, he divided the men into two groups, and sent one off with Masaru for spear practice in the usual place.

"Yells-at-Bears, did you pay attention during yesterday's lesson?"

"I did, Oyamada-san."

"We will start, as we did yesterday, with imaginary bow and arrow. Men, line up here!"

Once they had formed up, he added, "Yells-at-Bears, stand behind, so you can see what they do on each command. Try to do what they do."

He repeated the drill from the day before, first for the kneeling position, then for standing. And then he had the men shoot, one by one.

"Your turn," Isamu said, and handed the bow to Yells-at-Bears.

She drew an arrow from the stand and tried to match his shooting position.

"Feet farther apart. No, not that much." Jusuke was adding a translation in Kwak'wala, in case she had trouble with Isamu's Japanese. More surreptitiously, some of the spectators were placing bets.

"Fine, now the bow hand . . . easy up, yes . . . breathe deeply, in and out, from here, during the setup." He patted his stomach. "Begin the lift . . . hold it. Make sure you keep breathing. Now push out the bow hand . . . good . . . complete the draw . . . lower! . . . Now hold your breath . . . release when ready. . . ."

The standard target for novices was an *o-mato*, sixty-two inches in diameter, set eighty-five feet away.

Yells-at-Bears loosed the arrow. It fell short of the target.

"Take a new arrow from the *yadate* stand, and try again. Here, let me help you with the stance." Isamu came over and stood behind her, his front to her back. Once she had lowered the bow to shooting height, he put his left hand over hers. "A little higher," he whispered. As she pulled her right hand back, he touched it. "You can pull a little farther. Good! Take the shot. . . ."

This time, she hit the target, albeit close to the rim. "Better. Try again. . . ."

When she had shot all of the arrows she had been offered, she bowed to him, and said, "Thank you, Oyamada-san, for allowing me to shoot."

"Thank you, for volunteering." He dropped his voice to a whisper. "You did better than some of the sailors, actually."

Chapter 3

Camp Double Six, Texada Island

Something was different this morning, Yells-at-Bears mused as she slowly woke up. Then she realized what was different; she did not hear the sound of rain striking the roof of the building. She dressed and stepped outside. Not only was it not raining, the sky was not even grey. And the colors of the fall foliage, the yellows, oranges and reds, seemed more intense than they had the day before.

It was, she thought, an excellent day for an outing. She walked to Marsh Berry Lake, to pick a few berries and see whether the chum salmon had started spawning.

She had done this before of course, but always in the company of one or more of the Japanese, especially Isamu, or the ex-slaves Dembei and Jusuke. But there had been no dangerous encounters, either with man or beast, on any of the past occasions, and she decided this time to go alone rather than wait for one of the Japanese to escort her.

Not seeing the salmon in the lake, she went farther afield, walking alongside Marsh Berry Creek as far as she could without having to slog through marshland.

Isamu was walking toward the lakes when he heard a commotion ahead of him. Not knowing who or what might be the source, he drew his *katana*.

Suddenly, Yells-at-Bears appeared, running hard.

"You found salmon?" he asked.

"I found Indians! On Marsh Berry Creek!" she shouted.

"How many?" demanded Isamu. "And did they see you?"

"Three. But there could have been others, out of sight." She paused to catch her breath. "I don't think they saw or heard me. I had wandered somewhat away from the stream, collecting mushrooms. I was sitting down, examining one closely to make sure it was of a kind that was safe to eat, when suddenly, some birds took flight, heading north. I thought they must have been startled by something to my south, so I hid and waited. And then I heard the Indians coming up the stream. They weren't being stealthy, they were talking in the Tla'amin tongue about a woman one of them fancied."

That was somewhat reassuring; Isamu recalled Yells-at-Bears had told Tokubei that the Tla'amin were not especially aggressive, but rather needed to defend themselves from raids by the Laich-kwil-tach and the Haida.

"Did you see them, or just hear them?"

"I heard them first, then I saw them briefly, through a gap in the foliage. They walked up and down the stream, trying to decide on a fishing spot. I made my escape while they were downstream."

"Were they dressed for battle?"

"No. If they were here to fight, their faces would be painted black and their hair would be tied back."

"Ah," said Isamu. "So it couldn't be grabbed by a foe. Come back to camp, we need to have a council."

At Camp Double Six, he summoned Masaru, Fudenojo, Zensuke, Saichi, Dembei and Jusuke into the dining hall of the main building, and had Yells-at-Bears repeat her story.

"What weapons do the Tla'amin fight with?" asked Masaru.

"Clubs, daggers, spears, and bow and arrow," said Yells-at-Bears. "Weapons of stone, not iron. A few warriors might wear elk hide armor, but otherwise they wear ordinary clothing."

"What arms did the three you saw carry?"

"They had harpoons," said Yells-at-Bears. "And bows. Probably daggers, too. Weapons for fishing and hunting, that is all."

"We should go in force," said Masaru. "All of us, fully armed. Isamu and I should wear our full armor, and bring our *daikyu*. Tell them to leave, or else."

Yells-at-Bears frowned. "Excuse me, Deguchi-san, but that would be dangerous, in the long term. While this party is small, and we surely outnumber them, what if they go home and say we are a threat that must be dealt with? I do not know which Tla'amin band these Indians come from, but they might have hundreds of kinsmen living within a few days paddling of Sandy Bottom Bay. And soon, the families that lived apart during the summer will come together at the winter villages for matchmaking, feasting, dancing, storytelling, gift giving . . . and to plan raiding in the spring. Or even sooner, if they are angry about the actions of another band."

"We did not impose our will upon the Ainu of Ezochi by being timid," said Masaru. The Ainu were the aborigines who lived on Ezochi, the large island north of Honshu.

"Weren't we ordered to avoid conflict with the Indians?" asked Fudenojo.

"I thought we were just ordered not to leave Texada and go looking for Yells-at-Bears' people," countered Masaru. "These Indians have come to us, and we cannot ignore them. Surely you don't intend to cede control of Marsh Berry Lake and Creek to them, Isamu! We need the fish in those waters to feed ourselves over the winter."

Isamu spread his hands. "All of you make good points," he said diplomatically. "We will all go, but in two groups. The lead one will be small: myself, Yells-at-Bears, Jusuke, Fudenojo, and two more sailors who are good with firearms. I will have my two swords, but the rest will carry just short spears and half bows, which can be excused as hunting weapons."

"What about guns?" asked Fudenojo.

"Yes, you and your sailors may take those. The Indians will not know what our firearms can do; they will think them some sort of tool. And the presence of a woman will help reassure them that we are peaceful, neh?

"Masaru will command the reserve. He may wear armor and bring his *daikyu*, if he wishes, and I will loan him the Dutch spyglass Tokubei gave me, so he can watch from afar. His men will carry muskets, bows, spears and short swords, as their fighting skills warrant. He will keep the reserve as far back as he can and still see what is going on."

Masaru looked unhappy, but that was not uncommon. "I suppose that is acceptable. We can spread out in a crescent, so we can flank the Tla'amin."

"That's fine," said Isamu, "but let me be quite clear. You are to stay back unless either we are attacked or I signal to you by putting my left hand on my rump." He demonstrated. "If so, then advance to join us. Of course, if we are under attack, you will counter-attack.

"If I raise my left hand, you may advance, but only half way, and without drawing or raising weapons. My left hand, mind you, not my right."

"*Hai*."

"Fudenojo!"

"Yes, Oyamada-san?"

"Pick out a few trade goods. Nothing real fancy, we need to save those for tribal chiefs."

"I will, sir, but can Yells-at-Bears help me, please? I know how much we have of each kind, and how much they are worth to us, but she would have a better idea of what they would be worth to another Indian."

"Very well, so be it."

"And will our group carry the trade goods, or will Masaru's?"

"Each of our group may carry one small, light item of your choice, Fudenojo. The rest will be back with Masaru. Yells-at-Bears will divide them into batches of what she thinks the Tla'amin will consider to be of equal value.

"Masaru-san, if I scratch the back of my head with my left hand, it means send one man forward with one batch of trade goods."

"I will watch you closely," said Masaru.

When Isamu and his vanguard came into view, the three Tla'amin, who had been fishing in the creek, stopped what they were doing, and faced the Japanese. One whistled, and moments later Isamu could hear rustling in the bushes. It didn't take a sage to guess that there were more Tla'amin, now watching them from cover, and probably with bows ready. And it made Isamu uneasy to realize that he didn't know their number. Of course, they didn't know about Masaru and the reserve. Or did they?

Isamu waited a moment to see whether the Tla'amin took any more aggressive action, but the hidden Indians stayed hidden, and the fishermen stood their ground.

At a gesture from Isamu, Fudenojo and the two sailors held back, while Isamu, Yells-at-Bears and Jusuke continued to come forward. They stopped, however, well out of arm's—or spear's—reach.

Isamu gently tapped Yells-at-Bears' shoulder. It was her cue.

Yells-at-Bears raised both hands, showing that she was unarmed, and took a step forward. "I am Yells-at-Bears. I am the daughter of a chief of the Snuneymuxw," she told them in their own language. She spoke slowly, because it had been years since she last spoke Tla'amin.

One of the Indians matched her movements. "And I am Fast-Drummer. From your choice of speech, you already know I am Tla'amin. But the people with you are strange to my eyes." His own eyes were almond-shaped, surmounted by thick eyebrows.

"These people with me have great spirit power," said Yells-at-Bears. "They came across the ocean that lies west of the lands of the Kwakwaka'wakw and the Nuu-chah-nulth. The canoe they came on was larger than even the war canoes of the Haida, and it had wings that captured the wind so it could fly across the ocean without being paddled.

"They came to the Great Island, and found me living there. I had no living husband, and when they asked for people that could guide them to the Inner Sea, and speak with the people who lived there, I stood up."

That was a carefully edited version of the truth, since Yells-at-Bears had been living among the Gwat'sinux of the Great Island because she had been sold to them as a slave. She had no living husband because by tribal law, slaves could not marry. And she had been purchased by the Japanese, she didn't volunteer to join them. To admit that she had been a slave would immediately have reduced her status in Fast-Drummer's eyes and tainted the present negotiation.

"I would like to see this flying canoe," said Fast-Drummer. "Is it nearby?"

"No, but it has left a band here, with this man as its leader, to explore this island. It will return soon." She deliberately did not say when. "But if you know the Kalpilin Shishalh band, three of them saw the flying canoe in August. They can tell you about it, perhaps."

"Ah, we are from Wide-River-Bed," said Fast-Drummer. "We are two days paddling from Kalpilin."

Isamu coughed.

"Excuse me, the people I am guiding do not understand Tla'amin," said Yells-at-Bears. "I need to tell them what we have said so far."

"What language do they speak?"

"They have their own language, unlike any you have heard before, but a few of them understand Kwak'wala."

"I, too, speak Kwak'wala," he said, "so let us use that language from now on and it will be easier for you."

"I thank you," she said, and in Japanese, with the former castaway Jusuke's help, gave Isamu the gist of the conversation so far.

"Do you know where Wide-River-Bed is?" he asked.

"It is on the mainland coast," she said, "near the northern tip of Texada."

Isamu went back to consult Fudenojo, who had studied the up-time maps of British Columbia, and he said that this was most likely by the mouth of the Powell River.

Once the Japanese had plainly finished speaking, Fast-Drummer responded. "You are strangers from afar, and doubtless did not know better, but my grandfather's grandfather found this creek, and all of our band recognize that his descendants have the right—the exclusive right—to make use of it. We fish for salmon, we hunt deer, and we collect berries. So it has been, moon after moon, year after year, for many years.

"What do you say to this?"

Isamu came forward and conferred in a whisper with Yells-at-Bears and Jusuke. Through them, he answered, "We are indeed from afar, and we indeed did not know of your past use of this stream." He took care to say "use" not "right."

"Your fishing left no ripples behind, your hunting left no footprints. There was no sign of your past presence, let alone of your claim. Among my people, there is no claim to land without leaving a marker for others to see.

"The other members of your band know of your claim, but do the other bands of the Tla'amin? Of the Shishalh? Of the K'omoks?

"Nor do you live near here. Did you not say that Wide-River-Bed is two days paddling from Kalpilin? Then your band's winter home is at least as far from this place. But this is now our winter and summer home. Should not those who live nearby and year-round have the better claim then those who are occasional visitors?"

It was the Tla'amin's turn to whisper among themselves.

✣ ✣ ✣

Some distance away, Deguchi Masaru peered through the borrowed telescope. "He is taking a very long time to tell them to leave."

"At home, it is impolite to state your business right away," said Zensuke.

"Are the Indians' hands close to their weapons?" asked Saichi.

"No. But their expressions are hostile."

"May I look, Deguchi-san?" said Dembei. "I have lived among the Indians, you know."

Masaru passed the scope to him. "Put one eye here," he said, tapping the eyepiece, "and keep the other one open. If the view is blurry, make sure the telescope is fully extended and then slowly move the eyepiece section in or back out."

"I can't find them . . . wait . . . yes, there they are. Yes, they do look a bit angry."

"If we advance to where they can see us, then perhaps we can transform their anger into fear. It might speed up the negotiation, neh?"

"Forgive me, Deguchi-san," said Saichi, "but do we not have explicit orders to remain here unless there is actual fighting, or a signal from Oyamada-san?"

Masaru twitched. "I suppose. Yes, we will wait."

As Isamu waited for Fast-Drummer to reply to his speech, he wondered what Masaru was thinking . . . or doing. . . . Would he follow orders? Or would he do something that would spook the Tla'amin and frustrate this negotiation, perhaps leading to trouble in the future?

And if Masaru did follow orders, Isamu hoped that it would be for the right reason—obedience to Isamu's authority. As opposed to, say, the hope that the Tla'amin would kill Isamu, leaving Masaru in command.

Fast-Drummer cleared his throat. "If it is true that your people recognize rights only when you have marked the territory, like a dog or wolf, then where on this stream have you left your scent? We saw no sign of yours. So by your own words, and your own law, you have not established rights.

"And among my people, and the other peoples who live on the

Inland Sea, rights are established by voicing them when the band gathers for the winter, and none challenging them. And to be sure the right is recognized, one would give a potlatch for one's village, or even for several villages at once. And such is what my forefathers have done."

Fast-Drummer crossed his arms, signaling the end of his speech.

"But we did leave a sign," said Isamu. "Did you not come up this creek from the bay? Did you not see a stone pile, with a wooden cross on top like so?" He crossed his arms, one arm vertical, the other horizontal. "That was our marker, and by it we claimed the beach and the creek that flows through it."

"That may be so, but our claim came first, and there are tens of tens in our village that can attest to this." The implication, Isamu realized, was that there were hundreds that might fight to defend the Tla'amin claim.

Isamu asked, "Among your people, does a claim to a food gathering site last forever? Or can it expire, like smoke rising into the sky and disappearing?"

"If a site goes too long unused, another may claim it. But that is not the case here." Fast-Drummer explained that the rights were owned by his clan, and this year was his family's turn to use the stream, but in other years, other families of the same clan would come. And thus the clan maintained its right.

"And can a claim be traded from one to another?"

Fast-Drummer acknowledged that it could.

"We do not say you have no claim, but we say that we have a claim, too. Our village lies near the lake that gives birth to this stream, and this stream is the route by which we go down to the sea. So this stream is far more important to us than to you, who come from Wide-River-Bed. And we have marked our claim in accordance with our custom.

"We might be willing, however, to trade with you, so your claim no longer casts a shadow over ours."

"Even if I wanted to I could not bargain away my clan's claim. But you could bargain with me for the right to enjoy this stream for this year."

The bargaining then began in earnest.

In deciding what trade goods to take on the *Ieyasu Maru*, Tokubei had considered both what the Dutch had told him about trade with natives in other parts of the world, and what the Japanese traded to the Ainu of Ezo. The Ainu were eager to obtain rice, sake, salt, tobacco, lacquerware bowls and cups, ironware, thread, cloth, dye, and used clothing. Under Lord Yoshihiro, the Matsumae had often traded swords and armor, but Lord Kinhiro had thought better of this, favoring iron needles, smoking pipes, pots, kettles, knives and hatchets.

"For the right to lake, stream and beach, we will give you this," said Isamu. His party spread out a hemp blanket, the bulkiest item they carried. On it they laid out some polished wooden prayer beads, a red and black lacquer bowl, and some matching cups.

Fast-Drummer laughed. "They are pretty, but they are not enough for what you ask."

They continued bargaining, but Fast-Drummer was resistant until Isamu slowly brought out an iron-bladed hatchet. Fast-Drummer gingerly felt the edge of the blade. While he tried to conceal his reaction, it was obvious to Yells-at-Bears that he was impressed by its sharpness.

She pointed to a snag nearby. "See for yourself; try chopping that!"

He did, and there were excited murmurings from his companions.

"Think about how much faster you can chop wood with this spirit-metal blade than with an ordinary stone blade. Or, think what a canoe maker, or even a chief, would give for it," added Yells-at-Bears.

Fast-Drummer was plainly on the verge of agreement, but needed something more to clinch the deal.

"May I show you a special arrow?" asked Isamu.

Fast-Drummer nodded.

Isamu reached into his quiver and brought out a *kabura-ya*, a signal arrow. "When I shoot this, it makes a whistling sound. We use this—"

Yells-at-Bears motioned at him to stop speaking. "His people use it to chase away evil spirits and summon good spirits to come to their aid."

Fast-Drummer exchanged glances with his companions and then declared. "Very well, we have a deal. You may use this stream until this time next year."

"Excellent!" said Isamu. "And when our 'Great Canoe' returns, our chief can sail to Wide-River-Bed and tell all of your people of our claim, in accordance with your custom. And I am sure that he will give gifts of a kind you have never seen before."

"I look forward to this meeting," said Fast-Drummer. "But I warn you that I do not own the fishing rights to Clear-Sandy-Bottom, the bay that this stream leads down to. You fish there at your own risk."

"Are there any other bays on this island?" asked Yells-at-Bears.

"There are," said Fast-Drummer. "There is a large one in the north, nearer to Wide-River-Bed. And there may be others further south. But I doubt that there are any that are free of prior claims."

"We'll keep that in mind," said Isamu. *Once the* Ieyasu Maru *returns, we'll be able to negotiate for those fishing rights from a position of strength,* he reflected.

Chapter 4

Tayabas, Luzon, Philippines

Father Blanco lifted the coconut to his lips. His guide had just plucked it from a tree and punched a drinking hole in it for Father Blanco's benefit. The coconut water was a welcome relief.

Once Father Blanco tossed the husk aside, the guide motioned Father Blanco onward. They were on a meandering forest trail, and occasionally the guide had to draw his bolo and cut away intruding brush. The trunks of the trees were mossy, and their canopies were linked by vines. Once, a fern rustled, and the guide grabbed Father Blanco sharply by the shoulder, holding him in place. A moment later, a dark brown *ulupong*, a kind of cobra, slithered across their path.

Perhaps an hour later, they were in Tayabas, founded by Franciscan missionaries in 1578.

Tayabas was surrounded by thickets of *bayabas*, guava bushes, and its name was a contraction of the Tagalog phrase "among the *bayabas*." It had, as Father Blanco expected, a church, a town plaza, and a tribunal, the government administrative center. There was no fort. This town center was surrounded by a haphazard cluster of native dwellings.

Father Blanco was taken to the church, where he was welcomed by the priest, a mestizo.

"How do I get safely to Cebu?"

The parish priest shook his head sorrowfully. "Now? It is

impossible. There are Moro raids on the Tayabas Bay coast every week. Even if you could find a ship willing to make the attempt, it would take a miracle to reach Cebu without being spotted and overtaken. If you are lucky, you would just be held for ransom. More likely, you would be enslaved, or killed outright. Some of the Moros think that they earn their place in heaven by killing infidels."

"So, what do you suggest I do?"

"Wait. The Moros come up to the Visayas with the southwest monsoon. Each pirate squadron establishes a secret base near some Christian towns. Their little outrigger canoes fan out from there to capture hapless fishermen or raid small villages. Or the whole squadron, big ships and small, sallies against a town. The entire population is killed or enslaved, and the town burnt down."

"Isn't the southwest monsoon season over?"

"Yes, but they will wait until November, for the arrival of the northeast monsoon, to return home with their spoils. The wind is more favorable, and there is less chance of encountering a typhoon."

The northeast monsoon wind would also make it easier to sail to Cebu, Father Blanco realized. And he knew that the Moros were not to be trifled with. Why, the last archbishop of Manila, Hernando Guerrero, had been attacked at sea by six Moro galliots while attempting a pastoral visit to Mindoro. His ship made it to shore, but the pirates followed them in, and most of his party were murdered or captured for ransom.

"I will wait until November to attempt a passage. But considering the distance, it probably won't be easy to find a boat captain willing to take me to Cebu."

"That is true," the parish priest admitted. "There is no regular trade between us and Cebu. In times past, you would take a ship to Manila, and then from Manila to Cebu, but that trade has dried up. Perhaps, if you are lucky, a Chinese trader will come by to buy *lambanog*." That was a distilled coconut palm liquor, the local equivalent of sake or schnapps.

"Well, I should talk to the local boat captains in the meantime, try to line up a ride for November. Maybe someone who wants to sell *lambanog* in Cebu."

The parish priest frowned. "As you have no doubt noticed, Tayabas itself is some miles inland. There's a gravel road leading down to its port, Pagbilao. You can go down there and make inquiries, but be alert! It has the advantage of being set back, on Pagbilao Bay, and there's a wooden watchtower on one of the headlands, but the Moros' proas can escape notice at night, or the watchman may be distracted, asleep or absent altogether."

The Tayabas priest gave Father Blanco a new guide, and so Blanco said goodbye to the one from Bay. The new guide, a boy, looked suspiciously like the Tayabas priest, but Father Blanco kept his suspicions to himself. The boy spoke both Spanish and Tagalog, and he would be Father Blanco's interpreter, too.

They walked down to Pagbilao, and the boy asked Father Blanco many questions about Manila and Japan. The boy had never been to Manila, and he had never met anyone who had lived in Japan.

In Pagbilao, Father Blanco was an immediate sensation, and his companion basked in Blanco's aura of celebrity. Unfortunately for Father Blanco, that celebrity did not help him find transport. He did, however, hear many tales about Moro raids.

One fisherman told about how he and his fellows used to fish at night, by torchlight, when the Moros came among them in dugout canoes and captured them one by one. Fortunately, a cry for help had alerted him, and he was able to escape.

Another said in the early dawn, the Moros might have one or two of their number dressed like Christians, with the others lying flat in the hull, and come close, surprising fishermen at their fish corrals, or individuals on shore casting nets or gathering seaweeds, shellfish, salt or mangrove cuttings.

Even worse were the occasions when thousands of Moros landed on the beach and attacked a town. If the townspeople were very lucky, someone spotted them and rang the church bell. But unless the church had stout stone walls, their best course of action was to flee into the neighboring thickets. Under Spanish law, the Tagalogs could not bear arms, unless they were part of a militia company like the one in Manila.

If they didn't want to give up fishing and live inland, the best they could do was pray: "From the Moro fury, deliver us, Lord."

⁂

One of the fishermen invited Father Blanco to a fiesta in Sariaya, about sixteen miles west of Pagbilao. Father Blanco was anxious to ingratiate himself with the fishermen and accepted. It was almost the last thing he did in this life.

The day started off well enough, as he and his young guide were taken in a *bangka*, a double outrigger dugout canoe, to Sariaya.

The village plaza was thronged with people, not just the residents of Sariaya, but also partygoers from many nearby *barangays*. There was music, there was dancing, and of course there was *lambanog*.

Unfortunately, the local Tagalog and Father Blanco were not the only people attracted by the fiesta. That night, the Moro pirates beached their flotilla of *bangka* on the nearby coast, and worked their way slowly inland. It was their opportunity for a final coup before returning to their homelands in the south.

They moved silently from hut to hut on the outskirts of the village, surrounding it and then surprising the occupants, killing or trussing them up, and gathering up valuables.

Fortunately for Father Blanco and some of the other inhabitants, one of the Moros couldn't resist the temptation to set afire one of those huts.

As the fiesta became wilder and wilder, Father Blanco had moved to the sidelines, patiently waiting for his hosts to tire and offer him a ride back to Pagbilao. He prayed that they would not be so drunk that he would need to spend the night in Sariaya.

He had turned his back on the festivities—if these people must sin, best that he didn't witness it, he reasoned—and that's when he saw the fire. "What do you suppose that signifies?" he asked someone nearby.

"Moros!" the man screamed.

There was pandemonium. Father Blanco knew that he should run, but in what direction? He knew that if the pirates found him, he risked not only enslavement or death like the ordinary villagers, but death by torture. Their animosity for priests was considerable.

His guide tugged on his black cassock, a gift from the priest in Bay. "This way!" He was taken onto a trail leading into Sariaya's own *bayabas* thickets.

In their haste, their clothes were torn and their skin scratched by the thorns, but they were too keyed up to notice this until they stopped running and hid under the arching branches. And there they remained for a long, fretful night.

Father Blanco resolved to return to the relative safety of Tayabas until November. As Father Blanco and his guide trudged back to Tayabas the following morning, he reflected on the tragic irony of a Moro attack on a fiesta honoring the Virgin Mary, and more specifically, honoring her response to Pope Pius' prayer to her for victory over the Turks at Lepanto. The anniversary of that victory had been earlier that month.

Texada Island

West of Iron Landing, there was a small bay with a stream running into it. Beginning in October, the chum salmon had come there to spawn, and sailors of the exploration party had come there to catch them. Despite Fast-Drummer's warnings, they had not encountered any Indians here.

While the fish could be speared with the *yari*, it was more efficient to use a gaff hook, as salmon could work their way off a straight spearpoint.

The sailors stood on rocks, holding *yari* or gaff hooks in a ready position. While they studied the water, eagles swooped down out of the sky and grabbed salmon with their talons. Once a river otter made a dash from the brush along the stream and took a prize of its own.

Despite the competition, the Japanese collected a large number of fish. They brought them back in red cedar withe baskets made by Yells-at-Bears, and barbecued their lunch over an open fire.

There was a surplus of fish, and these were fileted and hung to smoke dry. Camp Double Six now had a separate smoke house.

The fishermen went into the main building and started gambling in the dining hall. Yells-at-Bears started to follow them but Isamu stopped her. "It is time you learned how to wield the *naginata*."

They went into his office, where the naginata was held in a stand.

"First, you should know how it is put together." Isamu removed a peg from near the top of the six foot long staff of the *naginata*, and that allowed him to pull the long tang of the blade out of the staff. He carefully unsheathed the eighteen inch blade so Yells-at-Bear could inspect it. The blade had a straight base and a curved tip.

"The edge is very sharp," Isamu warned her, "like that of my *katana*.

You can feel it safely with a finger if you tap it gently, but if you run a finger along it, it will slice you open. Because that's what it's designed to do."

"Understood."

"It's actually better not to touch it at all, but if you do, you need to oil the blade so it doesn't rust." He carefully put the cover back on.

"The *naginata* gives you a great reach," he declared. "All samurai women are expected to be proficient in its use by the time they are eighteen years old, but many men favor it, too. It is my favorite weapon, actually, as the bow is Masaru's."

"It is fortunate that you had an extra *naginata* for me," Yells-at-Bears said.

"Actually, I don't. But if you practice hard, and show me that you are worthy of it, I will give it to you. I can fight with my *katana*, of course, so I am not defenseless."

"But don't you want to have a *naginata* still?"

"Oh, I do. But before I left the *Ieyasu Maru*, I told Yoritaki that I was thinking of giving you my *naginata*, and that he should make sure that a new one is sent to me with the colony ship."

She smiled. "So you were thinking of me even then. . . ."

"Um, yes." He coughed. "Enough talk! You have much to learn!" He put the sheath back on the blade. "Lift it, feel the weight." After she did so, he told her to put it back in the stand and take the wooden staff that was leaning against the wall.

"This staff is the same length as the *naginata*, but lighter. Take it, and follow me."

Isamu and Yells-at-Bears went out into the assembly yard.

"Take a two hand grip near one end, palms facing opposite directions. Yes, that's right. Lift it above your head, bring it down to horizontal. Do this three times ten. Then up and to the right and down, three times ten. Up and to the left and down, three times ten. To the right and sweep forward, three times ten. To the left and sweep forward, three times ten.

"I must go now and check on the miners," said Isamu. "But do those exercises each day. When you are ready, I will give you the next lesson."

Yells-at-Bears saluted him with her practice staff, and began her exercises.

✣ ✣ ✣

A week later, Yells-at-Bears beckoned to Isamu. "Look," she said, pointing westward and skyward. The sun had just descended below the horizon but still lit up the clouds low in the west, making them look like red-hot embers. As Yells-at-Bears gaze crept upward, the sky colors changed, from yellow to white to ever darker shades of blue. At the zenith, and in the east, stars were already visible. Clear skies were unusual this time of year, but they happened.

"Pretty, yes?"

Isamu agreed. "And so are you," he added in a whisper.

"Perhaps we should take a walk into the woods a bit."

"Yes, let's do that," agreed Isamu. "Follow me."

He led the way, and tried to squeeze between two bushes. "Fuck! I am caught on something. . . . There are thorns everywhere! Yells-at-Bears, help me."

She laughed, saying, "Oyamada-san is caught by a big thorn bush. A *naginata*-bush." She pulled out her knife and hacked at some strategic branches, freeing him.

"Are you hurt?"

"In my pride. Maybe some other places, too."

"Take off your clothes. I must see if thorns are broken off in your wound. If so, the wound can fester."

Isamu complied. "Well?"

"Turn-around slowly. . . . Again. . . ."

When he completed the second turn, Isamu found that Yells-at-Bears was only wearing her necklace.

"No thorns, but a nice view," she remarked.

He reached for her.

"What's wrong, Isamu?" asked Yells-at-Bears. She had noticed that he was not eating with his usual relish.

"Our encounter on Marsh Berry Creek ended well, but it could have gone badly. What if they change their mind about our arrangement and come back in force? Or some other Indian group decides to come up that creek and see what they can find that is worth their while?"

Yells-at-Bears popped another berry into her mouth. Her appetite, at least, was undiminished. "What do you propose we do?"

"Find a good vantage point that overlooks Marsh Berry Lake and where concealment is possible, and station a sentry there, at least during the daytime."

"There are only eighteen of us, Isamu. And we already have sentries at Camp Double Six. Can we really afford to have another of our number keeping watch, rather than collecting water, food and other resources for surviving the winter?"

"Can we afford not to?"

Yells-at-Bears brooded about this for a few minutes. "I suppose that the sentry, on the way out to his post, could set out snares for small game, and then check them on the way back.

"But why by the lake, and not by the creek, somewhere downstream?"

"Because the lake is an obvious goal, and it can be reached without going upstream. From Saichi's survey, we knew that as the crow flies, it couldn't be more than half a mile from Marsh Berry Lake to the coast. Of course, it would be an uphill slog through the forest, without any trails we know of, but if you already knew the lake was there you could find it. And Fast-Drummer and his family certainly know about Marsh Berry Lake."

Yells-at-Bears wiped the berry juice off her mouth. "I am sorry to add to your troubles, but what about Rattling Bird Lake?"

"What about it?"

"We know a stream runs out of the northeastern end, but where does it go? If Indians can seek Marsh Berry Lake from the south, why not by Rattling Bird Creek from the north?"

"Yes . . . it is possible . . . but less likely. Judging from the *Ieyasu Maru*'s maps, from Rattling Bird Lake to the northeast coast is at least three times as far as from Marsh Berry Lake to the southwest coast, and that assumes that there is a straight path."

"If you aren't worried, then I am not, either," said Yells-at-Bears. "And I had best be off to weapons practice."

Isamu brooded over Yells-at-Bears' warning and by nightfall had decided that she was right. The Japanese had to know how accessible Rattling Bird Lake was from the northeast. For all they knew, there could be a village at the mouth of Rattling Bird Creek, wherever that might be.

He called Masaru into his office. "Masaru-san, I am going to explore where Rattling Bird Creek leads, make sure there is no cause for concern in that direction. Keep the men laying in food for the winter, and practicing with their weapons."

"Who are you taking with you?"

"I was thinking... just Yells-at-Bears."

Masaru frowned. "Then you better hope that there is indeed no cause for concern in that direction. How many natives do you think the two of you can fight off?"

"The point of keeping our numbers small is so we can move quietly and escape notice. And thus not need to fight off anyone."

"Ah, you will rely on vigilance. I hope then that you avoid... distraction."

Isamu didn't like the curl of Masaru's lip, but there was nothing plainly objectionable about what he had said.

Well, the bright side of Masaru's antipathy toward Yells-at-Bears was that he didn't have to worry about Masaru, the only other samurai on Texada, as a romantic rival.

"Should I bring my *naginata*?" Yells-at-Bears asked.

"No," said Isamu. Seeing her crestfallen expression he added, "It is not because of any failing on your part. The *naginata* is a pole weapon, you need room to wield it. That's why it is so often used in castle defense, or in battles on open fields. But we are going to be mostly in forest, and there it will be more trouble than it's worth. Take your knife and bow."

They left camp and walked at a brisk pace until they reached the head of Rattling Bird Creek.

The creek was a meandering thread of marshland. Where possible, they walked in the adjoining forest. As they did so, Yells-at-Bears told Isamu that given the lay of the land, later in the rainy season, the marsh might turn into a lake. Isamu found that of interest because there was higher ground in between Rattling Bird Lake on the west and this sometimes marsh-sometimes lake on the east. "A fort on that ground would thus have natural defenses," he told her.

They followed the stream and found themselves turning north. After a time they came to another lake, a narrow one, running north-south. Their arrival disturbed a flock of geese that had been floating on the lake. These took flight, honking angrily at the two explorers.

Yells-at-Bears immediately suggested the name "Angry Geese Lake," to which Isamu agreed. They made camp by the lakeshore for the night.

The next day, they pressed on. It turned out that beyond Angry Geese Lake was another, smaller lake, running in the same direction, and connected by a short stream. Naturally, this was dubbed "Gosling Lake." This, too had a north-running outlet, which they called Gosling Creek. First one stream joined Gosling Creek from the west, and then a second joined it from the southeast. Isamu wondered where these streams came from, but that was a question that would have to be answered another time.

After the second confluence, the stream became deep and fast, and the bank now provided a more solid footing.

The creek turned east, and after a time it was swelled by the waters of two more small tributaries. Knowing that they could not be far from the mysterious northeast coast, they slowed their walk, watching for footprints and broken branches, and pausing from time to time to listen for sounds that did not belong. But they found no signs of recent human presence.

They continued on until at last Gosling Creek opened onto a small V-shaped cove. They had reached the northeast coast of Texada Island.

To the east of the stream mouth, there was a sandy beach. Isamu and Yells-at-Bears, hand in hand, walked down to where the waters of the Malaspina Strait lapped onto the shore.

It started to get dark, and they retreated upstream and set up camp. After they had done so, Yells-at-Bears suggested they go to the hill overlooking the beach and see if they could get a better view of the opposite shore.

The view was a pleasing one . . . until the canoes appeared. There were at least a dozen of them, and Isamu guessed that they were forty or fifty feet long.

"War canoes," Yells-at-Bears told him. She spoke in a whisper even though there was no way the warriors on board could possibly hear her. "Haida."

Isamu knew from previous conversations that the Haida were a warlike people that lived on Haida Gwaii, the Queen Charlotte Islands, over three hundred miles northwest of Texada. Even the

Kwakwaka'wakw of Vancouver Island, with whom the *Ieyasu Maru* had a run-in the previous year, were wary of them.

"I hope they are not going to Kalpilin," Yells-at-Bears said fervently.

"Kalpilin?"

"It is a Shishalh village, on the other side of the Malaspina Strait, and to our southeast. My elder sister married a man from there. She is all the family I have left."

Isamu knew that she had been taken in a Kwakwaka'wakw slave raid, but until now she had refused to say anything about the exact circumstances, or her family, and Isamu had thought it best not to press her. But apparently their temporary isolation from the rest of the Japanese, or the memories stirred by the sighting of the Haida war canoes, had prompted her to open up.

"Why do you say that? What happened to your family?"

"I was on the beach with a few other girls, gathering clams, when the Laich-kwil-tach raiders surprised us and bound us. As we were carried off, we could see our village burning."

"That's horrible. But couldn't your parents have escaped the fire?"

"If they had, they would have ransomed me back. My father was the First-Man of our village, so he was wealthy. And he could have called for help from others. I was betrothed to a young man, of high status, from another village.

"Instead I was traded from one Kwakwaka'wakw band to another, until I ended up where the *Ieyasu Maru* found me."

"How old were you when you were captured?"

"I was just twelve." Isamu knew that she was now in her mid-twenties.

He hugged her. "I am sorry it took so long for you to regain your freedom. But you are one of us now."

She returned the hug. But later that night, as they lay under the stars, she wondered to herself, "What am I, really? Will the colonists really accept me as one of them?

"Of course, whether or not the colonists accept me, there's Isamu to look out for me.... But for how long? Will Isamu's eyes wander once there are Japanese women on the island? Will he decide that it might be better to marry the daughter of some Tla'amin or Shishalh chief, in order to gain advantage in trade deals?

"And if he abandoned me, what would happen if I return to the

Snuneymuxw? If I am known or even suspected to be an ex-slave, as seems likely, it would take a proper potlatch to restore my status, and I don't have the resources for it.

"They might not even consider me Snuneymuxw any more, given how I have taken to Japanese ways. Am I Snuneymuxw or Nihonjin? Fish, fowl or neither?"

It was several hours before she fell asleep at last.

Chapter 5

Cebu, Philippines
March 1635

The Cathedral of St. Vitalis in Cebu was squat and thick-walled, built to withstand both typhoon winds and the quaking earth. Father Blanco hoped that it was equally resistant to the two remaining elemental forces, the flood waters brought by the typhoon, and the flaming torches of the heathen Moro.

Getting to Cebu had been arduous. Merchant ships had once sailed between Manila and Cebu, but that trade had ceased since the Japanese occupation. The Tayabas fishermen had absolutely refused to sail several hundred miles just to deliver Father Blanco to Cebu.

Fortunately, while standing on top of a watchtower built to warn of Moro raids, Father Blanco had spotted a Chinese merchant ship. It appeared to be making for the mouth of the Palsabangon River, on Pagbilao Bay. Father Blanco borrowed a horse and raced there.

The ship was a junk with three masts, and when Father Blanco got close to it, he could see that it was armed with several cannon. Clearly, it was a long-distance trader.

Father Blanco waved to the ship, and a boat was lowered and sent to bring him on board. That, of course, didn't promise that he would win passage, only that he would have the opportunity to negotiate.

The Chinese captain spoke broken Spanish, so it was obvious that he had traded in the Philippines before.

The ship was, it turned out, a member of the Zheng family trading fleet, and its destination was the town of Cebu, as the authorities there had assumed governance of the Spanish Philippines after the fall of Manila.

The fare the captain wanted for passage was more than what Father Blanco had to spare, but Father Blanco explained why it would be to his advantage to take him on board after all.

"*Primus*, because it would be a most Christian act of charity, and would rebound to your benefit when your soul passes on."

The captain looked unimpressed.

"*Secundus*, because in your Buddhist faith, it would be a deed earning you positive karma."

The captain, unfortunately, wasn't a Buddhist, either.

"*Tertius*, because the Jesuit Vice-Provincial in Cebu, and the bishop of Cebu, will be most anxious to receive me, and they will make good the difference."

The captain indicated that would be most acceptable, had he not had experience with eminent Spaniards reneging on offers of payment after the job was done. Especially, offers made by a third party.

Father Blanco sighed. "*Quartus*, I was, until recently, in the city of Manila, and I can provide you with most useful intelligence as to the doings of the Japanese and Dutch in that city."

That, the captain conceded, would be beneficial to him and the Zheng family, but not, alas, enough to cover the gap between his price and Blanco's counteroffer.

"*Quintus*, I am able to read and do arithmetic, and perhaps I can be of assistance to your quartermaster."

It turned out that the captain didn't have a quartermaster, and was not very fond of taking inventories, doling out supplies, and the like. So, it was decided, Father Blanco would act as his quartermaster until they reached Cebu, he would answer the captain's questions about the situation in Manila, and, of course, he would attempt to secure the remainder of the fare from the authorities Father Blanco had named.

And at last Father Blanco had reached Cebu, without any further Moro pirate encounters. He was now waiting to see the bishop of Cebu, give him news of Manila, and hopefully get the funds he had promised the Chinese captain.

While cooling his heels, he inspected the image of the Child Jesus that Ferdinand Magellan had presented to Rajah Humabon after his baptism in 1521. It had been lost and then rediscovered in 1565; its survival was deemed miraculous. Until recently, it had been housed in the *Basílica Menor del Santo Niño de Cebú*, built on the very site of the rediscovery, but that church had burnt down in 1628 and its stone replacement was incomplete. So the painting had been moved to the cathedral for safekeeping.

The bishop's secretary found Father Blanco in the chapel where the Child Jesus was housed. "The bishop will see you now."

They spoke for about an hour. The bishop was most interested to hear that at least some of the Japanese and Filipino Christians had remained steadfast in the faith, but distressed by the other news Father Blanco brought: the Japanese remained in control of Fort Santiago and the Intramuros, the Spanish in Manila were being hunted down like dogs, and Moro piracy had ravaged the southern Luzon coast.

"I will recommend that the captain-general of the galleons take you on as chaplain for the return to Acapulco. The viceroy of New Spain should hear what you have to say. And I will take care of your debt to the Chinese merchant."

Father Blanco thanked him, and kissed the bishop's ring.

Madrid
April 1635

Lope Díez de Aux de Armendáriz, *marqués* of Cadereyta, waited patiently outside the *Salón de Reinos* in the *Palacio del Buen Retiro*. The palace had been built for Philip IV by his chief minister, the count-duke of Olivares. It was mostly used for court entertainments, and Lope wasn't sure why the king had chosen this location for a private audience.

Lope was, of course, in full court dress: a black doublet with red embroidery; a black ruff, and black hip-to-heel stockings. Since he was to enter the royal presence, his sword had been left behind with one of the royal servants.

A royal usher thrust open the doors and motioned Lope forward. Lope had not been in the *Salón de Reinos* before, so he took his time studying his surroundings. By the entrance there were individual portraits—surely done by Velazquez!—of Philip IV, his wife Elisabeth, and, in between them, above the door, their son Balthazar Carlos, prince of Asturias. Along the long walls, in between the windows, were more paintings, all of battle scenes. As a naval man, he took particular interest in one that appeared to be a depiction of the Spanish defense of Cadiz against Buckingham's 1625 expedition.

Above the windows were more paintings. There were ten of them, and from their number and appearance, they were plainly depicting the labors of Hercules. The official genealogies proudly identified Hercules as the ancestor of the House of Habsburg.

Lope's essay in art appreciation was interrupted by the appearance of a court functionary. "His Majesty approaches," he intoned.

Lope turned to face the throne, and bowed. As he held the bow, King Philip IV entered the reception room by the private royal entrance, and sat down on the throne. "Welcome to my *Salón de Reinos*, Marqués."

Lope held the bow an instant longer, then straightened. "Thank you, Your Majesty. How may I be of service to you and Spain?"

"You are, I understand, a *criollo*?"

"Yes, Your Majesty. I was born in Quito. My father was the president of the *Real Audencia* of the viceroyalty of New Toledo."

"You have served us well as both general and admiral in the new world."

"I am indeed Your Majesty's humble servant."

"I have decided to appoint you as my viceroy in New Spain. I need a viceroy with your naval expertise."

Lope bowed deeply. "Your Majesty is most generous. I will not disappoint you."

"See that you don't." King Philip IV stood up, and Lope bowed, holding the bow until the king had left the room.

Lope had much to think about. Not long ago, Lope had been invited to attend a grand junta, a joint meeting of the Councils of State and War. While a Dutch fleet had been defeated in the Battle of Dunkirk in 1633, thanks to betrayal by their erstwhile English and French allies, the Dutch remained a threat to Spanish interests in the Caribbean. Indeed, they had taken Curaçao in September 1634, not long after the USE ironclads and timberclads had forced an end to the siege of Amsterdam. It was surely only a matter of time before the USE began to meddle in the Caribbean.

And then there was the recent news from Cebu, in the Philippines. In March 1634, a joint Dutch-Japanese force had taken both the city of Manila and the fortified shipyard of Cavite. Word of that disaster had not reached Spain until 1635. Lope would have to find a way to cope with it, too, as Philippines were considered part of his new viceroyalty.

And these problems came on top of the usual ones of corruption and flooding in Mexico City, and Indian incursions on the northern borders of New Spain.

Sighing, his eyes were drawn involuntarily to Zurbarán's depiction of Hercules' second labor. Wearing only a loincloth, Hercules swept back a club, ready to swipe at one of the rearing heads of the Lernaean Hydra. Behind him, his nephew Iolaus held a firebrand, ready to cauterize the stump so it would not grow two new heads in place of the old. *It was*, Lope thought, *a fitting metaphor for his new assignment*.

Chapter 6

June 1635

The colony ship *Iemitsu Maru* had spent the night idling in the Juan de Fuca Strait, which separated Vancouver Island from the Olympic Peninsula.

As soon as the sun rose, the helmsman of the *Iemitsu Maru* unlashed the whipstaff, and the crew adjusted the sails to get the ship moving again. Sometime later, Captain Fukuzawa ordered the helmsman to put the ship on a new course, entering the Haro Strait. This was the broad channel between the southeast end of Vancouver Island and the northwest coast of San Juan Island. With the wind on their starboard beam, and the tide with them, he expected that they would make good time.

Looking back over the taffrail, Captain Fukuzawa could see the *Sendai Maru*, several cable lengths behind him. That was good. What wasn't good was that the *Mutsu Maru* and the *Unagi Maru* were still nowhere to be seen. A storm had separated the *Mutsu Maru* from the rest of the flotilla, and Fukuzawa, as commodore, had detached the *Unagi Maru* to look for it. That had been a week ago. With scurvy already present on the *Iemitsu Maru* and the *Sendai Maru*, Fukuzawa hadn't dared linger.

It was a sunny morning, with just a few puffs of cumulus dotting the blue sky. Captain Fukuzawa shielded his eyes against the sun. He studied the play of the water in front of his ship, watchful for any sort of navigational hazard. It was unlikely that there would be any—the report from Captain Haruno of the *Ieyasu Maru* was that the channel was so deep it could not be sounded—but Fukuzawa was a cautious skipper.

Fukuzawa was also alert for another kind of hazard—Indian war canoes. As long as he kept to the middle of the main channel, which was six miles wide at its narrowest point, there would be no chance of surprise in a daytime passage. Unfortunately, he would eventually have to thread his way through the islands of the San Juan archipelago, and according to up-time maps, the widest passages available to him would put him just a mile off several of those islands.

Neither the *Iemitsu Maru* nor the *Sendai Maru* were in ideal condition for a fight. Scurvy had weakened their crews as well as their passengers, and the gun deck and weather deck were cluttered by the passengers and their gear. Fukuzawa would be very happy when his crew received fresh food and the passengers were off-loaded.

As the *Iemitsu Maru* approached the first of the narrower passages, Captain Fukuzawa assigned several sailors to lookout duties. Despite the increased vigilance, no Indians were seen. Which of course, didn't mean they weren't there.

The *Iemitsu Maru* was welcomed to the more open waters of the Salish Sea by a spy-hopping orca. Fukuzawa had seen them only once before, when the *Iemitsu Maru* sailed past the eastern coast of Ezo, the land of the Ainu. But he had heard of the great beasts long ago. A friend of Fukuzawa had been hired by a captain by the Matsumae clan, which traded with the Ainu, and he had said that the Ainu thought they were gods.

Fukuzawa wouldn't go that far, but he admitted to himself that they were impressive creatures.

The two Japanese vessels sailed up the Strait of Georgia, and eventually the southeastern end of Texada Island came into view. Just to its west was a smaller but still substantial island, which an uptime map would call Lasqueti. And in between the two were many islets.

Captain Fukuzawa didn't fancy navigating through the passage between Texada and Lasqueti, and gave orders to put the ship on the port tack, to round Lasqueti. The *Sendai Maru* followed suit.

After they did so, Sandy Bottom Bay came into view, just to their north. It was, according to the *Ieyasu Maru*'s report, the best harbor on the west coast of Texada. But the samurai Haru, who had served on the *Ieyasu Maru*, urged Captain Fukuzawa to make for Iron Landing, where Isamu's scouting party had been left, and at last he agreed to do so.

Camp Double Six

Just in the nick of time, Isamu slid his cedar paddle underneath the shuttlecock—a cedar twig with three feathers attached—and sent it back up into the air, arcing toward Yells-at-Bears.

It was a game played by both adults and children in the region, and Yells-at-Bears had been pleasantly surprised to discover that Isamu had played a similar game. In Japan it was called *hanetsuki*, and it used a fletched soapberry nut. But no matter what side of the Pacific you came from, the goal was to catch the shuttlecock before it hit the ground and send it back into the air toward the other player.

Isamu was a pretty good *hanetsuki* player. More importantly, Yells-at-Bears thought he was enjoyable company. He had gone to the trouble of teaching her go, and *shogi*, and didn't sulk when, after many attempts, she finally beat him in the latter.

Yells-at-Bears was just about to return the shot when she was startled by the blowing of a conch trumpet.

"Signal sound!" she shouted.

"Yes, from the direction of Quarry Number One," Isamu acknowledged, the smile wiped off his face.

"What does it mean?"

"The long blast was to get our attention," said Isamu. "Now we listen for the explanation."

Three short blasts.

"Western-style ship," added Isamu grimly. "It could be the *Ieyasu Maru*. Or it could be the Dutch or the Spanish."

Isamu ran to the quarry, with Yells-at-Bears close behind him. The arrival of a Dutch ship would be mildly irritating. A Spanish visitation would be another matter entirely. The Spanish were an existential threat to New Nippon. They had a well-established colony of their own on the Pacific Coast of North America—New Spain, in Mexico—and each year galleons traveled between New Spain and the Philippines, with the eastbound galleon usually making landfall in southern California. When the *Ieyasu Maru* left Japan, its officers knew that the Dutch and Japanese had launched an assault on Manila, the capital of the Spanish Philippines, but not whether the assault had succeeded. Whether it succeeded or failed, it would guarantee that if the Spanish ever discovered the presence of a Japanese colony on the West Coast, they would retaliate as soon as they could assemble a punitive force.

Isamu assumed that there was already a Japanese colony at Monterey Bay, as Tokubei had told him that it was the planned destination of the First Fleet. And there was certainly a risk that the Spanish would stumble upon that colony, at some point. According to the up-time history books that the Dutch had brought to Japan, the Spaniards had discovered Monterey Bay in 1602, if not earlier, and colonized it in 1769.

While the Spanish were more likely to go to Monterey Bay, or San Francisco Bay, than the Strait of Georgia, it was not impossible for them to venture this far north. According to up-time sources, in old timeline 1775 they had made it as far as the Olympic Peninsula, and in 1792 they had stopped at Nootka Sound on Vancouver Island and continued up to the Alaskan Panhandle.

Zensuke, the second-in-command of Isamu's sailors, was at Quarry Number One, with several of the miners. He held the exploration party's precious spyglass, which he handed to Isamu.

"Is it the *Ieyasu Maru*?" asked Isamu.

"Definitely not," said Zensuke. "It is quite a bit larger than the *Ieyasu Maru*, but it has a similar shape. The *Ieyasu Maru* was of Dutch design, so perhaps this is a Dutch ship. I can't see the ensign; the wind is blowing it straight towards us."

"I am not worried about Dutch ships so much as Spanish ones. How similar are they?"

"I don't know, I have never seen a Spanish ship," Zensuke admitted.

The ship fired one of its cannon. There was no splash; that suggested it was fired without shot, as a signal rather than an attack.

"I guess they know we're here," said Zensuke.

"Raise the standard where they can see it." It was a long vertical blue banner with a red circle on it.

As Zensuke did so, Isamu continued to study the incoming ship with the spyglass. Suddenly he noticed something new. "Fuck! There's a second ship behind it!"

"Seems to be of a similar size," muttered Zensuke. "I hope that they are the colony ships that Tokubei was going to ask for."

Some minutes later, the lead ship lowered a longboat. While it was still making its way to shore, the wind slackened for a moment, and Isamu could see that the standard on the longboat matched his own. By the time the longboat arrived at Iron Landing, Isamu could see that one of the passengers was a samurai. Relieved, Isamu started making his way down to Iron Landing to greet him, and his men followed him.

The coast of this part of Texada Island was dominated by low, heavily broken cliffs. The "beach" of "Iron Landing" was really a great slab of rock sloping up from the water. It had probably fallen away from the cliff that rose behind it. Isamu fervently prayed to the Goddess of Mercy that the rocks that lay offshore would not rip a hole in the bottom of the approaching longboat. It would not be an auspicious introduction to Texada Island.

Because of the steepness of the slope of the slab, the broken water began close to the shoreline. On the longboat, the boatswain waited for the men on shore to notice what he was doing and move to face him. He steered the boat to face Iron Landing, and ordered, "Paddle hard!" The longboat leaped forward. Just as it entered the surf, he pulled strongly on the tiller, and yelled, "Port side draw!" The boat came around and the next big wave threw it on her broadside up onto the slab.

The samurai on board the longboat had already hitched up the legs of his "horse-riding" *hakama*, leaving his legs bare, just in case he had to walk through the surf. But this precaution was unnecessary. As soon as the boat stopped moving, he leapt onto the rocky shore.

The boatswain and his fellows clambered out of the longboat, and the Isamu's men, waiting on shore, rushed down to help haul her out of reach of the angry waters.

The newly arrived samurai was Isamu's former colleague, Terasaka Haru. They bowed politely to each other, the slight bow between equals. Like Isamu and Masaru, Haru's clothing bore the *Take ni Suzume*, the "sparrows and bamboo" *mon* of the Date clan, since he was in Date service. His clothing, however, was in good shape, whereas Isamu's had obviously been mended. And Haru's hair was neatly trimmed. Isamu's, not so much. But then, he hadn't expected visitors.

"Welcome back to Texada, Haru!" exclaimed Isamu.

"The blessings of the kamis and buddhas upon you, Isamu! I am happy, but not surprised, to see that you survived."

"Why have you come here on a ship other than the *Ieyasu Maru*?" asked Isamu. "It didn't sink, did it?"

"Not to my knowledge. But I left it at Monterey Bay."

"So the First Fleet arrived there, with the colonists?"

"It did."

"And our lord Date Masamune is well?"

"He is. As well as anyone could hope for, given his age."

"So how did you come to leave the *Ieyasu Maru*?"

"When the *Ieyasu Maru* came to Monterey Bay, it needed a refit, so I was put on the first ship returning to Japan to report on our discoveries. And I recruited ironworkers there, and have brought them back to this island. They are on the ship right behind me, the *Iemitsu Maru*." He gave Isamu the names of the *sannai* workers, the smith, and the iron caster.

Isamu's eyebrow twitched. *So who is in charge on Texada, now? Me or Haru?* Isamu liked Haru, but didn't want the shame of a demotion.

Haru obviously sensed Isamu's discomfort, because his next words were, "I will be your liaison to the ironworkers, but let me know whether there is anything else I can do to help out."

"I will. I am surprised that we need more than just a smith to get the iron out of the ore."

Haru laughed. "I received an education in that regard. Smiths haven't done their own smelting in decades. They buy the jewel-steel from dealers, who buy it from smelteries—*sannai*—in Chugoku. And those communities are very large. There's the smeltery foreman, the *murage*, and his assistant, the *sumisaka*. Then there are the charcoal burners, who cut down trees and make charcoal, the laborers who collect the iron sand, the firemen who add the charcoal and iron sand to the *tatara* smelter, the bellowsmen that supply the air draft, and the hammerers who break up the conglomerate of steel, pig iron and slag into manageable pieces. The jewel-steel, the *tamahagane*, goes to the smith, and the pig iron, the *zuku*, to the iron caster.

"Oh, I almost forgot to mention, we also have a priest of Kanayago, the goddess of the *sannai* workers, on board. He is going to want the *sannai* workers segregated as much as possible from the *kirishitan*. That is why there are no *kirishitan* on the *Iemitsu Maru*."

"They are on the second ship?"

"Yes, the *Sendai Maru*."

"Why does the priest want the *sannai* workers separated from the kirishitan colonists? Is he afraid that they will become Christian? The Shogunate Black Seal Edict for New Nippon says that anyone may worship whatever they please, as long as they don't interfere with anyone else."

"So the goddess isn't displeased by their heresies. The priest, Tanaka, says that if the goddess is displeased by their heresies, she will cause the *tatara* to fail."

"I will see what I can come up with. How many *kirishitan* colonists have you brought?"

"On the *Sendai Maru*, about sixty. Mostly *kirishitan* farmers and fishermen from southern Honshu. They have their own headmen. There are also samurai posted on board to make sure they went tamely into exile, but many of those will be returning to Japan. The *Mutsu Maru*, if it makes it here, has a similar passenger complement. The *Unagi Maru*, which went looking for it, is just a *war-jacht*, with sailors and a few samurai marines. No *kirishitan*."

"Hmm . . . It will take some hours to get everyone and everything ashore . . . Have your captains anchor in Sandy Bottom Bay. We will meet the boats on the beach there, and guide the colonists to the temporary lodgings we built for them."

"Excellent," said Haru. "I will have those instructions passed on as soon as we are finished speaking."

"Any news of interest from Japan?"

"In March of last year, we took Manila and Cavite from the Spanish. With Dutch help, mind you."

"That is wonderful news! Plainly, the kamis and the buddhas favor our people."

The boatswain of the *Iemitsu Maru* was sent back to the ship with Isamu's instructions, and Isamu took Haru to Camp Double Six. While Haru had been one of Isamu's companions on the *Ieyasu Maru*, he had remained on board, as part of the deck watch, so this was his first time setting foot on Texada.

The path from the landing site to the Japanese camp zigzagged up the coastal hills some two hundred or more feet, where it reached a shelf of sorts. Here lay the little quarry where the camp's small contingent of miners had first collected iron ore. Two oak trees flanked the quarry.

The path now went east, following what appeared to be an old game trail. At least, there was little in the way of undergrowth.

After about a mile, the path turned slowly left and upward, away from the game trail. It zigzagged up the slope. Pebbles, disturbed by their passage, skittered downhill.

Camp Double Six stood about two hundred feet above the quarry level.

Haru studied the wall protecting Camp Double Six with a soldier's eye. Back home, a bandit chief, let alone a daimyo, would have been ashamed of it, but he knew that manpower, time and materials had all been limited on Texada.

"Now that the colonists have come, you'll be able to have them build you something better," said Haru.

"True, but we will probably build a new fort closer to their settlements, rather than improve this one. But this will still serve as a refuge for the miners."

Isamu ushered Haru through the gate in the wall, and then into the main building.

"The *Ieyasu Maru* only left enough water for a couple of weeks, and enough food for a couple of months," said Isamu. "After that, we were on our own."

"You must have had a busy few months after your arrival."

"We did. I am not sure if we would have survived had it not been for Yells-at-Bears' knowledge of the Indian ways of finding food."

"Yells-at-Bears... she was the translator we left you? The one Tokubei bought?"

"That's right."

In the dining hall, the two miners were playing *ban-sugoroku*, while Saichi watched—presumably waiting to play the winner. They bowed to Isamu and then to Haru, the deep bow of commoner to samurai.

Isamu introduced Saichi to Haru. "Saichi here is our chief miner."

Haru explained why he had come to Texada. It was to establish an "experimental" *sannai*—an ironworker community—so the Texada iron ore could be smelted. At least, that was the hope. The ore was quite different from the iron sands mined in Chugoku, where the ironworkers came from.

Haru had also brought a smith and an iron caster, so the steel and cast iron produced by the *sannai* could be fashioned into tools, trade goods and weapons.

"That is wonderful news!" Saichi exclaimed. "We have mined iron ore, when we weren't needed to gather food and water, but it was frustrating to pile it up and not see it put to use."

"Is Yells-at-Bears here?" asked Isamu. "I want to introduce her to Haru."

"I think she is in the storage room," said Saichi. "I will fetch her for you." He strode off.

The other miners had, in the meantime, returned to their game. One rolled a pair of dice, and crowed when he saw that he had gotten a double-six, a *sugoroku*. He advanced his token twelve spaces and handed the dice to his opponent. Tokubei, the first mate, had told Isamu that the Dutch and Portuguese played a similar game, backgammon.

"And here is our mentor on wilderness survival, Yells-at-Bears," Saichi announced. He tilted his head slightly in her direction. Pointing fingers at a person was considered impolite.

Isamu made a similar nod in Haru's direction. "This is my friend, Terasaka Haru," Isamu declared.

"I am pleased to make your acquaintance," said Yells-at-Bears, bowing. "Any friend of Isamu is a friend of mine."

Haru's eyebrows rose, ever so slightly. First, because of how much Yells-at-Bears' command of Japanese had improved since the *Ieyasu Maru* had left her and Isamu on Texada the previous year. It called to mind a Dutch term that Tokubei had passed on: "a pillow dictionary."

And second, because it suddenly struck him that Yells-at-Bears was one of the natives whose features were such that they could pass as Japanese if properly attired. The grand governor's scholars had wondered about this, and the Dutch had told them that the up-timers' encyclopedias claimed that in the distant past, there had been a land bridge between northeast Asia and North America, and the Indians had passed over it.

"Yells-at-Bears will teach your colonists about what, where and how to fish, the many uses of the cedar tree, and what to do—or not do—if they run into other natives," said Isamu.

There was a note of pride—and perhaps something else?—in Isamu's voice, and Haru frowned.

"If that's all, I'd best get back to my work," said Yells-at-Bears.

"That's fine," said Isamu. "I am just giving Haru a tour of our part of Texada. We'll see you at dinner."

Yells-at-Bears bowed again to Haru, gave Isamu a look, and walked out of the dining hall, her hips swinging slightly from side to side.

"Pretty girl," volunteered Haru.

Isamu coughed. "Yes, quite. And very helpful."

"I'm sure."

Next, Isamu took Haru to Rattling Bird Lake. "We named it after the bird that led us to it. It made a rattling noise. Yells-at-Bears told me that her people danced to the sound of rattles and drums, and she had once owned a rattle in the shape of a rattling bird.

"It is a small bird with a big head." He put the heel of his hand on top of his head, fingers pointing up. "It has a shaggy crest, like so, colored the blue of . . ." He paused, then continued, "the blue of a faraway mountain. Yells-at-Bears says that it is a hunter of freshwater fish."

Haru looked down into the water. He could see little fish swimming in it. "Is the water safe to drink?"

"It is." Isamu cupped his hands, bent down, and collected some of the lake water.

He had just started drinking it when Haru abruptly asked, "Are you sleeping with her?"

Isamu started choking. Haru rapped him on the back. "Are you all right?"

"Yes," said Isamu, "no thanks to you. And, yes, I am sleeping with her, not that it is any of your business."

"Not officially, but I am your friend, and thus entitled to be nosy. Do you intend to bring her back home, as a concubine? Will you dump her once the colonists arrive, and you have more of a choice of women?"

"I didn't establish a relationship with Yells-at-Bears because she is the only woman on Texada. She has plenty of points in her favor, and not just her looks."

"I am sure she does. But I am not sure your family would see it that way."

"My family? " Isamu snorted. "For all I know, they have written me off. It's no secret that the shogun fears and distrusts the grand governor. Giving Date Masamune this posting was a way of taking him off the *shogi* board. The shogun might not have said so outright, but Date-sama is probably as much in exile as the *kirishitan*, and the same with his servants . . . like us. My family might not care who I marry at this point, if I am stuck in New Nippon for the rest of my life."

"I was able to go back," said Haru mildly.

"But the longer we remain in service among the *kirishitan*, the more likely we are to be banned," Isamu warned. "Perhaps . . . perhaps I should marry Yells-at-Bears."

"That's a crazy idea," said Haru. "You're in Date Masamune's service. You'd need his approval."

Isamu shrugged. "He might think it a form of diplomacy. Like the Chinese Emperor marrying off a Chinese princess to some Mongol or Jurchen chieftain."

"You forget, I was on the *Ieyasu Maru* when we bought her off the Gwat'sinux. Whatever her parents were, she's an ex-slave, not a fucking native princess. And I don't think Date Masamune will give his approval unless your clan is agreeable. Which they won't be."

Isamu held up his hands. "You just got here. Let's talk about this another time. I haven't said anything to her about marriage. And it's not as though I can beg Date Masamune's blessing today."

Haru sighed. "Agreed. Did you have more to show me?"

Isamu nodded. The two samurai headed southeast and came to a second lake. This lake was of an irregular shape, and surrounded by mossy bluffs. Isamu motioned Haru over to the marshy verge, and touched a viny plant. "This bears tasty red berries in the fall. We named this lake after them—Marsh Berry Lake."

Haru coughed. "Before I forget, Captain Fukuzawa says that Iron Landing is a horrible place to moor a ship. It is way too exposed."

"Fudenojo, our chief sailor, said the same thing," acknowledged Isamu. "Sandy Bottom Bay is safer."

"So I suppose we will have to smelt the iron ore up here, then transport any iron that is being sent to Monterey Bay or back home to Sandy Bottom Bay," mused Haru. "That is unfortunate."

"It's true that our original quarry, the one I showed you, is uncomfortably far from Sandy Bottom Bay. At least, if one is carrying big chunks of iron ore. But Saichi surveyed the land, and found richer outcroppings of iron ore over a broad area, running east from near Iron Landing, to within a couple hundred paces of Rattling Bird Lake. The outcrops were, he said, anywhere from two hundred to five hundred feet above sea level.

"We mined what was easy to collect from Quarry Number One, and then shifted our activities to the ones closer to Camp Double Six. Although we kept Quarry Number One as a lookout post. Now what's important is where the quarrying is done relative to where your *murage* puts the *tatara*."

Isamu took a breath. "If we head southeast, we reach Sandy Bottom Bay. It's about half a mile from here. We had best go there now and meet the boats from the *Iemitsu Maru* and the *Sendai Maru*."

"Lead the way!" exclaimed Haru.

Chapter 7

Sandy Bottom Bay

As one of the sailors from the *Iemitsu Maru* held the longboat steady, the smith Arinobu stepped into the knee-high water at the landward end of Sandy Bottom Bay, then turned.

"Umako, hand Haru-chan to me." She picked up their son, and Arinobu hoisted the boy onto his shoulders. "Wait, I'll come back for you."

He carried Harunobu—Haru-chan was what his mother and father called him—to the beach, and set him down there. "Don't move!"

Arinobu then went back to fetch Umako. She was wringing out the bottom of her kimono—while she had hitched it up in preparation to enter the water, a stray wave had caught her—when an unfamiliar samurai approached him.

It was plain that he had been living in the wilderness for a long time. His hair had grown over his ears and there was stubble along his chin. There was also a poorly repaired rip on one of the knees of his sea-blue *hakama*.

Well, Arinobu knew better than to call attention to the sartorial deficiencies of a samurai.

"You are Arinobu, the smith?"

"I am," said Arinobu. He bowed. "And whom do I have the honor of addressing?"

"I am Oyamada Isamu. I am in command here. When Haru-san arrived here, he told me about you. I am very pleased you came. With you here, we can do more than mine iron, we can make it into tools and weapons."

"That is why the Date clan's agents recruited me." Arinobu didn't elaborate. Some months ago, Arinobu had gone to Sendai, the capital of the domain ruled by the Date clan, to petition on behalf of his younger brother. The younger brother had been found guilty of selling stolen goods. He claimed that he hadn't known they were stolen, but the thief was a known friend of his, and, under torture, the thief had accused him of confederacy. Like most crimes that disturbed the Tokugawa sense of order, it carried the death penalty. The smith pleaded for leniency on account of the brother's age—he was only fifteen—the small value of the sale the brother had made, and the bad influence of the friend. Magistrates in Japan had a great deal of discretion in deciding what punishment to impose for a crime.

But those supposed extenuating circumstances proved less important than what Arinobu could offer the Date clan as recompense. Date Tadamune, who was ruling the domain in Date Masamune's absence, offered Arinobu a deal; he would commute the brother's sentence to exile from Sendai Domain provided that Arinobu served in New Nippon for five years. Arinobu agreed. And here he was, with his family, in the most remote finger of New Nippon.

You seem lost in thought," said Isamu.

"My apologies," said Arinobu, bowing his head. "I was. You should know that I can't get the iron out of the ore; you need Tetsue and his people for that." Tetsue was the *murage,* the smelter foreman, recruited by Terasaka Haru.

"Yes, I know. Tetsue came ashore about an hour ago. We were going to take him to the huts we have set up as temporary housing for the colonists, but he wanted to see the mine first."

Arinobu laughed. "That sounds like Tetsue. But since it will be a while before I have any iron to work with, I'd like to see where we'll be living. Do you know when our belongings will be brought ashore?"

"No. My authority ends where the water begins, I fear. You'd have to ask one of Captain Fukuzawa's mates. But I can take you to where you'll be living, at least for the next few days."

Isamu excused himself to talk to one of the sailors, and Arinobu and his wife studied what they could see of their new home. The tide was going out, and it left behind some tidal pools, whose denizens fascinated young Harunobu. There were anemones, crabs, sea stars, snails, fish, and even an octopus. The tidal pools also attracted the attention of a great blue heron and several seagulls. Harunobu tried chasing the seagulls, but they easily eluded him.

At last, a sailor called out to Arinobu that it was time for them to collect their belongings and take them to their temporary quarters. Those were just their personal belongings; his smithy equipment was stowed separately.

Isamu spotted them trudging up the beach and joined them. "I will guide you to where you need to go," he said. This was a great honor, coming from a samurai to a commoner. *But then again,* Arinobu reflected, *you would have to travel to Monterey Bay, over eleven hundred miles south of Texada, to find another swordsmith.*

Arinobu and his family did not, at least, have to negotiate Marsh Berry Creek. Isamu's scouting party had found it a rather inconvenient route for accessing Sandy Bottom Bay when they wanted to dig for clams or try to catch fish and, in the spring, had cut a trail on mostly higher (and drier) ground. Where it crossed Marsh Berry Creek, they had laid stepping stones and logs.

"With the additional manpower of the colonists your ship brought over, we can build a plank road," confided Isamu. "We can then use hand carts to transport goods in both directions."

The trail climbed to the east of Marsh Berry Lake and then turned left to pass between it and Rattling Bird Lake. It took them at last to a broad limestone terrace on which there was a sort of longhouse. It had a single sloped roof, making it evident that the builders expected that it would have to cope with heavy rains for part of the year. Coming closer, Arinobu could see that it was of a light construction, built in haste or with limited resources.

"So here we are. We call it 'Welcome House.' The frames are cedar poles tied together, and the walls are strips of cedar bark. The roofs are of bark, or leaves." Isamu spread his hands apologetically. "Yes, I know it is primitive. The natives build their longhouses with cedar timbers and planks, but we have only one carpenter, and most of our effort goes to feeding ourselves."

The temporary quarters for Arinobu and his family were just a curtained-off section of the Welcome House. "I am sorry, my dear," he whispered to Umako. "Sorry you and Harunobu had to cross an ocean."

"You did what you had to do."

Harunobu laid down on the cedar bough bedding that had been placed in one corner. He was soon fast asleep. Umako motioned to Arinobu to go out.

In the common area, he found Isamu. "You have had contact with the natives? What are they like?" asked Arinobu. "Are they like the Ainu?"

"When I was on the *Ieyasu Maru*, we had contact with some of the natives on the great island to the west, Vancouver Island."

"Is it as large as Honshu?"

"Oh, no. More like Kyushu. Anyway, we found some Japanese castaways, and they in turn helped us find some natives to serve as interpreters. We have two of the castaways, and one of the native interpreters, here now. Which is a good thing, because we did run into a small party of Indians south of Marsh Berry Lake."

"Did they attack you?"

"No, we reached an understanding, but there were some tense moments. And we know that some of the tribes are both numerous and warlike, so we are glad that the *Iemitsu Maru* and *Sendai Maru* have upped our numbers and fighting capability. As for the natives, they are hunters and fishers like the Ainu." He grinned. "I can introduce you to one now."

"That would be most interesting," said Arinobu. "But how would we communicate?"

"She speaks Japanese. Not perfectly, but she can certainly make herself understood, and understand the gist of what we are saying to her."

"How is that possible?"

"She came aboard the *Ieyasu Maru* about a year ago and she has been a diligent student."

"Well . . . even so . . . she must be quite clever. . . ."

"She is."

Yells-at-Bears was inside the Welcome House, treating the newly arrived sailors and colonists who showed symptoms of scurvy. Her remedy was "tree needle tea," made from the Douglas-fir trees that were common on Texada.

She was introduced to Arinobu as "*Kuma-san ni donaru hito.*" Literally, "a person who yells at a bear."

She took a moment to study the smith. He was of middling height, with thick eyebrows and prominent cheekbones. She guessed that he was in his thirties. He was wearing two swords, but no *hakama*.

"You are a samurai?" she asked.

"Oh, no. But as a swordsmith, I have the privilege of the 'large' and the 'small.'"

Arinobu had a question of his own. "Excuse me if this question is impertinent but your name in Japanese is unusual. Is it a translation of your name in your own language?"

"It is," said Yells-at-Bears.

"How did you come by it?"

Yells-at-Bears smiled impishly. "It was because of what happened when I was ten summers old. I was with two younger children, near a berry patch, and I saw a black bear walking slowly on all fours toward us.

"I didn't know whether it wanted to eat the berries or us, but had to assume the worst.

"I called the other children to me and had them hold me, so we looked like one big animal with many limbs, and I yelled at the bear. 'What do you think you're doing, Bear? Go away!'"

"You must have wanted to run."

"Can't run from a black bear; it says, 'I am prey, try to catch me.' Even backing away slowly is risky. And with a black bear, it does no good to climb a tree. They climb well. Better than children, certainly.

"Anyway, the bear stopped, and rose up on two legs, like a man. I don't know whether it was to scare us, or to get a better look at us, but that's what it did.

"And I guess it didn't like the looks of us, as it retreated." She paused. "But we didn't do any more berry picking that day."

"I don't blame you," said Arinobu.

Chapter 8

Isamu ordered that all of the members of his exploration party, as well as the newly arrived colonists, assemble in front of Welcome House. Captain Fukuzawa came, too, although Isamu had no clear authority over him. And he would be reporting to the shogun's agents, and perhaps also to the grand governor of New Nippon, on how Isamu conducted himself.

He looked around to make sure that Yells-at-Bears was present. Yes, there she was, wearing a pink rose in her hair. It was a flower that had just come into bloom this month. Isamu himself was now freshly groomed. He had even oiled his queue.

"Welcome to Texada Island. Some of you are followers of the kamis and buddhas." He gestured toward Tanaka, the priest of Kanayago-kami, and the ironworkers seated near him. Tanaka was a little shorter and stockier than Haru, but probably of similar age. He was wearing the everyday vestments of a Shinto priest: a tall, black *eboshi* hat, and a white *karaginu* robe.

"And others of you are *kirishitan*, who have come here to worship your *Deusu* in peace." He motioned toward the other new arrivals.

"All must obey the following Black Seal Edict, given under the hand of the shogun of Nippon, Tokugawa Iemitsu, court noble of the upper first rank:

"One. It shall be unlawful for barbarians, or people from outside provinces, to enter or exit New Nippon to trade with the Indians without the consent of the grand governor of New Nippon, or the shogun.

"Two. Within the province of New Nippon, freedom of worship is permitted, provided that it does not disturb public harmony.

"Three. It shall be unlawful for residents of New Nippon who are of the Christian faith to return to their former provinces without the consent of the shogun or his duly appointed representatives.

"Four. It is strictly prohibited to inflict injustices or crimes upon the Indians of New Nippon."

Isamu paused for effect. "This edict will be rigorously enforced. I call to your attention that freedom of worship is not merely that you may worship freely, it is also that you must not interfere with the freedom of another. Any attempt by *kirishitan* to convert a Shintoist or Buddhist to Christianity will be considered interference, unless you have received prior permission from me. But likewise, I will punish any attempt by a Shintoist or Buddhist to persecute a *kirishitan* on account of religion." He fingered his hilt of his *wakizashi*.

"Now, on to lighter matters. My companions and I have been here since August 1634, exploring the island and preparing for your arrival. I will introduce them to you, so if you have questions, you will know who to ask."

He named each of them, but it was only when Yells-at-Bears was introduced, as the native translator and expert on native fishing and foraging methods, that there was an audible stir in the audience. For most of the newcomers, it was their first sight of a Pacific Northwest Indian. Albeit one whose wardrobe had been influenced by her Japanese colleagues. She had even been persuaded to wear a kimono, purchased from one of the female colonists, for this occasion.

"I know that the Welcome House behind me is not ideal, but it is the best that we could do, given our numbers, and not knowing when or even if you would come, and how many of you there would be. But it will give you a place to lay your head until you can construct something better here."

The Shinto and Buddhist ironworkers, and the *kirishitan* miners, fishermen, farmers and artisans, disagreed sharply on matters of religion, but they did agree on at least one thing: they didn't find "Welcome House" particularly welcoming. The problem wasn't the overall design, but rather the detailed execution. Come winter, when (as one of the sailors from the exploration party told them) there would be heavy rain and strong winds, they would be shivering inside, with rain dripping from the leaky roof. At least until the whole thing blew down.

In fact, the sailor added, Yells-at-Bears had made scathing remarks about using sapling posts and beams where her people would insist on tree trunks nearly as thick as the *Ieyasu Maru*'s mainmast.

Soon after the *Iemitsu Maru*'s arrival, Isamu received petitions from the various colonist factions with regard to the location of the permanent settlement. The fishermen of course wanted the settlement to be near Sandy Bottom Bay, and the miners had an equally strong urge for proximity to the iron ore quarries, presently as much as three to four miles from the bay. The farmers wanted to see what arable land Texada had to offer before taking a position. Isamu's fear was that the Japanese would end up divided into three widely separated villages, which would be a nightmare to defend.

So, a few days after the *Iemitsu Maru* arrived, Isamu took the leaders of the *kirishitan* farmers to see the land he thought they could farm. Isamu made an expansive gesture. "This is Marsh Berry Lake. We thought that perhaps the shore could be used to grow rice. There is no lack of fresh water, yes?"

Hidezo, the headman of the farmers, nodded politely.

"And now, if you follow me, I'll show you Rattling Bird Lake. . . ." said Isamu as he walked northward. As he did so, he thought, *Marsh Berry Lake is only a mile from Quarry Two, and Rattling Bird is perhaps a little closer. If I can get the farmers to accept these fields, then I can at least put the farmers and the miners in the same village. . . .*

Wataru, another farmer, tapped Hidezo on the shoulder, and cupping his hand so Isamu couldn't hear what he said, complained to Hidezo. "Why does this samurai think he knows where rice can be grown? It's too cold here."

"I know," said Hidezo. "And we have been here a week, and it still hasn't rained. That native woman, Yells-at-Bears, says that this is the dry season. Whoever heard of a dry summer?"

"It is contrary to the natural order," Wataru agreed. "But so is a farmer convincing a samurai that he is wrong about anything."

"I know. If we tell him the truth, he may cut us down on the spot.

And if we don't, then we will labor for months and have nothing to show for it. That's why I am glad *you're* the headman."

The two farmers politely followed the oblivious Isamu to Rattling Bird Lake and listened to him extol its virtues. At last, he asked, "So, how many *koku* of rice do you think we can produce?" The *koku* was the amount of rice needed to feed a man for a year.

Hidezo gave Wataru a beseeching look. Wataru surreptitiously made the sign of the cross.

Hidezo bowed. "Most esteemed samurai, even back home, production varies greatly from year to year, and from plot to plot. Here, in a land whose soil and climate are unknown to us, only Deusu knows."

"But as an experienced farmer, you must have some idea of how much rice we can grow here, neh?"

Hidezo bowed again, even more deeply. "Tell me, where are you from?"

"From Sendai," said Isamu.

"And how does the weather here compare to that of Sendai?"

Isamu shrugged. "It is a bit cooler and drier."

"Well, we are from the southern end of Honshu. To us, it is as cold as Honshu would have been two months ago. Rice needs four months of warm weather to grow, and . . . and I don't think that on this island it will be warm enough, long enough. So sorry. . . ."

Isamu's first reaction was one of shock.

Wataru, belatedly feeling an obligation to support Hidezo, added, "I agree. And it may also be too dry. Rice is the thirstiest of crops. We can compensate somewhat by irrigation, of course, but I don't know whether it will be enough."

Isamu could feel his face turning red with embarrassment. He had bragged to Masaru about the significance of discovering the lakes. We will have no trouble growing our own rice, he had said. Now he would be eating his words, not rice.

The farmers, seeing his face, took several steps back, their faces now fearful. Isamu fought to control his anger. Commander Hosoya had told Isamu, when you are a commander, you must not blame the messenger for bringing bad news, lest no one give you the news until it is too late to salvage the situation.

Still, it would feel so good to break something right now. . . .

At last, he said, "I will ask Captain Fukuzawa to carry a message back to Sendai. They can ask the Matsumae clan whether they have any varieties of rice that will grow on Ezochi. I have heard that it has cool summers." Ezochi was the large island shown as Hokkaido on the up-time maps, and the Matsumae outpost at Hakodate in southern Hokkaido was about three hundred miles north of Sendai. "If so, they can send us Ezochi rice seeds."

The farmers praised his wisdom, and didn't point out the obvious problem that it probably would be two years or more before that "Ezochi cold-hardy rice" was delivered to Texada—assuming it even existed.

Isamu sighed. "So what can we grow here?"

The farmers exchanged glances.

"It would perhaps be better for us to explore more of the island before giving an opinion," said Hidezo.

"But what is wrong with this place for wheat, or barley?" prodded Isamu.

"For wheat or barley, it is too wet," said Wataru.

"But we are happy to look for some place better," Hidezo added hurriedly.

"Fine. I will hold you to that."

"It is all very troubling," Isamu told Yells-at-Bears. While Captain Yamada Haruno and Samurai Commander Hosoya Yoritaki of the *Ieyasu Maru* may have wanted Isamu's scouting party to make great piles of ore during the fall, most of their efforts had to go to accumulating enough food to last them through the winter. And in the winter, mining was limited by the frequent downpours.

The arrival of the *Iemitsu Maru* had led him to hope that they would at last have enough food-gatherers to have a surplus with which to feed the miners, so the latter could devote full-time to mining. But now there were not only the miners, but also the ironworkers to feed. And if the farmers he had been sent couldn't farm . . . well, you can't eat iron ore!

Yells-at-Bears couldn't make any suggestions as to where to put the farms, because she had only limited acquaintance with agriculture. Her people weeded beds of camas—a root vegetable that looked like an onion but tasted like a pumpkin—and sowed camas seeds directly into the soil as they harvested the bulbs, but they did not transplant camas seeds from one field to another.

Still, she understood that whatever the plant the Japanese were trying to grow, it was very particular about where it would grow—just like camas, which grew only in meadows with scattered Garry oak trees. And she also understood that Isamu needed her support.

She hugged him and said, "I am sure you will find a solution."

The next day, Isamu and Yells-at-Bears took the farmers on a tour of the area around Sandy Bottom Bay. At last they came to the top of the ridge defining the eastern shore of the bay. While it was stonier and not as level as they would have liked, they held out some hope. Perhaps, they said, one could grow wheat here. Or soybeans. Or, some of the cold-hardy vegetables, like potatoes.

"Isn't that just horse-fodder?" asked Isamu. Potatoes had been introduced to Japan around 1600, as an ornamental plant, but the Japanese were quick to discover a practical use for them.

Wataru shrugged. "If there is no rice, we eat barley and wheat. If they are not available, we eat buckwheat and millet. Potatoes are at least as good as millet."

"So, you will farm this land?"

"We are willing to try," said Hidezo. "In fact, we should plant soybeans right away. But we need to find fresh water nearby. It would be arduous to carry it from the lake."

"What about the bay water?"

"The salt would kill the crops."

The farmers' first suggestion was to get it from Marsh Berry Creek. However, that was the lowest, least defensible part of the ridge. Yells-at-Bears proposed that they explore the area east of Sandy Bottom Bay, looking for mountain streams, lakes and springs. About three-quarters of the way from the head of Sandy Bottom Bay to Sentinel Island, and about two thousand feet from the shoreline, they found a series of springs, in a north-south line.

"These will do for now," said Hidezo. "And when the heavy rains came in the fall and winter, we can collect the rainwater in wells or cisterns for future use."

What Isamu liked about this location wasn't the soil, but its position perhaps two hundred feet above the sea. The initial slope upward was perhaps forty-five degrees up to an altitude of perhaps a hundred feet. If the farming village were established here, at the top of the ridge, it would be difficult to attack it from the pebbly beach directly below it. Rather, the canoes would probably be beached at the head of the bay, and then the raiders would have to turn onto the ridge and follow it to the proposed farming village site, a distance of nearly two miles. That would give the Japanese time to spot them coming, sound the alarm, and assemble the militia. Once Isamu and his fellow samurai trained the farmers as militiamen, that is. At least the two colony ships had brought more arquebuses, shot and powder. And also some small cannon: swivel guns and three-pounders.

"All right," said Isamu. Just as he made this decision, he heard the "yewk yewk" of an osprey as it passed overhead. It winged over the bay, hovered for a moment, then plunged down into the water. It emerged triumphantly, a fish in its mouth . . . for just an instant, as it gave it a slight toss and swallowed it.

Isamu decided it was a good omen. "We will call this Sea Hawk Village."

The next morning, Isamu sent Saichi to explore the area near Sea Hawk Village. It would be ideal, Isamu told Yells-at-Bears, if iron ore could be found there; the village could then be the base for the miners, too.

Unfortunately, as a visibly tired Saichi reported that evening, the rocks in the vicinity of the planned Sea Hawk Village were quite different from those of the mining district west of Marsh Berry Lake, and he had found no sign of iron ore, or any other mineral of interest.

"So," Isamu complained to Haru, Masaru and Yells-at-Bears, "instead of having one village, easy to defend, it looks like we will have three: Sea Hawk Village by the springs; a fishing village at the head of the bay; and a mining and ironworking village by the present quarries. That's exactly what I was afraid would happen. I cannot be in three places at one time!"

"Nor should you be," said Haru. "I recommend that I take charge of the miners, as I already have a rapport with the ironworkers, Masaru take residence at Sea Hawk Village, and you watch over the fishermen, who I assume will be living just above the beach at the head of Sandy

Bottom Bay. That is the least defensible of the three locations, and also the most central. The most dangerous command should go to you as the supreme commander."

Isamu frowned. Haru's proposal was logical, but there was perhaps a hidden barb: the purpose of establishing the colony in the first place was to exploit its iron ore, which meant that whoever was in charge of the miners and ironworkers would probably get most of the credit for the success of the colony. Isamu didn't think Haru was doing this deliberately—after all, last August, Haru hadn't volunteered to stay on Texada—but Isamu feared that would be the result.

"Yes, I'll send Masaru to Sea Hawk Village." *Let him deal with the farmers' whining.* "But just as you have a rapport with the ironworkers, I do with the miners. We have lived together for almost a year, neh? And you have barely spent any time on Texada. So I think you should introduce me to your ironworkers, and take charge of the fishermen for now. You will need to find a fishing village site close to Sandy Bottom Bay, but with freshwater access and defensible. I will assign Fudenojo, who leads my sailors, as your second-in-command; he is familiar with Sandy Bottom Bay. Who is the headman of the fishing households you brought here?"

"Fukuhei."

"Bring Fukuhei with you when you scout out the possible sites. Otherwise, they are sure to complain about not being consulted."

He raised his voice. "Fudenojo!"

"Yes, sir!"

"Go with Haru here to see Fukuhei. You have some planning to do."

Haru told Fukuhei that the next day they would be scouting for a fishing village site. He in turn questioned Fudenojo about the types of fish that the exploration party had seen in Sandy Bottom Bay. But Fudenojo had to confess that most of their fishing had been for trout, in Rattling Bird and Marsh Berry Lakes, or for salmon in streams. In Sandy Bottom Bay, they mostly dug for clams.

"So, no one here knows what kind of fish you catch in Sandy Bottom Bay?"

"Well . . . perhaps . . . Yells-at-Bears. . . . But I am not sure that Isamu will be agreeable to her accompanying us."

"Why not?" asked Haru.

"Umm . . ." Fudenojo fidgeted.

"Let me guess," said Haru. "She is more than his interpreter. . . ."

"They indeed have a special relationship," Fudenojo admitted. "But Masaru gives Isamu a hard time about it."

"I'll talk to Isamu. We want to talk to her about fish, not cuckoo birds singing amidst the purple irises during the fifth month." Haru was alluding to a famous tenth-century love poem.

Haru and Fudenojo returned to Camp Double Six and persuaded Isamu to spare Yells-at-Bears for the next day. Part of the reason for their success was that Yells-at-Bears was enthusiastic, and nudged Isamu to give permission. She was curious about how the Japanese fishing methods differed from those of her people, and the sailors from the exploration party were not expert fishermen.

The next day, Haru, Fudenojo, Fukuhei and Yells-at-Bears walked to Sandy Bottom Bay. As they walked, Fukuhei talked about line fishing, gill nets, beach seines, boat seines, and encircling nets. Yells-at-Bears in turn told him how her people caught salmon by trolling or with a gaff hook, herring with a gill net or herring rake, and rockfish by jigging.

"What about sardines?" asked Fukuhei. Yells-at-Bears didn't know what that was at first, but Fukuhei described the fish and its habits, and at last she understood.

"Sardines are found further south, but probably not here," she told him. "So sorry."

When they reached the beach, Fukuhei pronounced himself pleased. At low tide, it was evident that the bay had a sandy, gently sloping bottom, at least for at least a mile out from the high tide line. That was perfect for beach seining, in which two net boats, or a single net boat working with a shore crew, dragged the seine onto the beach. They could be used to catch any kind of fish that schooled at shallow depths close to land.

The same conditions did make launching boats awkward, at least at low tide, because they would have to be carried to the water line. But if need be, a few boats could be kept on the narrow beach margins closer to the mouth of the bay.

Fukuhei wasn't the only fisherman on the beach this morning. Several oystercatchers, with black feathers and red beaks, were patrolling the water's edge for clams, oysters and snails. There was a great blue heron there, too, but it was standing statue-like. After a few minutes, it stabbed the water with its bill, and pulled a hapless fish up into the air, swallowing it an instant later.

"So, now we need to find fresh water," said Fukuhei.

"You know, the fishermen could live in Sea Hawk Village," said Haru, pointing in the direction of the site. Farmers, carpenters and sailors were already up there, working together to put up homes. "It's easier to protect one large village than two small ones, and there's going to be a spring inside the walls, so you can't be cut off from fresh water."

"No, it will be too far from the beach," said Fukuhei. "Being there would reduce our productivity."

"Let me take you to fresh water," said Fudenojo. He led the party to the mouth of Marsh Berry Creek.

"Yells-at-Bears, what do you think?" asked Haru.

"You would be very vulnerable to raiders here. They beach their canoes, and then charge the village. You are visible from the bay, and you have no height advantage."

"I agree," said Haru.

"When we explored Marsh Berry Creek, there was a tributary close to the mouth, coming from the east. Perhaps we should explore it," suggested Fudenojo.

They did so. Its confluence with Marsh Berry Creek was a couple of hundred feet from the high tide line, and they found that it ran parallel with the head of the bay for quite a distance. Farther upstream, they encountered a beaver dam.

"Did the Indians build this?" asked Fukuhei.

Yells-at-Bears laughed. "Oh, no, this is dam made by—" The word she used, of course, was the one in her native language, Halkomelem. It sounded like "sklow." She screwed up her face. "I don't know how to say it in Japanese. But it is an animal with big buck teeth and a flat tail. It can grow to be about this big"—she held her hands about four feet apart. "It can weigh almost as much as I do."

This excited some discussion, as beavers were not native, at least as far as they knew, to Honshu, the largest island of the Japanese archipelago. But Haru decided that beavers should be called "buck teeth," and the stream christened "Bucktooth Dam Creek."

They continued upstream, and found a place where a stream came down from the mountain to the north and flowed into Bucktooth Dam Creek. Here there was a profusion of ferns, with four-foot fronds, so they called this tributary, "Big Fern Run." Just beyond Big Fern Run, there was a jog in Bucktooth Dam Creek, the result of which was that there was a stretch of wood surrounded on three sides by water. At this point they were about three tenths of a mile, as the crow flies, from the high tide mark.

"This is good," said Haru. "We can put the village right here, where you will have fresh water, and the streams give a bit of protection on three sides—although I wish that they were wider and deeper! And while it is a little farther from the bay, I like it that the woods hide the village from the view of raiding canoes in the bay."

Fukuhei hesitated.

"This is probably a salmon run, too," said Yells-at-Bears. "So in spawning season, you can catch fish right on your doorstep. For that matter, the beaver dam we passed will slow down the salmon heading upstream, make it easier to spear them."

"I suppose it is doable," conceded Fukuhei. "But we would need boat sheds on the beach, so raiders would know that there is someone living nearby anyway."

"I don't think that's a problem," said Fudenojo. "There will be a trail leading to Sea Hawk Village, and the raiders will assume that the boats are theirs."

"Well . . ." said Fukuhei.

"Don't forget that Isamu-san wanted to put you by Welcome House. That would be a longer walk to the bay than even Sea Hawk Village, let alone this place." Sea Hawk Village was a little over a mile from the mouth of Marsh Berry Creek.

Fukuhei sighed. "Very well. We can also build a hut or two just above the high tide line. The fishermen can use them and perhaps a raider will think that the huts *are* the village and not look further."

They didn't return to Camp Double Six until twilight and, as they neared the camp, they caught a fleeting glimpse of a deer.

"You have deer roaming around this close to camp?" asked Haru.

"We do," said Yells-at-Bears. She pouted. "Masaru hunts them, since he's a Christian, but Isamu insists that he do so well away from camp."

Save for the miners, and Masaru, all of the Japanese in the

exploration party were Buddhists. As Isamu had told Yells-at-Bears, their sects only permitted the eating of deer, and for that matter of rabbit and wild boar, on special days, or when sick. Those who were ill could eat animal flesh in small quantities if prescribed by a physician.

"Well, now that we have all these *kirishitan* on Texada, perhaps Isamu should permit deer hunting for their benefit. While we can put fish on the table tomorrow, getting an edible crop is going to take a while," said Haru. "And if the *kirishitan* eat deer meat, there will be that much more fish and berries for the Buddhists."

"For that matter," said Fukuhei, "I think the iron workers you brought from Chugoku will not be averse to eating deer, even though they follow the way of the kami. Have you met their leader, Tetsue?"

"I have," said Yells-at-Bears. "You know, he was the first Nihonjin I met who had grey hair! He must be older than even Captain Haruno! Tetsue has a nice moustache, too. But he squints a lot."

"As a *murage*, he has to keep looking through a peephole in the tatara to make sure the fire is at the right temperature. His eyesight has probably deteriorated."

"I am sorry to hear that," said Yells-at-Bears. "But at least that won't interfere with his enjoyment of deer meat."

Haru told Yells-at-Bears that in the mountainous interior of Japan, where fish and grain were less available, people ate the flesh of wild animals throughout the year, albeit somewhat surreptitiously. They called rabbits "birds," explaining that their long ears were really wings. And wild boar meat was occasionally sold as "mountain whale."

"I, for one, think deer meat is very tasty," said Yells-at-Bears. "During the years I was kept as a slave, I hardly ever got to eat it." She paused. "If you bring me deer meat, I will tell Isamu that it is 'mountain seal.'"

The next day Yells-at-Bears met Haru for a deer hunting lesson. "I know your archery skills are far superior to mine," she said. "The first time I was allowed to shoot a bow was here on Texada. But there's more to deer hunting than taking the shot. I know because I listened when the boys were taught."

She made a face. "Masaru did not wish to hear my advice. But I can make you a better deer hunter than him. Even if he is the superior archer.

"Every male Indian is expected to be able to hunt deer. But he is not allowed to eat his first three kills, lest he grow up to be a greedy person.

"And the first thing he would be taught is how to make a proper deer call." She showed Haru how to make several different kinds. One was just a blade of grass; she held it lengthwise between her two thumbs as she formed a double fist with the thumbs in her mouth, and blew over it into cavity formed by the palms and other fingers.

Another was a strip of bark held between two pieces of wood. "Be careful using this if you go hunting on the mainland," she warned.

"Why?"

"It makes the sound of a fawn. Instead of attracting a doe, you might draw the attention of a bear or a cougar. They like deer meat as much as I do."

Haru went hunting, and took down a small buck. He boned out the meat, cut several saplings and some vines to make a travois, and dragged it home.

Most of the meat was divided in small portions among some of the *kirishitan*, as a treat after being on sea rations for so long, but the biggest cut he gave to Yells-at-Bears in thanks for her advice: "'Mountain seal,' as promised."

Chapter 9

While the ironworkers did not think that Welcome House was built stoutly enough to live in, they were perfectly happy to build their first *tatara* under its roof. It was only going to be operated for a few months, anyway, and the roof would protect the *tatara* from the occasional summer rain. Their own house could be assembled nearby.

Of course, if they succeeded in producing iron from the Texada iron ore, they would want a proper *takadono*, with a high roof, to house the *tatara* year-round. But that could be built near the Welcome House.

Isamu was pleased, as it meant that the *tatara* would be close to one of the iron outcrops.

"When will you be able to start work on the *tatara*?" he asked.

"Right away, if you can find others to put up our permanent quarters."

"I have a ship's carpenter, and the miners can help him."

"Then let's get started."

Getting started was easier said than done. There was a ritual associated with the creation of a new *sannai*, and it involved the priest, Tanaka, invoking the blessings of Kanayago-kami upon the enterprise. Kanayago's blessing was also needed for the *tatara* and the smithy, both inside Welcome House for the time being. The *sannai*, Iron Haven, would consist of Welcome House, and the new living quarters for the ironworkers. This would be a communal dwelling, like Welcome House, but more stoutly built.

Isamu had thought to quarter the miners with the ironworkers, but relented in the face of vociferous objections from Tanaka, Tetsue and Naoki. They were supported by Haru, who told Isamu that he had promised that the ironworkers would be protected from "pollution" by the *kirishitan*. So at last Isamu agreed that the miners would remain at Camp Double Six. The exploration party had dug cisterns there during the previous fall, so they did have a supply of fresh water.

The first task, however, was the construction of a small shrine to Kanayago-kami just beside Welcome House. Two ironworkers dug two holes for the posts of the *torii*, while the others worked under the supervision of Morimoto, the carpenter's mate. The posts and beams for the *torii* had been transported from Sendai, so all they needed to do was get then aligned and properly fastened together, with tongues fitting into their respective grooves, and then raise it so the butts of the posts slid into the holes. They then tied a straw rope to the posts, and attached paper streamers to it. This indicated that the path through the *torii* was barred.

Beyond the *torii* was the shrine proper, which was essentially a four-post hut, in which Tanaka reverently hung an image of Kanayago-kami.

Once Tanaka was satisfied with the shrine, all of the followers of Shinto gathered in front of the *torii*, and Tanaka cut the rope with a ceremonial knife. Led by Tanaka and the samurai, the worshippers passed through the *torii* gate and then left offerings in front of the shrine.

With that done, they could turn their attention to building the ironworkers' new quarters, so they could move out of Welcome House. With some prodding by Haru and Isamu, Tetsue and Tanaka grudgingly accepted the assistance of the miners from the exploration party, even though they were *kirishitan*. When they were done, Tanaka conducted a rite of purification in the quarters, thus dispelling any baleful Christian influence.

With the ironworkers moved, Arinobu's next task was to assemble the smithy, and two of the laborers brought over on the *Iemitsu Maru* were helping him. The rest of them were helping Tetsue build the *tatara*.

A week later . . .

"Is it deep enough, Master Tetsue?" asked one of the laborers, leaning on his shovel and breathing heavily.

Tetsue squatted beside the rectangular hole, and inserted a measuring rod he had cut previously to the desired depth. "Yes, it will do."

"Should we start putting in the charcoal, then?" asked Daichi, one of the two experienced firemen that had come with Tetsue from Izumo Province.

Tetsue reached down into the hole again, and grabbed a clump of earth. He raised it up to eye level, kneaded it with his fingers, then let it fall. "I'd prefer it to be a bit dryer. Let's build a fire inside, and bake it out."

The workmen followed his orders, and a few hours later, Tetsue pronounced himself satisfied with the result. He went to the Kanayago-kami shrine to pray for success.

The next day, the *tatara,* made of fire clay, was put into operation. For this first operation, it was using charcoal and iron sand brought over from Japan. So it should be successful, unless the climate here on Texada was unfavorable to iron smelting... or Kanayago-kami refused, or was unable, to bless operations so far from Chugoku.

After three days, the *tatara* was broken open, revealing the *kera*, the pig iron-and-steel conglomerate. The *sannai* celebrated, the *kera* was broken up, and the *tamagahane*, the steel, turned over to the smith.

Tetsue had a day to rest his eyes, and his workers a day to rest their arms and legs, and then the debris was cleared away and a new *tatara* built. For this second *tatara,* Tetsue decreed that they would still use the traditional charcoal, but would combine it with the Texada iron ore. The laborers used heavy sledgehammers to break down the latter into smaller pieces.

Tetsue was hopeful that this would work, because he knew, from words passed down from one *murage* to the next, that in ancient times, iron ore had been used on the San'yo side of the Chugoku, especially in Bizen, Bichu and Bingo. Whereas iron sand dominated on the San'in side, where Tetsue had learned his trade.

It took a couple days to rebuild the *tatara* with their Chugoku fire clay. Iron ore and charcoal were added, and the charcoal was ignited. Once the clay was warm enough, the bellowsmen increased their efforts, gradually raising the furnace temperature as other workers added more iron ore and charcoal. Through the peephole, Tetsue could see the color change, from the blood red color of the rising sun, to the white of the mid-day sun.

However, all was not as it should be. The slag was not coming out of the tapping holes as it should. Was the fire not hot enough? Or was there something in the Texada iron ore that was problematic?

Some hours later, Tetsue ordered that the bellowsmen slack off, allowing the charge to cool down to the color of the setting sun. And the following day, the furnace was allowed to die out, and the *tatara* was broken apart.

As Tetsue had feared, the bloom contained a great deal of slag.

Chapter 10

"Haru-chan, time for dinner!" cried Umako. The only answer was the rustling of the leaves in the wind. "Haru-chan!"

Umako saw Moriko, Naoki's wife, gathering some plants in the little herb garden inside the Texada *sannai*. "Moriko, have you seen Harunobu? Is he playing with your boys?"

"No, they were all out by Rattling Bird Lake earlier, but they came back. I haven't seen Harunobu since then. Is he at the smithy, watching your husband work?"

"No, that was the first place I checked."

"Perhaps he is at the *tatara*."

But Umako didn't find him there either. She wasn't allowed inside—the goddess was jealous of other women, and even on the other side of the ocean from Japan, the ironworkers didn't dare break that taboo—but Tetsue heard her yelling, and came out to investigate.

"What's the problem, Umako?"

She explained.

"Well, what I suggest you do is go to Camp Double Six and recruit Yells-at-Bears, or one of the samurai, to help you search."

She thanked him for the suggestion and ran as fast as she could to Camp Double Six, her long black hair streaming behind her.

"Yes, I will help you," said Yells-at-Bears. "We must first talk to the teenagers he was with earlier, and find out where he likes to go, or has expressed interest in going."

"I will take you to them. And we should stop at the smithy, and get my husband to help us."

"Yes." Yells-at-Bears grabbed a coil of rope, made of twisted dogbane fibers, that was hanging on the wall of the headquarters building, and the two of them set off.

"Are there dangerous wild beasts on Texada?" said Umako, her voice quavering. "Bears? Wolves? Wild Boar? Vipers?"

"None of those," Yells-at-Bears assured her. Her real fear was that Harunobu had fallen into a lake, or slipped off a cliff, but she didn't share those concerns with Umako.

At the smithy, they were joined by Arinobu and his assistants, so they had no lack of muscle power if they needed it for the rescue.

They raced over to Iron Haven, and called Moriko. Once she learned that Harunobu was still missing, she tracked down her sons and brought them out to be interrogated.

"Answer all questions," she ordered. "Hold nothing back!"

"We went to Rattling Bird Lake," said Taro.

"And we skipped pebbles across the water," added Jiro. "Maybe Harunobu went back to do it some more?"

"What was he wearing today?" asked Yells-at-Bears.

"Just a loincloth," said Umako. "It's been a warm day."

Yells-at-Bears frowned. The chance of finding a stray fiber on a plant, marking the path Harunobu took, was not good.

"Moriko, please ask around if there was anything near here that might have attracted Harunobu's attention. In the meantime, we'll search around both lakes. And we'd best hurry. Sunset is only a few hours away."

"You're right," said Arinobu. "We had best divide into two search parties, we'll cover more ground that way."

"I'll go with Umako and Moriko's boys to Rattling Bird Lake. You and your helpers, please check out Marsh Berry Lake."

Perhaps two hours later, both search parties had returned to Iron Haven, without spotting any sign of Harunobu. Naoki, Moriko's husband, waved them over. He was the chief of the *sannai*'s charcoal burners. He carried a walking stick, which he thumped on the ground to get their attention.

"One of my charcoal burners says that yesterday he saw a doe and a fawn at the edge of the woods near Iron Haven. They are creatures of habit, and perhaps they returned there this afternoon. If Harunobu saw them—"

"He might have tried to get closer, spooked them, and followed them into the woods!" exclaimed Yells-at-Bears.

"It is a possibility . . ." Naoki agreed.

"Show me where the deer were seen. . . ."

He did so, and Yells-at-Bears waved back the searchers, lest they spoil the ground. "Yes, there were deer here."

After a time, she found what she had hoped for: a child's footprint.

"Follow me," she ordered, "but stay ten feet behind. Keep your eyes and ears open." The searchers followed, with Arinobu and Umako in the lead, and Naoki close behind.

The ground dipped gradually as they proceeded; they were heading in the general direction of the coast. Yells-at-Bears didn't like that—the coast in that part of Texada took the form of sheer cliffs—but didn't share her misgivings with the other searchers.

They came up to an old game trail, running more or less parallel to the coast, and here Yells-at-Bears paused straining her senses. Beyond the trail, the slope steepened, and she was hopeful that the deer—and the boy—turned onto the trail.

"All of you, be still!" she shouted.

But it wasn't her eyes or ears that spotted the next sign, it was her nose. "Fresh deer scat, off this way!" She now stood a few yards down the trail, in the direction of Sandy Bottom Bay. Of course, she couldn't be sure that it was from the same deer, or that Harunobu was still following them if it was, but that was her only lead. And the sun had already turned red, so there was no time to lose if they want to find him before nightfall.

"Follow me!"

The trail rose, then descended. She paused all of a sudden. Was that crying she heard? She quickened her steps.

The trail took a sharp drop of several feet and there lay Harunobu.

Yells-at-Bears called out, and Arinobu and Umako ran to her.

"Don't pick him up yet!" she warned. "We need to know whether he is injured, and how. But you may speak words of comfort to him."

They followed her advice, albeit reluctantly.

"I don't like the looks of his ankle," muttered Yells-at-Bears. "Arinobu and Naoki, please lift him up slowly and carefully, and sit him in front of me."

They did so.

"The ankle is swollen and may be broken. He must be carried. We can make a stretcher, and—"

"No need," said Arinobu grimly. "I can carry him back to Iron Haven."

"Okay, if you can do so without touching his ankle, or letting it hit anything," said Yells-at-Bears. "But let me check his head first."

Harunobu's head was shaved, so this was easy enough. She didn't find any bruises there, and his pupils were of equal size. However, he had plenty of cuts and bruises on his shins and his hands were red. Plainly, he had managed to catch himself when we fell, and so protected his head.

"All right, as soon as you're ready, let's go," said Yells-at-Bears.

"Thank you, thank you, for finding Harunobu-chan," said Umako.

By the time they got back to Iron Haven, several stars could be seen in the sky, and the western horizon was a deep red.

Umako held open the door of their home, and Arinobu carried Harunobu inside.

Yells-at-Bears started walking back to Camp Double Six, but stopped when Arinobu came out and called her back.

He held in his hands a sheathed knife. "I made this with my own hands," he said solemnly. "I forged the steel into a blade, and put on the hilt made by another craftsman." He unsheathed the knife part way. "See, just under the guard? There's my mark."

He sheathed it again and held it in both hands, palms up. "I want you to have it. Thank you for finding my son."

"Children are precious," said Yells-at-Bears. "I did not search for Harunobu in the hope of a reward."

"I know you didn't, but you deserve one. Please take it."

"I will," said Yells-at-Bears. "Good night to you."

"And to you." Arinobu shut the door.

Yells-at-Bears pulled out the blade and studied it. She was no stranger to steel blades, having spent almost a year with the Japanese. But this was the first time she had ever met someone who could *make* a steel blade.

Among her people, craftsmen were thought to have animal spirit helpers who conferred spirit power upon them, the power of creation. Those skilled in working stone, for example, might have sea otter power. Yells-at-Bears had seen otters float on their backs and use a stone to crack open a shell.

But Arinobu's power, that was extraordinary. He could craft steel into a blade that was far superior to the stone axes and knives that Yells-at-Bears was accustomed to.

There was, from what Isamu had told her, more than one kind of steel power. Tetsue, who she had met earlier, had the power to transform ordinary stone into steel. But Arinobu could shape the steel into a knife blade.

That night, she had difficulty sleeping. In the morning, she walked to Iron Haven, and called upon Umako.

"How is Harunobu doing?"

"Better," said Umako. "We don't think the ankle is broken. Arinobu borrowed a little clay from Tetsue, and gently molded it around the ankle. It seemed to help."

Yells-at-Bears smiled. "Ah. You might strip off some cedar bark, and wrap the strips around the ankle. Even better, there are some herbs I can look for; you put them in water, heat it up, and soak the bark strips in that first."

"Thank you, I greatly appreciate all you have done for us."

"There is perhaps something else I can do for you," said Yells-at-Bears hesitantly. "For you and me, actually. Your husband will be making more knives out of steel?"

"He will be making more ironware. Not just knives, and not just from steel. Cast iron pots for cooking, for example. I can show you one."

"And what will he do with them?"

Umako shrugged. "Sell or trade them to the other colonists."

"And some of the colonists, they will trade them in turn to the Indians who live near Texada?"

Umako made a circle with her thumb and index finger. "I would assume so. But you're the only Indian that any of us who came over on the *Iemitsu Maru* have met, so far."

"That will change," said Yells-at-Bears. "The Tla'amin and the Shishalh come to Texada from time to time, and I think that once the *Ieyasu Maru* returns, it will visit their villages, and those of other tribes, too. And it will certainly engage in trade, as it did on the way here last year.

"But what I was thinking is that your fellow Japanese have no idea how to bargain with the Tla'amin, or the Shishalh, or any other

Indians. Whereas I do. If you let me sell your items for you, for a share of the proceeds, we will both do better than if you sold trade goods to the other Japanese."

"I will speak to Arinobu about it," Umako promised.

The next day, Umako told Yells-at-Bears that Arinobu had agreed that at least some of his ironware would be sold by her, on the commission basis that she proposed.

Late in the month, the *Unagi Maru* arrived in Sandy Bottom Bay. The weary captain reported to Isamu at the Welcome House. "We searched for the *Mutsu Maru* until half my crew was incapacitated with scurvy." Captain Araki's bleeding gums made it clear that he, too, was suffering from the scourge of the sea. "Then we sailed for this place. And if the winds hadn't been favorable, we'd be floating somewhere in the Salish Sea, our corpses rotting on deck, picked over by gulls. Now, is there anything you can do for my crew?"

"There is," said Isamu. "We have pine needle tea. It worked fine for the crews that came here before you." He smiled at Yells-at-Bears when he said this, remembering how in August 1634 she had collected the needles, brewed the tea, and nursed the afflicted sailors from the *Ieyasu Maru* back to health. "We also have kelp and some other wild plants that our Indian guide here says can help."

"I am most grateful for the assistance."

Chapter 11

Cebu Cathedral
July 1635

Father Blanco had spent the day in the Parian, the Chinese ghetto of Cebu, with his fellow Jesuits. It was missionary work, of a sort; the Chinese who lived there were mostly pagans. However, it was frustrating that he could not speak to them in their native language, as he could to the Japanese when he was in Nagasaki. Or, for that matter, to the *kirishitan* in Manila.

The day's experience had, however, brought the latter much to mind. The younger Kimura was of marriageable age, and Father Blanco had expected to offer him the sacrament of marriage when that happy day arrived.

He lit a prayer candle and placed it before a statue of Saint Vitalis of Milan. Then he knelt and prayed for the Kimura family, the other *kirishitan* of Dilao and San Miguel, the *kirishitan* still in Japan, and the millions of pagan Nihonjin that could lose their chance to go to heaven if they died before the missionaries returned and brought them into the True Faith.

Duty demanded that he serve as a chaplain on an Acapulco galleon for a time, but he hoped to preach in Japanese once again.

Welcome House, Texada Island

Isamu took a sip of Yells-at-Bears' latest tea imitation, taking care not to get his moustache wet. The *Iemitsu Maru* and *Sendai Maru* had brought some tea leaves, but the quantity was too small for tea to be drunk at any save special occasions, and then only by the privileged few. The farmers had brought both seeds and cuttings, but thought it unlikely that the tea plant would grow on Texada. The summers were just too cool. Even if they did grow, it would be three years before a tea crop could be harvested.

He made a face. This one might do as a medicine, like pine needle tea, but it would not be drunk for pleasure. So far, the imitation tea he liked best was the one made from strawberry and thimbleberry leaves.

There was a knock on the wood frame of the *fusuma*, the sliding door for Isamu's little office at the Welcome House. The paper for the *fusuma* was made by hand-pounding strips of the native cedar bark. Isamu would have preferred the more translucent mulberry paper from home, so he could see if someone were outside his door, but it was available only in limited quantities.

"Come in," said Isamu.

His visitor was Captain Fukuzawa of the *Iemitsu Maru*, the senior captain of the flotilla that had brought the ironworkers and the *kirishitan* to Texada.

"Welcome, Fukuzawa-san. How are your sailors faring?"

"Much better, thank you. They are now all recovered from their bout with scurvy."

"Excellent," said Isamu. "And what of the crews of the *Sendai Maru* and *Unagi Maru*?"

"I believe they are also restored to full health," said Captain Fukuzawa. "We captains are now putting the crews to work refitting and reprovisioning the ships for the return journey."

Isamu frowned. "I had hoped that you could put that off until September. First, at least until the *Ieyasu Maru* returns, we need your ships here as a deterrent against native war parties. And second, that would allow us to visit the neighboring tribes, for negotiation of trade terms and fishing and hunting rights, from a position of strength."

"I see. The problem is that the longer the *Iemitsu Maru* and the *Sendai Maru* stay, particularly in close proximity to your *kirishitan* colonists, the more they run the risk of being forbidden to return to Japan. For fear that our sailors' thinking has been contaminated by their heresies."

"But you shared the ship with the *kirishitan* on the passage here!"

"True. But we had the samurai guards to keep the *kirishitan* below decks, away from the crew quarters. Now, it is too easy for the sailors to mix with the colonists. I can't keep them confined on board for weeks on end when we aren't sailing anywhere. And they are all too aware that there are women among the colonists.

"The *Unagi Maru* can stay; its crew has special waivers, like those on your *Ieyasu Maru*. They can remain in New Nippon longer than we can without losing the right of return. I think it was intended that it serve as a scout for the *Ieyasu Maru* in the future."

"I understand your situation," said Isamu. "But please consider mine. The *Unagi Maru* by itself isn't big enough to be a sufficient deterrent. The presence of your two big ships until the *Ieyasu Maru* returns is essential to the safety of the colony. The Indians can put hundreds of warriors into war canoes, if they wish to do so, and I cannot hold them off without your help." While a few cannon had been delivered to the colony, most were still on the ships, and expected to remain there.

"You do not have the authority to order us to remain," said Captain Fukuzawa stiffly. "You were merely a squad commander under Hosoya Yoritaki."

Isamu's expression tightened. "You were told to obey the local authorities, neh? That's me, under authority granted me by Captain Haruno. Who represents Date Masamune, grand governor of New Nippon. Now, I grant that Captain Haruno expected to return before any colonists arrived, but there is no point in spitting against the sky!

"It is plain that this colony is very important to the grand governor. He didn't just send *kirishitan* here, there's a whole team of ironworkers! It is clear that the eye of the grand governor is upon us both."

Captain Fukuzawa muttered, "That may be true. But I won't linger if that means staying in New Nippon for the rest of my life. Not, at least, without a direct order from my superior."

"Suppose we have you move the *Iemitsu Maru* and *Sendai Maru* to northern Texada, and you stay there until September?"

Fukuzawa raised his eyebrows. "Why there?"

"We believe there's a bay there. It's far enough from Sandy Bottom Bay to discourage, ahem, casual visitation, but it can be reached if need be." Isamu didn't volunteer that his "belief" was based on Yells-at-Bears' recollection of tidbits of "friend-of-a-friend" geographical knowledge.

"Well . . . Well, I'm willing to take a look at it and see if it's a fit anchorage."

"Fine. I'd like to go with you, and take Yells-at-Bears and Saichi with me. Yells-at-Bears can help us find the bay and the stream, and Saichi can check whether there is anything worth mining up there in the future. We can take the *Unagi Maru* back to Sandy Bottom Bay."

With some reluctance, Isamu left Haru and Masaru in charge of the colony, and he, Yells-at-Bears and Saichi boarded the *Iemitsu Maru*. Fudenojo, the mate from the *Ieyasu Maru* who was Isamu's nautical expert, boarded the *Unagi Maru*; he wanted to get firsthand knowledge of how it handled. All three ships sailed out of Sandy Bottom Bay.

Fortunately for Isamu's relationship with Captain Fukuzawa, there was indeed a bay at the northern end of the island. In fact, there were two of them. Since the northern end had the shape of a three-clawed hand, and the Japanese dragon—the *tatsu*—has only three claws on each foot, he called them West and East Dragon Bays.

West Dragon Bay faced west, and Captain Fukuzawa did not like the looks of it. Fudenojo, as the commander of Isamu's sailors, had kept a weather diary, and it showed that all too often the wind in the vicinity of Texada Island came from the west.

East Dragon Bay, on the other hand, faced north, and there was a cove in the southwest corner that faced east.

The three explorers, with several sailors and marines, boarded a longboat and went ashore. Saichi examined the rocks in the area and reported to Isamu that the most common one was limestone. Back home, lime was used to make *shikkui*, a water- and fire-resistant plaster for buildings.

"Is that something we can sell back home?"

"It probably isn't worth the shipping cost," said Saichi. "But we can make good use of it here."

Saichi paused for thought.

"Well?" said Isamu. "Spit out what you're thinking."

"We know it rains a lot here during the winter. And anywhere there's limestone, and a lot of rain, should have caves."

Isamu raised his eyebrows. "You want to use the caves for storage?"

"If there are caves, there may be bats. And if there are bats, there is bat guano, which can be used to make saltpeter. One of the three ingredients of gunpowder."

A freshwater stream was located and the sailors from the *Iemitsu Maru* and *Sendai Maru* started building huts. The crews of the two transport vessels could refill their water casks, and forage for food. There were stores in the hold, reserved for the return passage, but it didn't hurt to have more.

While the *Iemitsu Maru* remained at anchor and on guard, the *Sendai Maru* would be careened so that barnacles could be removed and the hull inspected and recaulked. Once the *Sendai Maru* was fit to return to the open sea, it would take on guard duty and the *Iemitsu Maru* would be careened. That way there would always be at least one ship of force—at least by Pacific Northwest standards—on call, should Isamu send word that one was needed. With a favorable wind, a ship could sail from East Dragon Bay to Sandy Bottom Bay in a couple of hours.

Here the *Iemitsu Maru* and *Sendai Maru* would stay until September, safe from the baleful cosmic influence of the *kirishitan*, unless Isamu (or his presently absent superiors) gave permission for them to leave earlier.

Isamu would have preferred for them to stay in Sandy Bottom Bay, but he reminded himself of the adage, "even a cup of tea will stave off hunger for a while."

"What now?" asked Saichi. "Do we return to Sandy Bottom Bay?"

"Not yet," said Isamu. "We are here, with reinforcements to call on if need be, so let's explore northern Texada."

It was a good idea, but their timing was unfortunate.

Chapter 12

Shelter Point, where the Japanese had found the burnt Indian village, marked the southeastern end of Sandy Bottom Bay. Perhaps a hundred feet south of Shelter Point lay a small island.

When the Japanese first discovered the burnt village, they had been unable to venture onto the island because they had left their boat behind. On a later visit, they had discovered that at low tide, the island was connected to Shelter Point by an isthmus.

While they found nothing of special note when they followed the isthmus across to the island, they did consider the island to be a good place to post a lookout, and hence dubbed it "Sentinel Island." The top rose a hundred feet above the waters of the Salish Sea, and gave an excellent view in all directions once they had cleared away some trees.

Despite the advantages of having a lookout on Sentinel Island, Isamu had regretfully decided at the time not to station someone there, absent good reason to expect visitors. The exploration party was too small to easily spare a man to do nothing but sit on an island staring out to sea all day, and to be frank, even if raiders came to Sandy Bottom Bay, they were unlikely to venture as far inland as Camp Double Six.

Later, with Texada's Japanese population swelled by the arrival of the colonists, and with some of the colonists living close to Sandy Bottom Bay, Isamu had decided that it was time to have a full-time sentry on Sentinel Island, at least during the daytime. There were several teenagers among the colonists, and the duty was rotated among them. A small raft was built for the lookout's use, so he could come and go regardless of the tide.

Some of the teenagers considered sentry duty an occasion to just goof off, but Kaito wasn't one of them. After all, as the sentry, he was entrusted with one of the mission's precious spyglasses, and he never tired of using it to try to spot something interesting. Why, once he had seen a whale spouting!

Still, he couldn't sit or stand in one place for hours at a time, so what he did was periodically walk around the top of Sentinel Island, exploring. It was about three-quarters of a mile in circumference, and he would usually find something to amuse himself with. And from time to time, of course, he would look out at the water, in the hope of seeing a ship.

The sun was high in the sky, and Kaito was thinking about taking a nap, when he saw that a canoe was beached on the sand by the eastern jaw of Sandy Bottom Bay. It was nothing like the boats that the Japanese built, so it must be Indian-made. Kaito was upset that he hadn't spotted it while it was still at sea.

The spyglass revealed that the canoe was empty. What were its occupants up to? And how many of them were there? The canoe looked like it was large enough to hold a half-dozen Indians. He scanned the beach and the nearby waters, looking for additional canoes, but saw none. That was good news, but Kaito still needed to alert the Japanese villages that there was a possible threat.

He built up a fire, being sure to add some grass to the wood to make sure the smoke would be dark. He then covered it with a blanket, trapping the smoke. He counted to himself, then lifted the blanket. A single puff of dark smoke rose into the area. He covered the fire once more, reached for a sandglass that was stored nearby, and inverted it. When the time was up, he released another puff. He did this several more times, alternating short and long puffs. This was the signal, devised by Yells-at-Bears, for "unknown canoe sighted."

Splitter-of-Waves crawled slowly toward the seals. This was the birth season for harbor seals in this part of the Strait of Georgia and there was a sandbar near the southeastern lip of Sandy Bottom Bay where he knew them to come to give birth. He had beached his canoe about half a mile away, to avoid spooking them. He wore a sealskin and, as he came closer, occasionally barked, or rolled on the rocks, in imitation of a seal. This came easily to him because, besides being an expert paddler—hence his use-name!—he had "seal power." That is, he had gone on a vision quest and encountered a spirit seal, who had conferred upon him the ability to hunt and kill seals.

Just a few more yards, he thought. And suddenly there was a commotion and the seals barked and slid into the water.

He looked up and saw strange men, with bows and spears, on the slope above, yammering at him incomprehensibly. He dropped the club he had concealed beneath his seal skin, and raised both hands.

Two of the strangers half-ran, half-slid down the slope and pulled his hands behind his back, tying them together.

They started to try to walk him back up-slope, then thought better of it, and walked him to the head of the bay. There, he saw more strangers, pushing a boat into the water. The boat was not a dugout canoe, made from a single trunk, but appeared to be made from planks, like those used as the walls of a house. As his captors prodded him forward, the boatmen stopped what they were doing and stared at him.

His captors prompted him to sit down, and then they waited . . . and waited . . .

At last, two men came by to whom his captors plainly deferred. One of them spoke to him in Kwak'wala. "I am Jusuke, and this is Masaru, my chief. I will speak for him, since he does not know Kwak'wala."

How odd, thought Splitter-of-Waves. It had been plain from the very beginning that his captors were not Kwakwaka'wakw. Their dress was unlike anything he had seen before. But because the Kwakwaka'wakw were aggressive raiders, the chiefs of the Indian bands of the Salish Sea often had to parley with them. *What sort of band would pick a chief that did not speak Kwak'wala?*

"What are you doing here?" said Jusuke, translating for Masaru.

"Hunting seals, as I do here every year. As my father and grandfather did before me."

"Well, you can't do that here anymore. They are our seals now."

"How can that be?"

"We live on this island, and you don't," said Jusuke for Masaru. "Find seals somewhere else."

"Where do you live? I see no village here."

Jusuke and Masaru conferred in a strange language that Splitter-of-Waves did not recognize. At last, Jusuke said, "Near the bay. If your people and mine become friends, we will take you to the village. But for now, we just want you to leave and not cause any trouble. Can we trust you to do that?"

"I will leave. I will not cause trouble." *For now*, he added mentally.

The strangers untied him, and even handed back his club, although they kept their weapons ready. Their spears had spearheads made of an unfamiliar kind of stone, which gleamed in the sun. Splitter-of-Waves wanted to ask about the stone, but decided that this was not the right time to do so.

He walked back to his canoe, the strangers following at a distance of perhaps ten yards. It was, he knew, enough distance so that were he to turn and attack, they would have time to ready their spears. Worse, the archers had followed a parallel route, along the ridgeline, and could shoot at him. No, this was not the time to cause trouble.

As he passed the place where he had been stopped, he looked up slope, trying to spot the village he suspected was near there. But if that was the location of the village, it was set far enough back so that the houses were hidden by the slope of the land and the intervening trees.

His captors did not like what he was doing and all of a sudden he felt a shove from behind. Obviously, they wanted him to keep moving.

He did so, and at last reached his canoe. He eased it into the water and headed out of the bay. Looking back, he could see the strangers' boats in the bay. They seemed to be trawling for fish.

Do they think that all the fish of the bay are theirs, too? he wondered.

A week later, two Japanese fishermen were in a small boat, handlining, in the small bay east of Sentinel Island. They were intent on their work and did not notice the Indian canoe until it was well within spear throwing range. This canoe held a dozen Indians, and the fishermen quickly realized that they had no chance of escape. They threw up their hands.

The Indians took their catch, and their handline, sinkers and hooks. The metal hooks seemed to be something of a novelty to the Indians, as they were passed from one Indian to another, and then back again.

The lead Indian grabbed one of the fishermen's paddles. He cringed, expecting to be hit with it, but the Indian pointed with the paddle in the general direction of Sandy Bottom Bay.

The message was clear: go home, stay out of these waters.

When they finally made it back home, they complained to their headman, Fukuhei, who in turn complained to Haru. Why didn't the watchman on Sentinel Island spot the Indians and summon help? What were the colony's leaders going to do to protect fishing boats venturing out of Sandy Bottom Bay? Would the fishermen be compensated for their stolen gear and fish?

"Isamu is in command," said Haru. "We will take up the issue of protection as soon as he returns from northern Texada."

"And what about Sentinel Island?" demanded Fukuhei.

"Obviously," said Haru, "we can't entrust sentinel duty to teenagers anymore. Your fishermen should take turns standing watch. Talk to them and draw up a roster."

"Why not have your samurai do it?" protested Fukuhei.

"We don't have that many samurai, and they are most effective when grouped together as a fighting unit," said Haru. "There are lots of places that Indians can approach us—I have to worry about the miners and farmers, too, you know!—and I am not going to dribble our fighting strength away by posting a man here and a man there."

As Fukuhei stomped off, Haru thought. *When the fuck is Isamu getting back here?*

Chapter 13

Isamu said goodbye to the captains of the two transport ships and boarded the *Unagi Maru*. It dropped him, Yells-at-Bears and Saichi off at Iron Landing, then returned to Sandy Bottom Bay. The sky had the color of *seiji*, blue porcelain, lightest at the horizon and deepest at the zenith.

After checking on the progress of the miners, and eating lunch, Isamu and Yells-at-Bears visited Arinobu in his smithy. Arinobu had been producing a variety of small ironware suitable for trade: arrowheads, nails, fishhooks, hammerheads, bracelets and rings. Thus far, it had been from the blank stock he had brought with him, but soon, Arinobu hoped, he would be able to use Texada iron.

"Can you work metals other than iron?" asked Isamu.

"Yes, if need be," admitted Arinobu. "I was a country smith, so I worked copper and tin as well as iron. I didn't see much gold or silver, however. Why do you ask?"

"When we went to northern Texada, Saichi found some copper ore specimens. And he says that if there's copper ore there, it is more likely that we'll find silver, gold, zinc and lead ore there, too."

"That sounds promising! Although you must remember, finding a few specimens doesn't mean there's a big enough concentration of an ore-mineral to making a mining operation feasible."

Isamu sighed. "Yes, Saichi told us this. But we can hope. . . ."

Their conversation was interrupted by Arinobu's assistant. "Excuse me, Isamu-san, there is a delegation here to see you." It was a word that Isamu was not fond of. The term "delegation" implied people who want you to listen to their complaints. And expected you to do something about them, even if it meant offending someone else.

Isamu and Yells-at-Bears followed the bearer of ill tidings out of the smithy. It was a large delegation: Hidezo, the head farmer, Fukuhei, the head fisherman, and the samurai Masaru and Haru. Isamu fought back a groan; a large delegation meant a large headache.

Masaru described the two encounters, then summarized his position. "These Indians tried to hunt seals in our bay, and then they harassed our fishermen. The situation is intolerable, Isamu-san. If we don't teach the Indians a lesson, they will think we are pushovers, and their canoes will come into Sandy Bottom Bay and stop us from fishing even there. Bring back the *Iemitsu Maru* and the *Sendai Maru* to guard Sandy Bottom Bay. Or better yet, find out whether the Indians came from and shoot up their village."

"Didn't you provoke them by stopping them from hunting seals that you weren't even hunting yourself?" said Isamu.

"I was just defending our rightful territory," said Masaru, "as any samurai would." That was a barely veiled insult.

Isamu raised an eyebrow. "Did it occur to you that there are a lot more Indians than there are of us? A wise samurai also picks his battles, neh?"

Haru didn't wait for Masaru to respond. "There's no advantage to be gained by quarreling over who started the trouble, the fact remains, we can't tolerate the harassment. If we do nothing, it will only encourage the Indians to escalate."

"I agree that we can't do nothing," said Isamu, "but we need to avoid overly aggressive response. The harassment was of just an isolated boat, with just two fishermen on board, neh?"

"Yes, Isamu-san," said Fukuhei.

"Then from now on, you fish at least four fishermen at a time. One boat, two boats, I don't care. Keep a lookout. And the fishermen may carry spears, of the kind used for spear-fishing. If they are approached, they may show that they are armed, but they are not to fight unless they or their equipment are attacked. I think the Indians will hesitate to bother a larger, obviously armed group of fishermen.

"Also, if the Indians are fishing without interfering with you, let them. Even back home, some fishing waters were 'gray zones,' shared by several villages, neh?"

Fukuhei bowed his head. "Isamu-san, it is possible to do as you say, but the Indians may scare the fish even if they don't try to cut our lines and nets. Keeping a lookout means that one fisherman is not helping to put food on the table. And, yes, there were 'gray zones' back home, but the fishermen from the different villages would often come to blows over the catch from such places."

"And the authorities would then execute the troublemakers, neh?" said Isamu. "We need to keep a lid on this pot, at least until the *Ieyasu Maru* returns."

"I have a better idea," said Masaru. "We have a dozen more trained fighting men now." He was referring to the former *ronin* from the *Iemitsu Maru* and *Sendai Maru* that had agreed to remain with the colony. "Put them into guard boats at the mouth of Sandy Bottom Bay, and let the fishermen fish."

"The point, Masaru-san, is to discourage conflict," warned Yells-at-Bears. "If your samurai draw blood, or worse, kill someone, then the next thing you know, there will be war canoes beaching at Sandy Bottom Bay. A single war canoe might be fifty or sixty feet long and hold two dozen warriors. And I once heard of a forty canoe raid."

Her companions were silent for a moment. They knew that a raid by several hundred warriors—which Yells-at-Bears had made it clear, in previous conversations, was not unusual if the Indians were sufficiently motivated by greed or a desire for vengeance—would mean the end of the colony. Only Camp Double Six was fortified, and the colony did not have large numbers of trained fighters or cannon.

"Nor would those war canoes necessarily sail into Sandy Bottom Bay," mused Isamu. "They could land south or north of the bay, and have their warriors attack our settlements overland. I can agree to having one samurai—one I am sure is level-headed—go out with the fishermen each morning, to guide them if there's a confrontation, but the rest need to be standing watch at the settlements."

"I am wondering whether it would be prudent to build palisades around the villages," said Haru. "Or at least have a fortified building in each, where the villagers can take refuge."

"The Tla'amin and the Shishalh are not aggressive peoples," said Yells-at-Bears. "I think that they are unlikely to attack our villages directly as long as you haven't killed any of them. But that is more likely to happen if you arm your fishermen. We must tell the fishermen that they can only attack if they are themselves attacked, not merely to defend their equipment or their catch."

"I am not surprised that you would let the Indians do what they please, short of actually killing Japanese," said Masaru.

Haru quickly put a hand on Isamu's shoulder. "Let me respond," he whispered. And then he continued, more loudly, "It would be foolish to disregard the advice of Yells-at-Bears."

"I wasn't finished speaking," said Yells-at-Bears. "Word is going to spread that you are here. Eventually, the Haida, or the Laich-kwil-tach, or the Nuu-chah-nulth, will come. Isamu and I saw Haida canoes in the Malaspina Strait only a few months ago. They do raid villages without provocation. They behead the men and take the women and children back home as slaves. That's who you need to worry about."

"So we do need fortifications," said Haru.

"Will the miners and ironworkers help?" asked Hidezo. "It's difficult enough to feed them as well as ourselves when we can devote ourselves full-time to farming. If we are building fortifications, we aren't sowing, weeding, watering or harvesting. And it does no good to be ready to fend off an attack if we die from starvation. The supplies we brought over from Japan won't last forever."

"I have the same concern," said Fukuhei. "We can fish or fortify, but not both simultaneously."

"We'll build the blockhouses first," said Isamu. "That can be done relatively quickly, and they can also be used for storage. The miners can help. As for the ironmakers?" He darted a quizzical look at Haru, who waved a hand in front of his face. It was a gesture of negation. "I am not sure I can spare the ironworkers. But one way or another, we will get our defenses in order."

"I'd be happier," said Haru, "if we had a ship with cannon stationed here in Sandy Bottom Bay."

"So would I, but I told you what Captain Fukuzawa told me. When do you think the *Ieyasu Maru* will return?"

Haru shrugged. "It is in the hands of the buddhas and the kamis."

Chapter 14

Nootka Sound, West Coast of Vancouver Island

The sailor standing at the prow of the *Ieyasu Maru* hefted the lead sounding weight, and threw it forward. It splashed into the deep blue waters of the Nootka Sound. It was here that, in old timeline 1778, that the British Captain James Cook would make first contact with the "Nootka," and begin the Pacific Northwest sea otter fur trade that led to the British settlement of Vancouver Island.

The ship continued on its course and when the prow came directly over the weight, the leadsman called out the depth: "Forty *shaku*!" A sailor positioned midships repeated the call, as the wind driving the ship forward also made it difficult for the captain on the quarterdeck to hear the leadsman.

"Heave to," Captain Haruno ordered.

"You will anchor here?" asked Tokubei, the grand governor's special envoy to the Pacific Northwest Indians. "Not closer to shore?"

"I want to be outside arrow range of the shore," said Captain Haruno. "And have time to see and react if a bunch of war canoes suddenly head our way."

The name "Nootka Sound" was, Tokubei mused, a good example of the dangers of trusting too much to the up-timers' encyclopedias. On their last visit to Vancouver Island, they had rescued some Japanese who had been shipwrecked and enslaved by one of the Kwakwaka'wakw bands at the northwestern end of Vancouver Island. According to them—and to the Indian slaves they bought from the Kwakwaka'wakw—there was no such tribe as the "Nootka." The word did, however, sound like a phrase in their language that meant "circle around."

The Indians living on the shores of Nootka Sound were the Mowachaht, and they were one of the Nuu-chah-nulth-speaking peoples. If the interpreter had not misled them, there was a nearby village, Yuquot—"where the winds blow from many directions"—on the peninsula defining the north arm of the sound. The *Ieyasu Maru* was anchored in a shallow bay west of that peninsula, and its bow had been turned to face south. As long as the wind blew from any direction other than the southwest, south or southeast, the *Ieyasu Maru* could make a quick escape, should the Mowachaht prove hostile.

This was, in any event, supposed to be a short stopover, as Tokubei and Captain Haruno needed to check on the fate of the exploration party they had left on Texada Island. They would let the Mowachaht know that they were interested in buying sea otter furs, and settle on a price. They would buy what was available now and then give the Mowachaht time to hunt for more. They would collect the second lot of furs on the way home.

Everything the Japanese wanted to say to the Mowachaht would be translated first into Kwak'wala by Goemon, one of the castaways rescued by the *Ieyasu Maru* the year before. Then it would be translated into Nuu-chah-nulth by their Indian translator, Speaker-to-Strangers. He had recently adopted that name for himself.

After Tokubei purchased him from the Klaskino and freed him, making him Tokubei's "client," he decided that he would neither keep the slave name he had been given by the Klaskino, nor revert to the child's name he had among the Kyuquot, another Nuu-chah-nulth group.

Tokubei was well aware that double translation presented opportunities for misunderstanding, but it would be better than trying to communicate by pantomime.

The sailors heaved at the capstan, and the *Ieyasu Maru*'s anchor descended into the waters below.

Soon after the *Ieyasu Maru* anchored, a canoe had approached the ship, and one of the Indians in it stood up and gestured toward shore, while shaking a rattle. Another threw handfuls of what appeared to be a red dust in the direction of the *Ieyasu Maru*.

These were, Speaker-to-Strangers told them, peaceful gestures inviting them to land. That, however, Tokubei and Captain Haruno were unwilling to do. It was safer to have the Mowachaht come to them, preferably just a few at a time.

This first canoe returned to shore and, after some minutes, a half-dozen canoes came out. Tokubei was pleased to see that there were both men and women on board, as that made it less likely that the Mowachaht had hostile attentions.

This time, the invitation took a more elaborate form, further evidencing an eagerness for contact. On the largest canoe, an ornately painted and costumed individual stood up. His face was painted white, and his arms red. There were large feathers tied to his hair. He started dancing, while the other Indians in his canoe steadied it with deft paddle motions.

As he danced, the Indians in the other canoes sang, while striking the sides of their canoes with the butt ends of their paddles in time with the song.

"It is a song of welcome," Speaker-to-Stranger and Goemon told Tokubei.

What Tokubei and Captain Haruno wanted most were sea otter furs. While the sea otter could be caught in Monterey Bay, Date Masamune had placed restrictions on the catch.

And it did appear that the Mowachaht would able to supply those furs. Several of the Indians were wearing what appeared to be sea otter fur clothing, despite it being summer. Admittedly, July in Yuquot was about as warm as Edo in April.

Eventually, the Mowachaht came close enough for conversation, and Tokubei could put his translators to work. He had them insist that the canoes come no more than one at a time, and after this was communicated, he could see that there was some arguing and jostling among the Indians as to the order of precedence.

"Fish? Yes, we will take some fish. What do you want for what's in that basket?"

"Bear skins? Sorry, not interested. We want sea otter."

"Yes, I can see it was a very big bear. You are certainly a great warrior. But can you bring us some sea otter furs?"

After a few days trading, the *Ieyasu Maru* had acquired a substantial number of sea otter furs, and a few once fur-clad Indians were now naked. The Indians had been happy to take in exchange all sorts of metal items, but declined glass beads and clothing.

Tokubei visited the village of Yuquot and found it to be about twenty houses, laid out in a single row facing a sheltered cove.

Tokubei and Captain Haruno of course were still anxious to reach Texada and determine first, whether Isamu's party had survived, and second, whether their recommendation that colony ships be sent to the island had been acted upon.

With the supply of sea otter furs obviously dwindling, they told the Mowachaht leaders that soon they would need to depart. They softened the blow by promising to return in the Moon of Cutting Salmon to Dry, as the Mowachaht called September.

Yuquot, they were told, was only occupied in the spring and summer. In the preceding Moon of the Coming of the Dog Salmon, after the spawning runs had ended, the Mowachaht would move up a channel, about twenty miles deeper into the sound, to a place they called Tahsis—"gateway." There, where the climate was more pleasant, they spent the fall and winter, and traded by river routes with the Indians of the east coast of Vancouver Island.

Captain Haruno sent a longboat, with a Mowachaht guide, up the channel, taking soundings. He was relieved to find that the *Ieyasu Maru* would have no difficulty reaching Tahsis. With that issue resolved, they lifted anchor. It was time to return to Texada.

Chapter 15

Tetsue, the *tatara* foreman, was on break, puffing on a brass *kiseru* and sending a trail of smoke into the summer sky.

He had spent the month of July in furious experimentation. First, he tried mixtures of iron sand and iron ore, rather than iron ore alone. There were two kinds of iron sand: *masa*, which was used in the *kera oshi* process to make steel directly, and *akame*, which was used in the *zuku oshi* process to make pig iron. Tetsue found that the *akame* was more effective in increasing the fluidity of the slag. In fact, to obtain a good product, he had to use it in a ratio of one-to-four to the Texada iron ore.

But obviously, if the Texada operation were to prosper, he needed to find a local material to serve as a flux. He had his assistants collect samples of beach sand and mountain sand, and also pulverize the country rock in which the iron ore was found. This was a sort of *sekkaigan*, a soft rock found in caves back home.

Back to work, he ordered himself, and reentered the smelter house.

After several attempts, Tetsue had at last come up with a solution to the flux problem. This called, he thought, for a celebration, and Isamu agreed. However, the ironworkers, led by their priest Tanaka, balked at the suggestion that the *kirishitan* colonists be invited to participate.

Moreover, Tanaka insisted that Yells-at-Bears stay away, too, lest her presence offend Kanayago-kami. This irritated Isamu, who decided to send Haru to the ceremony as his deputy, and stay home himself.

The next day, Tetsue invited the smith Arinobu and the iron caster Imoji to see the product of his labors, *kera* and *zuku*. *Kera* was a solid mixture of iron, steel and slag. *Zuku* was pig iron. Since the *tatara* was about a quarter the normal size, he had produced about fourteen hundred pounds of *kera*, and four hundred pounds of *zuku*.

The *kera* was broken up by Tetsue's hammerers, and the choicest pieces—the *tamagahane*—would go to Arinobu. Arinobu guessed that this one *kera* had yielded five hundred pounds of *tamahagane*. The high carbon steel could be used to make blades for weapons, or armor.

The remaining material was called *bugera*. It would be heated until red-hot and then hammered to squeeze out the slag. Arinobu could forge it into metalware with less exacting requirements.

The *zuku* went to Imoji for casting. Like Arinobu, Imoji had gone to New Nippon because of his family. Unlike Arinobu, it was not because of a desire to aid his brother. Quite the opposite. Imoji was the younger, albeit more talented, brother and, when his older brother took over the family casting business, he treated Imoji like slag. Imoji was forced to leave Yamagata, and had moved from one town to another, always looked down upon by the resident casters as an outsider. In the last year, he had moved his workshop to Iwanuma, which was part of Sendai Domain. But he was arrested for being involved in a drunken fight. All of the judges in Sendai Domain were under secret instructions to advise the daimyo's administrators if any *ronin* or craftsmen were arrested. No doubt on the theory that such individuals might be persuaded that a trip to New Nippon would be good for their health.

And so Imoji had been recruited. At his "interview," Imoji had been shown a cannonball, and asked whether he could cast more like it. Imoji knew that he was a fish in a net; he quickly answered, "Absolutely!" It guaranteed him a place on board the *Iemitsu Maru*, and an indefinite stay in New Nippon, but that was better than receiving one hundred blows with a cane, the usual punishment for brawling. Or being decapitated, should any of those he injured die from their wounds.

Once Imoji had agreed to the Date clan's terms, his workshop in Iwanuma had been packed up for transport to New Nippon.

It was time for Imoji to figure out how to make cast iron

cannonballs. After all, there were canes—and swords—on Texada Island, too.

Before heading to northern Texada, the *Iemitsu Maru*'s captain had provided Imoji with a sampling of Dutch "three-pound" cast iron cannonballs. There were several marks that revealed to Imoji's skilled eye something of the casting process. First, there was the mold seam, running around the circumference of the ball. Plainly, two hemispherical molds were used. Second, there was a small imperfection on the mold seam. This, Imoji figured, was the remains of the filler hole sprue. Finally, at the center of one of the hemispheres, was another imperfection. That would correspond to the mold vent sprue.

Overall, the balls appeared to be quite round—they rolled easily, without noticeable wobbling. And when Imoji used a string to measure along the mold seam, they appeared to have almost identical circumferences.

The colony's carpenters and other laborers had erected a foundry for Imoji, close to where Tetsue's *takadono* had been built. A carpenter constructed the wooden frames that Imoji needed, and Imoji put in the appropriate amounts of sand and clay. He then pushed his model cannonball into the sand, first in one frame, then the other, then made minor corrections to the resulting sand molds to create a casting channel and a vent hole.

This would, Imoji expected, be a relatively easy job. The cannonballs were solid and therefore there was no need for a core, and they had smooth surfaces, without any decoration.

He recruited some of the miners and underemployed farmers to help with the next step, which required more than Imoji's two hands. They shoveled charcoal into his casting furnace, building up the temperature. The *zuku* had to be molten.

The mold frames, each containing a wet sand mold with a hemispherical cavity, were clamped together. The *zuku* was melted in the melting pot, and Imoji used a rod to remove any impurities that formed a scud on the surface. Then, with both hands holding the shaft of the ladle, he dipped its clay-coated bowl into the pot, and carefully poured the molten iron into the filler hole. He and his chief assistant stood on wooden planks, whose ends rested on the mold frames. This kept the molds from yielding to the pressure of the cast iron, but it also meant that the molten iron descended only a dozen or so inches away from the feet of Imoji and his helper.

Despite the danger, the process could not be rushed. If the flow were too fast, bubbles would be entrapped, which would weaken and also shift the center of mass of the cannon ball.

The molten iron flowed down through the filler hole in the top mold, ran through the horizontal channel at the seam level, and into the cavity formed by the fitted molds. The level of the iron in the cavity rose higher and higher, and soon Imoji heard a telltale hiss from the vent hole, as the iron forced air out of the mold.

Imoji carefully moved the ladle away from the molds, emptied the excess *zuku* back into the melting pot, and set down the ladle.

It was time to wait for the iron to cool and Imoji and his assistant did a bit of cleanup and then snacked on some berries.

All right, thought Imoji, *let's see what we have wrought*. He gingerly pulled away the top frame. He broke up the sand mold and pulled out the metal ball. With a hammer and chisel, he broke off the flash around the seam of the ball, and the sprues left by residual iron in the casting channel and the vent hole.

Once Imoji had cast eight cannonballs—eight was a lucky number—he showed them to Isamu and Yells-at-Bears.

"They look fine," said Isamu, "but let's try firing one of them."

They went down to the beach at Sandy Bottom Bay, and Isamu summoned the militiamen who had trained as a gun crew for the three-pounder stationed there. A *nobori*, a signal flag, was raised on the flagpole near the artillery piece, and one of the gun crew beat out a warning tattoo on a large red *taiko*.

The fishermen in the Bay slowly paddled out of the way, and at last Isamu judged it safe to fire a test shot. Even so, he ordered use of a reduced charge, both to minimize the danger to the fishermen and to conserve gunpowder. And he chose a line of fire well away from where the ships were anchored.

The militiamen were obviously excited as they sponged out the cannon bore then rammed first the charge and then the wad and ball down it. The gun captain checked the elevation and line of fire of the barrel and then turned to Isamu. "Permission to fire, sir?"

"Granted!" shouted Isamu.

The gun captain swung the linstock over the rear of the barrel, holding the lit slow match over the touch hole. When Imoji started to move closer, behind the gun, Isamu pulled him back. "Not safe!"

A moment later the powder ignited. The combustion gases propelled Imoji's ball out of the barrel and in a gentle arc into the waters of Sandy Bottom Bay. And the cannon recoiled on its Dutch four-wheeled naval carriage.

As the white smoke of the burnt black powder wreathed about them, Isamu grinned. "Well done, Imoji!"

Imoji bowed.

"We will need more cannonballs for the colony," said Isamu. "And the ships stationed in northern Texada will want replacement shot, too. I will ask Captain Araki of the *Unagi Maru* to go there and get samples for you of the six, nine and twelve pound shot used by the Dutch-made cannon on the *Iemitsu Maru*, as well as the small half- or full-pound shot used by her swivel guns."

"Yes, sir."

"And Imoji. A word to the wise. I know you were not a volunteer. If you want to return to Japan one day, I would suggest you train assistants to the point that they can build and run a cannonball foundry themselves."

Chapter 16

Town of Cebu, the Philippine Islands
August 1635

Pedro de Arce, the bishop of Cebu, watched as a procession of chanting Augustinian monks carried an image of San Raimundo de Peñafort to the galleon for which he was the patron saint. The image showed his most famous miracle. On Majorca, Raimundo had repeatedly reproved King James I of Aragon for keeping a mistress, to no avail. At last, the disgruntled cleric announced his intention to leave the king and return to Barcelona. The king ordered him to remain and threatened to punish any ship captain who offered to transport him.

Raimundo went down to the shore, pulled off his black Dominican cloak, tied its collar to his walking stick, and laid the hem on the water. He stepped on to it, placing the butt of the stick ahead on him on the cloak, and a wind carried him away, the stick serving as his mast, and the cloak as both hull and sail.

The bishop hoped that the wind would be equally kind to the galleon that bore the saint's name.

When the procession reached the shore, it halted. The galleon *San Raimundo* fired a seven gun salute. The image was then solemnly handed over to the galleon's new chaplain, the Jesuit Father Pedro Blanco, who boarded an elaborately decorated *barcaza* and was rowed out to where the galleon was anchored. He did not have far to go because there was deep water, with a sandy bottom, close to shore.

The galleons *San Raimundo* and *Nuestra Señora de la Concepción* had anchored in the calm water between Cebu and Mactan Island in July 1634. Their arrival in the sleepy Visayan town had caused great amazement. While Cebu was the first capital of the Spanish Philippines, the government moved to Panay in 1570 and Manila in 1571, to avoid harassment by the Portuguese and the Moros. Soon thereafter, the Chinese came to Manila with silk, porcelain, and other valuable merchandise, and the great Manila-Acapulco galleon trade began. The ambitious left Cebu and moved to Manila. Only a few hundred Spanish had remained in town. At least until Cebu's population was swelled by the arrival of refugees from Manila.

The appearance of the galleons was the silver lining in a very dark and ominous cloud. That cloud was the bitter knowledge that the galleons had diverted to Cebu because Manila had been conquered by the Dutch and Japanese in March 1634. A few months later, a Chinese vessel had delivered a demand from Manila's new masters that the Spanish surrender Cebu, too. Cebu at the time was defended by only a single company of soldiers, and the Chinese confided that the Japanese had sent more troops to Manila and were parceling out fiefs on Luzon.

Soon thereafter, most of the Chinese residents of Cebu had left town. Some may have feared reprisals—there were rumors that the Chinese in Manila had abetted the invasion force—and others no doubt expected Cebu to be attacked at any moment. If not by the Dutch and Japanese, then by the Moro pirates.

Fortunately, the galleons had brought a fresh infantry company over from New Spain. These were intended to replace a company in Manila that had finished its tour of duty, but now of course they were reassigned to Cebu.

A few months later, some Zheng family ships brought to Cebu all of the Spanish colonists—mostly soldiers, merchants and missionaries—that had been living in the Spanish settlements of northern Taiwan. The strengthening of Cebu's defenses was welcomed.

The Zheng also brought goods to trade. The last time that a galleon sailed from Cebu to Acapulco was in 1604, and it took time for the Fujian Chinese merchants—other than the ominously well-informed Zheng family, that is—to find out that the Acapulco galleons had safely arrived in Cebu. So goods trickled in. But if the quantity of Chinese wares sold to the Spanish and loaded onto the galleons was less than normal, it was made up for by other products, especially beeswax, pearls and cinnamon from Mindanao.

Normally, the galleons mounted their cannon only when they were cruising down the North American coast, where the risk of encountering English or Dutch pirates was greatest. However, with Manila fallen, the civil authorities in Cebu ordered that the galleons of 1634—the galleons *San Raimundo* and *Nuestra Señora de la Concepción*—be kept fully armed, guarding Cebu harbor, until the galleons of 1635 arrived.

The galleons usually arrived in Manila in July or August. And the galleons of 1635 should have been sighted off Cabo Espiritu Santo at least a month earlier, and diverted to Cebu. But it was now early August, and there was still no sign of them. It wasn't known whether they had been captured by the Dutch, lost at sea, or never sailed at all, but the bottom line was that they hadn't arrived. The decision was reluctantly made to wait for them no longer. The cannon were moved to the hold and the galleons laden with cargo and passengers. Many of the latter were refugees from Manila.

The secular authorities—that is to say, Captain-General Mendoza of the galleon *San Raimundo*, and the captain-general of Cebu, Don Cristobal de Lugo—had decided that insofar as possible, the ceremonies associated with the imminent departure of the "Cebu Galleons" for Acapulco should mimic those that had been customary in Manila. Hence, the present procession.

The bishop stood on a platform that had been erected for the occasion, so he could be seen by as many people as possible. From that platform, he could easily feel the *vendavales*, the west or southwest monsoon. The galleons rode the monsoon winds up to the higher latitudes, where they could pick up the westerlies for the transpacific leg.

He raised his hands, and waited for his audience to quiet down. Then he delivered a blessing on the ships and their crews. They would need it, as the passage from the Philippines to Acapulco was long and dangerous. And unfortunately, it was not only the southwest monsoon season, it was now also the typhoon season.

Only the wealthiest or most prestigious of the passengers on the *San Raimundo* were privileged to sleep in the temporary chambers constructed under the *tolda*, the half-deck running from the mainmast to the poop, or the forecastle. Father Pedro, as the ship's chaplain, was one of the lucky ones.

Other passengers had to sleep either in the vile and cramped between-decks, or on an open deck. And as open decks go, it was better to be on the top of the *tolda* or the forecastle than amidships, the aptly named "well." Finding space anywhere was difficult because profits were maximized if the deck was used for cargo. Some passengers had bribed their way onto the ship early so they could stake out and defend a place to lay their sleeping pads. They could also hang curtains for privacy, and tarps to keep dry in the inevitable storms.

Normally there would be several priests traveling on the galleon back to Mexico, but because of the fall of Manila, there was now a shortage of priests in the Philippines, and Father Blanco would have to content himself with secular company.

Back in Manila, Father Blanco had observed the departures of the Manila galleons whenever his duties permitted. He couldn't help but notice how different the passengers today seemed than those of past years. Usually, the passengers were richly-dressed and smug; they were people who had made a fortune in the China trade and were now heading back to New Spain, or even to Spain itself, to enjoy that fortune to the fullest. They might even buy land, and marry their daughters to impoverished noblemen.

But this time, many of the passengers were shabbily dressed and hangdog. These were mostly his fellow refugees from conquered Manila. If they were lucky—somewhat less unlucky?—they had been able to prove that they owned a share of the silver that had come in on the galleons, the proceeds of the last years' sale of Chinese trade goods. Otherwise, they were traveling on the charity of others, especially the church. The religious organizations in Cebu had claimed the assets of their unfortunate counterparts in Manila, both silver on the incoming galleons and *boletas*—tickets for cargo space—on the outgoing ones.

The galleon *San Raimundo* was the first to weigh anchor, followed by the galleon *Concepción*. Father Blanco weaved his way across the deck, exchanging friendly words with the passengers and trying to keep out of the way of the sailors. As he did so, he overheard one passenger say to another, "It's the fault of the missionaries." Both had their backs to Father Blanco.

Father Blanco sidled closer, so he could better hear the passenger's complaint. It was more difficult to hear what the complainant's companion was saying, but he apparently had just come over on the *San Raimundo* and, shocked to hear of Spain's defeat in Manila, had decided to return without delay to New Spain and try his luck there.

The passenger continued to complain. "My family used to trade directly with Japan. Then in 1614, the missionaries were kicked out, because they got involved in Japanese politics and picked the wrong side."

Father Blanco winced. He had served ten years in Japan, as a missionary, and then been forced to leave that year.

"Most of the missionaries left, but some were hidden by the converts and continued to preach in secret."

Father Blanco fought back a sigh. He had pleaded for the opportunity to be one of the missionaries who would hide and continue to serve the Japanese *kirishitan*, but the vice-provincial refused. Father Blanco was over six feet tall and even cloaked and masked, and seen at a distance, he could not pass as a native. His presence, the vice-provincial had declared, would put his hosts at risk.

"Moreover," said the disgruntled passenger, "Spanish merchant ships—including one I owned a share of!—were equipped with secret compartments by order of the governor so they could carry over more missionaries. My ship was inspected, and found to be carrying a missionary. The ship and its cargo were confiscated, and all on board were executed. That included my cousin! It is only through divine grace that I stayed in Manila that year, and thus was spared."

Father Blanco could not help but feel sympathy that this passenger had suffered so much when doing God's work. But of course, that work must still be done.

The rant continued. "Of course, it was incidents like that which caused the Japanese to forbid all Spanish merchant ships in 1625! Which meant that the Japan trade went to the Portuguese, and worse, the Dutch! And did Manila take the hint and stop sending missionaries to Japan? No, it sent them on Chinese ships. And that, my friend, is why the Japanese devils lost patience and drove us from our homes in Manila. And I fear that soon they will strike at Cebu."

Now Father Blanco was faced with a conundrum. Canon law said that a person who excites hatred or contempt against religion or the

Church is to be punished with a just penalty. The *Manileño* had certainly been critical of the Church. Should his words be reported to the captain-general, or even, on arrival in Acapulco, to the Inquisition?

Father Blanco decided against it. Criticizing the Church's missionary practices, if done temperately, did not violate canon law. This sufferer was just seeking sympathy from another Christian, not seeking to incite action against the Church. Hopefully he would seek confession and Father Blanco could lead him to a more balanced view. He decided to slip away without letting himself see the face of the critic, or the critic know that he had been overheard by the ship's chaplain.

Father Blanco sat on deck, reading a borrowed copy of Suarez' *Disputationes Metaphysicae* as the ship gently rolled with the swells. He heard a cough behind him, and turned.

"Excuse me, Father. I am Guillermo del Agulla, the pilot major. We are approaching the Embocadero. May we pray together for a safe transit?"

"Of course!"

After they did so, Father Blanco asked, "Are you pleased with our passage so far?"

"I am indeed!" Guillermo exclaimed. "It has taken us only two weeks to reach the mouth of the San Bernardino Strait. Had we come from Manila, it would have been longer. Indeed, there have been cases of it taking nearly two months."

"When do you think we will reach Acapulco?"

"My best guess would be, in December or January. But few ships have sailed from Cebu to Acapulco. The *San Pedro* left Cebu in June and reached Acapulco in October 1565. The *San Felipe* departed in June 1594 and reached Acapulco in November of that year. That's not much experience to base a forecast on, and we are leaving two months later than either of those ships did."

"Well, that's a good thing to hear, isn't it? Doesn't the galleon usually leave Manila in July or August and arrive at Acapulco in January or February?"

"Yes. But while the Cebu-Acapulco route is a month or two shorter, it is still dangerous. The Cebu galleon of 1597 never reached Acapulco. Cebu barely survived that loss."

✣ ✣ ✣

Despite the prayers, on the day that the Embocadero came into view, the pilot major found it prudent to anchor in a nearby cove. Even at the best of times, the Embocadero was dangerous, with numerous swirls and eddies. And the winds that day were not favorable to a safe passage.

That evening, Father Blanco was invited to the captain-general's table, where they were joined by Guillermo, the shipmaster, the surgeon, and the captain of soldiers, and a few of the more prominent passengers. Unlike most of the people on board, the captain-general actually had a table to eat at, and chairs to sit on. The common sailors had to spread cloths over their sea chests, and squat or kneel on the deck as they ate.

Captain-General Mendoza cleared his throat. "Father Blanco, did you meet my former chaplain, Father Almeida, before you left Cebu?"

"I did." said Father Blanco. "I introduced him to the more prominent of my fellow refugees from Manila. I am sure that he will do great service for the Church in these troubling times."

"If you pardon my asking," said the shipmaster, "why is it that you, who apparently know those refugees well, are now our chaplain, and the priest who served us for more than three months is no longer on board?"

"It is because I know the Japanese who live in Manila even better," said Father Blanco. "I was a missionary in Japan until 1614. After my return to Manila I was assigned to Dilao and San Miguel, the districts where the *kirishitan* who were banished from Japan and emigrated to Manila came to live. There I helped the *kirishitan* adjust to life in exile. When their pagan countrymen attacked Manila, they hid me. The bishop of Cebu intends that I report to the viceroy not just about the attack itself, but on the prospect that the *kirishitan* in Dilao and San Miguel could be used in some way against the heretic Dutch and pagan Japanese invaders."

"But how can we possibly trust any Japanese?" the captain of soldiers protested. "Didn't the Japanese in Dilao revolt in 1606?"

"Yes, but the Japanese in Dilao in those days were mostly pagans. Dilao was only predominantly Christian after 1614. And the Manila *kirishitan* saved my life. They saved other Spaniards, too."

"But did they take up arms against the Dutch and Japanese invaders?"

"Not as far as I know. But once they were given sanctuary in Manila, they were not permitted to own firearms, and only those of samurai rank were permitted to retain their swords. They saved more Christians by hiding us than they would have by throwing themselves, without any organization or coordination with the Spanish military, against the invaders.

"It is my earnest hope and expectation that Spain, under the Banner of Heaven, will retake Manila, and that I will once again guide my Japanese flock in the True Faith. Perhaps our most Holy Sovereign will even force the shogun to reopen the borders so I can be a missionary among the Nihonjin once more."

"Hear, hear!" said Captain-General Mendoza.

"How did you make it here?" asked Guillermo.

"The Japanese Christians arranged for their Filipino coreligionists to smuggle me out by way of the Pasig River and Laguna de Bay. From there I went to Tayabas Bay. I had to wait there for a time, but found a ship to take me to Cebu by sea."

"That's not a trivial journey," the pilot major remarked. "It's several hundred miles."

"Indeed. And I narrowly escaped capture by Moro pirates in the Tayabas area. But by God's grace, I reached Cebu in early 1635."

"We are glad to have you on board," said Captain-General Mendoza. "A toast to Father Blanco."

Glasses were clicked together.

The galleons waited in the cove for a week before the pilot major gave the go-ahead to proceed. A strong wind from the south or southwest was needed to force the galleons through against the current.

The *San Raimundo* and the *Concepción* at last threaded the gauntlet of the Embocadero and passed into the open sea, setting a north-northeast course. Around the twentieth parallel, the two galleons picked up the Kuroshio—the "black current"—that flowed northeast, parallel to the coast of Japan.

Unfortunately, that was not all they picked up. A storm came upon them, which they tried to ride out bearing just their storm canvas. Just when they thought the onslaught was at an end, and raised more sail, the storm delivered its final punch, hurtling the two ships toward the rocks of Batan Island. Expert piloting avoided a complete disaster, but both galleons lost some spars and sails.

The next mass was extremely well attended.

Life on board settled into a routine. Day and night were each divided into three watches, each four hours in length. As Father Blanco stood by the port handrail of the *tolda*, watching dolphins leaping in the water, he heard one of the pages call out, "one glass done, one filling, more sands run, God willing." Every half hour, one of the pages turned the sand clock, and sang out a bit of doggerel so the officers would know that they were awake and doing what they were supposed to do. On the seventh turn, they would call for the next watch to be ready. On the eighth, they would call "On deck, gentlemen! Hurry and get up, get up!"—and say a Pater Noster and an Ave Maria.

The pages were the youngest members of the crew. As such, they were considered the purest souls among the crew, and thus the best suited to deliver such prayers to Heaven. They ranged in age from eight to eighteen years, but the average was about fifteen. That was only a little older than Father Blanco had been when he first crossed the Pacific.

Father Blanco smiled when he thought about the voyage that changed his life. He had been raised in an orphanage in Mexico City. At the age of thirteen, he was selected to become a servant for a group of Jesuit priests who were going to Manila. When they were ordered to Japan, he accompanied them. There, he made himself useful by serving Mass, singing the liturgical responses, and learning Japanese.

He proved to have a knack for languages, and it wasn't long before he was acting as interpreter for new arrivals. This development did not go unnoted, and he was invited to become a novitiate in the Society of Jesus. He studied Latin, Japanese, humanities, philosophy and theology at the seminary in the domain of Harunobu Arima, a Christian daimyo. After he graduated, he preached throughout Japan until that fateful year, 1614, when Shogun Tokugawa Ieyasu ordered the expulsion of all Christian missionaries.

As the ship's chaplain, Father Blanco held services every Sunday. He also offered confession to those who wished it. During the first week after the *San Raimundo* left Cebu, most of the confessions related to fornication while in port. There were also a few cases in which the penitent confessed to theft or assault.

Alas, if the passenger who had said harsh words about missionaries was one of the penitents, he did not speak about his anger and grief to Father Blanco.

Chapter 17

August 1635

The waters of the Strait of Georgia were leaden, matching the color of the sky above. Sea foam surged past the bow of the *Ieyasu Maru* as it forged its way northwest toward Texada Island.

Captain Yamada Haruno, Dutch-made spyglass in hand, stood on the quarterdeck with Tenjiku Tokubei.

"Anxious?" asked Captain Haruno.

"A little bit," responded Tenjiku Tokubei. "We're getting back later than I expected."

"Orders are orders," said Haruno. After they arrived in Monterey Bay, the grand governor had sent them on a special mission, one that had delayed their return to Texada.

Haruno felt a raindrop graze the tip of his nose. Well, a little rain wasn't going to slow down the *Ieyasu Maru*.

"But it won't be much longer," he added. "If this east wind holds steady, perhaps three hours to the southern tip of Texada. And then another two hours to Sandy Bottom Bay."

The arrival of the *Ieyasu Maru* at the mouth of Sandy Bottom Bay caused, as might be expected, a strong reaction from the watcher on Sentinel Island. A smoke signal sufficed for the sighting of a canoe, but to warn of the approach of a western-style ship, the watcher fired off one of the signal rockets brought by the *Iemitsu Maru* for just such an eventuality.

The boom of the explosion did not go unnoticed on the quarterdeck of the *Ieyasu Maru*, either.

"We've been spotted," said Haruno.

"Yes," agreed Tokubei. "And it also means that at least one colony ship made it here. See that smoke trail?" He pointed at the sky to their northeast. "That was left by a signal rocket, and the exploration party we left didn't have any."

"Hopefully, our exploration party survived to greet and guide the colonists," added Haruno.

While the officers on board the *Ieyasu Maru* were thus expecting to find Japanese colonists on Texada, those colonists did not know whether the European-style *Ieyasu Maru* was Japanese, Dutch or even Spanish. Prudence dictated that they act as if the incoming vessel was hostile, until proven otherwise.

When the signal rocket burst, Haru was on the beach, where he could supervise the fishermen and hopefully forestall further conflicts with the Indians. His presence served equally well for maintaining order if a sailing ship came to Texada.

The fishermen had been told that if they saw or heard a rocket burst, they were to return immediately to the beach if they were in the bay, or row north to Iron Landing otherwise. It was expected that any western-style ship would approach from the south. While some remembered this directive, and complied, others had to be prodded by Haru. Which wasn't easy when he was on the beach and they were on the water, and could easily pretend not to see or hear him.

Fortunately, the colony ships had brought a few cannon as cargo, and some were placed in a battery defending the beach. Haru ordered a three pounder fired, without shot. The loud blast of the small cannon got the fishermen's attention. They hurriedly pulled in their nets and made for shore.

When the *Ieyasu Maru* sailed closer, Haru recognized his old ship, ordered the battery to stand down, and sent messengers to Isamu at Camp Double Six, Masaru at Sea Hawk Village, and Fukuhei at Bucktooth Dam Village.

". . . And this is the building housing our *tatara*," said Isamu proudly. He, Haru and Masaru had met the *Ieyasu Maru*'s boat at the beach, and welcomed Tokubei, Captain Haruno, and Commander Hosoya back to Texada.

"I am glad that you have not only survived, but prospered," said Hosoya soberly. "And I much regret that it took us so long to return to Texada. When we reached Monterey Bay, the grand governor had received news that his daughter Iroha-hime's ship had been wrecked, and after refitting and reprovisioning we were sent to San Francisco Bay to rescue her and search for her husband's gold hunting party."

"Heading north along the coast," added Haruno, "the winds and current would have been against us, and so we had to swing far out to sea and back. Between that and the search time, it was January before we were back in Monterey Bay.

"And in February, while we refitted, our companion Tenjiku Tokubei was honored by the grand governor with promotion to samurai status." Tokubei was proudly wearing both the long *katana* and the short *wakizashi*, the *daisho* of the samurai.

Isamu bowed politely to Tokubei, in recognition of this honor, even though Tokubei's status was of course still inferior to his own.

"And Captain Haruno was given valuable exclusive trading rights," said Tokubei.

"Then the grand governor said that he needed us to head south to search for signs of Spanish settlements," said Hosoya. "We sailed far south, past San Diego Bay, then returned to Kodachi Machi to report. And we refitted, and then came here. After trading with the Nuu-chah-nulth, that is."

"Each time we went north, of course, we had to make a big detour," said Tokubei. "Else the coastal winds would have been against us."

"Well, I am glad you made it here," said Isamu. "We were worried about you! Should I continue the tour?"

"Please do so," said Hosoya.

"We also have a smith, to forge the iron and steel into useful items for use by the colonists, or for trade with the Indians. Or for repair of the ironware on ships that call here."

"That reminds me," said Tokubei. "I want to talk to the grand governor about giving us a ship's smith."

"A ship's smith?" said Haruno.

"Yes. You know I have sailed on Dutch ships, as far as India. It is not unusual for European ships of a certain size to have a smith or armorer on board, and even a small forge, although they would usually make landfall if they needed to operate the latter."

"It's a good idea. In the old days, few Japanese ships were at sea long enough to warrant carrying a smith, but now, with sailing across the Pacific, it makes sense. I will support your proposal!" said Haruno. "In fact, now I hope to get a smith for the *Ieyasu Maru*!

"In the meantime, Isamu, if your colony's smith has time to spare, we can give him some billets to forge into trade goods."

"That would be prudent," said Isamu. "Yells-at-Bears says that the Indians would have difficulty working iron and steel, given that they have stone tools, so a steel knife would be worth far more in trade than a metal block."

Isamu's guided tour ended at Camp Double Six.

"Captain Haruno, may I have a word with you?" asked Masaru. "In private?"

Isamu frowned at Masaru. The most likely explanation for the request was that Masaru wanted to criticize Isamu's handling of the mission, without Isamu being able to defend himself. Isamu was still trying to come up with a good way to say this without implying that, indeed, his actions left something to be desired when Captain Haruno granted Masaru's request and thus took the matter out of Isamu's hands.

"That's fine," said Commander Hosoya, the commander of the *Ieyasu Maru*'s samurai marines. "I'll speak to Isamu while you talk to Masaru."

All right, then, thought Isamu. *I'll have the first word with Hosoya.*

Had Isamu been privy to Masaru's meeting with Captain Haruno, he would have been mollified. At least in part.

"Captain Haruno, I don't believe that Isamu has been utilizing my talents as effectively as he could. I would like to put in a request for transfer back to the *Ieyasu Maru*, Or for passage on the *Ieyasu Maru* to Monterey Bay."

"I will have to discuss your request with Commander Hosoya. It is not likely that we will make a decision until the *Ieyasu Maru* is ready to head south."

"Understood, sir."

✣ ✣ ✣

For that matter, Isamu's conference with Commander Hosoya took an interesting turn.

"I heard the good news, you are producing iron and ironware. Now tell me the bad news, please."

Isamu blinked. Hosoya's demand was unusually direct. It appeared that contact with the Dutch was rubbing off on him.

Isamu took a deep breath. "First, the climate here is very different than home, and the soil is poor, so the farmers are unhappy. More so than usual, that is. It might help if any future farmers are recruited from northern Honshu, or even Ezochi, and also if seeds from those areas are brought here.

"Second, while the lakes, streams and ocean are very productive, some of the natives living on other islands, or the mainland, are accustomed to coming here to exploit them, and that is creating conflict. Because of the orders for the ships to minimize contact between the *kirishitan* colonists and the Buddhist sailors, the *Iemitsu Maru* and the *Sendai Maru* have moved off to a northern anchorage and aren't really part of the colony's defenses. At best, they can retaliate if we are raided. And even that option will vanish when they return to Japan. We really need our own naval force!

"Third, while we have trained the miners, farmers and fishermen to fight, if need be, they are not the equal of full-time warriors. They can hold a spear, but it is doubtful that they can maintain ranks if they must advance in line under fire. They can fire a gun, but I am not sure they will hold fire until ordered to shoot, or hit their target when they do shoot. So we cannot take a firm position in these native encounters unless by chance a samurai is present or the numbers are greatly in our favor.

"Finally, we have too many people—miners and ironworkers—who aren't involved in food production."

Hosoya grimaced. "Giving you more samurai to deter the natives would not solve that problem. Indeed, it would exacerbate it."

"True, but if the natives were scared off, the fishermen might be more productive."

"I will consult with Tokubei. . . ."

"This is what we are going to do," said Tokubei. "We will visit the nearby tribes and impress on them that we are better friends than enemies."

"How do you propose to do that?" asked Masaru.

"Give them presents that they can't get locally. And, while they watch, blow something up with our gunpowder. My question is, where should we start?"

"With the Tla'amin, I think," said Isamu. "Most of the encounters have been with them."

"Where does their chief live?" asked Commander Hosoya.

"There is no one that tells all of the Tla'amin what to do," said Yells-at-Bears. "Each settlement has its own leaders. But the best place to go would be Camp-Overnight. It is a place at which the Tla'amin mingle with their kin, the Klahoose and the Homalco, and so the word of our strength would spread quickly."

"How do we get there?" asked Captain Haruno.

"I am sorry, I do not know."

Captain Haruno grumbled, "Is there anywhere else we can go? Where we can get a guide to Camp-Overnight, perhaps?"

"We should go to Wide-River-Bed," said Isamu. "It is where Fast-Drummer came from. I made a deal with him that we need to firm up."

"I hope you know how to get there," muttered Captain Haruno.

"Oh, yes," said Yells-at-Bears. "It is by what your map calls Powell River, on the coast of the Malaspina Strait, to our north and east. And Fast-Drummer, or one of his friends, could certainly guide your ships to Camp-Overnight, if you still want to go there."

"That sounds a lot better to me," said Captain Haruno.

"And we should also go to Kalpilin. Remember the Shishalh we met when we first came to Texada? They came from that village, and my older sister married a man who lived there. It, too, is on the coast, east of Texada."

"Fine," said Tokubei.

"Yells-at-Bears, you warned us about the Haida, and the Laich-kwil-tach," said Haru. "Should we be visiting them, too?"

She bit her lip. "I think that you should strengthen your defenses here before you bring themselves to their attention."

Chapter 18

Wide-River-Bed, a Tla'amin Village (up-time Powell River)

One August afternoon, Red-Feet ran into the longhouse where Calm-Water, the First-Man of the Tla'amin village of Wide-River-Bed, resided, together with his extended family.

"Where is Calm-Water?" he shouted. "I don't see him here."

Calm-Water's daughter looked up from the canoe bailer she was making from a strip of red cedar bark. "He is out back. What's wrong?"

He did not deign to answer, but ran for the back door of the longhouse. Red-Feet found Calm-Water standing by the berry-drying racks.

He spoke so quickly his words almost tripped on each other. "Excuse me, Calm-Water, but my friends and I were out fishing on the big water and we saw a floating island in the distance, near Pointed Nose."

Calm-Water laughed. "A floating island? Was it being towed by a whale?" Each winter, one of the elders told a story about the whale that supposedly lived in the pool at the base of the Powell River Falls, and made a noisy spout whenever the weather was about to change for the worse.

Red-Feet gave him an exasperated look. "I am serious, Calm-Water. We paddled here as fast as we could to warn you."

Calm-Water paused to consider what to say next. Red-Feet was a serious lad, not much given to pranks even on his peers. For him to try to embarrass an elder was next to unthinkable. But most likely, what he had taken for a floating island was just a mass of shore or river vegetation torn away by a storm.

"Exactly where is your floating island?"

"By the south end of Pointed Nose."

That was a little over six miles away.

"So why has no one else reported it?" asked Calm-Water.

"It is on the far side of Pointed Nose, so it is hidden from view."

"You are sure you are not confusing it with Place-to-Gather-Seagull-Eggs?" That was the little islet a mile west of Pointed Nose.

"Of course not!"

Calm-Water made a placating gesture. "Just making sure." He glanced westward at the sun. "We have enough time to get there and back before true night."

As they passed through the longhouse, Calm-Water called out, "Red-Feet is taking me to look at something by Pointed Nose, I'll be back in time for the evening meal."

Red-Feet and his three friends eased their canoe into the water, then held it respectfully to let Calm-Water board.

About two hours later, as the Tla'amin paddlers neared Pointed Nose, Red-Feet turned toward Calm-Water. "Perhaps we should beach the canoe on this side, and go overland, so we are more difficult to see?"

Even though Calm-Water thought Red-Feet was making much ado about nothing, he approved of Red-Feet's caution. The time might come when Red-Feet was leading his fellow Tla'amin against a Haida raiding party encamped near their village.

"That is a good suggestion."

Near the south end of Pointed Nose, there was a cove with a sandy beach, and that's where they beached the canoe.

They clambered uphill about fifty feet and then weaved through the forest, at last reaching a point where they could see the larger cove on the west side of Pointed Nose. Red-Feet and his friends went the last few yards on all fours, and Calm-Water somewhat grudgingly followed suit.

A moment later, he was glad he did. There was the floating island. He had expected that if he had seen one at all, it would be a flat green mass, with perhaps a shrub or two. But this . . . it was longer than their longest canoe. Longer than even a Haida war-canoe. As best he could make out in the twilight, it carried three tall burnt trees. How then could it float? The branches were even stranger. Two of the trees carried four pairs of horizontal branches, with each branch of the pair on opposite sides of the tree. The third tree was similar, but it had one opposed pair of diagonal branches, one branch rising the other falling, and together forming a straight line. It seemed profoundly unnatural, and Calm-Water fought back a shudder.

"We must warn the People," he whispered.

They retreated slowly, as silently and inconspicuously as they could. Once they were out of sight of the floating island, they hastened their pace. They launched the canoe and paddled furiously.

Calm-Water considered cautioning them to pace themselves but thought better of it. He wanted to put space between himself and the uncanny island as much as they did. He comforted himself with the thought that whatever beings might inhabit the island, they had no reason to direct it toward Wide-River-Bed. Nonetheless, precautions would need to be taken.

That night, Calm-Water called a tribal conclave inside his longhouse, which was the largest building in the village. He summoned not only the high-status adults but also the commoners. Only the slaves were excluded.

He welcomed everyone and called upon Red-Feet to describe his first sighting of the floating island. There was much muttering in the audience, but none were so impolite as to interrupt.

"Be seated, Red-Feet."

As soon as he sat down, another young man, one of higher status than Red-Feet, stood. "This is foolish talk, Calm-Water. I have gone to Pointed Nose many times, and I have never seen a floating island nearby. One might as well speak of fish flying over the trees!"

"I would agree with you," Calm-Water admitted, "if I had not seen the floating island myself, earlier today."

Standing-Bear, one of his fellow elders, cleared his throat. "It is a time when it is easy to mistake one thing for another."

Calm-Water didn't appreciate the challenge to his authority, but kept his expression deadpan. "When several people all see the same thing, it is unlikely that there is a mistake. And a refusal to accept the truth is dangerous."

Fast-Drummer, who was of high status, but too young to be a rival for Calm-Water, interjected, "Perhaps it would be prudent to move the women and children inland while we investigate further. There are the strange people I met near Clear-Sandy-Bottom, on *Sah yah yin*. They claimed to come there on a 'Great Canoe' that had wings instead of paddles. If canoes can flap their wings like birds, perhaps islands can float."

A few of the attendees slapped their thighs in approbation of this witticism.

"I agree," said Calm-Water. "But the move must wait until morning. T'al lurks in the forest, and she is most active at night." T'al was the Cannibal Woman, and she stole children.

Morning was too late. The sun's disk had only just cleared the horizon when the floating island was spotted by the lookout Calm-Water had quietly posted. Since it was coming out of the west, where the sky was still dark, it had not been easy to see, despite its size. He started beating on a drum to warn the rest of the village.

The warriors hastily grabbed their spears and bows and went down to the beach. The women were ordered to flee into the forest to the east, but many declined to do so. "We want to see this floating island," Calm-Water's principal wife said. "Time enough to flee if it comes to shore."

But it did not come to shore. It stopped about half a mile off. If anything, it was more uncanny than in the description given by Red-Feet and Calm-Water of their previous encounters. Not only was a moving island more threatening than a floating one, this one appeared to have white clouds hovering over it as it moved. Well, some of the Tla'amin thought they were clouds. Others insisted that they were flocks of seagulls.

The Tla'amin warriors remained tense even after it was clear that the island's movement had stopped. At last, one said, "I think I see people on the island. At least, I see them from the waist up. I *assume* they have legs." He laughed nervously.

"We should send warriors in a canoe to take a closer look," said Red-Feet. He puffed out his chest. "*I* am willing to go."

"The floating island came from the west. It must have broken off from the Land of the Dead," Standing-Bear declared. "We should have nothing to do with it."

"How could that be?" demanded Fast-Drummer. "The Great Island to the west is in the way." "Perhaps it is from the Land of the Dead, perhaps it is not," said Calm-Water. "It is easy to mistake one thing for another," he added pointedly.

"The people on the floating island have launched a canoe!" shouted Red-Feet.

"Then we will send a canoe to meet it," Calm-Water announced. "Fast-Drummer, you and Red-Feet may go. You may bring spears, but keep them out of sight unless you are threatened."

Red-Feet paddled, while Fast-Drummer steered. Fast-Drummer was of higher rank, and steering was the more prestigious task. The current was steady, so Fast-Drummer didn't need to make frequent adjustments. That left him free to study the mystery craft.

Fast-Drummer could see that the strange canoe was about twenty feet long, and had eight people in it. More remarkably, it had a small tree growing out of the center! And there was some odd artifact at the bow.

"Just two to greet us?" complained Yells-at-Bears plaintively. She was sitting near the prow of the *Ieyasu Maru*'s longboat, just behind one of the sailors.

"Better than being outnumbered," said Isamu, who was sitting behind her. He held one of the precious Dutch spyglasses to his eye. "And there are plenty of people on the beach, or back by the houses."

"Do you recognize anyone?" asked Yells-at-Bears.

"In the canoe? Well, one *looks* like Fast-Drummer. But I only met him once."

"May I look, please?" she held out her hand. She adjusted the focus slightly. "Yes, I am sure that's Fast-Drummer. But I don't remember the other one."

"I hope Fast-Drummer recognizes us." Isamu turned to speak to the helmsman. "Bring us closer to that canoe. Perhaps half the distance."

"I think one of them's a woman," said Fast-Drummer. "So we can chance getting a bit closer."

At last they came close enough that he could distinguish faces and he exclaimed, "I know two of them! I met them on *Sah yah yin*. One is Yells-at-Bears, a Snuneymuxw woman. The other is named Ih-sah-moo, and he claimed to be from across the Great Ocean."

Red-Feet made a warding gesture. "Doesn't that mean he is from the Land of the Dead?"

Fast-Drummer shrugged. "He was breathing just like you and me. His feet left footprints."

"I hope you are right," said Red-Feet. "So there is nothing supernatural about him?"

"Well . . ." Fast-Drummer hesitated. "In trade, he gave me my spirit-stone-axe. . . ."

"That axe! It's amazing!"

"Indeed it is." Fast-Drummer had demonstrated the axe's abilities several times, and it had raised his status in the community. Come winter, he intended to compose a song about it and perform it. Or perhaps a dance would generate more prestige. Or . . .

"Stop paddling, Red-Feet! They've stopped."

Red Feet raised his paddle out of the water. "Now what?"

"Now . . . We wait for them to make the next move."

The visitors, unfortunately, had adopted the same waiting strategy. Neither side had moved for some time.

"This is getting boring," said Red-Feet. "Shouldn't we do something?"

Fast-Drummer looked back toward shore. His fellow villagers had neither fled nor jumped into their canoes. Calm-Water was standing just as he had before Fast-Drummer and Red-Feet had urged their canoe into the water.

Fast-Drummer stood up—slowly, so as not to capsize the canoe—and held out both hands, fingers spreads, palms facing Isamu and Yells-at-Bears.

"He is showing that he is not holding a weapon," said Yells-at-Bears.

"He probably has them by his feet," said Isamu.

"We are armed, too," said Yells-at-Bears. "Your swords, the sailors' hatchets and arquebuses, and the swivel gun at the bow. And my *naginata*, of course."

"Be careful if you decide to swing that thing," muttered Isamu. "We are in rather close quarters here, and I'd like to keep my head in my possession as long as possible. But yes, I see your point." He stood up, started to lose his balance, and caught himself. "I hate small boats," he complained. Then he made a beckoning motion to Fast-Drummer.

"I . . . I think they want us to come to them," said Red-Feet. "Do you think that's wise?"

"One of us has to come to the other," said Fast-Drummer. "Unless we want to float out here for the rest of our lives. Start paddling. But slowly."

"Hail, Fast-Drummer, of Wide-River Bed," shouted Yells-at-Bears.

"Hail, Yells-at-Bears, of the Snuneymuxw. What brings you and your Great Canoe to Calm-River-Bed?"

"You gave us the right to use that stream on *Sah yah yin* for a year. But you know we want more than that, so we must speak with your clan. Indeed, we must speak with all who assert rights to hunt and fish on *Sah yah yin* and its waters."

"Then it is best that you speak to our chief, Calm-Water. Are you willing to take your canoe to Calm-River-Bed?"

Yells-at-Bears exchanged looks with Isamu. "We are."

"Then let us do this."

Fast-Drummer and Red-Feet turned their canoe about and started paddling slowly back toward Wide-River-Bed. The sailors on the longboat started rowing, too, and Fast-Drummer deliberately let the longboat come abreast of his canoe and stay there, making it plain to those on shore that he was not trying to escape it.

Calm-Water was quick to perceive that the interaction with the strangers had been friendly enough to prompt Fast-Drummer to invite them to Wide-River-Bed. He pulled back most of the warriors, and those that remained on the beach laid down their weapons. Although they were still within reach.

Once the longboat entered water shallow enough that the sailors could step over the side and walk the longboat up onto the shore, Calm-Water and the men accompanying him started singing a song of welcome. Hopefully, the strangers would understand it.

With the longboat secured, Isamu and Yells-at-Bears stepped out.

Calm-Water was quick to recognize that they were of higher status than the sailors and made a gesture of respect in their direction.

"Fast-Drummer! Red-Feet! Come here!" he called out. "Tell me about these visitors."

"What we took to be a 'floating island' is the Great Canoe I was told about on *Sah yah yin* several moons ago. They came to *Sah yah yin* across the Great Ocean in it, and they mean to live there."

"Why? Did another tribe force them from their home?"

"I suppose it is possible," said Fast-Drummer doubtfully. "But they have spirit-stone axes. Not just the one I was given in trade, but many." He gestured toward the hatchets the sailors had tucked behind their *obi*. He was oblivious to the arquebuses the sailors had shouldered, not yet having seen any demonstration of their capabilities.

"Also, you saw with your own eyes that their 'floating island,' their 'Great Canoe,' can move with the wind, without being paddled. So their warriors would not be tired from paddling before a battle."

"So . . . That implies that they have come to *Sah yah yin* for another reason. It cannot just be that their villages have gotten too crowded, and they want more land. Or they would just have taken more land on their side of the Great Ocean."

"I wish I knew that reason," said Fast-Drummer. "They wish to bargain with my family, and the other families of our clan, for our rights on *Sah yah yin*. If I knew what they valued on *Sah yah yin*, it might help us get the best price."

"Yes, you should try to find out," said Calm-Water. "And there are others from our village who own traditional rights on that island. But now, you must introduce me to our visitors."

Fast-Drummer did so, and food and drink was brought forward by Calm-Water's wife. Once the visitors partook of this, Calm-Water and the other Tla'amin noticeably relaxed. The visitors and the Tla'amin now had the relationship of guests and hosts; neither could attack the other without inviting the wrath of the great spirits, and both were obligated to protect the other if, during the visit, an attack were made by the Laich-kwil-tach or the Haida. Unless of course some grave insult were delivered that vitiated the guest-host relationship.

In the days that followed, gifts were exchanged. Calm-Water learned that the Japanese—who Calm-Water dubbed the "People-of-the-Flying-Canoes"—had come to *Sah yah yin* in the hope of collecting spirit-stone—iron—there. While normally this would have led Calm-Water and the other village leaders to up the price for the hunting and fishing on *Sah yah yin*, there was an incident that led them to be cautious about this.

There was a faction among the residents of Wide-River-Bed who were not enamored with the visitors. Their nominal leader was Splitter-of-Waves, who had had a negative encounter with the Japanese at Sandy Bottom Bay, and had responded in kind. He was secretly egged on by Standing-Bear, whose guiding ethical principle was to oppose anything favored by Calm-Water that was considered controversial by the free people of Wide-River-Bed.

Splitter-of-Waves argued against making any concession of Tla'amin hereditary hunting and fishing rights on *Sah yah yin* to the Japanese.

However, then came the "demonstration" of the "thunderbird spirit power" of the visitors. The *Ieyasu Maru* had been moved closer to Wide-River-Bed. Isamu had borrowed some cedar boards from Calm-Water and a couple of the sailors used these to construct a target. After making sure that there was no person or other structure in line with the target, the *Ieyasu Maru* fired its twelve pound chase gun. The cannonball punched a ragged hole through the cedar target and buried itself deep into the backstop positioned behind it.

The Tla'amin watchers were deeply impressed, not just by the hole but also by the smoke, the flash and the sound. "They must be favored by the Thunderbird," said Red-Feet. "Was the flash not like the lightning the Thunderbird releases when it blinks its eyes? Was the roar not like the sound the Thunderbird makes when it flaps its wings?"

Another chimed in. "The ball of spirit-stone it threw makes me think of the balls of ice that the Thunderbird rolls out of its cave when someone comes too close."

Isamu ceremoniously gave the cannonball as a present to Calm-Water. Calm-Water gasped as he took it. It was heavier than a stone the same size would have been.

After his guests retired for the night, Calm-Water took out one of his deer bone awls, and tried scratching the cannonball. He was able to do so. But on further study, he found that the iron was far tougher than either bone or stone.

"What is this material?" he wondered aloud.

"Stop making noise and go to sleep," commanded his principal wife.

The next morning, his question still unanswered, Calm-Water met again with the Japanese.

"So you want to go to Camp-Overnight," said Calm-Water. "Why?"

"So we can address all of your people, as well as the Klahoose and the Homalco, about the benefits of trade and peace with the Japanese," said Yells-at-Bears.

Calm-Water frowned. He was not keen on sharing the unique trading opportunities provided by the Japanese with other villages. On the other hand, he didn't want to offend the visitors.

"It is true that many of the People will be at Camp-Overnight for the winter ceremonies," he admitted.

"Winter, huh?" muttered Captain Haruno. "When exactly are we talking about?"

Calm-Water shrugged. "In five moons."

Captain Haruno made an expression of surprise. "That long? We visited the Mowachaht, and they go into winter quarters in late August."

"The Mowachaht live on the Outer Coast. Their fishing season is shorter than ours."

Captain Haruno thought about this. "I don't fancy being in these waters come winter. Perhaps we will forego a visit to Camp-Overnight and head on to Kalpilin."

"I think that would be best for you," said Calm-Water solemnly. *And even better for us*, he thought.

Chapter 19

On the* San Raimundo, *in the Pacific

It had been over a decade since Father Blanco had last sailed on a galleon, and he had forgotten what a benighted lot the sailors, officers, soldiers and passengers were. Six at least of the seven deadly sins—lust, greed, sloth, wrath, envy, and pride—had been displayed during Blanco's time on board. Only gluttony had failed to make an appearance, no doubt because of the unappealing nature of the provisions. Punishments had been decreed for fornication (there were a few female passengers on board), gambling, theft, inattention to duty, cursing, and brawling.

Strictly speaking, only the cursing was formally within his purview, and then only when it took the form of blasphemy. But the misbehavior left a sour taste in his mouth. He could not help but contrast it with the soberness, honesty and piety of the Japanese Christians he had served in Manila. How he wished he was back with them!

Wide-River Bed, Tla'amin Territory

Learning that the *Ieyasu Maru* was planning to visit Kalpilin, both to trade and to look for Yells-at-Bears' elder sister, Fast-Drummer suggested to the Japanese that they let him paddle first to Kalpilin to warn them. Otherwise, he explained, the Shishalh too might think that the *Ieyasu Maru* was some sort of supernatural visitation, and hide until it left. It had been a near thing at Wide-River-Bed, he added.

They accepted his offer. "We don't want to scare away prospective customers," said Tokubei.

Fast-Drummer's friends helped push his canoe into the water, and then jumped in to join him. The canoe's bow was carved into the shape of a seal's head, so Fast-Drummer could imagine that he was riding a seal slicing through the swells as they paddled south along the coast.

While Fast-Drummer indeed intended to assure the Shishalh at Kalpilin that the *Ieyasu Maru* was manned by human beings not unlike themselves—although possessed of formidable spirit powers—he had an ulterior motive in making this proposal. At Calm-Water's urging, he would tell the Shishalh the trade terms negotiated by Calm-Water, and cajole the Shishalh to insist on the same terms rather than undercut the Tla'amin.

Those terms did not speak of sea otters, as those were not common in Tla'amin waters. What the Tla'amin had to trade were beaver skins, inner cedar bark, clams, and smoke-dried meats—eulachon, salmon, deer and seal. Some of these would be consumed by the Japanese and the remainder could be traded by them to the Indians of the outer coast.

Five days later, Fast-Drummer and his friends returned, and the *Ieyasu Maru* set sail for Kalpilin.

There, they were greeted in an elaborate ceremony, not just by singing, but also dancing, and gift-giving. The chief here was named Holds-a-Bundle, which they surmised was a reference to his possessions. His house was decorated with many carvings and paintings of animals—eagles, ravens, bears, whales and beavers.

Like the Tla'amin, the Shishalh did not hunt sea otters. However, they fed their guests smoked sturgeon and surf smelt, which were goods they traded to the Tla'amin and other tribes.

On inquiry, the Japanese discovered that Fast-Drummer had described the "thunderbird-spirit-power" of their cannon, and if anything, the tale had grown in the telling. It therefore was not necessary to repeat the demonstration.

When the immediate translation needs of the visitors had been satisfied, Yells-at-Bears decided that it was only fair that she take some personal time. She wanted to find her sister, Salmon-Berry. She was so named because she had been born in June, when the salmonberries ripened.

"First-Man, my sister Salmon-Berry married one of your people. Where can I find her?"

"Do you know her husband's name?"

"I am sorry, I don't. I was young and it was long ago."

"How long ago did they marry?"

"More than a decade ago."

"And you are of the Snuneymuxw?"

"Yes."

"It is rare for our men to go across the Strait for a bride. But Tall-Post was a great trader. I think he married one of the Snuneymuxw. She changed her name after her marriage. I don't remember her old name. She is now 'Chickadee.'"

"Where would I find them?"

"Little-Raccoon can take you to them. Where is the young rascal? Little-Raccoon, come here!"

While Yells-at-Bears went off to find her sister, Isamu sought a private conference with Commander Hosoya.

"What do you think of Yells-at-Bears?"

"She is certainly a great asset to our mission here."

"And to me personally," said Isamu. "I have been thinking of asking her to marry me, but I am not sure how to go about this. There are no professional go-betweens on Texada!"

"That is hardly your only problem," said Hosoya. "First, your family has not been consulted, and may well have already arranged a marriage for you back home. Second, you are a samurai, and therefore require your lord's permission to marry. And third, she is not of the samurai class, or even Japanese, which will probably prejudice both your family and Date Masamune against the marriage."

"Once it became known that I was going to New Nippon in Date Masamune's service, probably for many years, the other family broke off the betrothal. I think my family has written me off insofar as marriage alliances are concerned."

"That may be true, but the grand governor may feel that he needs some communication from them to the effect that they deem you free to marry as you will."

"It would be a year before I could get their reply, assuming that I could send it back with the *Iemitsu Maru*."

"Nonetheless, I recommend you try," said Hosoya. "What of my other points?"

"If a samurai family adopts her, she becomes samurai, and is no longer a commoner. And there are a few samurai here who know Yells-at-Bears. I might be able to persuade one of them to help."

"True, but adoption is usually a family decision, in which one's parents and other family elders are consulted."

"I know, but I imagine it depends somewhat on the terms of the adoption."

"Perhaps so."

"Well, thank you for your advice."

Little-Raccoon was, Yells-at-Bears discovered, Holds-a-Bundle's grandnephew, and was about twelve years old. He was quite happy to serve as Yells-at-Bears' guide, as it allowed him to escape, at least for the time being, a chore he did not find especially enjoyable.

As they walked down the row of houses, he kept up a constant chatter. This person had the best hunting dog in the village. A second had just started building a canoe. A third had a daughter who had just gone into her *qaieqa*, her seclusion for her first period. Was Yells-at-Bears staying long enough to enjoy the *solomates*, the puberty feast, that her parents would give when she emerged?

The house of Tall-Post was two-thirds of the way down the row from that of Holds-a-Bundle. That suggested that his family was not especially prosperous.

Little-Raccoon put his hands around his mouth to form a speaking-trumpet and yelled, "Hey, Tall-Post, you have a visitor from far away!"

A woman came out. "Tall-Post is out hunting."

Yells-at-Bears said uncertainly, in Halkomelem, the language of the Snuneymuxw, "Salmon-Berry? Is that you?"

"I was once Salmon-Berry," she responded. "I am now Chickadee. Who are you?"

Salmon-Berry didn't look quite as tall as she had when Yells-at-Bears was twelve, but she was still recognizable. Yells-at-Bears couldn't help but notice that Salmon-Berry was wearing a dentalia shell necklace. Dentalia were found in the deep waters west of Vancouver Island, not in the Strait of Georgia. Here, on the inner coast, they were expensive. Well, Holds-a-Bundle did say that her husband Tall-Post had crossed the Strait. Perhaps he had gone as far as the lands of Mowachaht, where they could have been obtained more cheaply.

"I am your younger sister, Yells-at-Bears."

"Yells-at-Bears? How is that possible? You were taken by the Kwakwaka'wakw. And they never made a ransom demand."

Yells-at-Bears understood the significance of that statement. It could mean of course that they had entirely wiped out Yells-at-Bears' village, so there was no one to deliver a ransom demand to. Or the raid was motivated not merely by economics, but by a serious grudge that could not be satisfied by ransom. Or that the raiders were unsure of their ability to resist a counter-raid if they identified themselves by presenting a ransom demand.

But wait . . ."How do you know this?"

"Our parents survived the fire the raiders set. Messengers were sent to those in other villages who were related by blood or marriage, including to us." Kalpilin was only about thirty-two miles from Nanaimo; just a few days' paddling. "But no trace was found of you or the other captives. What happened to you?"

"We were taken by the Laich-kwil-tach," said Yells-at-Bears. "They sold me to the K'wagu'l, who sold me to the Gwat'sinux. I was their slave until a year ago, when the People-of-the-Flying-Canoes freed me."

She paused. "I saw the fire as the raiders carried me off. I thought everyone in our village was dead."

"I am so sorry, Yells-at-Bears," said her sister. "But now you know they are alive."

"So, how has life been among the Shishalh?"

"I can't complain," Chickadee said. "Tall-Post is a good hunter. We have two grown daughters, both married." She smiled ruefully. "Of course, paying the bride's price for them both wasn't easy, especially since we couldn't look for help from the Snuneymuxw side of the family."

"Because of the fire?"

"Yes, Father and Mother lost most of their possessions, one way or another, and he lost status, too. The moon after the raid, he was supplanted as First-Man."

"Sad."

"Yes, though not as sad as your own story. But at least yours has taken a turn for the better."

"Yes, it has," admitted Yells-at-Bears.

"So what is life like among the People-of-the-Flying-Canoes?"

Yells-at-Bears talked at some length about the Japanese and their ways.

"It sounds as though you are sweet on this Ih-sah-moo."

"I am."

"And does he reciprocate these feelings?"

"He does."

Chickadee lifted her shoulders and then relaxed them. "It's a pity he can't marry you. Since he is one of the leaders of the People-of-the-Flying-Canoes, he must be of noble status, as you once were. You were enslaved too long without being ransomed, so you are slave status now. There is no marriage between noble and slave, just concubinage."

"The People-of-the-Flying-Canoes freed me."

"How?"

"By declaring it among themselves."

"That is enough by their laws, perhaps. But by the laws of the Snuneymuxw, the Tla'amin, and the Shishalh, you are still a slave. You just now belong to the People-of-the-Flying-Canoes."

"My status can be redeemed by potlatch," said Yells-at-Bears.

"Yes, but who will throw one of sufficient generosity?" asked Chickadee. "Not me, we are in straitened circumstances because of the two bride-prices. Not your parents, they were ruined by the fire."

"That was a dozen years ago. Perhaps they are prospering now."

"Perhaps, but I don't know."

"You are not in touch with them?"

"Not really. It is probably ten years since I last visited them, and they have never visited us."

Plainly, Chickadee was long estranged from Father and Mother. Whether it was out of outrage over their failure to rescue Yells-at-Bears, or over a lack of support for Chickadee's new family, Yells-at-Bears couldn't guess. Her mind shifted back to her own problem.

"The People-of-the-Flying-Canoes, perhaps, will give a potlatch on my behalf if I asked them to."

Chickadee frowned. "I am not sure that counts. But for it to have a chance of benefitting you, they must throw the potlatch for your old tribe and its allies, as it is they who were shamed by your own disgrace."

Yells-at-Bears made a gesture of affirmation. "In the meantime, please say nothing about my enslavement by the Gwat'sinux to anyone."

"I won't, but Tall-Post knows you were taken and not ransomed. And so you must have been either enslaved or killed. And Holds-a-Bundle, or one of the other elders, may remember hearing from me that the 'sister of Chickadee' was taken in a raid."

The conversation then turned to lighter topics, and Yells-at-Bears was invited to stay to meet Tall-Post and have dinner with him and Chickadee. She, at least, was willing to treat Yells-at-Bears as a free woman, since even commoners would not dine with slaves.

At dinner, Yells-at-Bears invited Tall-Post and Chickadee to come aboard the *Ieyasu Maru* and sail with them to Texada . . . and, if Yells-at-Bears had her way, to Nanaimo.

They agreed, provided Tall-Post's canoe could be taken on board. That way, they could leave whenever they wished.

The next day, Tokubei and Captain Haruno gave approval for Tall-Post and Chickadee's excursion. However, they were not willing to sail to Nanaimo, let alone go there to throw a potlatch to remove the stain to her honor.

Yells-at-Bears had explained to them that a potlatch was a ceremonial feast in which the host gave out gifts to those attending. Usually, its purpose was to win public confirmation of the status of the host but when given on behalf of an individual who had been disgraced in some way, it was to obtain public acquiescence in the rehabilitation of that individual In this case, her.

"Nanaimo doesn't having anything we need, nor is it a threat to us," said the captain. "So there is no reason for the *Ieyasu Maru* to go there. And as long as you live among us, you are a free woman, and it doesn't matter to us what your status is in Nanaimo. I assume you are not foolish enough to tell the Tla'amin or Shishalh that you were a slave! But even if you do so, it wouldn't bar our using you as an interpreter, it would just cramp your social life.

"Besides, didn't you say that it is your family that must throw the potlatch, not outsiders like us?"

"It is customary," she admitted. "I don't know which tribes would accept a potlatch thrown by outsiders as a purification of my status. At the very least, they might expect more generous gifts to dissuade criticism of the . . . irregularity."

"What if *you* threw the potlatch?" asked Tokubei. "Don't you count as part of your own family?"

"Well . . . It might work . . . Or I could give them the goods on the sly, and then have *them* give the potlatch. But I don't have that kind of wealth. . . ."

"Not yet," said Isamu. "But you have a deal with the smith. And I have some money, too, to buy trade goods. From the ships, or from the colonists."

"Thank you!"

Isamu turned to Captain Haruno. "Would you be willing to give us the use of the *Unagi Maru* for a few months?"

"I suppose you have earned it. It will be needed in the spring, as a guard ship for Sandy Bottom Bay, unless the *Ieyasu Maru* is here, or we can set up a strong enough battery. But for now, the Indians are moving into winter quarters."

"Thank you very much!" said Isamu, bowing deeply to him.

Chapter 20

The *Ieyasu Maru* sailed back to Sandy Bottom Bay, and Isamu, Yells-at-Bears, and their guests disembarked.

As they walked down the new cedar plank road to the Welcome House, they saw and greeted a group of *kirishitan* women, who were gathering huckleberries from the nearby bushes.

"I know you need to hold a bunch of boring meetings, now," Yells-at-Bears said to Isamu as they continued walking.

"I hope they are boring," said Isamu. "If they are boring, it means that there are no crises to resolve."

"I understand," said Yells-at-Bears. "Before we left, Tetsue had succeeded in making Texada *tamahagane*. I want to talk to Arinobu, and find out what he's made with it. If I am to give that potlatch to redeem my status this coming winter, I need to act quickly."

Isamu waved her on. "Go, and good luck!"

Yells-at-Bears ran to the smithy, where Arinobu greeted her. "And here you go," he said. "The first knife made with Texada iron." He bowed slightly as he presented it.

"What wood is the handle made of?" asked Yells-at-Bears. "It's not cedar."

"No, I tried cedar. It's too soft for my taste. This is the wood of what we named 'the flaky-orange-bark tree.'"

"You carved it?"

"Oh, no. Morimoto, the carpenter's mate from *Ieyasu Maru*, is making knife handles for me. But the blade, that's my doing, of course."

Yells-at-Bears held the blade up to the light, and rotated it. "The finish is different than on the knife you gave me."

"Yes, this is *kuroichi*. The blade retains the black scale from the forging process. The knife I gave you previously had a hand-hammered finish—*tsuchime*—so every blade is distinctive."

He cocked his head. "Which style do you think will fetch the best price from the natives?"

"I am not sure," said Yells-at-Bears. "But which is more work to make?"

"*Tsuchime*, certainly."

"So we should sell those at a higher price," she said. "And perhaps only to those of high status."

"All right."

"What else do you have in stock?" asked Yells-at-Bears.

"Three more *kuroichi*, made from the same batch. And the metalware I made from the smelted Japanese iron that was brought over. *Kama* pots, pans, fish hooks, arrowheads, spearheads, ax and saw blades, hammer heads, chisels, files.... Some are cast iron, some wrought iron, and some steel, depending on what part of the *tamahagane* I use and how I treat it."

"How long does it take to make a knife?"

"Two or three days if it has a *kuroichi* finish. Twice that if you want *tsuchime*."

"Hmm..." she pondered this. "I'd like to go over what you have, and figure out what would most appeal to the Tla'amin and Shishalh. In fact, I have Shishalh guests—my elder sister and her husband—and I can take them here and get their opinion."

"That makes sense, but what do the natives have that *I* want? Or that the colonists want?"

Fortunately, Yells-at-Bears had thought about this when she visited the Tla'amin and the Shishalh.

"First, elk, mountain goat, or bear hides for use as outerwear or blankets during the winter. I know from Isamu's complaints last winter that it is cooler here than in Sendai, and many of the *kirishitan* come from southern Honshu, or even Kyushu.

"Second, venison to supplement the diet."

Arinobu winced. "Not for me."

"The colonists are *kirishitan*, they will happily eat meat," Yells-at-Bears pointed out. "And for that matter, I know that some of the miners and ironworkers do so."

"Yes, they come from the mountains. Farming is more difficult there, so they are permitted to eat game. Especially if they worship just the kamis, not the buddhas. But aren't there deer here on Texada?"

"There are," she agreed. "But other than the samurai, hardly any of the Japanese here are good archers."

"True enough, although firearms are now part of militia training. And it takes less time to train a musketeer than an archer. Anything else?"

"Eulachon. It's an oily fish, a great delicacy. And we use the dried fish as torches."

"Curious. But will the colonists like them?"

"If they don't, then we can trade them to other Indians that live further away from the eulachon spawning grounds."

"How good a trade do you think we can get?"

Yells-at-Bears sighed. "It is very difficult to predict. But we can first ascertain what price the colonists will pay, and then use that as a floor."

"That sounds reasonable."

Yells-at-Bears fidgeted.

"Is something the matter?"

"Trading for things the Indians have that the colonists want will give us a quick profit, but a small one. The big money is in trading for things that are wanted back home, or in China, like sea otter pelts."

"But then we won't get paid for a year or two."

"That's right," said Yells-at-Bears. "Unless we trade our trade goods to the officers and crew of the *Ieyasu Maru*. They pay us in coin acceptable to the colonists, and then they use those to buy the sea otter pelts. We won't get as good a profit as if we were buying the sea otter pelts ourselves, of course. But Isamu and I have many friends on board, so we can trust them to deal with us fairly."

"I thought that the *Ieyasu Maru* was remaining on this side of the Great Ocean."

"It is," said Yells-at-Bears. "But its officer and crew will give their pelts to Captain Fukuzawa of the *Iemitsu Maru*, to be taken to Japan and then sold on their behalf by Date Masamune's agents."

"You have given me much to think about. I will discuss the options with Umako and get back to you."

"It is an important decision, of course, but please do not tarry. Isamu and I will want to sail while the weather is still good. There is a reason that my people spend the fall and winter indoors as much as possible."

Yells-at-Bears gave Tall-Post and Chickadee the "grand tour" of the Japanese settlement, from the mines to Sandy Bottom Bay. While Tokubei had thought it a good idea to have Indian visitors, this still caused Isamu a little anxiety—until the relations with the Tla'amin stabilized, he would have preferred not to give any of them a preview of the Japanese defenses. Which, to be honest, were not as strong as he would have liked.

One concession that Yells-at-Bears made was not to show them the hidden Bucktooth Dam Village; they were allowed to assume that the fishermen lived at Sea Hawk Village, which was visible from Sandy Bottom Bay.

Tall-Post and Chickadee oohed and aahed over the smithy's wares, as well as many other goods they saw at the Japanese settlements. They helped Yells-at-Bears figure out what would sell best among the Tla'amin and Shishalh, and were given some small gifts in return for this help.

Arinobu and Umako reached a decision about how to proceed, reserving a quarter of their goods for the sea otter skin trade, and the rest going for the more immediate return.

"Very good," said Yells-at-Bears. "Since the fur trade is with the Nuu-chah-nulth, on the outer coast, I'll pick out the goods most likely to appeal to them, and entrust them to Tokubei on our behalf. And then I'll sail for Tla'amin country."

Yells-at-Bears, Isamu, Tall-Post and Chickadee stood on the beach of Sandy Bottom Bay, waiting for the boat from the *Unagi Maru* to pick them up. The *Unagi Maru* was a three-masted *jacht* of sixty tons burden, of very shallow draft. It had a crew of twenty, and several samurai marines. It was no pleasure craft; it was armed with eight cannon firing three-pound balls and four swivel guns.

"We have something to show you up north," said Yells-at-Bears mysteriously. "Then we will visit the Tla'amin, and finally take you home."

The passage north was short, but slow, the wind being adverse. Fortunately, the *Unagi Maru* was equipped with sweeps, so it could make progress under those circumstances.

They at last arrived at East Dragon Bay. The surprise that Yells-at-Bears had alluded to was the presence of the two great transport ships, each about three hundred tons, substantially larger than even the *Ieyasu Maru*. At Isamu's urging, Yells-at-Bears refrained from explaining that these ships, which plainly carried cannon, were leaving Texada the next month. Better that word spread that the Japanese had ships even larger and presumably more powerful than the *Ieyasu Maru*.

They overnighted here and Isamu conferred with the captains of the transports. The next day, they continued on to Wide-River-Bed, the Tla'amin village. They were welcomed there and Tall-Post and Chickadee helped Yells-at-Bears with the trading.

A few days later, they continued on to Kalpilin, where they did more trading. And they had a surprise reunion, too.

When the *Ieyasu Maru* had first come to Sandy Bottom Bay, it had a friendly encounter with three Shishalh from Kalpilin, who had tracked a pod of orca there. They weren't hunting the orca, they were trying to decide whether the baby orca in the pod was the reincarnation of a fellow tribesman who had died by drowning at about the same time that they had witnessed the birth of the baby. That required studying the newborn calf's markings and behavior and deciding whether they were in any way reminiscent of him.

The three had come to the hut where Yells-at-Bears had set up shop (after suitably compensating its owner). They recognized her immediately, as she had acted as the translator that day.

"So," asked Yells-at-Bears, "what did you decide about that baby orca? Was it your friend reborn?"

"No," they told her sheepishly. "The baby orca rolled over, and its underside didn't have a long white pattern stretching toward the tail."

"Oh," said Yells-at-Bears. "The baby was a *girl* baby."

"So," said Isamu. "Is your share of the take sufficient to buy back your good name?"

"I think so. Besides my trading, I received gifts from the chiefs of both villages. And hopefully my parents will be able to make *some* contribution."

"When should we go to your old home?"

Yells-at-Bears bit her lip. "The timing is a little tricky. The families are still in their summer camps. In mid-winter they will congregate at the winter ceremonial site, and that is where potlatches are held. That is near what your map calls 'Departure Bay.' They will remain there until early spring."

"So you are figuring on holding an early potlatch, soon after arrival at the ceremonial site?"

"Yes. But preparations would have to be made before then, while my parents are still in their summer camp. They would need to bring food for the guests; we don't have that."

"Then we will sail for your parents' village now, and set the potlatch preparations in motion."

"Thank you, Isamu."

Yells-at-Bears felt hope and uncertainty in equal measure.

Chapter 21

From Kalpilin to the heavily mountainous southern tip of Texada Island was about eleven miles and, with a good wind, it took a little over an hour to get there. From there it was another fifteen miles to the mouth of the Nanaimo River.

Yells-at-Bears' childhood home, Kwalsiarwahl, was one of a string of five villages on the lower Nanaimo. It was in fact the one closest to the mouth of the river, and thus enjoyed the most varied assortment of foods during spring and summer. Unfortunately, that had also made it the one most vulnerable to Laich-kwil-tach raiders.

The arrival of the *Unagi Maru* created something of a stir. Canoes rowed out to meet the Japanese *jacht.* While the Snuneymuxw had weapons at hand, the tensions were defused when Yells-at-Bears, standing by the prow, called down to them in Halkomelem, and told them, "I am Snuneymuxw, I am Yells-at-Bears, I am the daughter of Four-Fingers and the sister of Salmon-Berry. I am coming home."

The *Unagi Maru* anchored and Isamu and Yells-at-Bears boarded the *jacht*'s yawl and were rowed to shore by a party of sailors.

"Is the village as you remember it?" asked Isamu.

"It's smaller. Sadder, too."

Yells-at-Bears asked to be shown to Four-Fingers' house and a young man offered to lead her and her party there.

Some summer camps just offered simple lean-tos, with poles holding up mats of cedar, but Kwalsiarwahl featured several true longhouses. In the winter, when it was time to move to Departure Bay, the planks and roofing would be gathered up and loaded into canoes, leaving just the frames behind.

The carved and painted house post by the main door of Four-Fingers' new longhouse was unfamiliar. No doubt the original one had been burnt in the fire.

Yells-at-Bears stood at the entrance and yelled, "Four-Fingers! It is Yells-at-Bears, your daughter! I have returned! Father, are you there?"

"I heard the rumors of your arrival, but they are nonsense," a voice quavered. "My daughter Yells-at-Bears was taken captive long ago. She is dead or a slave now. You are an impostor. Or an evil spirit sent to plague me."

"I am no spirit!" cried Yells-at-Bears. "The People-of-the-Flying-Canoes freed me from the Gwat'sinux."

"I have not heard of the People-of-the-Flying-Canoes."

"Well some of them are here with me. We came here on one of their flying canoes."

"Only a spirit would sail in a flying canoe," the voice muttered.

"The canoe doesn't really fly, Father. It just means that it moves without being paddled. It has mats that catch the wind, like the leaves on a tree."

There was no immediate response.

Yells-at-Bears tried again. "Please, Father, come look at me, you will see I am flesh, not spirit. And I am no impostor, either."

Four-Fingers came to the entrance to look her over. "You look a little bit like Yells-at-Bears. But you look different, too."

"Of course I look different, Father! I was twelve when I was taken. I am twice that now. Where is mother?"

Four-fingers' head dipped. "She died two years ago."

"I am sorry to hear that. May her spirit be at peace."

"At peace," he echoed, and made a warding sign.

"May I come in?" asked Yells-at-Bears.

"Tell me something that only my daughter would know."

Yells-at-Bears thought for a moment, then reminded her father of how she had once gone shellfish collecting and found herself trapped on a tiny island when the tide came in.

A voice came from behind Yells-at-Bears. "Four-Fingers, who are these strangers that are blocking the door?"

Yells-at-Bears turned to look and see who spoke. It was a woman she had never seen before. She looked to be about Yells-at-Bears' age.

"I am Yells-at-Bears, second daughter of Four-Fingers. Who are you?"

"I am Rain, his wife."

Yells-at-Bears saw that Rain was not merely his new wife, but his visibly pregnant wife. That was a most unfortunate turn of events.

Four-Fingers was surely planning a potlatch to celebrate the birth of his new child. He would not want to spend additional resources on redeeming the status of Yells-at-Bears. And his new wife would not want Yells-at-Bears' status restored, as it would raise her to a place above that of her own child.

This was a disaster. But she had gone to the trouble of trading for potlatch goods, and had made the journey here. She should at least ask. . . .

Yells-at-Bears took a deep breath, and then explained that the Japanese had freed her, she was living with them now, and she had no plans to live at Kwalsiarwahl. That, she hoped, would placate Rain. She just wanted a potlatch to remove the shame of her captivity and restore her status to that of a member of the upper class, so she would be a suitable match for Isamu, one of the leaders of the Japanese. And she would provide all the potlatch gifts, all that Four-Fingers and Rain needed to do was to invite all the right people and feed them.

Rain pointed her finger at Yells-at-Bears. "You! You have been gone for what, twelve years? And you think to rejoin the community? Not merely as a commoner, but as a noblewoman? My equal?

"Why, you can't even speak Halkomelem properly anymore. You speak it with a Kwak'wala accent! You sound like one of the Kwakwaka'wakw, our greatest enemies. You cannot return. You should not have even tried to return."

Yells-at-Bears' face turned red. "We're leaving!" she snapped at Isamu. "Back to Texada!"

"What did they say?" asked Isamu. Isamu didn't know Halkomelem, the language that Yells-at-Bear had been speaking (or at least trying to speak). He could see that she was upset, but had no idea why. He raised his eyebrows quizzically.

"I'll explain later," said Yells-at-Bears, grabbing his arm, and pulling him away from the entrance to the longhouse.

"It's almost sunset. It's not safe to sail back to Texada now," said Isamu.

"Then we'll sleep on the *Unagi Maru*, and sail back first thing in the morning."

She stormed off, Isamu and the sailors following.

But in the meantime, a large crowd of the Snuneymuxw had gathered near Four-Fingers' longhouse, anxious to get a glimpse of the mysterious visitors. And word that one of them claimed to be the long-lost Yells-at-Bears had spread, too.

"Yells-at-Bears! Wait!" cried one of the women. "It's me, Bluebird!"

Yells-at-Bears stopped short, and one of the sailors narrowly avoided running into her.

"Bluebird? Is that really you?" Bluebird had been one of her father's slaves, and a childhood companion for Yells-at-Bears. She had been sick the day of the raid, and hence had not been taken by the Laich-kwil-tach along with Yells-at-Bears and her friends. Yells-at-Bears had assumed that she perished in the fire. But here she was!

It was obvious, however, that she had not escaped the fire unscathed, as she had a burn scar on her face.

"It is!" cried Bluebird. "I am so glad to see that you survived that awful day!"

"I did. I am a translator for the People-of-the-Flying-Canoes. And a trader."

"That sounds exciting. I do what I have always done." She lowered her voice. "Only, when I can get away with it, a little more slowly."

"Bluebird! Stop gabbing and get back to work," someone shouted.

"Who is that?" asked Yells-at-Bears.

"My mistress. Your father sold me after the fire. I best get going. . . ."

"Wait!" Yells-at-Bears approached Bluebird's mistress. "I would like to buy Bluebird."

The sailors had been carrying a sampling of the goods that Yells-at-Bears had intended for her redemption potlatch, to show to her father. She pulled out one of them. "Will this do?"

Bluebird's mistress' gaze went back-and-forth between Bluebird and the trade good. "She is healthy and a good worker. She's worth four of those, but since you grew up here, I will let you have her for just three."

"Make it two," said Yells-at-Bears. "And she comes with her clothing and personal items. You won't see goods like these again for a long time, as we are leaving, and I don't expect to come back. Ever."

"Two it is," the mistress agreed, and took possession of the items. She left without even saying goodbye to Bluebird.

"So I am to go with you?" asked the latter.

"Yes," said Yells-at-Bears. "Go run and grab your possessions."

"Right!" said Bluebird, who ran off to her former mistress' longhouse. She was back soon after, wearing a rain hat and a blanket, and carrying a basket. "I am ready."

A few minutes later, they were back at the landing beach. The sailors pushed the yawl into the surf and helped Isamu, Yells-at-Bears, and Bluebird get on board. The oars bit into the water and soon they arrived alongside the *Unagi Maru*.

Once Bluebird was helped on deck, Yells-at-Bears spoke. "You are now a free woman. Like me."

Camp Double Six

Isamu put his writing brush back in his *yatate*, and studied the letter he had just written. This, he thought, was surely the final draft of the letter to his family. Admittedly, he had thought that about each of the three previous drafts.

But time was running out for tinkering with the wording. The *Ieyasu Maru* was going to leave soon for East Dragon Bay, to meet up with the ships that would be returning to Japan after trading with the Nuu-chah-nulth. Captain Haruno had promised to personally deliver Isamu's letter to Captain Fukuzawa of the *Iemitsu Maru*.

He reread the letter, skipping over the ornate salutations, the polite inquiries regarding the health of his extended family, and the humbly worded descriptions of his own achievements.

"Respected elders, with Japan at peace under the Tokugawa, the opportunities for my advancement are limited. There is conflict only in the Philippines and in New Nippon. But the Philippine forces are led by persons who are no friends of the Date clan, our patrons. And the Date clan's fortunes are now firmly tied to New Nippon.

"As for marital prospects, few women of the samurai class would be willing to travel to New Nippon. As far as I know, the only ones who have come here so far are either members of Date Masamune's own family, and thus far above my station, or are *kirishitan*." And, he mused, any other exceptions had probably done so because there was something in their background that would preclude them finding a good match back home.

"Nor do I think that we would want to ask one of the families long associated with our own to ask one of their daughters to endure the hardships of life in the wilderness of New Nippon. And if we did so, they would surely demand a very high price from our family.

"I of course would not consider marrying one of the *kirishitan*, and thus tainting our blood in the eyes of the shogun.

"But that leaves only the option of marrying one of the native women, and I met one who is of their chiefly class. She has learned Japanese and is well respected by the leaders of his expedition."

He humbly beseeched them to consent in writing to this match, and to send it by the next ship going to Texada, with a copy going directly to Date Masamune at Kodachi Machi.

And now, I hope for a favorable response. Until then, I will say nothing to Yells-at-Bears. She has had enough disappointments this year to last a lifetime.

Chapter 22

Pacific Ocean
September 1635

On the galleon *San Raimundo*, at noon each day, Guillermo measured the sun's altitude. The day came when he determined that the ship had reached the thirty-fifth parallel, about even with Edo, the capital of Japan. "Very soon," he told the shipmaster, "it will be time to turn the ship eastward, to cross the Pacific."

Late in the afternoon watch of that day, in his small workroom, the carpenter of the *Concepción* cursed. "We're out of varnish!"

"How much do you need?" asked his apprentice.

"Just a cupful," the carpenter admitted. "But bring up the whole cask. It will save time in the long run."

"Yes, sir."

The carpenter's apprentice went outside and grabbed one of the ship's lanterns. In the alcove holding the lantern there was flint and steel. He opened the horn window of the lantern, and pulled out the candle. He lit it and placed it back in the lantern.

Carrying the lantern, he opened a hatch and descended into the hold. Were it not for the rather dim light cast by the lantern, it would have been pitch black, as virtually every nook and cranny was filled with merchandise, leaving just a narrow passageway. He continued to descend, deck after deck.

At last, he reached the orlop deck. It was so dark here that he couldn't see well even with the lantern. Horn was translucent at best, and the horn was covered with soot. Grumbling, he opened up the window. There, that was better. Now he had a better chance to find what he needed.

He found the barrel at last. With no one about to hear him, he cursed. It looked heavy, and by now it was the end of his watch. He didn't fancy spending his leisure time manhandling the barrel up several decks. Surely there was a can here that he could use to get just what was needed? Yes, that one would do.

He set the lantern down, removed the bung from the barrel, and placed the can beside the bunghole. Now, where was a spigot? He started rummaging around for one. As he did so, a rogue wave hit the *Concepción*, causing it to heel over to port. The lantern tipped over, and varnish came streaming out of the bunghole and into the lantern. An instant later, and the varnish was on fire. The fire arced back to the barrel, and the barrel exploded, covering the carpenter's apprentice in burning varnish, and releasing varnish vapor into the air. He screamed, and rolled about, frantically and unsuccessfully seeking to put out the flames. They consumed him.

The fire spread to other barrels, and then to the sail locker. There were combustibles everywhere, and the orlop deck filled with smoke and flame.

It was fortunate for the crew and passengers of the *Concepción* that the weather was mild and hence no one slept below deck. Also, that one of them had a keen nose that had not been completely dulled by the normal stench of a galleon at sea. "Smoke!" he yelled. "I smell smoke! God preserve us!"

It soon became evident that the smoke was coming out of every hatch, rather than from just the cookstoves of the sterncastle.

Captain Atondo hesitated for a moment. Close the hatches to smother the flames? Open the hatches and chop holes in the deck to pour water down?

The decision was taken out of his hands. Flames shot up through the hatches, attacking the masts and sails.

"Abandon ship!" he ordered.

The watch on the *San Raimundo* saw smoke rising from the *Concepción*'s hull and sounded the alarm. Despite the hazard to his own ship, Captain-General Mendoza ordered the *San Raimundo* to draw closer to the *Concepción*. Fortunately, the *San Raimundo* had been sailing in the *Concepción*'s wake, so it did not need to come about, a time-consuming maneuver.

Of course, there were limits to how close Captain-General Mendoza would dare come, especially once there was burning wreckage and oil in the water. The ship's longboat was in the water already, towed behind the *San Raimundo*, and this was pulled in close so sailors could board it and cast off. The longboat crew rowed frantically toward the *Concepción*.

The *Concepción* had its own longboat, towed behind the galleon. There was no time to board it properly; sailors jumped into the water and those who knew how to swim did so. Some, especially those who had thought to grab a hatch cover or other wood object to use as a flotation device, made it to the craft, or at least stayed afloat long enough for it to reach them. Many, unable even to tread water, sank into the depths.

The rescue vessels went back and forth between the wreck and the *San Raimundo*, rescuing as many of the distressed mariners as they could. But by the third visit, all they found were bodies, floating face down.

Father Blanco led all on board the *San Raimundo* in a prayer of thanksgiving for the rescued, and commiseration for the souls of those who had perished. Over the protests of some of the passengers, some of the deck cargo had been tossed overboard to make room for the refugees from the *Concepción*. The captain-general assured the passengers whose merchandise had thus been sacrificed that the loss would be shared proportionally by all who held *boletas* for cargo space on the *San Raimundo*. And he also pointed out that at least they were better off than those whose cargo had been on the *Concepción*.

Despite this measure, the deck was still overcrowded. Hence, the captain-general ordered that the surviving crew of the *Concepción* would have to take turns riding in the two longboats that were now towed behind the *San Raimundo*. While that was better than clutching flotsam in the open sea, the longboats would be in peril if the *San Raimundo* encountered a storm. If there was adequate warning, the longboats would be brought on board, of course, and their passengers would have to find space below-deck, but a squall could strike quite suddenly.

Deck space was not, in any event, the greatest concern. The fire had spread so quickly that food and water had been left behind. The supplies on the *San Raimundo*, intended for a crew of one hundred twenty and about one hundred passengers, would now need to be stretched to accommodate another hundred souls.

And that would put considerable strain on their provisions. Even if the *Concepción* had not burned down, it was customary for the Acapulco-bound galleons to put the crew on half rations for part of the passage, and to rely in part on rainwater collected en route. That way, more paying cargo could be squeezed on board.

The next day Father Blanco led all on board in a prayer of thanksgiving. It was indeed a blessed result that so many had been saved. But as he stood on the poop deck, looking down at the assembled crews and passengers, his eyes strayed to the rigging. There, many dozens of Chinese-made porcelain water jars were hung. Father Blanco knew that many more were stowed below deck, but he couldn't help but wonder whether there would be enough so that they could reach Acapulco without anyone dying of thirst. He prudently included in his sermon the prayer, "O God, grant us gentle rain, sufficient to meet our needs. . . ."

He was not the only person on board thinking about drinking water. That evening, Juan de Molina, the *San Raimundo*'s water constable, stood, wool *bonete* in hand, just inside the Great Cabin. This was beneath the *toldilla*, the poop deck at the stern.

Captain-General Mendoza beckoned him forward. "What is our water situation?"

"In Cebu, we took on about one hundred eighty *pipas* of water, Your Excellency. We have drunk about twenty so far. Since there has been little rain thus far, the empty jars were refilled with seawater and taken down to the bottom of the hold to serve as ballast."

"How long will the remaining water last us?"

"That depends, Your Excellency. How many people did we rescue from the *Concepción*?"

"About one hundred," said Mendoza, "by God's grace."

Juan scrunched his face as he did some mental mathematics. "If we keep to full water rations, and do not stop for water, or collect any rainwater, then we will run out in about two months. That would be before we reach Acapulco."

Mendoza turned to Guillermo. "Where can we stop for water?"

"We are better off just staying on course, Your Excellency. The nearest land is Japan, but—" Guillermo spread his hands. Even if the Japanese hadn't attacked Manila in 1634, the Japanese had banned all Spanish ships in 1625.

"What about the Islas de los Ladrones?" The "Islands of Thieves" were what an up-time map would call the Marianas, thus named in 1667 after a Spanish queen.

"They are now well to the south. Much time would be lost in diverting there."

"There are no other choices?"

Guillermo fidgeted.

Mendoza stared at him. "Spit it out, man!"

"Rumor has it that the maps of the up-time heretics show the Kamchatka Peninsula north of Japan, and the Aleutian Islands to its east." Guillermo was plainly being careful not to admit to possession of those maps. While there had been copies in Manila, their use had not been officially approved.

"I see. . . ." said Mendoza.

"But even if we felt we could rely on them, those lands reportedly lie above the 50th parallel, far north of the approved galleon route. Not only would we lose time by going there, we would risk encountering icebergs.

"I recommend we make our crossing of the Pacific between the 40th and 44th parallels, as many of the galleons have done. The westerlies are stronger there, and it also rains more frequently, than if we cross in the Thirties as planned. Of course, the route will be longer."

"De Molina, put the crew and passengers on half-rations of water," Mendoza ordered. The normal ration was about three quarts of water. However, it also included a quart of wine, as well as some vinegar and olive oil, and those weren't cut. The crew, eating salted meat and fish, and doing heavy labor, would certainly complain, but they wouldn't die of thirst.

De Molina bowed and left the Great Cabin.

✣ ✣ ✣

A week later, when the sky darkened with the threat of rain, mats were hung everywhere possible. After the storm passed, the water absorbed by the mats was squeezed out into some of the used water jars. Encouraged by their entry into the "rain belt," the shipmaster ordered restoration of full rations.

It was an act of misplaced optimism.

Chapter 23

September 1635

The *Ieyasu Maru* sailed to East Dragon Bay to collect the *Iemitsu Maru* and *Sendai Maru*. Then, under a mackerel sky—the Japanese called it *iwashigumo*, a "sardine" sky—all three ships sailed for Yuquot.

When they arrived at Yuquot, they were surprised to find a large number of canoes, perhaps twenty, awaiting them.

Tokubei frowned. "I thought the chief said that his people would be farther inland, at their winter quarters, by now."

"He did," said Goemon.

Speaker-to-Strangers, his fellow translator, had been studying the greeting party carefully. "Those are not Mowachaht. The canoes are wrong, the face and body paint are wrong."

Captain Haruno overheard this and reacted instantly. "All hands! Prepare to repel boarders!" he shouted. Some of the sailors and marines loaded the cannon with hailshot, and others rigged boarding nets or climbed up into the tops with muskets or bows. Signals were made to the other Japanese ships to ensure they took similar precautions.

The natives could not have understood everything happening on board the three Japanese vessels, but they definitely realized that they were not being invited to come closer.

Speaker-to-Strangers could hear the natives calling out to each other, but he couldn't make out what they were saying. But eventually they appeared to recognize that the Japanese were dismayed by the size of their force. Most of the canoes drew further away, but one large canoe, approached them. One of the Indians, ornately dressed, stood up and started making gestures.

"He is signing that he wants to parley," said Speaker-to-Strangers.

"Should we fire, sir?" asked one of the sailors.

"Hold your fire," said Captain Haruno, "but keep your matches lit." While there were plenty of men just on that canoe—Haruno estimated that there were about forty—the sides of the *Ieyasu Maru* were high enough that they would find it difficult to board it.

He turned to Speaker-to-Strangers and Goemon. "Can you figure out what he wants?"

"We'll try." And they did try, but the wind made it difficult to hear what the Indian emissary was saying.

"Sorry, sir, either you'll have to let them come closer, or we'll have to go to them. May I have a look through your spyglass?"

Captain Haruno handed it over and a moment later, Speaker-to-Strangers said, "From the looks of them, I think they are Kwakwaka'wakw, not Nuu-chah-nulth." He gave the spyglass to Goemon, who quickly agreed with this judgment. Neither was willing to speculate as to which Kwakwaka'wakw tribe they were affiliated with.

"I am not letting forty men of uncertain intentions come any closer, and that's a fact," said Captain Haruno. "And I don't want to give them a hostage." Tokubei made a gesture of acknowledgment. "Speaker-to-Strangers can take the smallest boat, and keep out of arm's reach."

Captain Haruno was doubtful. "Forty oars can bring him into arm's reach very quickly."

"And if they try, we blast them," said Tokubei. "But we either need to find out what is going on here, or leave the coast for the season."

Captain Haruno drummed his fingers on the railing of the quarterdeck. "Fine. But signal to the other ships, so they are ready to cooperate. If we fire, those other canoes will be paddling furiously toward us. They will need to give us covering fire while we recover the boat."

The *Ieyasu Maru*'s smallest boat was suspended from davits astern. It had just four oars and no mast. Goemon was forbidden to go, but Speaker-to-Strangers was accompanied by four sailors and one of the samurai marines.

The boat was lowered and freed from the suspending cables. The sailors started rowing. The samurai had his composite bow laid just out of sight, and the sailors had muskets, pikes and hatchets similarly close at hand.

When the boat came into view from the canoe, the Indian negotiator sat down and his men reached for their paddles.

As soon as they did so, Speaker-to-Strangers stood up and raised his right hand to shoulder height, palm outward, then moved it sharply to the left and downward.

The Indians stopped what they were doing, and Speaker-to-Strangers told the sailors to paddle slowly toward the canoe. They stopped about a hundred yards away. An Indian arrow could certainly travel that far, but its effective range was more like sixty yards, and out on the open water, fired from an unstable firing platform like a canoe, it would be less.

Speaker-to-Strangers had a speaking trumpet, and it doubled as an ear trumpet. "Who are you, and why are you here?"

"We are Klaskino, and we are here to sell you sea otter skins."

Speaker-to-Strangers had hoped he would never see another Klaskino as long as he lived. At least the speaker had not recognized him as a former Klaskino slave. That was the advantage, he supposed, of having his forehead shaved Japanese style, and wearing a kimono and obi.

As these thoughts passed through his mind, the Klaskino leader added, "That is why your Great Canoes have come here, yes?"

"It is," Speaker-to-Strangers acknowledged. "But why are *you* here, in Mowachaht waters?"

"To make sure you come to us before you return to trade with the Mowachaht."

"You come in great numbers. Why not send just a few canoes, to lead us to the villages of the Klaskino?"

"The Mowachaht would not permit it, and we did not know where you made your home. Where might that be?"

Speaker-to-Strangers knew better than to answer that question. "Why wouldn't the Mowachaht permit you to wait here to meet us?"

The answer was the one Speaker-to-Strangers expected. "They want to be the only ones to trade with you. After they sold you all the sea otter skins they had on hand, they came to us and asked us to sell them our skins. We were suspicious—why would they need skins from us, when the sea otter favors their waters, too?—and so we persuaded one of them to tell us more."

Speaker-to-Strangers could imagine the form that this persuasion took.

"And for what price would you trade us skins?"

The Klaskino leader named a price that was somewhat more than the price agreed to by the Mowachaht.

"Why would we pay you more than we paid the Mowachaht?"

"Because you can't reach the Mowachaht now." The Klaskino leader gestured toward his fleet of canoes.

"I will take your words to our Council of Elders. We will speak again tomorrow."

Speaker-to-Strangers made a Kwakwaka'wakw gesture of respect, and signaled to the samurai that they should return to the *Ieyasu Maru*.

Before dark, the three Japanese ships moved to mid-channel, and anchored in the nautical equivalent of a wagon circle. The ships' boats, carrying lanterns, were set out to patrol around the anchored ships. Fortunately, there was also moonlight to see by.

"I think we should just tell these Klaskino that we'll buy sea otter skins from them at the same price we do the Mowachaht," said Commander Hosoya. "We don't care who sells us the skins, just that we get a good price for our trade goods."

"And if the Klaskino refuse to lower their price?" asked Captain Haruno. "Do we charge past them, take their deal, or leave?"

"Charge past them, of course. Fire a warning shot. I think that they'll be put off by the sound and smoke, not to mention the big splash where the ball hits."

"And if that doesn't work?"

"Sink one of their canoes."

"I understand your position," said Captain Haruno. "But they have perhaps four hundred warriors in those canoes. We have trained gunners, but I doubt those on the *Iemitsu Maru* and *Sendai Maru* have ever fired a cannon in earnest. And those warriors could put a lot of arrows into the air while we are reloading the cannon. Or come close enough to board us."

"Attempt it, at least. We have a good six feet of freeboard," said Commander Hosoya. "I grant that arrows can be shot quickly. But I daresay that they would be much disordered by a round of hailshot."

"May I point out the obvious?" said Tokubei. "Dead Indians can't trade. Also, if we charge past them, as you propose, then while we are up-channel trading with the Mowachaht, they could call for reinforcements and ambush us as we try to head back to sea."

"So what do you propose?" asked Captain Haruno.

"Tell them that if they won't lower their price to match the Mowachaht, then we will leave, and they will get nothing. And the Mowachaht will also get nothing more and will blame them for it."

"That's logical," said Commander Hosoya. "And to carry the logic one step further, we will get nothing more . . . and our superiors will blame us for it."

"If I may say something?" asked Goemon.

"I would not have invited you to join us if I didn't want you to contribute," said Tokubei.

Goemon bowed. He was, after all, a fisherman who had gotten shipwrecked, enslaved, and then cajoled into service as an interpreter. He was not of samurai rank. "This humble person apologizes for the interruption. If you sell to the Klaskino, the Mowachaht will be angry with us. If we return next year for a new collection of skins, they may raise their price or even attack us for breaking our word."

"It's not our fault that they left this waterway undefended," said Captain Haruno.

"Even so, they are likely to blame us rather than themselves," said Goemon apologetically.

"Suppose we say this," said Tokubei. "We will divide our trade goods in half. One half will be traded to the Klaskino, and the other half to the Mowachaht. But only if the Klaskino honor the same price as the Mowachaht, and only if they let us trade with the latter as we promised to do. Otherwise, we will leave, and everyone will be unhappy.

"Also, we can tell them that if the trading goes well this month, we will return next year with more trade goods, and we will visit the Klaskino at home before we come to the waters of the Mowachaht. Coming from Japan, that is the easiest route."

"I am agreeable," said Captain Haruno, "but I doubt that the grand governor will permit the *Ieyasu Maru* to sail to Japan. The *Sendai Maru* and *Iemitsu Maru* of course are intended to do so."

"Then perhaps one or both of them can call on the Klaskino. Or we can send word home to send out another trading ship."

"Very well. It appears we are in agreement. Hopefully, we will get through the night without incident."

They did, but there was a new development the next morning. "Captain!" the maintop lookout cried. "There's a fleet of canoes coming from the north!"

"How many?" he yelled back.

"At least two score."

Captain Haruno turned to Tokubei. "What do you think this means?"

"They are almost certainly the Mowachaht, come to dispute access to us."

"Or they have decided to join up with the Klaskino, attack us, and divide the spoils," muttered Commander Hosoya.

"Commander Hosoya, have Goemon and Speaker-to-Strangers roused and brought to the quarterdeck."

By the time Goemon and Speaker-to-Strangers answered the summons, there were further developments. A Klaskino canoe—at this distance it couldn't be determined if it was the same one that participated in the negotiation of the day before—approached the Mowachaht line, and a Mowachaht canoe went forward to meet it. Plainly, those two forces were negotiating.

"I wish we knew what they were saying to each other," Commander Hosoya told his lieutenant.

"The Klaskino are outnumbered two-to-one, so I would imagine the Mowachaht are saying 'get lost . . . or else!'"

The leaders of the Japanese expedition met once again, and made plans for various contingencies: one side or the other withdrawing, both remaining and seeking trade, and outright battle between the Klaskino and the Mowachaht. It was quickly agreed that their prior dealings with the Mowachaht did not commit them to take the Mowachaht's side if there was a clash of arms.

✣ ✣ ✣

It was not much later that the Klaskino leader once again approached the *Ieyasu Maru*. Speaker-to-Strangers went out in the small boat again to speak to him.

"The weather has taken a turn for the worse," the Klaskino said. "We are going home, and we invite you to follow us."

Speaker-to-Strangers fought back a snicker. While the sky was overcast, it was evident that the "bad weather" in question was the arrival of the Mowachaht.

"Why should we follow you, when we could trade here, and when you wanted to charge us more than the Mowachaht?"

The Klaskino leader waved this point away. "If you are willing to come to our home waters, we will drop our price down to theirs. And our sea otter skins are cleaner. Theirs were full of lice, were they not?"

Speaker-to-Strangers had been advised that the Japanese ship captains were not interested in clawing their way north to Klaskino territory unless the Klaskino were willing to make major concessions. And this counteroffer didn't qualify.

"We look forward to enjoying Klaskino hospitality in the future," said Speaker-to-Strangers. "But our crews are homesick, anxious to return to their homes across the Great Ocean. Perhaps one of our Great Canoes could call on you next spring or summer."

The Klaskino leader lowered the price demanded for a skin, undercutting the Mowachaht, but did not lower it to the level that Speaker-to-Strangers had been coached would be good enough to warrant a trip north.

Speaker-for-Strangers had been given a gift to pass on to the Klaskino leader to soften the blow of the refusal. This gift, which he passed over, somewhat nervously, in the basket of a long handled pole, was a small ceramic *anka*, a charcoal-burning foot warmer, with a dragon design on it. Speaker-for-Strangers explained how it was used. The Pacific Northwest Indians already made charcoal for use as a black pigment, so the Klaskino would have no trouble providing it with fuel.

He could see that the Klaskino puzzling over it. There was nothing quite like a Japanese dragon in Kwakwaka'wakw art, although it could be compared with their Two-Headed Serpent. And while the Kwakwaka'wakw made baskets and stone and wood carvings, he had never seen them make pottery.

In return, Speaker-to-Strangers was given a necklace of sea lion teeth. He knew that such necklaces were worn by dancers in some ceremonies.

With the Klaskino gone, trade with the Mowachaht could be resumed. However, once their trade rivals were out of sight, the Mowachaht were inclined to renegotiate terms. This did not sit well with the Japanese.

"What now?" asked Captain Haruno. "Do we accept a poorer rate of exchange?"

"It sends the wrong message to let them renegotiate with no change in circumstances other than chasing away some of the competition," said Tokubei.

"Then do we go home with unsold trade goods?"

"We could take them to the Klaskino," said Commander Hosoya. "Or to the Tla'amin and Shishalh, if we are willing to buy something other than sea otter skins."

"That's certainly an option," said Tokubei. "But there's a stratagem I'd like to try first. . . ." He explained, and the ship's council agreed to it.

The Japanese exchanged gifts with the Mowachaht envoy, then invited him on board. Through the interpreters, Tokubei explained that the Japanese were the People-of-the-Thunderbird, and they would consult the great Thunderbird Spirit directly as to whether to accept the Mowachaht's revised offer.

"Time to sing!" Tokubei shouted.

Goemon and Speaker-to-Strangers had advised Tokubei of the importance of song in Nuu-chah-nulth rituals. Hence, Tokubei had briefed the sailors on what they needed to do. The sailors sang a folk song that began "Drink, drink sake!" Of course, it was meaningless to the Mowachaht envoy, but they were reasonably on key. When they finished, they all bowed, and at a signal from Tokubei, one of the cannon was fired off.

Startled by the sound and smoke, the Mowachaht envoy ran for the ship's side and dived into the water. Speaker-to-Strangers called out to him, "The Thunderbird has spoken! He is saddened that you would go back on your word to us."

The envoy, eyes wide and teeth chattering, assured Speaker-to-Strangers that there was a big misunderstanding. They were happy to trade sea otter skins at the previously agreed-upon price.

And in due course, the three Japanese ships sailed off. The sea otter skins were transferred to the *Sendai Maru* and the *Iemitsu Maru*, which were sailing for Japan, while the *Ieyasu Maru* turned south. Tokubei and Captain Haruno intended to check out some possible new settlement sites, report to the grand governor, and return to Sandy Bottom Bay in the spring. Of course, the grand governor might order them to go somewhere else.

"Hopefully we can find a better route north from Monterey Bay to Texada than the one we just took to avoid the adverse winds by the coast," grumbled Haruno. "Tokubei thinks we should consult the Dutch when they come to Monterey Bay with the Third Fleet."

"If you know the disease, the cure is near," said Hosoya.

Chapter 24

Pacific Ocean
October 1635

On the *San Raimundo*, down below the main deck, Diego de Aro, the quartermaster's mate, barked orders to a squad of seamen. The steward had run out of several items at once, and he wanted them right away.

"Enrique, get two baskets of garlic and two of onions. Jose, a *quarto* of sardines." That was a barrel about three feet high and two feet in diameter. "Ernesto, a *quarto* of chickpeas. And no dawdling, any of you!"

Enrique's load wasn't heavy, but it was awkward. He lost his balance, falling against one of the Chinese porcelain water storage jars. It broke.

"*Tonto*! You've wasted—"

Diego cut short his diatribe when he saw that no water was leaking out. "Enrique, set down your baskets and fetch the lantern." The lantern—properly shielded, as no one wanted a repeat of the fire that had doomed the *Concepción*—hung from a hook on the ceiling. Enrique gingerly took it down and awaited further instructions.

"Yes, shine the light on the jar you broke."

Diego lifted off the lid. There was not a drop of water inside. What was there instead was merchandise—porcelain plates, faience bowls and figurines, and silks. Contraband merchandise.

"Carry the food to the steward then return here. Bring some empty baskets or bags. Say nothing of this discovery to anyone."

While his squad was on their kitchen errand, Diego examined the broken jar further. He did not, of course, expect to find any of the shipper's marks that were listed in the official manifest. However, whoever was responsible for the smuggling would probably mark the jar in some way so it could be shunted aside when they arrived in Acapulco. Preferably, in a way that did not reduce the sales value of the jar itself. However, he found nothing of note.

When the squad finally returned, Diego told them to help him gather up the pieces of the jar and the contraband. They carried them all up to the main deck.

There, he paced nervously, back and forth, for a few minutes. Normally, Diego would report the discovery to the officer of the watch. But that was at this moment the shipmaster, Juan Andres de Molina, the second-in-command. Who, judging from his surname, was some sort of relation of the water constable, and hence not to be trusted in any investigation of the possible crimes of the latter.

Diego therefore decided to instead inform Guillermo de Agulla, who as pilot major was the third-in-command. He led his men to Guillermo's cabin, but not before first making sure that the shipmaster was busy somewhere else and would not observe their movements.

Guillermo de Agulla glumly studied the pieces of the broken smuggler's jar. There were two problems, he knew. One was logistical: determining how many other water jars had been misappropriated and figuring out the effect on the water supply. The other was political: determining and holding accountable the guilty party.

It could of course be the water constable, but he was protected by the shipmaster, who outranked Guillermo. It could be the shipmaster himself, because he accounted for all of the ship's cargo and oversaw the provisioning and outfitting of the galleon. For that matter, they could have conspired together.

But perhaps the perpetrator was Francisco Arquin, the boatswain. He was responsible for the loading and unloading of cargo at port, and for making up the manifest. And he too was involved in the loading of supplies for the journey. Francisco was fourth-in-command, and thus inferior to Guillermo. But he was Diego's immediate superior.

Under the circumstances, Guillermo decided to consult with Captain Atondo, the erstwhile skipper of the *Concepción*. While he was not part of the chain of command of the *San Raimundo*, he was a nobleman, and his word would carry great weight with the captain-general.

In acknowledgment of Captain Atondo's rank, the captain had been given the quarters normally occupied by the shipmaster. The shipmaster, in turn, slept in what should have been the pilot major's quarters, and so on down the chain of command. Unfortunately, since he had not been assigned an official function on the *San Raimundo*, his principal occupation was brooding about the trial that awaited him and his surviving officers when they reached New Spain.

Captain Atondo was willing to participate in Guillermo's investigation. He advised Diego to inform Antonio de Bolaza, the captain of seamen and infantry, of the situation, as it might be necessary to post guards over the evidence or even to use force to arrest the culprits. A page was sent with an invitation to de Bolaza to visit Captain Atondo at his earliest convenience.

De Bolaza arrived after two turns of the sand-glass, expecting that the invitation had something to do with the welfare of the survivors of the *Concepción*. He came accompanied by his ensign, Antonio Garcia.

"Hide what you have already found here," said de Bolaza grimly after being briefed. "Ensign Garcia will wait with you, and I will send a squad of soldiers here. Once they arrive, one will stay here and the others will join you, under Ensign Garcia's command. You may then go down and conduct your inspection."

Diego, Guillermo, Captain Atondo and Ensign Garcia followed de Bolaza's advice. The movements of the soldiers did attract attention, but when questioned, by the shipmaster, they referred him to Captain de Bolaza. Even at the best of times, there was no love lost between the soldiers and the sailors, and the soldiers had been warned against confiding in the shipmaster, the water constable, or the boatswain.

Diego's party found forty-seven more storage jars that were nominally marked as water jars but actually contained trade goods. They were not all in one place, but the party gathered them together in one place to make them easier to guard.

Leaving the soldiers and Ensign Garcia behind, they returned to the *tolda*. There they collected the original evidence and went to the Great Cabin. The soldier that had stood guard there was sent to summon Captain de Bolaza to join them.

At first, the steward, Geraldo de Polduian, was reluctant to admit them. But on Captain Atonzo's insistence that the matter was urgent, he ushered them in. By that time, Captain de Bolaza had arrived.

First Diego and then Ensign Garcia told their tales. Then the baskets and bags of evidence were opened for Captain-General Mendoza's benefit.

"Forty-seven jars, you say?" His face was red.

"Forty-eight, begging your pardon, if you count the original find. And we only checked the water jars on the one deck. It is the lowest, and whoever was involved in the scheme doubtless hoped that those jars would never be opened while they were on board."

"Captain de Bolaza, have your men take the shipmaster, the boatswain, and the water constable into custody. They are to be held in such manner that they are not able to communicate with each other, and then they are to be questioned about the water jars. I want to know how and by whom the jars were purchased, brought on board, inspected and stowed. Captain Atondo, if you would do me the honor of supervising the questioning."

Captain Atondo bowed, de Bolaza and Ensign Garcia saluted, and they left to carry out this order.

"Diego, were the contraband jars all stowed in one place?"

"No, Your Excellency. I found them in different parts of the lowest deck."

"Then once the three suspects are in custody, have all of the contraband jars brought up to the *toldilla* for inspection in full sunlight. And have some good jars brought there as well, but be sure to keep them separate. I want a painstaking comparison between the contraband jars and the good ones."

"As you command, sir."

Diego studied the water jars. All of them were blue and white porcelains, variously painted with flowers and birds. The blue and white design wasn't very helpful, as it was typical of lower quality Chinese porcelain.

Diego scratched his blond hair. It was very vexing. He could find no obvious outside feature that would signal to a conspirator that a particular jar held contraband and therefore had to be treated differently from the others.

He reluctantly reported his failure to Captain Atondo.

The captain was not surprised. "It could have been a mark that was washed off as soon as the jars were brought down to particular alcoves. And the mark was to be reapplied when we neared Acapulco." He sighed. "We will have to hope that the interrogations are more productive."

A ship's page knocked on the door of the tiny cabin that Father Blanco had been assigned. "Begging your pardon, Father, but Captain Atondo requests that you attend him."

Father Blanco looked up from his reading, which was the pontifical history by Gonzalo de Illescas. "Of course. Is he in his cabin?"

"No, Father. But I will lead you to him."

Father Blanco was surprised when the page led him into the part of the ship governed by Captain de Bolaza, that is to say, the part where the soldiers were quartered.

He was even more surprised when he was brought to Captain Atondo and the captain said, "The captain-general has requested that I investigate a serious crime committed on board, and I would like your assistance."

"Is the crime of an ecclesiastical nature?"

"No, it is the use of water jars to convey contraband goods rather than water, thus imperiling the health of all on board."

"I see. And how am I to assist you?"

"As you know, I am new to this ship," said Captain Atondo. "I would like your opinion as to the moral character of the suspects. They are the shipmaster, the water constable, and the boatswain. And I would like you to watch their testimony and advise me whether you think they are telling the truth."

Father Blanco frowned. "It pains me to say this, but I see two impediments. *Primus*, I only joined the ship's company in Cebu, so I do not know the suspects much better than you. *Secundus*, I am the confessor for all on board this ship, including the suspects you have named. My opinions could be influenced, unconsciously, by what they have told me under seal."

"I understand. But then I would like you to swear in the suspects, and any witnesses that may be called, and record the proceedings."

"That I can do with a good conscience."

The shipmaster, Juan Andres de Molina, admitted that he had ordered the water for the journey to Acapulco, and that he had chosen the suppliers of the water. He pointed out that they might have subcontracted the water collection and delivery to others, and it was up to them which water jars to use. He claimed that it was the boatswain who supervised the loading of the water and decided where the water jars were stowed.

Juan de Molina, the *San Raimundo*'s water constable, testified that he had no say in the selection of the water supplier, or of the water jars, or in their stowage. All he did, he claimed, was bring water jars up to the main deck and dole out the proper ration for each person on board.

Captain Atondo asked Juan whether he had inspected the water jars as they were brought on board, or once they were stowed.

"I only open a water jar when we are ready to use it for the men, Captain."

"Was it not part of your duties to inspect all water jars when they came on board to make sure they were full and the water was clean?"

"Absolutely not, Captain. If we were in Cavite, that would have been done by a port official." Cavite, at the southern end of Manila Bay, was the shipyard and port for Manila.

"And was that done here, in Cebu?"

"I do not know, Captain. I assume so."

"But you did not attempt to find out?"

"I am just a water constable, Captain. It is not meet for me to contact port officials. I only deal with the crew and passengers."

The final suspect to be deposed was the boatswain, Francisco Baptista Arquin.

"Yes, I supervised the loading and stowage of the water jars," he admitted belligerently. "But not just the water jars. I was in overall charge of the loading of all cargo and all provisions. There were hundreds of boxes and other containers. You think I had the opportunity to give special attention to the water jars?"

"So who did?"

"I don't remember who supervised their loading and stowage. Maybe it was Diego de Aro."

"He was the one who found and reported the contraband water jar," said Captain Atondo. "That is inconsistent with him being the one to hide it in the first place."

"Or it could have been Juan de Molina, the water constable."

Atondo raised his eyebrows. "He testified that he doesn't deal with the water jars until it's time to dispense the water."

"Then he is either incompetent, or a liar. If he does not at least watch the water jars be stowed, how will he know where to find them? And is he not the best person to decide where they should be stowed, so they are easy to access, they are not broken when the ship heaves and rolls, and their contents remain wholesome?"

Diego de Aro, who had previously been deposed as to the discovery of the contraband, was recalled to testify as to his role in the loading and storage of the water jars.

"Captain Atondo, I was in charge of the ship's boats at that time." The *San Raimundo*, besides the longboat that was towed behind it, had a couple of smaller boats that were broken down and stowed once the ship was ready to depart Cebu, in order to make more room on deck. "I don't think we transported over any of the water jars. It's possible, but more likely they were carried by a lighter hired by the supplier, whoever that was. Perhaps Francisco remembers. . . ."

"Please be seated," said the captain-general. "I have read the transcripts. Who do think is guilty?"

"I think we can absolve the shipmaster," said Captain Atondo. "I am not so sure about the boatswain and the water constable."

"Even if they were not deliberately seeking to sneak contraband on board, they seem to have been most cavalier about assuring the safety of the water supply," said Captain de Bolaza.

"I agree," said Captain Atondo.

"And what punishment would you recommend, gentlemen?"

Captain Atondo rubbed his chin. "The punishment for smuggling is usually a fine or imprisonment, but that would be imposed in Acapulco."

"True enough. Although this was more than smuggling, as the

water could be said to have been stolen. The punishment for theft is flogging. At least a hundred lashes."

The captain-general grunted. "Such a sentence would certainly be appealed. It would have to be held in abeyance until we reached Acapulco. And unless a confession can be obtained, either from the suspects or some accomplice on board, I am not sure that the authorities in Acapulco would uphold the sentence. At best we have evidence of negligence, not criminality."

"Then," said Captain Atondo, "fine them, or demote them."

"Yes, let them both be reduced to ordinary seamen," said Captain de Bolaza.

"So be it."

The boatswain's mate was promoted to boatswain, and one of the soldiers was made water constable. Diego de Aro was given a cash reward and, at his request, was made boatswain's mate. As he confided to Father Blanco, he had been made quartermaster's mate because he could read, write and cipher, but it was something of a dead-end position, with no promise of action and no prestige or power. As the boatswain's mate, he would order the sailors at the prow, and he would command the ship's boats.

By now, of course, it was well known among the crew, and even among the passengers, that there was less water on board than expected. However, some of the rumors made the deficiency much greater than was actually the case. Many of the crew complained about not having enough to drink. Several sailors became convinced that they were dying of thirst, and had to be brought to the sickbay.

One sailor drew a knife on the new water constable, claiming that he had given another sailor more than his proper allotment. Since the water constable was considered an officer, albeit a relatively lowly one, had the attacker drawn blood, he would have had his knife hand nailed to a mast. But since he merely threatened the constable, he was placed in the stocks.

Watching the punishment, Diego de Aro crossed himself. He couldn't help but think the incident a harbinger of more trouble to come.

Chapter 25

November 1635

Tensions rose further when, in November, more than a week went by without rain. The pilot major was summoned to the Great Cabin.

"The crew is on edge about the water situation," said the captain-general. "How soon will we make landfall?"

"We are back down to the 40th parallel now, and on a southeast course. Normally we would make landfall at or below the 36th parallel. However, if we follow the 40th parallel east, we should strike Cabo Mendocino." The cape was given that name several decades earlier to honor Antonio de Mendoza, then viceroy of New Spain. Captain-General Mendoza claimed to be a descendant of that viceroy. "About ten miles south of the cape, there is supposed to be a river mouth. We can collect fresh water there."

"Make course for Cabo Mendocino," the captain-general ordered.

The first sign that the *San Raimundo* was nearing the California coast was when a large raft of seaweed floated past the galleon. The lucky sailor who spotted this was given a chain of gold by Captain-General Mendoza, and many pieces of eight by the passengers. The ship's bell was rung, and a day of misrule was declared. Several sailors, dressed in togas, set up a mock court under a canopy. The captain-general was tried for the crime of drinking so much wine that the ship had to be retrimmed, the pilot for "quarreling with the sun," and the surgeon for being "an excellent executioner." The sentences were commuted in return for the condemned sharing out some of their precious private stores of chocolate, sugar, and good wine.

The next day, the smaller ship's boats were reassembled, and the cannons and anchor cables hauled out of the hold. The cannons were wanted because there was a risk of English or Dutch pirates lurking off the coast of California or New Spain.

Sometime later, they came across a small group of *lobos marinos*, or "sea wolves." These were harbor seals, which usually didn't travel far from shore. More lookouts were posted; the seals liked rocky shores better than the sailors did.

The following day, one of the lookouts spotted Cabo Mendocino. One of its distinguishing features was a huge haystack-shaped rock just offshore. The *San Raimundo* turned south and nosed its way down to the mouth of the Mattole River.

The main problem with this stopover was that it was a completely open roadstead. One could gain some shelter from the winds by heading upriver, but the deepest part of the mouth was only twelve feet deep, and the river was generally much shallower.

The galleon's crew took down most of its sails, and dropped several anchors. The ship's boats were launched, under Diego's direction, carrying both sailors and soldiers. The soldiers established a defensive perimeter and then the sailors began filling water jars.

The forest hugged the riverbanks, meaning that any natives in the vicinity could come quite close before being spotted. Once a soldier thought he saw movement and fired. There was no return fire, and, when a scouting party was sent out to investigate, they found no footprints or other signs that an Indian had made the disturbance in the foliage.

As the sun set, the soldiers returned to the boats—not without nervous glances back toward the forest—and the boats were rowed back to the *San Raimundo*.

In the Great Cabin that evening, Captain-General Mendoza consulted Guillermo once again.

"We will follow the coast down to Cabo San Lucas," Guillermo declared. That was the southern tip of Baja California. "However, we dare not get too close—the coast is shoaly and foggy. From Cabo San Lucas, we head for Acapulco."

Hopefully there will be no further bad news, thought Mendoza.

Chapter 26

"Sail ho! On the port bow!"

Guillermo ran to the bow of the ship and started scanning the seascape with his spyglass. He saw nothing of interest. He shrugged, and climbed the ratlines to the foretop. Holding the mast with one hand, and his spyglass with the other, he repeated the search process. At last, he spotted the other vessel. It came in and out of view, depending on its position relative to the waves. It had a single mast, and it was presently hull down.

Even if it were crammed with pirates, it would be little threat to the high-sided *San Raimundo*. But its presence here was curious. As far as Guillermo knew, while the Chumash of the *Islas del Canal* to the south built wooden boats, they did not use sails. Cabrillo's report on them was from 1542, and it was conceivable that they had copied the Spanish sails, but it also seemed improbable.

Could it be a fishing vessel from New Spain? If so, what was it doing so far north? Unless matters had changed drastically since the *San Raimundo* left Acapulco, the most northern Spanish settlement was at Chametla. It was a base for pearl fishermen. But from Chametla it was a good 250 miles to Cabo San Lucas, the tip of the Baja California peninsula, and from there it was another 1200 miles to their present position, somewhere near the Bahía de Monterrey.

Could it be a captured Spanish fishing boat that was only pretending to be fishing? Perhaps pirates had established a base somewhere nearby. In which case it was probably here as a sentinel, to give warning of the arrival of the Manila galleons, that they might be waylaid by the pirate squadron somewhere further south.

Guillermo pressed the objective end of his spyglass against the mast, to close it, and clambered down. He reported his observations and reasoning to the captain-general, who ordered that the mystery vessel be boarded.

There was a flurry of orders, and the *San Raimundo* altered its course to bear directly on the presumed pirate scout boat. The latter tried to escape, first by heading south and then, when it realized the greater speed of the *San Raimundo*, heading east into the shoals of the coast. However, its turn came too late to make a difference.

As the *San Raimundo* came closer, more details of the mystery vessel became visible. It was an open deck vessel, but with some sort of thatched roof fore-and-aft. There was a large rudder and a high prow. The sail was a single square sail, stayed fore-and-aft. And most puzzling of all, the men on board were wearing colored robes and large, slightly conical hats.

Once the *San Raimundo* came alongside, the boatmen abandoned all attempts at fleeing, and just sat down in despair.

Did a Chinese fishing boat been blown to California? the pilot major wondered. *Or had the Chinese, who had come to Acapulco on galleons past, built boats in New Spain and ventured up here?*

A sailor approached. "We tried hailing them, and they didn't respond."

That made the second possibility less likely. Although there were Philippine Chinese who spoke little Spanish, despite living in Manila for years, those were people who spent almost all their time in the Parian, the walled and guarded Chinatown. There was no Parian in Acapulco.

"Go find Señor Escalante. He is one of our merchant passengers. I have heard that he dealt with the Chinese many times."

A few minutes later, Señor Escalante joined the pilot major by the railing overlooking the apprehended boat.

"How may I be of service, pilot major?"

"You speak Chinese, do you not?"

"A smattering. The words and phrases needed to do business."

Guillermo pointed at the boat. "Find out who they are and where they are from."

Señor Escalante spoke to the boatmen in a mixture of Spanish and what the pilot major presumed was Chinese, with many gesticulations.

The boatmen made some attempt to respond. After a time, Señor Escalante shook his head.

"I didn't understand much of what they were saying. They said 'por favor' at one point. So they know that much Spanish, at least. But whatever they said in their own language, it didn't sound like any Chinese I knew. I know this sounds crazy, but could it be Japanese?"

Japanese? The pilot major admitted to himself that if a Chinese fishing boat could be blown across the Pacific, a Japanese one could, too.

"Señor Escalante, would you do me the favor of fetching Father Blanco? And do not talk of this situation to anyone else."

A few minutes later, Father Blanco arrived at the waist of the *San Raimundo*, and greeted the pilot major. Guillermo asked Father Blanco to question the boatmen, and he agreed to make the attempt.

However, he found conversation to be difficult, with the wind blowing and sailors at work behind him. "Lower me down to their deck, please."

"Are you sure, Father? I will not be able to guarantee your safety."

"They do not seem to be armed, or belligerent, my son."

"No, Father, but we don't know what they have hidden under their clothes, or those awnings. And even the tools of the sailor can serve as weapons, in a pinch. Let me at least have a couple of soldiers board their boat before you."

"I thank you for your concern, but I think that I will get a more honest answer if I go alone."

The pilot major at last gave in, and ordered a rope ladder lowered for the priest. He descended the ladder and entered the boat.

Guillermo held his breath while Father Blanco spoke with the boatmen. His anxiety increased further when the priest was conducted under the awnings, thus vanishing temporarily from sight.

The pilot major was ready to order the soldiers to board the boat when Father Blanco came back into view, and held up his hand. He made the sign of the Cross, and to Guillermo's astonishment, the mysterious boatmen returned it.

Once Father Blanco came back on board the *San Raimundo*, he remarked, "Well, they told me a tale to rival anything out of *Orlando Furioso*. I think we'd best go directly to the captain-general."

"Very well," said the pilot major, "but I will make sure that boat doesn't go anywhere in the meanwhile." He gave the necessary orders and then escorted Father Blanco to the great cabin.

"So," said Father Blanco. "The boat is a fishing boat, and on board are five Japanese fishermen."

"Remarkable!" said the pilot major. "Was their boat dismasted by a storm and carried here by the currents before they could repair the damage?"

"No. It was carried here, disassembled, by a colony ship. The Japanese have apparently founded a settlement north of here. I think, from the description, on the coast of the Baja de Monterrey."

"*Madre de Dios*! The Japanese, our new foes, so close to New Spain!" exclaimed the captain-general.

"Ah, but there is more to the story. They claim to be Christians! All five of them openly wear the cross on a necklace."

"A ploy, you think?" asked the pilot major. "Their settlement is close enough to New Spain so that the Japanese carry the cross, in case they are apprehended by a Spanish warship? They had time enough to put the necklace on, between when we gave chase and when you questioned them."

"If so, then the ploy was well-thought out, as they knew some catechisms."

"I don't understand how Japanese Christians would come here. Did those in Manila, or Macao, sail here in secret?"

"The fishermen say that the shogun of Japan announced that those Christians who surrendered to the authorities within a set period of time would be allowed to sail into exile in a faraway land they called 'New Nippon,' and they would be permitted to practice their religion there. Bahía de Monterrey, it would appear, is this 'New Nippon.'"

"And whose ships did they sail in?" asked the pilot major.

"Some were Japanese-built, others were Chinese or Dutch," said Father Blanco.

"Dutch!" protested the captain-general. "Then they may be heretics, not true Christians! Have you inquired into this?"

"I will. But it would appear that even if their transporters were Dutch, their original instruction, back in Japan, was in the True Faith, else they'd not have been exiled. May I ask that they be brought on board, but protected from those who might wish to harm them because of the misdeeds of their pagan countrymen?"

"It shall be so," said the captain-general. "But we need to question more than just their religion. I think we need to know as much as possible about this New Nippon. How many colonists are there? How are they armed? What is the role of the Dutch in this colony? The questions are nigh endless."

And troubling, he thought. *How could this have happened, especially with the Crown knowing nothing about it?*

Chapter 27

Guillermo consulted with the captain of soldiers, and handpicked and carefully instructed men escorted the Japanese fishermen to the brig. There, they were further questioned by Captain Atondo, with Father Blanco serving as translator.

Subsequently, a council of war was called, with all of the high officers of the ship, as well as Father Blanco, Captain Atondo, and Diego de Aro, present.

Atondo cleared his throat. "From the interrogation, it appears that the fishermen at least consider themselves to be good Christians, although their doctrinal knowledge is shaky."

"Which is to be expected," Father Blanco interposed, "as at the height of our missionary efforts, there were perhaps a hundred missionaries to instruct a hundred thousand Japanese Christians, and most of the colonists have not seen a priest since 1625, when we lost the opportunity to smuggle in priests on Spanish trading ships. Or even since 1614, when the shogun ordered the expulsion of the missionaries."

"There are not even any native priests among them?" asked the captain-general.

"Apparently not," sighed Father Blanco. "Nor any of the *iruman*, the Jesuit brothers. Only a few *dojuku*, the lay catechists who know no Latin and recite the catechisms by rote."

"So, then, there are none to administer the sacraments to them."

"Indeed, they can only be baptized, since that sacrament does not require a priest. The fishermen said that in their community, there is a *mizukata*, a water official, who baptizes the babes."

"Your pardon, Father, but I think there are more pressing concerns than the religious life of these Japanese intruders," said Captain Atondo.

"Yes, we must know what threat they pose to New Spain," agreed the captain of soldiers.

"Unfortunately, the fishermen cannot count beyond the limits of their fingers and toes," complained Captain Atondo. "So we don't know the numbers. However, they came over in September 1634, in what they call the 'First Fleet.'"

"That sounds ominous," commented the captain-general.

"This First Fleet included more than twenty ships of substantial size, each at least comparable in size to a *fluyt*."

The shipmaster frowned. "Even if there were only twenty, they were all just hundred tonners, and carried what our Ministry of Trade considers a legal load for the Atlantic trade, that would mean something like a thousand passengers."

"Given the uncertainties, it could be double," said Captain Atondo.

"Or triple," said Father Blanco. "The Japanese are more tolerant of crowded conditions than we are, and the *kirishitan* might have been anxious to leave Japan before the shogun changed his mind."

"The news gets worse, for a 'Second Fleet' arrived a few weeks ago. Some of this second lot of Japanese went to the original four settlements, and some to a new settlement that they call Maruya," added Captain Atondo.

"That name is the Japanese corruption of the name of María, the Blessed Virgin," Father Blanco pointed out. "That is consistent with their assertion that they are followers of the True Faith."

"With the Japanese in five settlements, we may assume that they number several thousand. That suggests that it would take a substantial force to dislodge them," grumbled the captain-general.

"How many of those passengers were warriors?" asked the captain of soldiers.

"In Japan, I would guess that something like one in twenty people is a samurai," said Father Atondo. "But the impression I had from the fishermen was that the proportion of samurai in the colony was higher than that. It made them . . . uncomfortable. Not only because the samurai have the right to kill a commoner, but because few of the samurai were Christian."

The captain-general raised his eyebrows. "So, at Bahía de Monterrey, we have a cadre of pagans ruling at least nominally Christian commoners."

"Not entirely," said Father Atondo. "While the person they call the grand governor—Date Masamune—is believed to be a pagan, I was told that his son publicly converted to Christianity. He was baptized 'David Date' when they reached the American coast. The fishermen were very impressed by this act."

The captain-general scratched his head. "That name—Date Masamune—I have heard it before."

"He is one of the kings of Japan," said Captain Atondo.

Father Blanco corrected him. "He is a daimyo. More like a duke, but with more autonomy than one of our dukes would enjoy. He sent an embassy to the Pope some years ago. It visited Spain, France, and of course Italy. I believe it left Acapulco, returning to Japan, in 1619 or thereabouts."

"Then he may have some leanings toward Christianity," mused the captain-general.

"Or the embassy was a ruse, so he could spy on Spain and find out our strengths and weaknesses," said the captain of soldiers.

"He was friendly with the Franciscan Luís Sotelo," said Father Blanco. "Sotelo went to Spain with the embassy."

The captain-general held up his hand, interrupting this digression. "Whatever his religious tendencies, the presence of the Japanese here is a threat to New Spain. Especially given their alliance with the Dutch, who can use Bahía de Monterrey as a base for operations against Acapulco. We need to spy out their fortifications."

"Preferably without them realizing we are doing so," said the captain of soldiers.

"And we have the means to do so," said Diego de Aro. "I can take the captured fishing boat, and dress our men in the fishermen's clothing. As long as we don't get close enough to another boat or the shore for their faces to be seen clearly, we should be fine."

"I am concerned about the presence of the Japanese Second Fleet," said the captain of soldiers. "If Diego reconnoiters the bay while all those ships are present, he is likely to be detected and apprehended."

"The fishermen did not think that the Second Fleet would remain more than another week or two," said Father Blanco. "Are we willing to dawdle in these waters that long?"

"Probably not," admitted the captain-general. "But from the up-time map I was shown, the bay is very large. Where do the ships anchor?"

"Once they have finished discharging passengers at the various settlements, they congregate in the north, near their main settlement, Kodachi Machi."

"Then Diego should be able to explore most of the bay without fear," said the captain-general. "We would like to know about Kodachi Machi, of course, but he should approach it cautiously, if at all, if the ships are still present. It is paramount that the Japanese not notice our presence here. Especially if there are warships among this Second Fleet of theirs. What do the fishermen know about that?"

"There are indeed warships, sir, but the fishermen are incapable of judging their strength," said Father Blanco.

"So spy, but spy cautiously, Diego," said the captain-general. "And have Father Blanco come along, in case you are hailed by another boat and must answer in Japanese."

"I will not disappoint you, sir!"

But privately, he couldn't help but worry that the Japanese would spot them, identify them as intruders, and capture or sink them.

Chapter 28

"Must I wear this ridiculous clothing?" complained one of the sailors, holding one of the Japanese fishermen's broad-brimmed bamboo hats.

"You must indeed," said Diego. "Put on the hat!"

The sailor, still grumbling, complied.

"There, now, you look like a proper Japanese. Perhaps a pretty Japanese wench will swim out to you from shore, and give you a kiss!"

The other sailors chosen for the reconnaissance mission laughed. They already had their hats on. One joked, "Have her send for her sisters!"

They clambered down into the fishing boat. Diego pulled out a spyglass and confirmed that it was in working order. It was fortunate that this fishing boat had an ordinary square sail, not the strange, battened lugsail of the large Japanese junks.

His sailors could handle the fishing boat's sail well enough. He sent one man back to helm the tiller, as he would want to take station up front.

The Japanese fishermen's catch was no longer on board, having been appropriated and added to the *San Raimundo*'s store of provisions. However, the fishy smell lingered.

According to Guillermo's cross-staff measurements of the altitude of the Pole Star, the *San Raimundo* was presently at thirty-six degrees north latitude. However, even on land, cross-staff measurements could be a full degree off.

When first assigned to captain this espionage mission, Diego had been worried about the wind. More precisely, about the fact that since they made landfall, the wind had blown from the north or northwest, which meant that sailing north from their present position, southwest of the southern cape of Bahía de Monterrey, back to the mouth of the bay, could be extremely slow and laborious.

They would have to take advantage of sea and land breezes and other occasional favorable winds—which would be time-consuming and chancy—or lower their sails and row. There were sweeps on board the fishing boat, so rowing was certainly an option.

But when the Japanese fishermen were questioned, it turned out that if you stayed close to shore, there was a north-setting current. That current was apparently seasonal—from November to February—but it was running now. In addition, at this time of year there were occasional gales from the southeast.

Taking advantage of this nearshore current was not something that Diego would want to do in a large ship like the *San Raimundo*—it had a deep draft, and the California coast was shoaly and often foggy—but in this little fishing vessel, it should be safe enough.

Safe enough from the elements at least. Staying close to the coast meant being more easily studied by coastwatchers on shore.

"Well, let's be off," said Diego.

"Wait sir!" said a sailor. "It's bad luck to sail a pagan ship without renaming it."

Diego stroked his chin. "Well, we'll call it *El Anzuelo*—the 'fish hook'—since we'll be snaring information."

The interrogation had revealed the number and general location of the Japanese settlements in the vicinity of Bahía de Monterrey, but not what the Spanish most wanted to know: the defenses of each settlement. That the Spanish would have to find out for themselves—preferably without revealing their presence to the Japanese.

Carried by the current, *El Anzuelo* edged closer and closer to the nearest Japanese settlement, Maruya. Through the spyglass, Diego could see several fishing boats beached on the shore, and a giant cross. Diego guessed that it was twenty feet high. Diego motioned Father Blanco forward and handed him the spyglass. "Look at that, Father Blanco."

He did so. "Remarkable. I would say it serves as confirmation of the story that the Japanese on this coast are exiled Christians."

"Couldn't pagans put up a cross to mislead any passing Spanish ship?" asked Diego.

Father Blanco shrugged. "They could, of course. But the fishermen know more of our Faith than I would expect pagans of their place in society to know." He handed the spyglass back to Diego.

The fishermen had revealed that Maruya was not on the beach, but up the Carmel River. Unfortunately, the terrain blocked the Spanish scouts' view of Maruya. After some fruitless maneuvering to get a better sight line, Diego decided it was time to move on.

El Anzuelo continued its journey north, circling the Monterey Peninsula. When it came abreast of Punta de Piños, the wind shifted to the west and Diego had to make a decision; follow along the bay, or make for the opposite point. If he took the first option, the next settlement *El Anzuelo* would pass would be the captured fishermen's home port of Andoryu. And there was therefore a risk that if their boat was seen passing Andoryu rather than docking there, it would arouse suspicions. However, heading straight for Kodachi Machi to the north might be even more suspicious. So he decided to just follow along the bay, still taking advantage of the inshore current.

Andoryu was on the site of up-time Monterey. The spyglass revealed that as the fisherman had told their Spanish interrogators, this was a fortified village, with walls and a watchtower.

Following the arc of the bay counter-clockwise, the Spanish came abreast of Kawamachi, by the mouth of the Salinas River. Observation revealed a keep on a hill. Presumably there were also homes nearby, but Diego couldn't spot them. He feared that if he came closer, for a better look, sentinels on the top of the keep would realize that there was something suspicious about *El Anzuelo*.

Hence, after Father Blanco finished making a sketch of the keep, Diego ordered the boat on to the next Japanese settlement, Niji Masu. This was at the mouth of another river—someone with an up-time map would identify it as the Pajaro. Beyond the village, Diego could see some kind of fortification on a hill. Diego tried to bring *El Anzuelo* closer, but broke off the attempt when a boat emerged from the mouth of the river, heading straight for *El Anzuelo*!

A guard boat? Diego wondered. Even if it were a fishing boat, Diego didn't want to linger and explain his presence. He ran to the tiller and helped the helmsman bring *El Anzuelo* about.

The wind, unfortunately, was from the northwest. If they wanted to make directly for their final target, Kodachi Machi, they would have to row. And row they did.

Fortunately, the boat that was trying to intercept them—for whatever reason—had the same problems.

El Anzuelo was longer than the boat from Niji Masu, and apparently also had the larger crew. The distance between the boats increased, and after some minutes, the Niji Masu boat gave up the pursuit.

Diego breathed a sigh of relief. His greatest fear had been that the pursuit would be seen by, or reported to, the authorities in Kodachi Machi—the fishermen had said that was the capital of "New Nippon," and had the largest fortress—and that guard boats or even warships would be sent out from Kodachi Machi to cut off *El Anzuelo*'s escape.

The question now was whether it was safe to proceed with reconnaissance of Kodachi Machi. Diego was well aware that his superiors would not be happy if his report didn't include the main Japanese fortress. On the other hand, the capture of *El Anzuelo* would be potentially disastrous. The Japanese would know that the Spanish were aware of their presence on the bay and the *San Raimundo* would not have the information Diego had been sent to collect. And warships in the bay could be sent to find the *San Raimundo*!

"Take down the sail!" Diego ordered. That would make the boat quite difficult to spot. The tide was going out, as was evident from the movement of flotsam, and that would carry them west, closer to Kodachi Machi.

Unfortunately, even at their closest approach they were still too far away to properly observe it. When Kodachi Machi was due northeast, they threw out a sea anchor to keep themselves in place. Diego waited until nightfall. Waited further, until the late November moon, a little before full, had climbed further into the sky.

It gave enough light to steer by. And the wind was still from the northwest, although it had slackened somewhat. "Haul in the sea anchor! Raise sail!" They could now head straight for Kodachi Machi. And the view of *El Anzuelo* from the Japanese fortress would be a head-on one, more difficult to spot than a profile one.

Some minutes passed. "Drop the sea anchor!" Diego feared coming any closer.

There were what appeared to be huts of some kind on or just behind the beach. Behind them, on a higher ground, was some sort of palisaded settlement. And, on higher ground still, there was a more substantial fortress, with multiple towers. This was all consistent with what the fishermen had told them, although they had only rarely visited the fishing village of Kodachi Machi, and had never been inside the fortress or the other settlement.

It was impossible to judge how many soldiers presently manned the fortress, or how many cannon it was equipped with. But Diego's best guess was that it was the same size as Fort Santiago, the citadel of Manila. A Spanish fortress of that size could hold a substantial garrison. Several hundred, at least. And conceivably it could offer some shelter to several hundreds of Japanese civilians, assuming that it had enough food and water on hand.

As for the harbor, there were several ships of substantial size there. None were as large as the *San Raimundo*, but they were certainly over a hundred tons. Some of these, presumably, were the ships of what the fishermen had called the "Second Fleet," and would be leaving once they were refitted and reprovisioned. But others might be a permanent naval defense force stationed at Kodachi Machi.

In the moonlight, at their present distance, Diego couldn't make out gunports. And he had no intention of waiting for daybreak, or coming any closer. If he were close enough to make the observation, he would be close enough for the cannon of the fort, sited on elevated ground, to target him. The additional information that might be gleaned wasn't worth the risk of *El Anzuelo* being captured or sunk.

"Take us about," Diego commanded. "Heading due south."

And even though they weren't safely back on board the *San Raimundo*, he couldn't help but breathe a sigh of relief.

Chapter 29

After the return of *El Anzuelo*, another council of war was held on board the *San Raimundo*. Diego and Father Blanco had been called before it because of their firsthand knowledge. Diego stood uncomfortably at attention, knowing that any of the officers might ask questions . . . and find his answers wanting.

He nonetheless knew that the council was really *pro forma*, since it was obvious that the *San Raimundo* could not act alone against the Japanese settlement. And it was equally obvious to Diego that the captain-general did not want to take any chances that he might be faulted by higher authority for failing to bombard Kodachi Machi.

All of the officers of the *San Raimundo*, as well as Captain Atondo of the unfortunate *Concepción*, signed the finding that it would be extremely imprudent to risk the cargo of the *San Raimundo*, and lose the advantage of surprise, by taking further action against the Japanese at this time.

There was a bit more debate on the subject of whether it was better to scuttle *El Anzuelo*, or keep it. It was at last decided that as long as it could keep up with the *San Raimundo*, or be safely towed behind it, it could be used as supplemental accommodation, and if need be as a scout. And, once they arrived at Acapulco, it would serve as further proof of the Japanese presence.

Of course, the captured fishermen were the best proof of all. Father Blanco pleaded with the captain-general that they be allowed exercise on deck, and attend all religious services, and Mendoza agreed. They would of course, have to be guarded when outside the ship's brig, but that was as much for their own protection as to prevent their escape.

"And there is the matter of their religious instruction," Father Blanco added. "It cannot be denied that some of their beliefs would be classified as heretical. But I firmly believe that their heresy is merely material, not formal. It has been decades since any of the Japanese had regular contact with one of our priests, and even when they did, there were formidable language barriers. I would like to correct their errors . . . before we reach Acapulco."

The captain-general nodded his understanding. "I will need to turn over the records of the interrogation to the authorities in Acapulco, and they will certainly transmit them to Mexico City. It is possible, even likely, that the Holy Office of the Inquisition will see the documents and launch an investigation."

"That's right. And I want to make sure that if there is an investigation, they are acquitted of wrongdoing. We have wrenched them from their homes and families; the least we can do is prepare them for a Christian life in New Spain."

"Before the expulsion, how much instruction in the faith was customary in Japan?"

Father Blanco shrugged. "For the common people, like these fishermen? A week. Ten days if we were lucky."

"Then you best get started. Guillermo thinks we will reach Acapulco in a few weeks."

The *San Raimundo* proceeded southward, with double the usual number of lookouts. Spielbergen had taken a Dutch squadron to Acapulco in 1615, and Schapenham an even larger one in 1624. With the Dutch known to have brought Japanese colonists to Bahía de Monterrey in 1634 and 1635, there was reason to expect that after offloading their passengers, they had sailed south to lie in wait for the Manila galleons. There were many possible places the Dutch could use as bases—Cape San Lucas, the Tres Marías islands, and even Zihuatanejo on the Mexican coast.

Father Blanco offered daily prayers that the Dutch had left the coast. Someone seemed to have been listening, as the only peril faced by the *San Raimundo* on its final leg was one posed by nature: a fierce squall that tore away one of the topsails before they could furl it. They did encounter boats, but these were the simple wood canoes of the Chumash, who inhabited the Santa Barbara Islands. They were propelled by oars, not sails, and observed the *San Raimundo* from a respectful distance.

December 1635

When the *San Raimundo* descended to the twentieth parallel, the winds died down. It was a dark cloud with a silver lining, because at night several sleeping sea turtles floated close to the ship, and were taken. These ended up on the captain-general's table the following evening. Father Blanco was one of his guests and was surprised to find that the turtles tasted more like beef than like fish, despite living in the sea.

A small gale blew in, close to midnight, but Guillermo did not dare take full advantage of it until morning, lest the ship be blown onto the shoals along the coast.

Soon thereafter, the *San Raimundo* arrived at Puerto de la Navidad. The ship's boats were used to bring the sick passengers ashore and thereby alleviate the crowding on board the *San Raimundo*. The boats and the passengers were of course carefully searched to make sure that they were not carrying any Chinese goods, as those had to go through customs in Acapulco. Captain Atondo also left the *San Raimundo* at this point; he went to the royal shipyard, where he was given a horse and would ride, changing horses at the post stations, to Mexico City to report the arrival of the *San Raimundo* and the loss of his own galleon. He had insisted on serving as courier, no doubt feeling it best that the first report of that loss come from him, rather than another.

About two weeks later, the *San Raimundo* finally found itself in front of the great outer harbor of Acapulco. The mouth of this harbor was divided by the Isla de Chinos into two channels, the Boca Chica and the Boca Grande. Coming as they did from the north, they took the Boca Chica. They rounded the Punta Grifo, and the inner harbor, with the Castillo de San Diego standing on the opposing headland, came into view. It had five bastions, about forty cannon, and a permanent garrison of about a hundred men. It probably had more soldiers than that right now. Reinforcements would have been sent, for the security of the *San Raimundo* and its treasure, as soon as Captain Atondo reached the capital.

The *San Raimundo* reduced sail, and dropped anchor. It saluted the castle with seven guns, which responded with three. The crew was assembled on deck and Father Blanco led them in singing the "Te Deum." Many of the passengers joined in the singing of this hymn, too.

A pirogue, sent by the castellan, brought an ox, fowls, bread, sweetmeats and lemons as treats for the ship's officers. Soon thereafter, it returned with the castellan himself, the comptroller, and the surveyor, and the captain-general solemnly handed them the bill of lading for the *San Raimundo*, the original bill for the *Concepción*, and the list of goods lost when the *Concepción* sank. They also collected the king's duties, which were a great many pieces of eight.

Diego took them to see the water jars that had been used to carry contraband, and gave them the depositions of the individuals questioned in connection with their discovery. The three suspects from that inquiry were taken into custody for further questioning at the castle.

Naturally, given that contraband had already been found in the course of the voyage, the surveyor and his men made a very painstaking search for additional contraband, which took several hours. At last, they grudgingly pronounced themselves satisfied.

Father Blanco slowly ascended the steps leading up to the quarterdeck. His slowness was not because of any physical infirmity, but rather a spiritual one. He was worried about the fate of the Japanese fishermen that the *San Raimundo* had captured. He feared that they would be turned over to the Inquisition, and burnt as heretics, on account of their doctrinal errors. Or merely imprisoned for life, as citizens of a hostile state.

The captain-general was a man of great influence in the viceroyalty of New Spain. Father Blanco hoped to persuade him to intercede on their behalf.

"We must give thanks to our Lord for our safe arrival in New Spain," Father Blanco remarked.

"We must indeed."

"And how wonderful it is that the Japanese Christians who came into our hands will be able to attend sermons, partake in the Eucharist, make penance, and perhaps even marry."

The captain-general shrugged. "Before that can be considered, they will come with me to Mexico City, to be questioned by the highest military authorities. Perhaps even by the viceroy himself. The Crown would expect us to make sure we have extracted every possible nugget of useful information concerning the Japanese settlements on this coast. And the situation in Japan itself, and the Japanese-occupied territories in the Philippines."

"I trust that I will be permitted to come along to serve as translator . . . and to make sure that if they continue to be cooperative, they are treated kindly."

"I would welcome that," the captain-general conceded. "It is doubtful that there is anyone in Mexico City with your fluency in Japanese. And, of course, you participated in their original interrogation, so you would notice any discrepancies."

"And after their further interrogation I would like to place them in the care of my order. While they cannot return to Japan, or to Bahía de Monterrey, my fellow Jesuits can find the *kirishitan* who immigrated to Mexico after the expulsion of the priests, and those can help our captives integrate into Mexican society. As you know, I have already met with the poor souls on several occasions to correct their understanding of the True Faith."

The captain-general sighed. "I know. But I doubt that the viceroy will accept your word, or mine, that they are now orthodox. I still expect that the viceroy will send their files to the Holy Office of the Inquisition. Since, by their own admission, they have been baptized, they can be guilty of heresy. And I have read the transcripts of their interrogation, and even a lay Catholic would realize that they came to us with heretical beliefs. Why, they equated the Virgin Mary with the Holy Spirit!"

"I know. Collyridianism. And as a corollary, they believe that God the Father was once one, but divided himself in three. But they knew the Sign of the Cross, the Hail Mary, the *Salve Regina* and the Apostle's Creed. They knew the Ten Commandments. Their heresies were innocent, the result of learning the church's teachings from fellow *kirishitan* whose own understanding was imperfect, as it was imparted long ago from priests who did not speak Japanese well. I have explained to these fishermen the errors of their ways. Accepting the correct teachings will be sufficient to protect them from the Inquisition. I hope."

"I will pray that you are correct. It is a pity that you cannot serve as their advocate if they are put on trial."

Father Blanco shrugged. As a Jesuit, he had been carefully trained, not only in canon law, but in the judicial practices of the Church. It had been almost a century since prisoners had been allowed to select their own counsel. Moreover, the advocate served the tribunal, not the prisoner. An advocate who forgot that was likely to face the Inquisition himself.

"I made a sworn statement concerning the conditions of baptism and religious instruction in Japan before and after the expulsion of the mercenaries, my admonitions concerning their theological errors, and their willingness to correct them. I pray that will be enough."

Chapter 30

Holy Office of the Inquisition
Mexico City, Viceroyalty of New Spain
January 1636

In due course, the Holy Office of the Inquisition launched an investigation of the Japanese fishermen. Father Blanco was allowed to serve as translator, and to testify as a witness as to their recent instruction, but as he expected, he was not permitted to serve as their advocate.

Three *calificadores*—theological assessors—were appointed by the Inquisitor, Doctor Bartolomé González Soltero, to review the preliminary array of evidence.

The master *calificador*, Juan de Noval, was dressed in the white tunic and scapular, and long black cloak and hood, of the Order of Preachers. The Dominican summoned his colleagues to order. "Well, this is an unusual case," he muttered. "Japanese fishermen, apprehended in Californian waters."

Gabriel de Morillo fingered the triple knotted girdle that secured his brown Franciscan habit. "Does the Holy Office even have jurisdiction over them? They are citizens of Japan. In general, foreigners who have lawfully entered the Spanish dominion, without representing themselves to be Catholic, are not prosecuted for heresy unless they make their heretical views public. After all, we have tolerated English sailors and merchants in Spanish ports since the Treaty of London in 1603. And they entered the viceroyalty of New

Spain under compulsion, as a result of their capture outside of New Spain by the *San Raimundo*, so their presence cannot be treated as unlawful."

Geronimo Castellete, the blacked-robed Augustinian, disagreed. "But they were living on the coast of *Las Californias*. It is Spanish territory under the terms of the Treaty of Tordesillas. Having entered the Spanish dominion unlawfully, they may be examined by us for heresy, assuming of course that they were baptized."

Gabriel de Morillo was unconvinced. "But they are present in *Las Californias* as exiles from their homeland. They were given the choice of exile, martyrdom or apostasy. They chose the only path that permitted them to live as Christians. And the Crown does not presently administer *Las Californias*. I would contend that they should be treated like a foreigner who enters New Spain as a result of shipwreck of a civilian vessel."

Geronimo shook his head. "What do you think, Juan?"

"I would focus not on their citizenship, but on their assertion that they are Christians. I think that if they claim to be Christian, and were in fact baptized, they are within our jurisdiction."

The *calificadores* agreed at last that the Holy Office had jurisdiction if there was a valid baptism.

"The next issue, then," said the master *calificador*, "is whether they were properly baptized. Four of the five fishermen have no personal recollection of their baptism, and appear to be young enough to have been born after, or shortly before, the expulsion of missionaries in 1614. So it is possible that they were not baptized by a priest."

"Lay baptism is permissible, in cases of necessity," said Castellete.

De Morillo nodded. "Yes, but how do we assess necessity, when there are no witnesses to the baptism?"

"I think that the fact of the expulsion of the missionaries is sufficient to justify an inference of necessity."

"Fine! But we have the testimony of Father Blanco that the last bishop of Japan, Luís de Cerqueira, decreed that since there was a shortage of holy oil, anointment could be dispensed with."

"Typical Jesuitical accommodationism," Castellete muttered.

Juan shrugged. "That said, the formal requirements are the application of water and the use of the Trinitarian formula. A baptism without anointment may be illicit, but it is valid."

"I agree," said Castellete.

"I will defer to my colleagues," said de Morillo at last. "I would hesitate to declare the instructions of a bishop, even a Jesuit, concerning baptism to result in invalidity *per se*."

Juan folded his hands. "So, since they have been baptized, they can be heretics. You have read the transcript of Father Blanco's initial interrogation. There is no doubt, is there, that when first apprehended, these fishermen were guilty of at least material heresy?"

The others shook their heads.

"But Father Blanco's interrogation also revealed that the four younger fishermen had not, since reaching the age of reason, had contact with a priest, and that the senior fisherman had not had such contact within the last twenty years. That at least raises the possibility that their heresy was merely material, the result of ignorance. As Alciatus said, 'one whose understanding of the Trinity is wrong is not a heretic unless he persists in his error after being admonished.'"

Castellete shook his head. "Admonition is unnecessary for heresy if the accused already knew that his views were contrary to Church doctrine. So say Sanchez, Cajetan, Vasquez—"

"You need not put your scholarship on display," de Morillo complained. "There is no testimony that the accused knew of their errors."

"But their ignorance is culpable, when the doctrine is well known. And there is no doctrine better known or more central than that of the Trinity."

"Were the accused living in New Spain, or the Philippines, your point would be well taken. But I doubt that the doctrine of the Trinity was well known in Japan in 1614."

The master *calificador* coughed. "Perhaps we can set that point aside, for now? Even if we accept that the fishermen were guilty only of material heresy at the time they were taken on board the *San Raimundo*, Father Blanco has testified that he has instructed them over the course of the month between their capture and their delivery to Acapulco. If, despite that instruction, they persist in any of their heresies, then they are being pertinacious, and are guilty of formal heresy, for which they may be tried and punished."

"Indeed," said de Morillo, "but their most recent testimony suggests that they now have a proper understanding of the Holy Trinity."

Castellete snorted. "Actually, all it shows is that Father Blanco knows what they need to say to satisfy the Holy Office. He was their translator. We have no idea what they actually said."

The master *calificador* sighed. "You are accusing Father Blanco of intentional false translation? To protect heretics?"

"I accuse him of being a Jesuit."

"Do you think we should find another priest, a Franciscan, or Dominican, or Augustinian, who speaks Japanese as well as he does?"

"I do."

"And do you know of such a person here in Mexico City?"

"Well, no. But we could send to Madrid for such a scholar. . . ."

"No! Absolutely not! The inquisitor would be furious if I made such a suggestion. Months to send out the request. Months to pick someone. Months for the scholar to get here. And then what? Suppose he and Blanco disagree? How do we know which is right?"

"Well . . ."

"Perhaps then we send out for another scholar, of even greater repute. From the Vatican, say? And hope that he sides with one or the other . . . rather than saying that both are wrong!"

The other two *calificadores* were silent.

"We have a letter from Father Blanco. I wish to read it aloud:

> *"As the Tribunal is aware, I had the privilege of preaching the faith in Japan for a decade, and subsequently, of ministering in Manila to the Japanese Christian exiles.*
>
> *"You have read the testimony of the sailors who first boarded and inspected the vessel of the accused. So you know that they did not find any pagan idols or other improper possessions. And you know that the accused, when taken into custody by those sailors, were wearing crosses and rosaries.*
>
> *"Likewise, you have read the testimony of the soldiers who guarded the accused while they were in the custody of the* San Raimundo. *They observed the accused in prayer, and did not observe any forbidden practices.*
>
> *"All of the religious orders that have labored in Japan know of the difficulties that were experienced in communicating the Faith to the Japanese people.*
>
> *"Primus, there was the language barrier.*

"Secondus, the existence of deeply rooted and sophisticated, although of course erroneous, native religions.

"Tertius, the fierce opposition of the Buddhist and Shinto priests to our teachings.

"Quartus, the reluctance of the people to give up customs contrary to the Faith, such as polygamy.

"And lastly, quintus, the vile whisperings of the Dutch merchants in the ears of the shogun.

"Our goal was to spread the Faith as quickly and widely as possible, and as a result, perhaps a hundred thousand souls were baptized, but they were served by only a hundred or so priests... few of whom spoke Japanese well.

"Even if one were to question our converts then, at the height of the mission, no doubt one would have found all sorts of foolish beliefs. Had it not been for the poisonous actions of the Buddhists and the Dutch, it would not have mattered; the errors would have come to the notice of our priests and been gently but firmly corrected. Given time.

"But time was not on our side. Instead, the priests were expelled—I was one of those sent away!—and the few that escaped expulsion, or slipped secretly into Japan at a later date, labored under even greater difficulties.

"It should not be a wonder that these poor fishermen, seeking to preserve even tatters of the Faith despite persecution and neglect, developed some heretical beliefs. But let us not forget that despite those errors, they resisted all attempts to compel them to adjure the Faith. These fishermen had relatives and friends who died as martyrs to the Faith, and they went into exile, across the great Pacific, in order to remain Christian. We should honor them, not chastise them!

"Lastly, Holy Inquisitor, I refer you to the words of Saint Augustine:

*"'Those are by no means to be accounted heretics who do not defend their false and perverse opinions with pertinacious zeal (*animositas*), especially when their error is not the fruit of audacious presumption but has been communicated to them by seduced and lapsed parents, and when they are seeking the truth with cautious solicitude and ready to be corrected.'*

"I have met with these fishermen and they have evidenced that readiness to seek the truth. Hence they should be acquitted of any wrongdoing.

"Your fellow servant in Christ, Pedro Blanco, S.J."

"He doesn't mention that the Jesuits did their best to push the other orders out of Japan," said Castellete sourly. "Or their willingness to excuse ancestor worship as a mere secular expression of respect for one's ancestors, in order to win so-called converts."

"True," said the master *calificador*. "Nonetheless, it is a powerful letter."

"So it is," said de Morillo.

The master *calificador* put his hands on the table. "This is my recommendation, with which I hope you will agree. Let the Japanese be excused and allowed to live with their fellow Japanese who have already taken refuge in New Spain, as Father Blanco suggests. Let the Jesuits be their shepherds, if they so wish. But should our agents report that the Jesuits are tolerating heresy on the part of these Japanese, well, then there will be a reckoning. . . ."

Chapter 31

Camp Double Six, Texada Island
Omisoka (Great Last Day of the Year)
Kan'ei 12, Month 12, Day 30 (February 6, 1636)

Bluebird placed a bamboo basket just outside and to the left of the entrance to Camp Double Six. She then put pine branches inside the basket, and tied them together with cedar strips so they would all stand neatly upright.

Yells-at-Bears had told Bluebird that this was what the Japanese called a *kadomatsu*, a gate decoration heralding the coming of the New Year. Tradition called for this to be made of pine, bamboo, and a plum blossom.

The pine, according to Yells-at-Bears, symbolized longevity because it kept its leaves all year. Finding it was easy enough, as the western white pine grew on Texada.

Bamboo, on the other hand, was not a native plant. The Japanese colonists had brought cuttings for "arrow bamboo," thinking to grow it into thickets for the protection of their settlements. The fallen leaves could be used as fuel, and the stalks harvested for use as fencing, pipes, and, when, split, in basketry, lattices and screens.

This bamboo basket, which had been brought from Japan and admittedly had seen better days, would do fine as the second component of Bluebird's *kadomatsu*. Yells-at-Bears told her that bamboo represented rapid growth and resiliency.

Now, for the finishing touch: the plum blossom. Well, the imitation plum blossom. According to Yells-at-Bears' boss (and boyfriend) Isamu, the Japanese plum tree would bloom even when it was still cold and snowy, and its blossom was white or pink, and sweetly scented. Yells-at-Bears had told Bluebird that she, aided by a few colonists, had made multiple attempts to find a similar tree on Texada, without any luck. So the "plum blossom" in this *kadomatsu* was artificial, made from a scrap of silk and then dyed and scented.

She fastened it in place and admired her handiwork.

Bluebird had only half-believed Yells-at-Bears a couple of months ago when she told Bluebird that she was a free woman. After all, everyone knew that to free a slave, there must be a potlatch, with a feast and a distribution of gifts. You couldn't just say, "You're free, go do what you want for the rest of your life."

But when they reached Yells-at-Bears' "flying canoe," Isamu, who was obviously of the noble class from the way everyone else on board treated him, told her the same thing. Albeit in really bad Kwak'wala. Apparently, the Japanese didn't like slavery at all, and as far as they were concerned, if you lived with them, you were free.

Of course, Bluebird wasn't about to live on her own. She was free, not crazy. The Japanese, she discovered, were divided into occupational groups. There were farmers, fishermen, miners, craftsmen, and warriors. It also seemed very strange to Bluebird, since as a slave she could collect camas bulbs, dig for clams, make baskets, and cook food, all in one day. But the Japanese had built canoes that could move without oars, so perhaps they knew what they were doing.

Or maybe they just knew how to build flying canoes.

What next? Right, I need to hang the shimenawa *over the entrance,* thought Bluebird. Yells-at-Bears had told Bluebird that the Japanese—well, some of them—believed that the Sun was a great female spirit, and when her brother mistreated her, she hid in a cave. Heaven and earth were shrouded in total darkness. So the other great spirits tricked the Sun into coming out of the cave and then hung a sacred rope across the entrance so she couldn't go back inside. The *shimenawa* was a sacred rope. Even the Japanese who didn't believe in the Sun Spirit, Amaterasu, used it that way. It was supposed to be made of something called "rice straw" but since that wasn't available, the Japanese on Texada used cedar bark strips.

Anyway, Bluebird didn't like any of the Japanese occupations, and offered to be Yells-at-Bears' servant. After all, Yells-at-Bears was the only person she knew on the entire island, and, moreover, Yells-at-Bears knew what it was like to have been a slave, and could be expected to treat Bluebird well.

Yells-at-Bears had protested at first—"if you serve me, you'll just act like my slave, not a free woman"—but eventually agreed. But she insisted that Bluebird call herself Yells-at-Bears' assistant, not her servant.

As Yells-at-Bears' assistant, Bluebird had lots of different things to do. Of course, Bluebird had to do many of the same tasks she did as a slave for the Snuneymuxw. But she had many more interesting tasks, too. In particular, to help Yells-at-Bears teach the Japanese, who came from across the Great Ocean, how to survive on Texada. That is, what plants were good to eat, or had medicinal value, and which to avoid. How different fish behaved and how to catch them. How to read the weather. And how to talk in Halkomelem and any other languages Bluebird knew.

Right now, of course, Bluebird's job was to get Camp Double Six ready for the New Year festivities. And since the New Year's foods were cooked in advance, her work was just about done for today.

Japanese New Year (O-shogatsu)
Kan'ei 13, Month 1, Day 1 (February 7, 1636)

Bluebird rose at the crack of dawn to collect water from Camp Double Six's cistern. As instructed by Yells-at-Bears, she chanted, "I draw golden water," in Japanese. Of course, she didn't yet understand much Japanese, but she had memorized the syllables in advance.

She had also been cautioned that if she met someone along the way, she must not talk to him or her. "Not a problem," she said, "because I don't speak Japanese and the Japanese don't speak Halkomelem." But in any event, she was the first one up on this auspicious day.

Coming back inside, she heated the water in one of the *kama* pots on the camp's *kamado*, a terracotta stove with openings on top. She added Yells-at-Bears' latest tea substitute, dried blackberry leaves. As she did this, she couldn't help but think about how tasty the berries themselves were. But they wouldn't be out until April. The only problem with berry hunting back in Kwalsiarwahl was that the black bears of the Nanaimo River valley were just as fond of berries as the people were, but had bigger teeth.

Yells-at-Bears had assured Blueberry that there were no bears on Texada. So Blueberry was looking forward to bear-free berry hunting expeditions come spring.

The current residents of Camp Double Six were Isamu, Yells-at-Bears, Bluebird, and the miners.

After breakfast, Bluebird, Yells-at-Bears and Isamu went down to Welcome House, where many of the Japanese were gathered. Near Welcome House, there was a small Christian chapel that had been erected by the *kirishitan* soon after arrival. And while the first Shinto shrine built was to Kanayago, the ironworkers' goddess, there now was a second shrine with images of Hachiman, Ebisu, and Inari, for the benefit of the samurai, the sailors and fishermen, and the farmers, respectively.

Bluebird noticed that some of the *kirishitan* visited both the chapel and the shrine. She asked Yells-at-Bears about this. She smiled and said that while those *kirishitan* thought Deusu was the greatest spirit, it wasn't wise to offend any of the others.

Bluebird also noticed that some *kirishitan* were wearing elk hides to keep warm. These, she had been told, had been brought to Texada as a result of Yells-at-Bears' trading with the Tla'amin and the Shishalh.

An impromptu game of *hanetsuki* started up. Bluebird watched, and had to admit that the two women playing were both good at keeping the shuttlecock in play. At last one missed, after making a desperate attempt to slide her *hagota* paddle under the shuttlecock and falling on the ground. Both shrieked with laughter, then set the paddles down.

There was a tap on her shoulder. It was Umako, the wife of the man with the "metal power." She pointed at the paddles, mimed swinging one, then pointed at herself and Bluebird.

Bluebird was flabbergasted. In Kwalsiarwahl, even commoners, let alone those who possessed spirit powers, or owned ceremonial rights of great value, did not play games with slaves. Well, Yells-at-Bears had been an exception, but even she had been careful to do so only when she and Bluebird were alone and at a safe distance from the village.

And it was at a time when they were both children, and children were given more leeway than adults.

Bluebird pointed to herself, then spread her hands, as if to ask, “Me?” Umako repeated her gestures and then went to pick up the paddles offering one to Bluebird.

They played for a few minutes and then Bluebird heard Yells-at-Bears calling to her, and missed the shot.

“Sorry, I didn’t mean to spoil your game,” said Yells-at-Bears. “I was thinking that if there are more paddles, we can play the game Snuneymuxw style.”

She turned to Umako and explained, “In my village, we played a similar game, but any number could play. We formed a circle and each person batted the shuttlecock to the person on his or her right.”

“That sounds like fun,” said Umako, who ran off to fetch more paddles. Yells-at-Bears and another woman joined the circle. A crowd gathered and soon more women went off paddle hunting. At the peak, there were ten women in the circle.

During the day, Yells-at-Bears had kept a surreptitious eye on Bluebird, to make sure she was doing all right. And Isamu, as the *daikan* for the Texada Island colony, had to meet and exchange gifts with his fellow samurai, the captain of the *Unagi Maru*, the head miner, and the headmen of the fishing and farming villages.

So they didn’t have much time with each other.

That evening, however, they had some privacy, and they took advantage of it.

Kan’ei 13, Month 1, Day 2 (February 8, 1636)

Isamu was normally an early riser. Not today though. Bluebird was also asleep, so Yells-at-Bears heated up some *miso* soup. Soybeans were planted in June, very soon after the *kirishitan* arrived, and had done pretty well, despite their popularity with Texada Island’s rabbit population. But while the colonists got to eat less *miso* than expected, they did eat more rabbit. . . .

Suddenly, Yells-at-Bears was grabbed from behind. She shrieked, but before she could actually struggle, she realized it was Isamu in a playful mood. The Japanese were not keen on public displays of affection, but their living area in Camp Double Six was curtained off. And the Japanese were also very good about not noticing things that they knew they were not supposed to see or hear.

"So," said Isamu, "tell me about your *hatsuyume*? Did you dream about Mount Fuji?"

"Why would I dream about a mountain I have seen only on a painted scroll?"

"It's the highest mountain in Japan, and therefore a source of inspiration. So if you dream about it on the first night of the New Year, it means that you will have a great inspiration in the coming year."

"Sorry, I didn't even dream about the mountains of Vancouver Island, let alone Mount Fuji."

"Was there, perchance, a hawk in your dream?" asked Isamu. "You've seen hawks before." He paused for thought. "I think an eagle would do, too."

"Sorry, no."

"Too bad. A hawk flies high, too. And it's a powerful bird. Very auspicious. What about eggplants?"

Yells-at-Bears stifled a laugh. "No. You think I would dream about a vegetable I have never eaten? And why would an eggplant dream be lucky, anyway?"

"Well . . . think of the other meaning of '*nasu*.'"

"Oh." The sound "nasu" could mean either "eggplant" or "to fulfill."

Isamu continued his attempt to find a harbinger of good fortune in Yells-at-Bears' first dream of the new year. "What about a treasure ship? A rising sun? Moonlight? An earth—"

"Before you ask me about any other auspicious elements that might have been in my dream, perhaps I should just tell you what I dreamt."

Isamu bowed his head. "I suppose that makes sense."

"I was teaching you how to speak Kwak'wala, and suddenly I realized I was stark naked."

"I see. You know, perhaps we should go back to our futon and discuss this more privately."

"I think that's an excellent idea," said Yells-at-Bears.

Chapter 32

Welcome House
April 1636

After the Welcome House was no longer needed as a temporary residence for the colonists, or a shelter for the *tatara*, it still served as an informal gathering place. Isamu and Yells-at-Bears were there when word came that a new ship had arrived from Japan.

"Well, that's a pleasant surprise," said Isamu. "They actually listened to me when I said that it was best to send colonists so they arrived at the beginning of the growing season, not the middle."

"Didn't you also say not to send farmers at all? That you wanted fishermen, miners, lumberjacks and carpenters."

"I did, but I am well aware that there are a lot of *kirishitan* farmers, so we can expect to get some. Hopefully, they only sent us upland farmers from Tohoku." Tohoku was northern Honshu. Many of the farmers on Texada were from Kyushu, over five hundred miles to the south, and lowlanders to boot.

Isamu and Yells-at-Bears walked to Sandy Bottom Bay. There were now three ships in the harbor: the war yacht *Unagi Maru*, which they had used in Yells-at-Bears' ill-fated visit to her homeland; the larger *Ieyasu Maru*, which had returned recently from Monterey Bay, after some further exploration; and the new ship. They saw that unlike the Dutch-inspired *Ieyasu Maru* and *Unagi Maru*, the new ship was junk-rigged. However, the hull lines looked European. It seemed about the size of the *Ieyasu Maru* so it probably was not carrying a large number of colonists.

Haru greeted them. "A fine sight, neh? I hope they brought rice. And sake. I miss them both."

"Let's take a boat out to them, and speak to the captain."

The ship was the *Tohoku Maru*. They were ushered into the cabin of Captain Miyoshi. He welcomed them, and showed them the passenger list and cargo manifest. "And I have a letter for you, Isamu-san. From Sendai."

Isamu took the letter with some trepidation. Yells-at-Bears looked at him curiously, but he whispered, "I'll explain later."

The captain offered them a tour of the ship, which they accepted. They discovered that while the shape of the hull was European, the ship had watertight compartments, as was the practice in Japan and China.

"So, what's going on?" asked Yells-at-Bears.

"It's a letter from my family," said Isamu. "Would it be all right with you if I read it in private? If it contains bad news, I'd rather be alone."

"Are you sure?"

"Yes, I think that will be best."

"All right. I will go for a walk, look for herbs."

"Thank you, I appreciate it."

Isamu's reaction to the letter was similar to his reaction to the passenger list and cargo manifest; could have been better, could have been worse.

His family said that they understood that as a third son that he did not see a future for himself in their little fief. However, they were concerned that he was contemplating a marriage too soon. What if Date Masamune decided to transfer him back to Sendai? Or to a part of New Nippon where his proposed bride did not have useful connections?

Also, the norm would be that the family would have the opportunity to meet the proposed bride, and her family, before any agreement was made. They recognized that it was impractical for them to come to Japan so they could get to know each other. Isamu mentally substituted "interrogate her" for the latter.

Given that Date Masamune, as Isamu's lord, would need to approve Isamu's marriage, they thought it best to require that he personally inspect the bride on their behalf. If he approved of the marriage, then they would, too. And he, or his designee, could act in their stead for the actual ceremony.

It was obvious to Isamu that they expected that the grand governor would refuse approval. But Isamu had quietly collected testimonials from the Japanese who knew Yells-at-Bears best, swearing them to secrecy.

He didn't know, of course, whether she would consent to marriage, but he hadn't wanted to ask her until he knew that his family wouldn't block it. And with this letter in hand, he thought that Envoy Tenjiku Tokubei, or Captain Yamada Haruno, or even perhaps Commander Hosoya Yoritaki, would be willing to adopt her, thus making her part of a samurai family.

Yells-at-Bears returned from her walk, her basket filled with various plants.

"It appears you had a successful hunt," said Isamu.

"I did," said Yells-at-Bears. "How is your family?"

"No great tragedies," said Isamu. He paused and then continued, abruptly, "My family gives me permission to marry you if my lord, Grand Governor Date Masamune, after meeting you, gives his consent. Which I would need in any event. If he consents, would you be willing to be my wife?"

Yells-at-Bears dropped her basket. "Would you repeat what you just said?"

"If my lord, from whom I must get approval, consents, will you marry me?"

"I can't marry you, Isamu. You know that!"

"Why is that?"

"Because I was a slave, and therefore lost status, I am no better than a commoner now. Whereas you are a samurai." While in Snuneymuxw society, intermarriage between commoners and those of chiefly status was not unheard of, Yells-at-Bears was now not merely a commoner, but one tainted by slavery.

"Your enslavement by the Kwakwaka'wakw would have no bearing on your status in Japan."

"But in Japan, I would be considered a foreigner, neh? What is the status of foreigners? Can they marry samurai?"

"I know that there have been English, Dutch and Portuguese merchants and sailors who took Japanese wives. I am sure that most of those wives were commoners. But I think that the English pilot, William Adams, was made a *hatamoto* and took a samurai wife."

"A *hatamoto*?"

"A samurai in the direct service of the shogun."

"Well, it is not likely that I will be made a samurai, is it?" Strictly speaking, only men were samurai, but the female children of a samurai were *bushi*, that is, of the samurai class.

"There is a way. If you are adopted by a samurai, then you enter the samurai class, and a samurai may marry you. The question is, do you want to marry me?"

Yells-at-Bears took a quick look around, to make sure no one else was nearby, and then hugged him. The Japanese frowned on hugging in public. "Of course I do. But who would adopt me?"

"I will ask Haru first. Then Tokubei. And if need be, Captain Haruno and Commander Hosoya."

Yells-at-Bears smiled impishly. "I notice you didn't suggest asking Masaru."

Equally impishly, he responded, "Oh, would you like to call him 'Father'?"

"No, I have enough names for him already."

"Very well, I will find you a samurai father, and then I will need to get authorization to leave my post and take you to Kodachi Machi to meet the grand governor."

Isamu had good reason for naming Terasaka Haru as his first choice. His family had served the losing side at the Battle of Sekigahara, over thirty years ago. So he had been a *ronin* before Date Masamune had recruited him. He had served as a bodyguard for traveling merchants, a bouncer for inns and brothels, and a bandit hunter. He had even had to write letters for illiterate peasants. Fortunately for him, one of Date Masamune's clansmen had seen him defeat three would-be robbers single-handedly and, impressed by his fighting skills, brought him to Date Masamune's attention.

Still, given his checkered past, he was less likely to look down on

Yells-at-Bears than, say, a samurai of distinguished lineage who had never suffered a stain on his honor.

Isamu invited Haru to join him for a drink.

"More sake?" asked Isamu. His hand was on the handle of the *tokkuri*. It was a narrow-necked porcelain bottle with a lustrous black and silver *urushi* lacquer, a gift from Captain Haruno.

"If you please," said Haru, lifting his *ochoko* with both hands, and Isamu filled it. He passed the *tokkuri* to Haru, who then poured for him.

Isamu raised his cup. Haru matched this gesture, and Isamu shouted "*Kanpai*!" The two samurai slowly sipped the rice wine.

He explained his marital situation to Haru. "So . . . would you be willing to adopt Yells-at-Bears, so I can marry her?"

"I'll do it."

They exchanged bows.

Haru took another sip of sake. "Now, if you had wanted me to adopt a man, I would have to consult with my family, since that would affect inheritance. But a daughter is no problem. As long as you don't expect me to dowry her . . ."

"No, you needn't worry about that."

Commander Hosoya read the letter from Isamu's family, and then handed it back to him.

"So you want to take a leave of absence so you can present Yells-at-Bears to the grand governor?"

"Yes, sir."

Commander Hosoya stroked his chin. "Well, there would be some advantage in having you state the case for further development of the Texada colony in person. You can present the grand governor with a sampling of the island's products."

"I look forward to doing so."

"And it's true that Yells-at-Bears can give the grand governor a special perspective on the Texada colony's situation. That said, I will want you to stay here until the fall. Then I can spare the *Unagi Maru* to take you, Yells-at-Bears, and the samples to Kodachi Machi. Hopefully Imoji will have a full set of cannonballs by then. Perhaps he can think of something else to cast that would make a nice present for the grand governor, neh?"

Isamu bowed. "I will tell him. Thank you, sir."

"And who would you suggest be placed in charge of Texada Island in your absence?"

"Terasaka Haru. He recruited the ironworkers, and they have succeeded in smelting iron. And he has also kept an eye on the fishing village."

"Not Masaru?"

"No, sir. He has a belligerent attitude toward the natives, who far outnumber us."

"Well, I will give Haru a chance."

It was, Isamu told Yells-at-Bears, the best arrangement that he could have hoped for, given his family's attitude. Now, it was up to the two of them to persuade the grand governor to approve the match.

Chapter 33

Letter from Lope Díez de Aux de Armendáriz, marquess of Cadereyta, viceroy of New Spain, to His Catholic Majesty, Philip the Fourth of Spain:

"This humble servant of Your Majesty kisses your Royal hands and feet. I am pleased to report that the treasure galleon San Raimundo *has successfully returned from the Philippines with Chinese silk and porcelain. Your Majesty was previously informed, by my predecessor's communication of late 1634, of the fall of Manila to a treacherous surprise attack by Japanese and Dutch forces. In view of the no-doubt temporary occupation of Manila by our enemies, the galleon had been diverted by Your Majesty's servants in the vicinity of the San Bernardino Strait to the town of Cebu, which is serving as the temporary capital of the Philippines.*

"To avoid its occupation by the Dutch or Japanese, Your Majesty's representative on the Isla Hermosa made a temporary arrangement with the Chinese. I attach his letter explaining and justifying the arrangement and withdrawal. I must note that this arrangement was made without any prior consultation with me, and leave it to Your Majesty's wisdom as to whether it should be praised or condemned.

"However, I will note that there is a threat to Cebu from both the Dutch and Japanese in Manila, and the Muslims in Mindanao, and the withdrawal from Hermosa to Cebu has

served, according to local authorities, to strengthen our position in Cebu.

"Based on reports from refugees, and our spies among the natives, the authorities in Cebu estimate the Japanese forces in Manila at this time as being on the order of ten thousand troops. That greatly dwarfs the forces in Cebu and consequently we cannot regain Manila unless Your Majesty chooses to send an army to the Philippines. While the Japanese probably would not be able to transport all their troops at once, even a tenth of that number would be a serious threat to the normal garrison of Cebu, which was but a single company.

"The authorities in Cebu are grateful to now have the three companies from Hermosa. Additionally, three of the six companies stationed on Ternate have been pulled back to defend Cebu, and the San Raimundo *delivered one company that was destined for service in Manila.*

"But there is even graver news. Captain-General Mendoza of the galleon San Raimundo *reports that in the vicinity of the Bahía de Monterrey, he encountered a Japanese fishing boat. The fishermen were interrogated and it was discovered that the Japanese have established settlements on the shore of that bay. The captain-general investigated and confirmed that this was the case. Indeed, there are four settlements, at least two of them fortified, on the bay proper, and a fifth on a smaller bay just to the south. The first wave of settlers arrived there in September 1634, and a second a year later. It is believed that there are several thousand settlers already in place, and more expected to come in the fall of 1636.*

"It is the opinion of the captain-general that this colony could not have been established without the assistance of the Dutch, and it is therefore likely that the Japanese have offered the colony as a naval base for the Dutch, from which they can seek to intercept the galleon trade between Acapulco and the Philippines, and even perhaps the movement of silver from Peru to the Isthmus of Panama. I have sent avisos *to Panama and Callao to inform the* audiencia *of Panama and the viceroy of Peru of this threat.*

"I urge that we conduct an assault on this Japanese colony before it can be strengthened further. The prospects of success would be increased, of course, if our sea and land forces in the Pacific are reinforced. In view of the recent developments in the Caribbean, I cannot in good conscience recommend to Your Majesty that we move any of our forces there to the Pacific. Hence, the reinforcements would need to come from Spain.

"I would further point out that it would be easier to confront and humble the Japanese on this coast, than at Manila, or their homeland. Here, their line of supply is long, and ours is short, and in Asian waters, the reverse is true.

"Your Majesty no doubt has confidential servants in Grantville. It is possible that there are books or maps there that would have information about the climate and terrain in the vicinity of Bahía de Monterrey that would be helpful in the planning of a military operation, and I hope that Your Majesty will see fit to command his servants there to expeditiously collect such information and have it sent with your instructions.

"Curiously, Captain-General Mendoza reports that the captured Japanese fishermen claim to be Christians, and that the settlement is primarily of Christians. When captured, they were wearing crosses, and they had some knowledge of the catechism. Consequently, the fishermen were brought to Mexico City and questioned by the Office of the Inquisition. Although they do not appear to have been contaminated by the Protestant heresy, they were found to have many heretical notions inspired by their native religion.

"Hence, I do not believe that the colonists' profession of Christianity should dissuade Your Majesty from the proposed assault.

"The fishermen themselves will be brought back to a proper understanding of the True Faith by lodging them with Japanese Christians who long ago immigrated to New Spain, and thus can serve as an example to them. They will, of course, be closely watched by the Inquisition.

"We trust that after Spanish forces triumph over the Japanese at Bahía de Monterrey, and Spanish rule is

established over the settlements there, their fellow Japanese can likewise be reformed.

"May Our Lord guard and increase the Royal Catholic person of Your Majesty, with increase of greater kingdoms and dominions, as Christianity has need and we, the servants of Your Majesty, desire."

Chapter 34

Panama
June 1636

The *guardián* of the *San Diego del Milagro*, the flagship of the *Armada del Mar del Sur*, had one hand on the gently swaying mainmast and the other on his spyglass. The lead ship of the Armada, the patache *San Bartolome*, had been sent ahead to verify that the Panamanian coast was free of pirates. It would not do for His Catholic Majesty's Peruvian silver to fall into the hands of the Dutch or English, as it had in 1579. The perpetrator of that calamity, the infamous Sir Francis Drake, was no doubt roasting in the fires of Hell for his many sins.

The *guardián*'s thoughts turned to happier topics, such as his winnings the night before at *triunfo del basto*. And the use to which he would put those winnings after the Armada came to anchor.

As he meditated on this most secular topic, he continued to scan the horizon. Today, the waters of the Gulf of Panama were slate-blue, with scattered whitecaps. The pilot major of the Armada had advised that a wide berth be given to the Archipelago de las Perlas, as it offered many havens for freebooters. Of course, one could not avoid the islands closest to the port of Panama, but the *San Bartolome* would sniff out any lurking enemy pinnaces in the shadow of Taboga or Taboguilla.

Wait! Was that the *San Bartolome*? Yes, yes, it was. And it was flying yellow and red flags, the agreed-upon signal. It was safe to proceed. He yelled down the news to the pilot on the poop deck.

A few hours later, and the Armada was anchored off Perico Point, seven miles southwest of the town proper. That was as close as the galleons could come, lest they be stranded at low tide.

August 1636

Don Bernardino Hurtado de Mendoza y Larrea, general of the *Armada del Mar del Sur*, wiped sweat off his forehead while he waited impatiently to meet with Enrique Enriquez de Sotomayor, the president of the Audiencia de Panama and governor of the Province of Tierra Firme, the Spanish Main. It was a hot day even for Panama in August.

More than a month ago, he had offloaded his silver at the port of Panama. It had been taken on muleback across the Isthmus to Portobelo, to be exchanged at the annual fair there for goods from Spain.

When he received an urgent summons to the chambers of the Audiencia, he hoped that it was to be informed that the fair had finally taken place and he would soon be able to raise anchor. Panama was a swampy, malaria-ridden hellhole, and the sooner he could get back to Callao, the better. But it was true that one of his galleons, the old *Nuestra Señora de Loreto*, in service since 1621, had benefitted from a refit.

These thoughts were interrupted when an aide opened a door and said, "The Governor will see you now."

After an exchange of pleasantries, the governor sprang an unpleasant surprise on him: "You are commanded by the direct order of His Catholic Majesty, Philip the Second of Spain, to sail at the earliest opportunity to Acapulco."

"Acapulco? Why Acapulco? And what about the goods that I am supposed to take back to Callao?"

"You are to meet the Manila galleon at Acapulco."

"The Manila galleon? I heard a rumor that Manila has fallen to the Dutch and Japanese infidels."

"The rumor is true," said the governor. "Some of the refugees went to Acapulco, and thence to Ciudad de Mexico. But a galleon sailed from Cebu to Acapulco, and brought word that the Japanese have a colony on the coast of Alta California, upon the bay that Sebastián Vizcaíno discovered in 1602."

"Ah! My armada will join with the Manila galleon, and we will destroy the Japanese colony! We will have our revenge for their attack on poor Manila!"

"Indeed, we will," said the governor. "The joint force will be called the *Armada de Retribución*."

"And I will command the joint force?"

"No. His Majesty had intended that my predecessor, Sebastián Hurtado de Corcuera y Gaviria, would be the next Governor-General of the Philippines. Indeed, he is already in Acapulco, with the reinforcements intended to go to Cebu. They were to be led against our foes in the Philippines, you understand, but the Japanese in California are a riper target. He will be in overall command of the *Armada de Retribución*. Once the invaders of California are dealt with, he will continue on to the Philippines and you will return to Callao."

Don Bernardino wrinkled his nose. So his own mission was to be massively disrupted, yet he would not even receive the honor of commanding the *Armada de Retribución*? The only consolation was that the *Armada de Retribución* appeared to be poorly constituted for its purpose. The Manila galleon, after all, was a large merchant-galleon, not a war-galleon, and he could only supply two of the latter.

"Striking against the Japanese in California makes sense. But why weren't warships sent to Acapulco from the Atlantic fleets, or even Spain itself? Why deprive the viceroy of Peru of his maritime defense force?"

"I believe that His Majesty was advised that the passage of the Straits of Magellan would be too dangerous," said the governor.

Don Bernardino snorted. It was the same excuse the government had given in the past for not reinforcing the *Armada del Mar del Sur*. But Don Bernardino suspected that concerns over the dispositions and activities of the Dutch and the United States of Europe in the Caribbean might also be at play.

"And surely," the governor continued, "a Japanese settlement in California is a threat to Callao as well as Acapulco."

Don Bernardino conceded the point. It wasn't as though he had a choice. But if the Dutch or English attacked Callao in the meantime, he suspected that Luis Jerónimo Fernández de Cabrera Bobadilla Cerda y Mendoza, count of Chinchón, viceroy of Peru, would blame Don Bernardino.

And there was another problem. "Even if we have a quick victory, it will be at least six months before we can return here to pick up the merchandise for Peru. And then another three months or more before we can get it back to Callao."

The governor spread his hands. "What of it?"

"The Lima merchants will be distraught. They will have neither their silver nor their goods. Some may go bankrupt."

"They are mere merchants. Gadflies on the body of the state. You need not worry about them."

As Don Bernardino walked back to the dock, his thoughts were on those gadflies. The Lima merchants had little influence in Madrid, but they had much to say on local matters. Such as the command of the *Armada del Mar del Sur*.

He would send an urgent message to the Portobelo factors for the Lima merchants, suggesting that they hire some coasters to take their merchandise home.

And he would try to leave before they could reply, and whine for him to leave one of his ships behind.

Chapter 35

Acapulco, Viceroyalty of New Spain
November 1636

Sebastián Hurtado de Corcuera y Gaviria, commander of the *Armada de Retribución*, paced back and forth on the King's Bastion of the Castle of San Diego, the main fortress of Acapulco. A chachalaca squawked angrily at him from its perch on the parapet, disturbed by his movements, then flew off to raid the castle garden. A sudden gust of wind tried to steal away the wide-brimmed, plumed hat he was wearing, but he rescued it in the nick of time.

De Corcuera was in poor temper, and it was his turn to squawk angrily at his aide. "They call three ships—one of them a mere patache, and another an ailing grandmother of a galleon—an armada? Did they pay no attention to my report? The Japanese aren't living in beach huts, they have an actual fortress set back from the coast."

The three ships of the *Armada del Mar del Sur* had at last arrived in Acapulco. It had been a slower passage than Don Bernardino's pilot had expected. With some fairness, he blamed the *Loreto*. It had lumbered behind the other two ships, so much so, that it took an inordinate length of time just to clear the Gulf of Panama. Its captain blamed contrary winds and currents.

De Corcuera was inclined to blame everyone involved.

His aide coughed. "Don Bernardino said that in both 1634 and 1635 the Conde de Chinchón sent the Crown 200,000 pesos for the construction of four new large galleons for the Armada del Mare del Sul, but the ships have yet to arrive."

De Corcuera laughed mirthlessly. "They will never arrive. The money has doubtless been spent on something else by now."

"At least Don Bernardino's flotilla brings us up to five ships," said the aide. He was counting the galleon *San Raimundo* and a patache that de Corcuera had commandeered from Acapulco.

They heard footsteps behind them and turned. It was Guillermo del Agulla, the pilot major of the Manila Galleon.

"About time," grumbled de Corcuera.

Guillermo doffed his cap. It was not as grand as what de Corcuera was wearing. It was just a red woollen *bonete*. "How may I assist you, my lord?"

"If we were to leave this week, how long would it take us to get to Bahía de Monterrey?"

"If we follow Vizcaíno's route, we should allow six or seven months."

De Corcuera's eyes widened. "That long?"

"Knowing that was our destination, I looked up the details. He left Acapulco on May 5, 1602. He reached the harbor of San Diego on November 10. He rested there until November 20, and didn't round the Punta de los Pinos, the southern end of Bahía de Monterrey, until December 16.

"Cabrillo, a half-century earlier, fared a bit better. He left Navidad, which is a good three hundred miles closer to Monterrey, on June 27, 1542 and reached San Diego—he called it San Miguel—on September 28. He made several stops after that, and I am not sure when exactly he passed Monterrey, but my best guess is that his total sailing time from Navidad to Monterrey was four months. Unfortunately, I do not know how his route differed from Vizcaíno's."

"But you made it from Bahía de Monterrey to Acapulco in a month!"

"Indeed. We made landfall at Cabo Mendocino, a little above the fortieth parallel. From there we followed the coast all the way to Cabo San Lucas. The wind was most often from north-northwest, so we were running before the wind. And there was a strong current bearing south, some miles off the coast, which aided us, too. Returning the same route, we will face contrary wind and current."

"Can they not be avoided?"

"At the cost of going far from the direct path. We can go south to pick up the trade winds, head west, then go north to pick up the westerlies in the forties, and finally descend from Cabo Mendocino."

"And how long would that take?"

He shrugged. "No man can say, as the route has not yet been tried. If we don't go west far enough, we will still be caught in the contrary winds, and will have lengthened our journey rather than shortened it. If we go too far, then we lose the advantage the trades and the westerlies would otherwise give us.

"Also, remember that in the northerly leg, we will be crossing the horse latitudes, where calms are common and rain infrequent. We know the best places to cross the horse latitudes in the Atlantic, but not in the Pacific."

"Hmmph. Let's see what this looks like on a map. You brought one, I hope."

"I did, sir." He held up a leather tube. "But let us move out of the wind, into an alcove. Or better yet, indoors."

They found a place to spread out the map. The map in question was one of the new ones prepared by the cosmographers of the House of Trade in Seville since the Ring of Fire. It copied the North American coastline from some up-time map, but with only the positions of down-time settlements marked. And with all names in Spanish, of course.

"All right," said de Corcuera. "I see where Cabo Mendocino, Bahía de Monterrey, and Cabo San Lucas are. And it seems to me that there is a military advantage in coming to Bahía de Monterrey from the north. The Japanese fishermen said that the main Japanese fortress, Kodachi Machi, is on the north coast of the bay. So we are much more likely to surprise it if we come from the north than from the south."

"That is true, sir," said Guillermo. "Especially if the wind is northerly, which would delay the armada's crossing of the bay from south to north."

Guillermo crossed his arms. "But I cannot recommend risking an entire squadron on a completely untried route, my lord."

"And if I were to order its use?"

"I would of course comply, but I would want a document acknowledging that I warned of the risks and uncertainties and was absolved of responsibility if the route proved worse than the direct one."

"That's an extraordinary request."

"Oh? Pilots Major have been executed if they were deemed responsible for the loss of a single war-galleon. What would a court of inquiry do to one whose piloting doomed five ships? In fact, I think it best that I hold a council with all the pilots, and we make a joint recommendation as to how far to sail west before turning north."

"Fine. Hold your council, and do so quickly. In the meantime, I will try to get supplies enough for a six month passage, just in case the offshore route is no better than the direct one."

The pilots from the five ships met at the Fort of San Diego, and the area of greatest disagreement was with regard to how far west to go before turning north. No one knew how far out to sea the coastal winds extended. One favored going only as far as the longitude of Cabo Mendocino, then turning. According to the up-time maps, that was near the 124th west meridian, whereas Santa Cruz was on the 122nd.

At the other extreme, one of the pilots from Callao remembered that two explorers had successfully sailed north in the mid-Pacific. First, there was Mendaña, who left Callao in 1567. He had passed through the Marshall Islands. And then in 1605, Quirós had passed between the Marshall and Gilbert Island chains. Both had ultimately turned east and made landfall in western North America. The up-time maps showed that the Marshalls and Gilberts were between the 180th meridian and the 165th west meridian.

If the pilot major did not want to take the slow but sure way up the coast, taking advantage of the land and sea breezes, then he should attempt to turn north some place west of the 180th meridian, the Peruvian said.

The pilot major shook his head. "So you want to sail more than halfway to Asia? Just how long is that route?" They were pilots, not cosmographers, so none knew for sure. They did know that the map distorted distances as one moved away from the equator. But their best guess was 2500 to 3000 *legua geographica*. If there were good winds along the entire route, the trip might take two months. But chances were that the northerly leg would be quite slow so . . . who could say?

"Come, my friends! What do you think de Corcuera will say if we give him this advice? He is no cosmographer, but he can look at a map!

"Suppose we were to turn between the 155th and 160th meridians. That is where the up-time maps placed the Hawaiian Islands. If the voyage is overly slow, that would at least provide a place to reprovision."

"Do we know anything about those islands?" one asked.

"I have not heard of them being visited by any of the Manila galleons," said the pilot major. "But if we are running low on food or drinking water, well, God willing, they will serve."

The pilots at last agreed that the northing should be attempted between the 150th and 170th meridian, the precise timing to be at the discretion of the pilot major.

After the meeting of the pilots, the pilot major had dinner with Father Blanco at an inn in Acapulco Town.

"It is all so absurd, like a story of Don Quixote," said Guillermo.

"How so?"

"We only know our longitude by dead reckoning," said Guillermo. "And the further we sail, the greater is the uncertainty, unless we come to a place of known longitude. So where we turn north is really based on a wild guess!

"There was a story told in the House of Trade in Seville that described what happened when three pilots from the same flotilla compared notes on the same day of their journey. One said that they were two hundred leagues from the coast, the second said that they were only fifty, and the third confessed that by his calculations, they were on top of a mountain range."

"I will pray for you," said Father Blanco.

The boatswain of the galleon *San Raimundo* blew his whistle. The men on board the galleon shouted, "God save you, Lord Captain-General!" and a single cannon was fired. A moment later, the other ships of the newly formed *Armada de Retribución* followed suit.

Once the white smoke cleared, Sebastián Hurtado de Corcuera y Gaviria, the captain-general of the *Armada de Retribución*, boarded the *San Raimundo*. He wore a white cloak and tunic, and on the back of the cloak was a green Greek cross, symbolizing that he was a Knight of the Order of Alcántara.

De Corcuera had assumed command of galleon *San Raimundo* and made it his flagship, it being the largest vessel in the armada. The former commander of the galleon *San Raimundo*, the captain-general of the galleons, had taken ill a few months earlier. It had come as no surprise to anyone, Acapulco being a notoriously unhealthy port. He had been sent to Veracruz to recuperate.

De Corcuera's second-in-command was Don Bernardino Hurtado de Mendoza y Larrea, in the galleon *San Diego del Milagro*. Today, de Corcuera knew, Don Bernardino wore a black cloak and tunic. The red cross of St. James embroidered above his heart signified that he was a Knight of the Order of Santiago.

De Corcuera fought back a twinge of annoyance that Don Bernardino's Order of Santiago, although newer than that of Alcántara, was wealthier and more powerful.

Today, the cargo of the *San Raimundo* was not porcelain or silks. It was soldiers. Soldiers stood at attention, shoulders touching, on the main deck of the *San Raimundo*. There were so many of them that most of the sailors were hanging from the rigging rather than standing. And there were more below deck.

Captain-General de Corcuera made a gesture to Father Blanco, the chaplain of the *San Raimundo*. "Father, you may proceed with the prayer."

Blanco cleared his throat. "Lord, have mercy on us . . ."

De Corcuera was pleased that his dread majesty, Philip of Spain, had at last ordered the viceroy of New Spain to send a punitive expedition against the Japanese. Not against their homeland, where they were strongest. Nor against Manila, the former jewel in the Spanish imperial crown, where they reportedly had ten thousand troops, repaired fortifications, and Dutch warships to resist any attempt to recapture the city. But against their new colony on Monterey Bay. The Japanese had overextended, and their loathsome tentacle in the New World would be cut off by Spanish might.

"Our Lady of Victory, pray for us . . ."

The Virgin Mary had been accorded that title in 1571, after the Christian forces triumphed over the Turks at the Battle of Lepanto. Once again, the Church Militant sallied forth against the pagans, this time those of Japan.

De Corcuera quickly suppressed the passing thought that it had been reported that the Japanese of Monterey Bay were actually

Christians. The report, surely, was in error, as the Japanese suppression of the Faith had begun decades ago. And only last year, when the Japanese took Manila, they had gone to special pains to hunt down the Christian priests, like Father Blanco.

The prayer came at last to an end, and the assembly was dismissed. De Corcuera turned to the pilot major. "Raise anchor, and signal our escorts to do the same." Guillermo saluted, and started barking orders.

For most of the voyage from Cebu to Acapulco, the guns of the *San Raimundo* had been stowed below deck, the better to cram cargo on board. Not so today. Still, the role of the *San Raimundo* in the present expedition was intended to be that of troop carrier. Shore bombardment, or engagement of enemy warships, would be primarily the task of the two war-galleons that would be accompanying the *San Raimundo* on this expedition.

The two war-galleons were both about 600 *toneladas*. They were thus considered large galleons, although the *San Raimundo*, as an armed merchant-galleon built for the Acapulco-Manila run, was larger still. The *San Diego del Milagro* carried 44 guns, some as heavy as third- and quarter-cannons, and the *Nuestra Señora de Loreto* was built to the same plan and was similarly armed. Unfortunately, the *Loreto* had been in service since 1621, and its pilot had already made disparaging but accurate remarks about its seaworthiness. De Corcuera sincerely hoped that this would not be a problem, but he couldn't afford to leave it behind; there were too few capital ships on the Pacific Coast.

At least he didn't have to worry about the *San Diego del Milagro*. It had come into service in 1631 and had replaced the *Loreto* as the *Armada del Mar del Sur*'s flagship.

A two-masted, hundred ton patache, the *Galgo*, was the first ship to leave the harbor, followed by the one hundred-and-fifty ton patache *San Bartolome*. Each carried just two guns, not counting swivel guns. These light vessels were followed by the *San Diego*, the *San Raimundo*, and the lumbering *Loreto*. All were flying flags with the red Cross of Burgundy on a white field.

They passed though the Boca Chica and out into the open sea.

The die was cast; the Spanish campaign to annihilate New Nippon had begun.

Chapter 36

Kodachi Machi (Santa Cruz), Monterey Bay
November 1636

Kodachi Machi lay to the west of the San Lorenzo River, on the site of modern Santa Cruz. It was really three towns in one: a fishing village called "Lower Kodachi Machi"; a farming village called "Middle Kodachi Machi"; and a castle called "Upper Kodachi Machi" or "the High Fortress." The fishing village was originally the Uypi Indian village of Aulintak. The natives still lived there, but the village had expanded in size, and now included some Japanese fishermen's huts and, further from the beach, a couple of more substantial buildings.

A guard boat hailed the *Unagi Maru* as it approached the mouth of the San Lorenzo. "Who are you?" bellowed the samurai in command.

"Oyamada Isamu, samurai in the service of Lord Date Masamune."

"Ah. You are free to proceed but for my records, what is the name of your vessel?"

"The *Unagi Maru*. I am here with confidential reports and goods from the north for the grand governor. Where will I find him?"

"At the High Fortress. Water levels in the San Lorenzo are low right now, so unless your ship draws no more than three feet, you'll need to requisition a horse at the fishing village." He pointed at the beach behind him. "And carts, if you have cargo to deliver."

Torakichi, the first mate of the *Unagi Maru*, called out, "where should we anchor?"

The guard boat samurai gave him directions.

The headman's house was easy enough to find as it was made of wood. Beside the headman's house was a small stable, and the harbor guard's barrack. These, too, were made of wood.

In contrast, the fishermen's huts were of a cruder construction. Torakichi, who had come to Kodachi Machi previously, when he was the third mate on the *Ieyasu Maru*, told Isamu and Yells-at-Bears that the fishermen's huts were constructed like the nearby homes of the local Uypi, one of the many bands of Ohlone Indians in central California.

The Japanese, copying the Ohlone, fastened bundles of tule rush to a framework of bent willow poles. The tule was a giant sedge found in the marshes that dominated the central coast of Monterey Bay. Torakichi called it *iwashiba,* which was the name for a sedge found in Japan.

However, the Japanese favored smaller huts, housing a single family, whereas some of the Ohlone huts were large enough for two or three.

Isamu found the Japanese headman and identified himself. He signed out a horse and several carts, and the sailors who had brought him to Monterey Bay loaded up the carts. Getting the headman to spare an ox for each cart proved difficult and ultimately Isamu had to bribe him.

There was then a further delay as Yells-at-Bears refused to come near the horse. She had never seen one before—the Japanese had not brought any to Texada yet—and she did not like the look of its teeth, or the way it snorted. Isamu finally persuaded her to board the last cart, the one furthest from the horse. He was thankful that the colonists on Texada had brought a few oxen, so they weren't strange to her anymore.

Bluebird's reaction was similar to Yells-at-Bears', but she reluctantly sat beside Yells-at-Bears for the ride up to the fortress.

Following the headman's instructions, they rode north along the west bank of the San Lorenzo River. After a mile or two, they came to a guard post, which lay just west of what the headman had told them was the most southerly fording point on the river. Of course, having come up the west bank, they hadn't had to plod through the ford, which was just as well.

The guardsman told them to take the road away from the ford. It would run west, past the farming village, and then curve toward the High Fortress.

The farming village, they saw, was situated on a bluff perhaps eighty feet high. The bluff was the tip of a huge, arrowhead-shaped ridge that pointing southeast. The village had a wooden palisade and a couple of watchtowers. However, they were not challenged as they passed them.

As they rounded the village, they gradually ascended, until at last they were at the same level as the village. It was clear that these were benchlands, and the farming village was on the first bench.

The High Fortress appeared to be on a southeasterly spur from the second bench, perhaps two hundred fifty feet above sea level. On the near side, its southeast side, there was a steep drop-off down to the first bench.

Isamu saw that their road led, by a couple of switchbacks, to the south corner of the fortress. Isamu's party followed the road and eventually they saw that it led to a narrow but deep ravine separating the southwest side of the fortress from an adjacent spur. The road went up the ravine to a western gate tower covering both sides of the top of the ravine.

Well, thought Isamu, *I wouldn't want to be part of a unit trying to take that gate. . . .*

The grade was such that only one sailor stayed on each cart, the others walking behind it to help push.

They were challenged as they approached the gate tower. Isamu this time indicated that he was the acting *daikan* of Texada Island, and was here to report.

The gate opened and Isamu's party entered the dark gate tunnel. They emerged into a small courtyard, and turned right, where there was a second gate. This brought them into a second courtyard, where they turned right again. The tallest building, of course, would be where they would find Date Masamune, but Isamu was curious and he walked over to the north battlement, Yells-at-Bears following. Here, he saw, was a long drop, down to the river valley.

So, as he pointed out to Yells-at-Bears, the triangular High Fortress was well-situated. The only place where the ground in front of the walls was level was at the west corner, where there was a small keep containing the gate tower. Of course, if artillery could be brought up to the second bench, it would be at the same height as the High Fortress and could do serious damage if it were close enough, but given that the second bench was heavily forested, that wouldn't be easy.

Isamu and Yells-at-Bears returned to their party and continued on to the central keep. There, they delivered the reports and goods to the grand governor's steward, and were shown to a room in which to await the grand governor's summons. That came several hours later. The summons was just for Isamu and Yells-at-Bears; Bluebird was left in the waiting room with Captain Araki and First Mate Torakichi.

The audience room inside the central keep would not have impressed Date Masamune's fellow daimyo back home, but Yells-at-Bears was awed by it.

Date Masamune, wearing a baggy-sleeved black *kataginu* and a skull cap, was seated cross-legged on a *zaisu*, essentially a cushion with a chair back. The sharkskin-wrapped hilt of his katana was barely visible under the folds of his garment. His cushion, of course, was on a raised dais.

Isamu bowed and folded himself into the formal *seiza* position, his buttocks resting on his heels. Yells-at-Bears also bowed, but instead adopted the "sideways sitting" position that was more comfortable for women in traditional dress.

"Welcome, Oyamada Isamu! Welcome, Yells-at-Bears of the Snuneymuxw!"

Both of them bowed again.

"Isamu. I have read your report, and those of your colleagues, and I am very pleased with what you have accomplished on Texada. I understand that you have brought me the first Texada-made cannonballs."

"Yes, sir. Also a war fan, decorated with scenes of Texada, and a helmet with 'thunderbird wings.' Both cast from Texada iron."

"Excellent! And I have some presents for you." He gestured toward the items on a *chabudai*, a short-legged table, placed against one of the walls.

"Thank you, Date-sama."

"Now, I understand that the two of you would like to get married, which of course would require my permission since you are in my service."

Both Isamu and Yells-at-Bears tensed, slightly but noticeably. "Yes, sir. Yells-at-Bears has been adopted by Terasaka Haru, who is also a samurai in your service, so this would be a *bushi*-to-*bushi* marriage."

"And your family has asked me to evaluate the prospective bride for them."

"That is true, my lord. Our fate rests in your hands."

"Well, I have no absolute objection to marriages between Japanese and the natives. Yells-at-Bears appears to be in excellent health, and you brought me letters testimonial on her behalf from Captain Yamada Haruno, Commander Hosoya Yoritaki, and Negotiator Tenjiku Tokubei. And of course Terasaka Haru's actions speak in her favor! However, while I respect those individuals, I do not know them that well.

"Your family has imposed a grave responsibility upon me. Your Oyamada clan has served the Date clan for generations, and it would be inappropriate for me to decide on the basis of this brief meeting whether Yells-at-Bears is a suitable bride to enter your family."

Isamu's expression relaxed ever so slightly. There had been the possibility that the grand governor would reject the marriage out-of-hand.

The grand governor continued, "I think it best if Yells-at-Bears spends a few months here, where she can be observed by my chief advisors, my family, and myself. According to the testimonials, and Isamu's report, you have learned Japanese. Is that true, Yells-at-Bears?"

Isamu gently nudged the somewhat awestruck Yells-at-Bears.

"I speak Japanese," said Yells-at-Bears, "but I cannot read it, Masamune-sama. I only know a few *kanji*."

"Well, I have a proposal for you," said Masamune. "I want you to spend a few months here at Kodachi Machi, teaching the Indian languages you know to my scholars. Explain the cultures of the different peoples of your territory to them, too. Perhaps you may also help them learn some of our local Indian languages, since you are obviously a natural at picking up new languages. And in turn, you may learn to read and write Japanese."

It was, Isamu knew, more of a command than a proposal. He did not like the thought of being separated from Yells-at-Bears by a thousand miles, but he could not think at first of how to phrase this in a way compatible with his duty of fealty.

At last, he replied, "Thank you my lord. It is our pleasure and duty to serve. I hope that I, too, may serve you here at Kodachi Machi for a few months."

Date Masamune was silent for a few moments, and Isamu feared that he dared too much. After all, he had already left Texada in Haru's hands for the time needed for the round trip between it and Kodachi Machi. Would the grand governor consider a further absence to be dereliction of duty? If so, he could lose both his position and the prospect of marriage to Yells-at-Bears.

"You were the acting *daikan* for Texada Island. It will be difficult to find a position of equal or greater responsibility here in Monterey Bay, especially since you intend to return to Texada."

Isamu bowed. "I do not mind taking on a lesser position here in Monterey Bay for a few months. It would be wonderful to have the opportunity to observe how you have developed this colony."

"Hmm . . . The ship you came on, the *Unagi Maru* . . . According to your report, it has both sails and oars? And it is shallow draft?"

"You have virtually exhausted my nautical knowledge, Date-sama, but that is all correct."

"Well, I am going to have to ask you to leave your sweetheart behind for a month or two. I want you to lead an exploration party down south along the coast. You will take my mining engineer and a Chumash translator with you. We know that there is jade in the Big Sur region and I want the coast checked for jade deposits. Then visit the Chumash at Morro Bay and the *eta* village nearby. Question them about mineral deposits, too. Finally, sail to San Diego Bay and look for any sign that the Spanish have reached it. Then return here.

"You should be able to head south under sail, and return with the aid of the current that runs north along the coast in November through February. At least, the part of the coast we've explored so far. But if it doesn't run as far south as San Diego, well"—he shrugged—"you may try to find a favorable wind, or you can row.

"I will give you additional samurai since you are going into unknown territory. Once you return, I will give you a post here in the castle, or nearby, if Yells-at-Bears isn't finished with her work for me."

Isamu pondered this proposal. It would mean a separation, but at least he would not be a thousand miles away from Yells-at-Bears.

"Thank you, my lord!"

"You are excused. My steward will assign quarters. Please tell Captain Araki I will be calling for him shortly."

After Isamu and Yells-at-Bears left, Date Masamune called out, "Chiyo-hime, you may come out now!"

His daughter Chiyo-hime had been listening from behind a screen.

"So, I want you to make friends with Yells-at-Bears. Get a sense for what sort of person she is, and whether she would be a suitable wife for a samurai destined for bigger things."

"I can do that, Father. But it is a pity that you must separate the two lovers."

"It is deliberate, Chiyo-hime. I do not know to what extent this attachment is a matter of happenstance. She was the only woman in the Texada exploration party and on Texada they were never apart for more than a few hours or days at a time. If their match is destined by Heaven, it will survive this separation."

"Yells-at-Bears? Is that you?"

Yells-at-Bears turned. The speaker was Heishiro. He was one of the Japanese castaways that the *Ieyasu Maru* had rescued from the Nakomgilisala, a Kwak'wala-speaking tribe living at the northern end of Vancouver Island. She had known him for only a couple of months, since they parted ways when the *Ieyasu Maru* left Yells-at-Bears on Texada, but she had learned her first Japanese words and phrases from him. And of course they had the bond of both having been slaves of the Kwakwaka'wakw.

And now, here they both were, in the inner courtyard of the High Fortress.

"I am glad to see you are well, Heishiro."

"And I am pleased to say the same about you.

"You are here to help the grand governor's scholars learn your languages?"

"So I have been told. How does that work?"

"When I arrived here, I was asked to try to remember words and phrases in the Nakomgilisala dialect of Kwak'wala, and write down how they are pronounced and their meaning in Japanese."

"You know *kanji*?" Those were the tens of thousands of Chinese characters used by the Japanese.

"Oh no," said Heishiro. "Just *katakana*." That was a syllabary. "I write down the Nakomgilisala words phonetically."

"The *katakana* has symbols for all the sounds of Nakomgilisala?"

"Unfortunately, no. We had to invent some. And a scholar sits down with me and adds the *kanji* for the translation."

"And how are these lists used? Are there Nakomgilisala here?"

Heishiro crossed his arms. "None that I have met. No, the lists are sent to Japan, and I think they are supposed to be given to the colonists sent to the 'Thousand Island' *han* so they can study them before they arrive."

"It's a good idea, but we have received two batches of colonists on Texada, and none of them spoke any Kwak'wala before they arrived."

Heishiro shrugged. "I am not surprised. The *bakufu* bureaucracy loves to collect paper. Actually helping people, not so much."

"Who's in charge of the language study, and where do I find him?"

"Her actually. In theory, at least. One of the grand governor's daughters, Chiyo-hime, made friends among the local Indians. Some of them learned Japanese, and some of our people learned the local languages, so they formed a 'corps of translators.' There are now pairs of translators stationed at each of the settlements.

"She will probably want to know about how your people live, but she'll leave word list compilation to one of the old men. Probably Yamaguchi Takuma, a commoner like us."

Yells-at-Bears winced, but held her peace. Heishiro didn't know that Yells-at-Bears had lost chiefly class status as result of her enslavement, and hence that she was sensitive on the issue of rank.

"He used to be a merchant in Nagasaki, but he can read, write and count, so now he's a minor administrator. He will probably be the one to quiz you about word meanings and record them for the *bakufu*."

"So are you a full-time language scholar now?"

Heishiro laughed. "Hardly. I have a fishing boat again." Heishiro had been the captain of a fishing boat wrecked by a storm near Japan and carried by the North Pacific currents to Vancouver Island. "And one of my sons fishes with me."

"And the other?"

"He is a servant here at the High Fortress. I came here today to visit him. We are also paid to practice our Kwak'wala regularly, although it doesn't seem likely that we would ever get to use it again."

"What is this 'Thousand Island' *han* you mention?"

"Well, you know what a *han* is, it's a domain ruled by a daimyo. The shogun sent three commissioners here and they decided that New Nippon was too big for the grand governor to rule it all directly. So they divided it into three *hans*, and the one in the north is called 'Thousand Islands.'"

Yells-at-Bears pondered this. It was true that there were many small islands between Vancouver Island and the mainland, but as far as she knew, the Japanese had only settled on Texada. Did the new name mean that the Japanese planned to expand? Few of the islands were as little used by the Indians as Texada, and even so there had been conflict.

"And who is to be the daimyo of this Thousand Islands *han*?"

"That has not been publicly announced, and the grand governor doesn't confide in me."

The following day, while Isamu met with Iwakushu, the grand governor's mining engineer, Yells-at-Bears and Bluebird answered a summons from Chiyo-hime.

One of the things that both Yells-at-Bears and Bluebird, like the Ohlone Indians, found strange about the Japanese was their preference that each nuclear family have a house of its own. That was, indeed, one of the reasons that the Japanese colonists on Texada moved out of the "Welcome House" as quickly as they could. In contrast, the Snuneymuxw spent at least the winter in longhouses, each holding an extended family.

The central keep of this castle seemed to the two women to be like one giant longhouse. In the Pacific Northwest, a longhouse was divided by woven mats into separate compartments for each family. Here in the keep, there were wooden walls.

A servant ushered them into Chiyo-hime's receiving room, whose floor was covered by *tatami* mats. Only a few of the Japanese homes built the past year or so in Texada had *tatami*.

The room was on one of the upper floors of the keep, and hence it had a window, closed by a *shoji*, a sliding screen covered with white paper. But since this was a room in a fortress, there were also wooden shutters that could be barred in place.

On one wall there was a painting, which appeared to be of a large black and white bird, with outstretched wings, flying over the very top of the castle.

Yells-at-Bears and Bluebird sat on a *tatami*, Bluebird copying Yells-at-Bears' posture as best she could.

Chiyo-hime entered the room, and they inclined their heads to show respect. The grand governor's daughter was wearing a black silk kimono, with orange flower and white butterfly embroidery.

"Welcome to Kodachi Machi," said Chiyo-Hime. "Yells-at-Bears, my father has asked to make sure you settle in comfortably here at the castle. Is there anything you need?"

"Your father's steward has been most helpful in getting us settled in."

"My father shared with me the reports he received about Texada—and you—from Tokubei, Captain Haruno and Isamu. It appears that you are one of those people for whom the wheel of karma keeps turning. I am happy that you are now prospering."

"Thank you, my lady."

"But the reports didn't say anything about your companion. Please tell me about her."

"Her name is Bluebird, my lady. We were childhood friends, but we were separated for many years, and I only recently found her. I am training her to be my assistant."

"Ah. Does she speak any Japanese?"

Yells-at-Bears spoke to Bluebird in Halkomelem. Since Rain's slighting remark about Yells-at-Bears' accent, Yells-at-Bears had tried to speak to Bluebird in her native language, rather than Kwak'wala, whenever possible.

"*Watashi wa nihonjin ga sukunai*," said Bluebird. It meant, literally, "I have little Japanese." The phrasing was awkward, but Yells-at-Bears didn't correct her. Nor did Chiyo-hime.

"Well, it takes time to learn a new language. Please, translate what I say for Bluebird, so she doesn't feel left out. I know only a little of the languages that the Indians of Monterey Bay speak. It doesn't help that there are at least three of them. Awaswas here on the north side, Mutsun near Niji Masu, and Rumsen near Kawamachi, Andoryu and Maruya. I know Rumsen best, because I have a good friend that is of one of the Rumsen bands. Are there many different languages spoken up north?"

"Dozens," said Yells-at-Bears. "But there is trade and intermarriage, and so in each village, there are people who know the languages of nearby tribes. Nuu-chah-nulth and Kwak'wala are especially widely known."

"Interesting. Here, the nearer Indians have been learning some Japanese. We hope that it will become the common language for all the tribes of Monterey Bay, but that will take time."

"Excuse me," said Yells-at-Bears. "Let me explain to Bluebird what we have been discussing." There was a hurried interchange, and Yells-at-Bears added, "Bluebird reminds me that some tribes, especially those on the mainland, have hand gestures, too." The Snuneymuxw had close relations with several of the coastal mainland tribes, especially the Sto:lo of the lower Fraser River.

"Interesting. The reports tell me about the work you do for the colony. But what do you do to amuse yourself?"

"To amuse myself?" Yells-at-Bears was not quite sure how to answer the question. "Over our first winter on Texada, Isamu taught me how to play go, and *shogi*, and *sugoroku*. And we have also played ball games."

"Ah, so you have exercised both the mind and body."

"Well, an even better exercise for my body has been practicing archery and *naginata-jutsu*."

"*Naginata-jutsu*? You can be my sparring partner!"

"I would be honored, my lady."

"We can ride together, too."

Yells-at-Bears made a face. "Horses are evil-looking beasts."

"To do our language research, we may need to travel to visit the Indians in their villages, as some are not willing to come to Kodachi Machi. We can travel at lot faster on horseback than on foot. Being able to ride a horse is as important here as being able to row a canoe is in the Salish Sea."

It was time for Isamu to commence his expedition. Yells-at-Bears and Bluebird rode on one of the carts taking supplies down to the *Unagi Maru*, and Isamu was on horseback.

When they reached the harbor, Isamu helped Yells-at-Bears off the cart. "You really are going to need to learn to ride a horse."

"So Chiyo-hime has told me. But what use will that skill be when we return to Texada?"

"We have no idea when, or even if, that will happen. But I think horses will be brought to Texada eventually. It would make it easier to coordinate the defenses of the different villages."

"I suppose. Well, if I have to learn to ride a horse, you should learn how to sail a boat!"

"I will ask Captain Araki to teach me," Isamu promised. "I can promise him that I have no bad habits to unlearn."

"Make great discoveries, to impress the grand governor!" demanded Yells-at-Bears. "But don't take stupid risks and justify them as following the code of Bushido!"

"I won't. Wasn't I the voice of reason on Texada?"

"Maybe. Most of the time, at least." Yells-at-Bears fought back a sniffle. "Come back to me."

"I will. Stay away from handsome samurai until I return."

Yells-at-Bears put her fists on her hips. "All right . . . but don't dawdle."

Chapter 37

Valley South of San Francisco Bay
November 1636

Iroha-hime, the eldest daughter of Grand Governor Date Masamune, and her party had traveled north along the west bank of Coyote Creek all day. The stream itself ran along the Diablo Range, the east side of Santa Clara Valley, and was heavily braided, with the main channel perhaps eighty feet wide and the outer banks separated by at least double that distance. The gurgling of the water served as a counterpoint to the calls of the birds. The wet season had only begun a month ago and so the water levels were still low, with only the main channel running. The banks were open, save for the occasional silver-barked sycamore tree, and some shrubs.

She was dressed for riding, more or less like the men in her party, a butterfly hairpin in her hair being her only feminine concession. And she rode as they did, the European custom of forcing women to ride side-saddle never having caught on in Japan. For that matter, the missionaries had failed to persuade the Japanese that their horses should wear horseshoes nailed to their hooves. Instead, Nihonjin steeds wore straw shoes that were tied to their legs and replaced as needed.

In mid-afternoon, they entered the Lesser Narrows, where the valley, which had been five miles wide when they entered it from the south, narrowed to just two miles. On their right, on the other side of Coyote Creek, was grassland. To their left, there was a valley oak savanna. This continued for about three miles before giving way to more grassland.

As the sun dipped beneath the peaks of the Santa Cruz Mountains to their west, they could see ahead of them the Greater Narrows, perhaps a mile and a half across. Sanada Jiro, who had led the first overland expedition to the South Bay, was in the lead, and he raised his hand. He motioned for Iroha-hime to come join him.

Sanada Jiro pointed northward. "See the hill in front of us, Iroha-hime? Would it not make a wonderful site for a fortress? It commands the Greater Narrows."

She could see that it did. It divided the Greater Narrows in half, with Coyote Creek passing to the northwest of the hill. "How tall do you think it is?"

He shrugged. "Perhaps five hundred feet."

"And I assume that it has fresh water . . . at least when Coyote Creek is running."

"Not just from Coyote Creek," said Jiro. "There's a long lake that runs southeast from the hill, parallel to the creek. I don't know what it's like at high summer in a dry year, but it's had water every time I've passed this way. And on one side, near 'Fortress Hill,' there's a willow grove."

Iroha knew that willows were thirsty trees. "And how far is it to the Bay coast?"

"Another day's ride."

She sighed. "That is too far for it to serve as a refuge for the colonists at Sausuendo. But perhaps we should send some farmers here at some point. Have them see whether it might be possible to grow rice here, neh?"

They continued on, passing through another stretch of valley oak savanna and then into grassland once more. By this point, they were close to Fortress Hill, and the eastern sky was a *konio-iro* blue.

Her senior guardsman, Matsuoka Nagatoki, called, "Make camp!"

Iroha-hime dismounted with some relief. Having to entertain the shogunal commissioners that had come to Monterey Bay with the Third Fleet meant that she hadn't ridden for a month, and her thighs had been reminding her that it was imprudent to ride long distance after such a period of inactivity.

This was her second full day in the saddle, and she was looking forward to escaping to the privacy of her tent, when her maid Koya could apply a salve to Iroha's reddened thighs.

The tent poles were dragged behind one of the pack horses on a kind of travois. Koya and the other servants unloaded the tent poles, stays, canvas, and *tatami*, and set up the two tents, one for Iroha and Koya, and the other for the samurai. Both were adorned with a repeating pattern of the Date *mon*.

They ate deer stew—none of them were devout Buddhists—and then retired. Iroha slept uneasily. She had been given a great responsibility and wondered whether she could shoulder it.

At daybreak they broke camp and continued on. Soon, they left the hills behind.

When they stopped to let the horses drink, Date Iroha-hime shaded her eyes and looked north. Was that the south end of San Francisco Bay ahead? Or just haze? The land here was very flat, the flood plain for the Guadelupe River and Coyote Creek.

"Jiro-san!" she called out.

Sanada Jiro brought his horse alongside hers. "How may I be of service, my lady?"

"How much farther do we have to go?" It had been Jiro and his brother Saburo who had blazed the trail from the south end of San Francisco Bay to Niji Masu, on Monterey Bay.

Jiro studied the shapes of the mountains to either side of them. "I think we may be able to reach Sausuendo by sunset."

"Then let's quicken our pace."

At last they reached the village of Sausuendo.

"Wait, my lady!" Date Iroha-hime's senior guard, Matsuoka Nagatoki, steadied her horse, and Iroha dismounted.

"Well, it appears that Daidoji Shigehisa has been busy," she muttered. Two years ago, she and her shipwrecked companions from the *Sado Maru* had arrived here by raft. Until she was rescued by the *Ieyasu Maru* in December 1634, she had lived in what she had dubbed "Sadomaru Palace," a lean-to made of salvaged ship timbers and sailcloth, and traded Japanese goods for food produced by the local Tamyen Indians.

After the *Ieyasu Maru* completed its search for other survivors of her husband's *Sado Maru* gold hunting expedition, she had been brought to Monterey Bay. There, in February 1635, she had pointed out to her father the strategic advantage of a settlement at the southern end of San Francisco Bay, which could be reached by land from Monterey Bay. She had urged, unsuccessfully, that she lead the settlers back there.

Instead, he had placed them under the command of Daidoji Shigehisa, her deceased husband's former guard commander. The *Miyagi Maru*, one of the Second Fleet ships, had transported some of the new arrivals from Monterey Bay to Sausuendo, and to a second settlement on the east side of San Francisco Bay. It did not return to Japan; it was used for communication among the settlements of San Francisco Bay.

Shigehisa was now bowing to her. "Welcome back, Iroha-hime. Allow me to escort you to suitable quarters." A servant standing behind him also bowed, but more deeply.

Iroha thanked him, and turned to address her maid. "Koya . . ."

Koya was engrossed in conversation with two of Iroha's guards, Sanada Jiro and his younger brother, Sanada Saburo.

"Koya! Attend me!"

Jiro and Saburo showed a sudden interest in adjusting their saddles.

The maid bowed deeply, her face flushed, and responded, "Yes, my lady?"

"Lead our pack horses to the stables. Shigehisa-san's servant will show you the way."

Koya complied with these instructions and headed off, the little tambourine-like jingles hanging from the pack horses' saddles clinking together musically.

When the Sanada brothers started to move in the same direction, Matsuoka Nagatoki called them to heel.

"How was your journey?" asked Shigehisa.

"Uneventful," admitted Nagatoki. "No natives approached us."

"I am not surprised. They do not have horses, and those who have never seen ours think a horse-and-rider is some strange monstrosity, more dangerous than even a grizzly bear."

Iroha saw that many of the houses were made Ohlone style; that is, with bundles of tule rush tied to a framework of bent willow poles.

"Commander Shigehisa, are there natives living among us?"

"Only a few," he said. "But I understand why you think that." He waved toward the tule huts. "This was a matter of necessity. While there are sycamore, cottonwood, oak and other trees within a few miles of Sausuendo, and they could be cut and floated down the Guadeloupe River or Coyote Creek, it was much easier for the colonists to build with the materials found close to the shoreline."

That said, Iroha could see that Sausuendo had several wooden constructions: the stables, a tall watchtower, a residential building, and several *funaya*. The *funaya* were two-story boat houses, with the boats housed on the first floor, and the family living above them. Their presence suggested that some of the colonists had once lived on the Sea of Japan.

The residential building stood on pilings—no surprise, there was a flood risk here—and was just a single story, but it had a tiled roof. The tiles, which were in the style common in Nagasaki, had no doubt been carried over on one of the Second Fleet ships and intended to mark the home of a village headman.

Shigehisa led Iroha and her entourage to the house with the tiled roof. That was, as she expected, his own home as the administrator of the colony.

The main course at dinner was shellfish, dug up from the mudflats at the southern end of the bay. These came in great variety: mussels, clams, oysters, abalones, and more. Shigehisa had a folding screen depicting a scene from the *Matsukaze*, a three-century old Noh drama, displayed in his dining area. It showed the exiled courtier Ariwara no Yukihira seated on a beach on the Bay of Suma, chatting with two half-naked female saltmakers. The artwork was a bit crude; it was probably the work of one of the *kirishitan*.

"Does San Francisco Bay make you think of the Bay of Suma?" asked Iroha-hime.

"Only when the moon glistens on the waters," joked Shigehisa. He was referring to a later scene in the *Matsukaze*, in which the two saltmakers, collecting brine at night, see the moon reflected on the water and try to catch it in their ladles.

They continued to talk about cultural matters throughout dinner. But after dinner was taken away, it was time to turn to business.

"To what do we owe the honor of your visit, my lady?"

"Last month, the Third Fleet brought three shogunal commissioners to Monterey Bay. They told my father that the shogun gave the Dutch barbarians permission to found a colony at San Francisco and look for gold. However, my father would be responsible for making sure they accounted to the shogun for his share of any gold they collected."

"I see."

"And what do you think of that arrangement, Commander?"

"I think it puts your father in a difficult position, my lady."

"Indeed! It is an absurd arrangement! The only way to make sure that the Dutch turn over any gold is to send samurai with the Dutch gold miners and take the shogun's share on the spot. The most likely outcome is that the Dutch would give lip service to the demand, and pay nothing. My father would then lose face when the shogun's agents turned to him for an accounting. It might even serve as a pretext for removing him from office." What went unsaid was that perhaps that was the shogun's true purpose.

"You are your father's daughter."

"Have the Dutch been seen?"

"Their presence has not been reported to me, but we do not venture often to the Golden Gate area. The *Miyagi Maru* remained in the bay, but it travels mainly between Sausuendo and Daikoku." Daikoku, a mining settlement, was on the eastern shore of the bay, near up-time Oakland.

"We should have the *Miyagi Maru* investigate," said Iroha. "But I didn't see it at anchor."

"It should be back any day now. It sails regularly between here and Daikoku." Daikoku was named after one of the Seven Gods of Luck. The *Ieyasu Maru* had discovered *outtekou* and *oudoukou* deposits in the "Leona Heights" district of "Oakland" in January 1635. They were pyrite and chalcopyrite, respectively, and could be roasted to yield sulfur. With sulfur from Daikoku, saltpeter from manure, and charcoal from local woods, the Monterey Bay colony could eventually make its own gunpowder. But right now its population was too small to support significant saltpeter production.

"You should also know that my father wishes a third settlement to be established. One suitable for rice cultivation."

"Where will that be?"

"He leaves the exact location up to you, but he assumed it would be on the San Joaquin-Sacramento Delta. You explored there last year, and reported to my father that it is a good place for rice paddies," said Iroha.

The attempts at growing rice in the Monterey Bay area had not been particularly successful and the Japanese hoped that the wet Delta region would prove more productive. Of course, peasants back home usually ate millet, buckwheat or radishes, but it was important to feed the samurai well.

The commander grunted acknowledgment. "It is. But the farmers I have spoken to have some concern about flooding. It might be better to establish a settlement on the shore of the Carqinuez Strait. The farmers can plant rice in the mudflats, but live on higher ground nearby. And the natives in the area are the Karkin, who speak a language more similar to that of the Indians of Monterey Bay."

"Did you have a particular place in mind?"

"Yes," said the commander. "Exploring the straits, we found a rocky peninsula, perhaps a hundred feet high, with mudflats lying northwest of it. If you look at the up-time map of 'San Francisco and Vicinity,' it is between Benicia and Vallejo. More specifically, opposite the stretch between Crockett and Porta Costa. Compared to anywhere on the delta, it is more defensible."

"Against the Indians?"

The commander shrugged. "Or the Dutch. Both the Carquinez Strait and the delta are on the route that the Dutch will be taking to get to the gold fields. There is a potentiality for conflict. But we can't build fortifications on the delta islands, since they flood. And the Dutch *jachts*, at least, would be able to enter the delta channels."

"Would their warships be able to enter the Carquinez Strait?"

"Most likely they could, since the *Miyagi Maru* was able to do so. But the strait is only a half-mile wide at that point, and a fort would have a hundred-foot height advantage."

"It would be best to establish the settlement . . . and the fort . . . before the Dutch arrive. My father sent several ships of the Third Fleet to Daikoku with the intent that they carry colonists to the new settlement. They left last month."

The commander blinked. "The northward passage is always a difficult one. But if they are not there this month, they should arrive next month."

"Also, the shogunal commissioners required him to divide New

Nippon into three *hans*: Monterey Bay, San Francisco Bay, and the Northlands. Daikoku will be the capital of San Francisco Bay *han*."

"And who will be its daimyo? Some favored nephew of one of the shogunal commissioners?"

"No, someone better suited." Iroha smiled. "You. *Lord* Shigehisa, as you may call yourself from now on. After all, you are one of the few to have explored that way. You will still be subject to Date Masamune's authority as grand governor, of course. And he to the shogun, naturally."

"Naturally.

"And who will command here?"

"My father says that you may leave Sausuendo in my hands. He has appointed me as his *daikan*." That meant that she would be the magistrate and civil administrator. "Matsuoka Nagatoki will be my guard commander and military advisor."

Lord Shigehisa frowned for a moment and then smoothed his expression. "I am sure he is capable of ensuring the safety of this settlement against any Indian threat. But you must send word to me, or your father, if the Dutch prove . . . obstreperous."

"Of course. But I think it will be you that bear the brunt of dealings with the Dutch, as the route to the gold fields passes by the delta and nowhere near Sausuendo."

Lord Shigehisa harrumphed. "If I am to plan this new settlement, I will need to know how many *kirishitan*, and how many samurai, are coming."

Iroha-hime grimaced. "About that. The shogunal commissioners brought orders that the samurai who came with the Third Fleet are to return with it. The shogun doesn't want them exposed to *kirishitan* any longer than necessary." He gave her an apologetic look. Iroha-hime had been secretly converted by Luis Sotelo in 1612, and she now openly wore a cross, hanging from a necklace.

Iroha-hime knew that there were samurai on board each colony ship to make sure that the *kirishitan* couldn't take it over and sail it back to Japan. But until now, most of the samurai had remained in New Nippon, to protect the colonists from the Indians and the Spanish, and to keep order.

"So who is to protect the new settlement in Karkin territory?"

"In the short term, my father will move some samurai from

Monterey Bay to here. Actually, he expects that he will need to send more troops to our iron mining and fur trading colony on Texada, too. The Indians in that part of the Americas are supposed to be much more warlike than those in California. But in the long term, the Date clan will hire *ronin* and bring them to New Nippon. Pay them with profits from the fur trade."

"I don't like hearing that he is weakening the defenses of Monterey Bay. . . ."

"What other option is there? The Indians in that region haven't given us much trouble so far. There was the flare-up between the Ixchenta and the Achista, near Maruya, but that's settled. And the conflict over the cinnabar mine. But nothing that can't be handled."

"Unless the Spanish come. . . ."

"True. But the commissioners expect them to either try to regain Manila, or to attack the homeland. One of the commissioners told my father they want the samurai back to defend Manila. And, if the Spanish prove too weak to counterattack, to drive them out of the Philippines altogether. That would deprive them of a forward base for sending missionaries to Japan."

"What is the present situation in the Philippines?"

Iroha-hime took a sip of tea. It was real tea, imported from Japan, rather than a local imitation. "Well . . . Bearing in mind that the news is at least six months old . . . We reportedly control most of Luzon now, and the Moslems have forced the Spanish out of Mindanao. The Spanish still hold Cebu, and some of the other islands, but they have recalled their forces from Formosa and the Spice Islands."

"I wonder why the shogunate is calling troops back from California, when there are still plenty of *ronin* in Japan," mused Lord Shigehisa. "Is it because the shogun wants the grand governor to fail?"

"Perhaps. But remember, in the Philippines, the troops will be exposed to Christians, both Spaniards and native converts. The shogunate may be of the opinion that the troops that escorted the *kirishitan* here are already tainted, so better to use them in the Philippines than expose fresh troops to Christian heresies."

Iroha pushed the empty teacup aside. "My father says that having so many samurai here is unsustainable in the long run anyway. The samurai don't produce any food. Back in Sendai Province, only one in twenty are of the samurai class, and half of those are female. Here, close to one in five are samurai, servants of the samurai, or artisans. And to make matters worse, food production is uncertain here, because the farmers don't know the land or the climate."

"Your father is very wise. I cannot dispute any of that. But we can expect the Indians, and the Spanish, and perhaps eventually the Dutch, to test our right to be here."

"That is why he decided last year to train a militia."

"I am sure that will help, especially for holding a castle, or repelling the natives. But peasants, even with firearms, are not the equal of trained soldiers, be they Japanese or Spanish. At least on a battlefield."

In the room assigned to her, Iroha-hime studied her reflection in a hand mirror and told herself, "Well, that went better than expected. At least, he didn't openly question my appointment. . . ."

She took the butterfly hairpin she had been wearing out of her hair and placed it in a lacquerware box.

Iroha-hime had tried, ever so hard, to be a proper wife to her late husband, Matsudaira Tadateru, the present shogun's uncle. But he hadn't made it easy. First, he had disgraced himself to such a degree that he had been forced to divorce Iroha and become a Buddhist monk. Then, a couple of years ago, he had been provisionally rehabilitated and given command of a gold-hunting expedition to San Francisco Bay. Against her father's advice, Iroha-hime had joined him. He had managed to get his ship wrecked and left Iroha-hime on the beach with a few guards and set off in the ship's boats for the gold fields.

Iroha-hime and her companions had made the best of it, rafting along the west coast of San Francisco Bay, and setting up camp at its southern end. Here, at what was now known as Sausuendo.

It was a disaster. It was also an opportunity. Iroha-hime had taken charge, had parleyed with the natives, and survived until the messengers she sent reached her father's Monterey Bay colony and summoned a rescue ship.

It had taught Iroha-hime that she was capable of more than just giving birth and raising children. That she deserved more responsibility.

Lord Shigehisa did not fall asleep until late that night. It wasn't because he doubted Iroha-hime's abilities. Date Masamune had told him about various clever remarks she had made in her youth, and lamented, "Imagine if she had been born a boy!"

During the *Sengoku*, the civil wars of the sixteenth century, it had not been unusual for a daimyo to leave his wife in command of his home castle while he took his army elsewhere. But after the Tokugawa clan triumphed over its last rivals in 1615, Japan had been at peace, and women were less likely to be given positions of authority.

Back home, Iroha-hime would certainly have led a circumscribed life. But here in New Nippon, Iroha-hime, her brother David Date, and her half-sister Chiyo-hime, were Date Masamune's only blood relations, and few others would enjoy the same level of trust. And Iroha-hime had demonstrated her talents by establishing friendly relations with the Indians near Sausuendo when she was just a castaway.

Iroha-hime had another qualification for the task. Shigehisa knew that Iroha-hime had secretly become a Christian over two decades ago, during the time that Father Luis Sotelo was preaching in Sendai. Were she to publicly acknowledge her conversion—and the cross she wore was a big step in that direction—that would forge an immediate bond with the *kirishitan* colonists in Sausuendo and beyond.

Iroha-hime could certainly govern Sausuendo. The reason for Shigehisa's unease was that it was clear that the shogun would not shed a tear if Date Masamune failed and the *kirishitan* colonists perished.

Chapter 38

A week later, as the *Miyagi Maru* eased out of its anchorage at Sausuendo, Captain Shiroishi saw a gull swoop out of the November sky and snatch a fish hanging from the beak of another seabird. He couldn't help but wonder whether it was a portent sent by some buddha or kami.

The current mission of the *Miyagi Maru* was to look to see whether the Dutch had yet arrived at San Francisco and if so, remind them of their financial obligations. But Captain Shiroishi feared that they would not only disregard those obligations, but snatch the gold fields, and perhaps even the entire coast of San Francisco Bay, away from the Japanese.

Fortunately, it was not Captain Shiroishi's problem. He just needed to search the coast for signs of the Dutch, and then deliver his distinguished passenger, the new daimyo of San Francisco Bay, Lord Daidoji Shigehisa, to Daikoku. And if the Dutch were found, Lord Shigehisa would negotiate with them.

Captain Shiroishi shook his head. Any Dutch presence at San Francisco would be a threat to both the copper and sulfur mining at Daikoku and the rice-growing at Suiden, the new settlement that Lord Shigehisa was planning. The Dutch could fortify and interdict the Golden Gate. If so, supplies for the Daikoku and Suiden colonies would have to travel overland from Monterey Bay to Sausuendo, which would be a great inconvenience.

The shogun should have fortified the Golden Gate before letting the Dutch into the Bay, thought Shiroishi. Not that the shogun had asked his opinion.

Shiroishi shrugged. Rumor had it that the Dutch had suffered a big naval defeat in a faraway ocean, and their very homeland was in danger. It might be years before they came to San Francisco. Or they might come, and end up shipwrecked, as Lord Matsudaira, Iroha-hime's ex-husband, had. Or their naval defeat might have taught them humility . . . although that seemed unlikely. . . .

The *Miyagi Maru* sailed up the west coast of the Bay to Yerba Buena Cove. This was where the town of San Francisco would have been founded in the year 1776 of the old timeline, and hence the most likely place for the proposed Dutch colony.

There were no Dutch ships or houses on the shore of Yerba Buena Cove. Still, to play it safe, Captain Shiroishi ordered a boat lowered and the shore searched for more subtle signs of a Dutch visitation. There were none found. There were, however, shell mounds left behind by the as yet unseen natives.

"So," said Lord Shigehisa hopefully, "we beat them here."

"Not necessarily," said Captain Shiroishi. "Any footprints would have been erased by the tide, or the last rain. And if they left behind any artifacts, those would have been scavenged by the natives after the Dutch left.

"Lord Shigehisa, do you wish to go now to Daikoku?"

"No, we'd best explore the coast as far as the Golden Gate first," said Lord Shigehisa.

"As you wish."

They found the Dutch in another cove, closer to Golden Gate. While Lord Shigehisa was expecting to find a Dutch ship eventually, the presence of a squadron of six Dutch ships was an unpleasant surprise. Two were *jachts*, but the other four were larger.

"Do they really need that many ships for a gold prospecting mission?" he asked. "Have they brought hundreds of miners over in the hope that they would find the gold?"

The ship captain shrugged. "I don't know about that. What I do know is that they outgun us."

The only consolation was that the Dutch seemed equally taken aback by the arrival of the Japanese. Nonetheless, the Japanese were greeted politely and Captain Shiroishi and Lord Shigehisa were invited to dine with the leaders of the Dutch colony.

The Dutch settlement, Fort Maurice, was on top of a small bluff, which, their hosts explained, corresponded to "Fort Mason" on some up-time map of San Francisco. The settlement was already protected by a wooden palisade, which implied that they hadn't just arrived.

At dinner, the main course was rice with pieces of fish added. The rice, Lord Shigehisa suspected, had been brought over from Batavia, but the fish were perhaps caught locally. And either the Dutch did not like vegetables, or the colony was too new to harvest any yet. The Dutch were politely evasive on the subjects of how old the colony was, and how many settlers had been brought over.

"Have you sent out an expedition to the reputed gold fields, yet?" Lord Shigehisa asked.

"We have not," said the chief merchant. "We hope to do so in the spring."

"I assume that you will sail to the top of the bay, and then boat up the Sacramento River."

"That would be the logical route," admitted the squadron commander, van Galen. He was red-haired and blue-eyed, and several inches taller than Lord Shigehisa. He also had not bathed recently, but what could you expect from a Southern Barbarian?

"We have a colony on the east side of the bay," said Lord Shigehisa. "If you look at your up-time maps, it is in the area of the up-time town of Oakland, but about five miles inland. Once you have mined gold, you may leave the shogun's share there, and one of our ships will pick it up."

The commodore and the chief merchant exchanged looks.

"Actually, the tithe doesn't apply until we have recouped the costs of establishing the settlement," said the chief merchant. "And even then, it applies to the net, after operating costs."

"That's not what I was told," said Shiroishi. "Do you have the grant here? With the shogun's red seal?"

"Alas, no," said the chief merchant. "That would be in our headquarters, in Batavia."

"No doubt an authenticated copy would have been sent to the grand governor of New Nippon," said Lord Shigehisa. "I will send a message to him. We should have an answer by the spring, if not sooner."

"Be sure to consult the Dutch version," said the chief merchant.

"And if there is conflict between the Dutch and Japanese versions?" asked Shiroishi.

The chief merchant shrugged. "Then no doubt there would be further communications between the Governor-General of the Dutch East India Company, and the shogun of Japan." Which, as the Japanese were well aware, would take years.

After leaving the Dutch settlement behind, Captain Shiroishi and Lord Shigehisa discussed what they had seen.

"They surely didn't need six ships to establish a new colony," said Captain Shiroishi. "Did they come here to attack Sausuendo or Daikoku?"

"I doubt it," said Lord Shigehisa. "They would not have known those settlements existed. Sausuendo was founded by Iroha-hime and her fellow survivors of the *Sado Maru* shipwreck, and Daikoku when the *Ieyasu Maru* came here to search for those survivors. That was after the Dutch ships of the First Fleet had left this coast."

"Why so large a force?"

"Two possibilities. First, so they could interdict the Golden Gate, so no other ships could enter San Francisco Bay," mused Lord Shigehisa. "Thus preventing the Spanish from accessing the gold fields to the northeast."

"That would be awkward for supplying Sausuendo and Daikoku."

"Indeed, but both have indigenous food supplies. Fishing and farming at Sausuendo, hunting and gathering at Daikoku. And there's the overland route from Monterey Bay. I suppose we'll have to move some samurai to Sausuendo and Daikoku until we're sure of the Dutch intentions, however."

"And what is the second possibility?" asked Captain Shiroishi.

"That they intend to use San Francisco Bay as a base for attacking the Spanish coast. They could sail south and lie in wait for the Manila galleon, with its Chinese silks and porcelains, or go after the silver being brought from Peru to Panama."

"If they do, then the Spanish, trying to find that base, are likely to stumble upon our Monterey Bay settlements."

"Indeed. It is a point I will address with the grand governor. Fortunately, they are unlikely to engage in any offensive action prior to the spring. I will get the grand governor's instructions as to whether to attempt to dissuade them, or merely insist that they notify us before proceeding."

After Captain Shiroishi excused himself, Lord Shigehisa brooded over their topic of conversation. The Dutch had been staunch allies of the Japanese since 1634, and good trading partners before then. Was that about to change, now that both were expanding in the San Francisco Bay area? And what would it mean for the future of New Nippon?

Chapter 39

December 1636

A brown pelican landed on the bowsprit of the *Osaka Maru* as it turned into the emerald waters of the Carquinez Strait. This prompted an argument among the sailors as to whether this was a purely natural occurrence or an omen of some kind. The event was called to the attention of the ship's officers, so they could make the difficult decision as to whether to shoo the bird away, offer it fish, or simply ignore it. They, in turn, consulted the samurai among the passengers.

However, these learned men could not recall any legend regarding pelicans. Cranes, of course. Pheasants, likewise. But not pelicans. In fact, none of them could remember even seeing a pelican in Japan.

Therefore, the more learned of the *kirishitan* colonists were brought into the deliberation. One of these recalled having seen art depicting a similar bird—albeit white not brown—and being told that it was a symbol of Jesus Christ. Given that the settlement was of Christians, the pelican's appearance would seem to be a good omen.

The captain therefore ordered that a fish be solemnly offered to the pelican. However, by the time this decision was made, the pelican had already spread its wings and sprung into the air. After a few minutes, it suddenly stopped flapping its wings, and dived. Just before it hit the water, it folded its wings against its body. There was a splash, and then nothing. Just as the sailors began to doubt that the bird had survived the dive, it bobbed up to the surface, lifted its beak skyward, and swallowed.

"What does this omen mean?" the captain whispered to Lord Shigehisa, who shared the place of honor on the quarterdeck.

"The bird's successful hunt tells us that this settlement will find food easily, and be successful," Lord Shigehisa announced.

The *kirishitan* whose turn it was to stand on deck prayed that Lord Shigehisa was right. They were, like their fellows in the hold, a mixed lot; farmers, fishermen, laborers, servants, shophands, and a smattering of artisans.

A few months earlier, they had arrived in Monterey Bay, and their headman was honored with an audience with Katakura Shigetsuna, chief counsellor to Date Masamune, grand governor of New Nippon.

Shigetsuna told him that the new arrivals were being spread out across New Nippon, so as not to overtax the ability of the land to support them. His group was being honored with the opportunity to found a new settlement, several hundred miles further north.

The headman was not entirely sure that this was an honor. It surely was easier to fit into an existing settlement than carve a new one from the wilderness. But he recognized that there was no point in "spitting against the sky."

In October, he and his fellows, who all came from villages in the same province, were placed back on board one of the Third Fleet transports, the *Osaka Maru*.

It made a circuitous passage north from Monterey Bay to the Golden Gate, and then sailed to Daikoku. This, they discovered, was a copper mining settlement. And there the eminent Lord Shigehisa, with a squad of samurai, joined them. He would guide them to Suiden, their new home.

Sausuendo

The *Osaka Maru* was not the only Third Fleet transport to enter the San Francisco Bay. Others had brought additional colonists to Sausuendo and Daikoku. These had come from five villages—Nata, Hakozaki. Hakata, Fukuoka, and Meinohama—on the shores of Hakata Bay, in northern Kyushu. Iroha-hime welcomed then to their new, shared home.

Iroha-hime's immediate concern was to avoid conflict between the new colonists and the local Indians. Realizing that the Japanese, with their superior boats and nets, could catch more fish faster than the Indians, she negotiated a deal in which the Japanese would do the fishing and would give a share of their catch to the Indians. Since that share was more than what the Indians could catch on their own, they were happy with the arrangement, and devoted more manpower to hunting and acorn-gathering in consequence.

All went well . . . at first.

A half dozen fishermen from Kata slowly walked toward shore, dragging a long beach seine across the mudflats north of the village of Sausuendo. When the water was less than knee-high, the fishermen at the far ends curved inward, forming a three-sided box.

One of the fishermen was inspecting the surfperch wriggling in the net when he felt something sting his shoulder. He turned, and saw one of the fishermen from Hakozaki glowering at him.

"What the fuck do you think you're doing?" said the man from Hakozaki.

"What does it look like we're doing? We're catching our supper. Did you throw something at me?"

"One of these," he said, and picked up a beach pebble. "It's what you deserve, for poaching on our beach."

"Your beach?" He put the edge of his hand flat against his forehead, as if he were shielding his eyes from the sun, and mimed looking left and right. "I don't see the village of Hakozaki here."

"I don't see the village of Nata, either. And we were the first to fish here, so it's our beach."

By this time, several of the other Nata men had set down the net and joined the one who had been struck. One of these said, "Both Nata and Hakozaki men only came to these shores a week ago, it is not time enough for anyone to claim exclusive rights. It is first come, first served."

A second added, "Back home, Hakata Bay was *iriai*—common fishing territory for Nata and Hakozaki. Hakata, Fukuoka and Meinohama, too, since all our villages were on its shore. This is also a bay. It stands to reason that it would be treated the same way."

The injured man rubbed his shoulder. "Anyway, there are six of us and one of you—so get lost!"

✣ ✣ ✣

Iroha was from Sendai Domain, in northern Honshu. Her knowledge of conditions in northern Kyushu was minimal. So she was a little unsure of how to proceed as the fishery dispute intensified.

"I had expected that the farmers might have trouble adjusting to life here. The summers here in California are dry, whereas those in Kyushu are very wet.

"But there still is no lack of food. Clams, mussels and oysters on the mudflats; smelt, sardines and rockfish in the surf; deer and rabbit in the woodlands. Acorns, too. So why are these new colonists fighting?"

Matsuoka Nagatoki grimaced. "According to the colonists from Fukuoka, there has long been rivalry between the fishermen of Nata and Hakozaki. They have centuries of grievances against each other. . . . At least there have been no serious problems with the fishermen from the other three villages, Hakata, Fukuoka and Meinohama. . . . So far. . . ."

Iroha-hime had the headmen of the Nata, Hakozaki, Hakata, Fukuoka and Meinohama contingents summoned to her audience room. Without naming names, she warned that those who disturbed the harmony of the community would be severely punished. All five earnestly assured her that they, at least, were the most amiable of men and would not start any trouble.

She presented each of them with a map she had prepared, dividing the bay and the mudflats among them.

They thanked her for taking the time to consider their needs.

A few days later, the Nata complained that the Hakozaki were poaching fish from Nata waters. The Hakozaki's defense was that they had seen the school in Hakozaki waters and had merely exercised their time-honored right of pursuit.

And the Hakozaki made a counter-complaint that the Nata were encroaching on their part of the beach. In their defense, the Nata urged that the Hakozaki were setting some of their nets in such a way as to divert the fish from the Nata beaches, and the Nata were only reclaiming their fair share of the shoreline.

✣ ✣ ✣

Iroha-hime handed Nagatoki the record of the complaints and counter-complaints prepared by her scribe. "Is there any chance we could send one of the warring contingents to Suiden?"

"So sorry, sending them would be a confession that you couldn't settle the dispute by less drastic means. It would not be a good way to start your tenure as *daikan*."

"How would such a dispute have been handled in Kyushu, do you think?"

"If there were identified perpetrators, they would be sent into exile, or beheaded, depending on the severity of the offense. If no one confessed, the headmen of the problem villages would be punished."

"There are so few Japanese in New Nippon, let alone Sausuendo, that I would prefer to find a different path," said Iroha. "Is there some unpleasant task we might have them perform?"

"Your father has sent some offenders to the cinnabar mine. But that is a form of exile, and not conducive to a long life."

"Inform the headman from Nata and Hakozaki that I have dismissed all complaints and counter-complaints," said Iroha-hime. "Tell them that I am extremely displeased that they have not been able to work out the details of the division of the waters and shores without causing a disturbance.

"Both headmen, and their wives and children, are hereby assigned to night soil collection duty for the coming week.

"And they are to be told that if there are further problems between them, I will assign all of their fishing and beach use rights to the contingents from Hakata, Fukuoka and Meinohama. They may then live off nuts and berries, if they wish."

January 1637

There was a knock on the door of the chamber in which Chiyo-hime and Yells-at-Bears were practicing *naginata-jutsu*.

The two combatants stepped away from each other, and bowed.

"Enter," commanded Chiyo-hime.

"Your father wishes me to inform you, and your companion, that Oyamada Isamu has returned," said the servant.

"Returned?" exclaimed Yells-at-Bears. "Where is he now?"

"On his arrival he went straight to the grand governor, of course," said the servant. "They are closeted together now, but he will be sent on to you as soon as their conference is completed."

The servant bowed and left the room.

"Should we continue our *katas* until Isamu comes for you?" asked Chiyo-hime. "It will make the time pass more quickly."

"All right," said Yells-at-Bears. And she tried but kept making elementary errors.

"I see that your mind is not on your weapon," said Chiyo-hime. "We had best stop before you are injured."

"Yes, please. Do you think that your father will give us permission to marry? Will we be able to return to Texada?"

"On the first matter, I can say that I have spoken in your favor," said Chiyo-hime. "But Father doesn't always share his thoughts with me."

"I have a new mission for you, Isamu," said the grand governor. "Were you aware that I appointed my daughter Iroha as *daikan* for Sausuendo?"

"Vaguely, sir. And I must admit that I only have an imperfect idea where Sausuendo is. Somewhere on San Francisco Bay?"

"Yes, the south end, a few days ride from here. That's right, you weren't on the *Ieyasu Maru* when it rescued her. Well, before the rescue, she did a fine job of making contact with the local Indians. And so, when I promoted the *daikan* of Sausuendo to daimyo of San Francisco *han*, I chose to have her take over Sausuendo.

"But trading with the Indians is a bit different then keeping order among our people, neh?" The grand governor chuckled, and Isamu dutifully joined in. "And Shigehisa is no longer by her side to give her advice. He's at the new colony of Suiden, a few hundred miles away.

"So I want you to pay her a visit, seeing as how you have experience with the birth pains of a new colony."

"Then I should introduce myself as her new advisor?"

"Perish the thought! You may say that you are there to observe the local Indians and consider whether any of their practices might be useful back at Texada, where you were acting *daikan*."

The grand governor smiled. The smile was as broad as the one on a statue of Ebisu, the *kami* of Good Fortune. "Of course, if she does happen to ask you for advice, you may freely provide it." He paused.

"And when you return, I will want your confidential report on how she is doing."

"Given that she is your daughter, and you have given her this very responsible position, there is a possibility that she will not be fooled by that excuse for my presence," said Isamu.

The grand governor steepled his fingers. "You have a better excuse in mind?"

"Indeed I do," said Isamu. "Yells-at-Bears has already made the acquaintance of your younger daughter, Chiyo-hime. You would not want Iroha-hime to feel slighted, and so Yells-at-Bears should visit her, too. Since I have officially sought Yells-at-Bears' hand in marriage, it would be natural for me to accompany her on such a visit."

The grand governor looked amused. "I suppose it would be. But can she ride a horse?"

"While I was away, Chiyo-hime insisted that she and her maid Bluebird get daily lessons. They aren't ready to ride independently, but they should be able to follow me at a walk or trot, and let their horses follow mine.

"It would be good if we can get a boat ride to Niji Masu, and pick up the horses—and a guide who know the way to Sausuendo—there."

"My steward will make the arrangements."

Isamu hesitated. "Before I go, sir, I would like to know—do we have your permission to marry?"

"You ask again, rather than just wait until I am ready to speak?" said the grand governor, his brows furrowed.

"Unless you enter the tiger's den, you cannot take the cubs," replied Isamu. It was an old proverb, of Chinese origin.

The grand governor smiled. "I will make the decision when you return."

Chiyo-hime and Yells-at-Bears met Isamu just outside the grand governor's audience room.

"It's about time you showed up," said Yells-at-Bears.

Isamu shrugged. "Susanoo wanted me to tarry in the south." Susanoo commanded the winds and waves.

"Was your mission successful?"

"It was."

"Did . . . did the grand governor say anything about our future?"

"He has another mission—one for both of us—and will give us his decision after it is completed."

"Then we should start it soon . . . but not today. Come back to our quarters." She gave Chiyo-hime a significant look.

"I will leave the two of you to get reacquainted," said Chiyo-hime hastily.

The arrangements took a few days. On the day before Isamu was to leave, the grand governor's steward handed him a sealed scroll.

'What's this?" asked Isamu.

"It's a personal message from the grand governor to Iroha-hime," said the steward.

"I will make sure she gets it," promised Isamu.

The *Unagi Maru* took Isamu, Yells-at-Bears and Bluebird to Niji Masu, where they were warmly welcomed by Moniwa Motonori, the local *daikan*. That evening, Isamu and Motonori enjoyed a long drinking bout in which they exchanged somewhat exaggerated stories about their service to the Date clan.

The next morning, Motonori assigned them a guide who had ridden to Sausuendo several times before, and wished them a pleasant journey. The guide found a couple of easygoing mounts for Yells-at-Bears and Bluebird, and a finer one for Isamu, and then they were off.

The riding distance from Niji Masu to Sausuendo was close to sixty miles. The guide usually covered it in two days but with two inexperienced riders in their party, it took four. The most difficult part of the journey was when they went over the Santa Cruz Mountains. While the pass wasn't high, they were forced to work their way around a rockslide. It hadn't been there when the guide had last ridden the route. Looking back from the top of the pass, they had a fine view of Monterey Bay.

They descended into the Santa Clara Valley. Yells-at-Bears pointed out to Isamu that it was evident from the vegetation that this area got less rain than the Monterey Bay coast, and their guide agreed with her.

As they approached Sausuendo, they could see small fishing boats out on San Francisco Bay. Yells-at-Bears suddenly found her mouth watering. Hopefully, they wouldn't have to wait long for dinner.

They were greeted by Sanada Jiro, who identified himself as one of Iroha-hime's guardsmen. He had a servant take them to their quarters.

Later they were taken to dine with Iroha-hime. Isamu handed her the scroll, and she tucked it into her obi. It would have been impolite, of course, for her to open and read it on the spot. Instead, Iroha-hime plied them with questions about her father, brother and sister in Kawachi Machi. Yells-at-Bears answered most of the questions, as she knew Chiyo-hime and her brother "David Date" better than Isamu did.

The conversation was very mellow until Iroha-hime suddenly asked, "Did father send you just to check on me, or to take my place?"

It was obvious to Isamu that she had guided the conversation as she had in order to take him by surprise with this question, and thereby glean a truthful answer.

"Neither!" exclaimed Isamu. "I am here as an escort for Yells-at-Bears. Who in turn is here to entertain you with stories of the lands from which she comes."

"And of the mischief that your sister Chiyo-hime and I have gotten into," Yells-at-Bears added.

"Of course, if you order me to regale you with stories of my mistakes in managing the Texada colony, I would certainly comply," said Isamu.

"And I can tell you if he leaves any out," added Yells-at-Bears.

Iroha-hime stared at them, and then laughed. "Well, I can see that the two of you will be more entertaining than watching a puppet play. Not that there any puppet plays to watch, here in Sausuendo."

After the visitors were escorted to their quarters, Iroha-hime opened the scroll. "Greetings, daughter. You have no doubt been told that I have sent Yells-at-Bears to you so she may entertain you as she did your sister Chiyo. However, I have an ulterior motive. Oyamada Isamu, her companion and my retainer, has asked for permission to marry her. Spend time, with them, alone and together. Draw them out in conversation. Watch how they act, and have your servants watch them too. Give me your opinion as to whether I should grant this request."

Chapter 40

Monterey Bay
February 1637

The gamble had been successful, Captain-General de Corcuera mused as the *San Raimundo* rolled with the swells. *And hopefully, the weather will hold.* Most of the sky was fair weather blue, but there were clouds on the western horizon.

The armada had made landfall, north of the thirty-seventh parallel, in just three months. They would reach Monterey Bay in about half the time it had taken Vizcaíno to sail there from Acapulco. And the pilot major had explained to de Corcuera how the armada could use the curvature of the northern coast to conceal themselves from the enemy until they were very close to Kodachi Machi harbor.

Unfortunately, depending on their time of arrival, there was a risk that the armada would be discovered by Japanese fishing boats out of Kodachi Machi. According to the captured fishermen, while most only went a few miles from their port, some—like the captives themselves—ranged much further. It all depended on the season and the kind of fish the fishermen were looking for.

The armada followed the California coast, southeast. In due course, they spotted Año Nuevo, a rocky, windswept point so named because Sebastián Vizcaíno had seen it on January 3, 1603.

Continuing, they kept a wary eye on the shore. The weather of the California coast was often stormy, and there were no safe anchorages here. The Santa Cruz Mountains ended in sheer, beige-colored cliffs. The sky was already overcast, although the sun could be seen hazily through the cloud cover.

The coast gently changed direction, from southeast to east. At last, the pilot major, who had transferred to the lead vessel, the *Galgo*, discerned that it had turned northeast. Based on the up-time maps copied by Spanish agents in Europe, they were now about five miles from the mouth of the San Lorenzo River. According to last year's reconnaissance, the harbor was close to it.

The pilot major and the master of the *Galgo* faced northeast. Both held spyglasses.

"See that point?" asked the pilot major. "The harbor should be just past it."

"Yes, I see it." The point in question was what an up-time resident of Santa Cruz would have called Seal Rock.

The master called for a casting of the log. A seaman threw a lead-weighted wooden board attached to a knotted line out from the stern of the ship, and flipped a half-minute sandglass. When the sand ran out, he locked the reel and hauled in the log, counting the knots as he did so. He reported the count to the master, who made a quick calculation of the ship's speed.

"We should make the point in two turns of the *ampolleta*." Each turn of the sand clock used for timing the changes of the watch was half an hour, and on the galleons, the pages responsible for the sand clocks would recite a psalm whenever they flipped them. Here on the *Galgo*, there was only a single ship's boy to monitor and announce the passage of time, and he would just ring a ship's bell.

The disadvantage of taking a route that hid the armada from the Japanese was that it also hid the Japanese from the armada. They did not know whether there were any hostile ships in the harbor and they wouldn't know this until they passed Seal Rock.

They were also close enough that the chance of discovery by a Japanese fishing boat was significant. Whether they could board or sink it before it could bear warning back to the harbor would depend on the relative positions of the harbor, the fishing boat, and the incoming armada when it was spotted. And, of course, the wind and current.

The masts of the *Galgo* were not particularly lofty, and hence its sighting distance was limited. However, watches were also maintained on the three galleons, whose mainmasts reared perhaps a hundred feet above the water. They could hope to spot a fishing boat ten to fifteen miles away, depending on air clarity and wave height.

On the *San Diego*, which was behind the *Galgo* and *El Anzuelo*, the lookout did see a few fishing boats well out into Monterey Bay. When he reported this, the master deigned to climb up himself for a better look. He came down a few minutes later, and brushed raindrops off his face.

"Well, you're smiling from ear to ear," said Don Bernardino. "No fishing boats?"

"A few, but they are far out in the bay, so even if they were to try to reach Kodachi Machi, we would get there first. And I doubt they can see us."

"I don't know whether to hope that the harbor is free of Japanese ships, or not," said Don Bernardino. "Their absence will facilitate our attack, but it would be more satisfying to begin the campaign by sinking their colony ships than by burning a few fishing boats and huts. And even better if there are Dutch warships present! An opportunity to demonstrate the superiority of Spanish arms and the True Faith!"

When they were almost even with Seal Rock, the pilot major commanded, "signal to fleet, heave to." There was no standardized signal system in the Spanish navy, each commander devised his own signals. But this was one that had been agreed to at a previous council of war, when the pilot major had pointed out the need to reconnoiter. Two flags were raised on the mizzenmast, one indicating that the command was from the pilot major.

The *Galgo* had been towing behind it the *De Anzuelo*, the captured Japanese fishing boat. The boat was untied and the skipper, one of the senior seamen from the *San Raimundo*, brought the *De Anzuelo* ahead of the *Galgo*. He and his two crewmen were to check the harbor and report. They wore the clothing taken from the captured Japanese fishermen, but this was an uncertain disguise. Since the Japanese had shaved heads, while the Spaniards had a full head of hair, they wore hats. Even so, they would be in trouble if another boat came within hailing distance, as they did not speak Japanese.

The *De Anzuelo* passed Seal Rock, and one of the crewmen made a pretense of rod fishing. It was quickly apparent that there were no western-style ships in the harbor. Whether they might be somewhere else in Bahía de Monterrey was unknown, but if prisoners were taken, they might know the answer. In any event, there was no reason for the armada not to proceed with the attack.

The *De Anzuelo* could not reverse course, because of the direction of the wind, but it turned south and, when the *Galgo* and San Diego came into view, it lowered and raised its sail once.

In response, the San Diego raised and lowered a red ensign on its mizzenmast.

The *San Raimundo* was hove-to a hundred yards behind the *San Diego*. Captain de Bolaza saluted the captain-general. "Sir, the *San Diego* signals that there are no warships in Kodachi Machi harbor."

"Direct the pilot major to signal the armada to advance to the attack!"

A few minutes later, red ensigns were raised on the foremast and mizzenmast of the *San Raimundo*. As soon as the *San Diego* was seen to have resumed motion, the *San Raimundo*'s pilot major ordered its sailors into action. The backed main topsail was braced to its normal position, and the *San Raimundo* surged forward. The maneuver was then copied by the *Loreto* and the *San Bartolome*.

As soon as the harbor came into view from the *San Diego*'s main deck, it fired a broadside. The main target was a small guard post by the mouth of the river, and the wooden buildings nearby, but cannonballs also struck the huts.

When the *San Raimundo* came past the point, it was apparent that there was no advantage to it firing, as the fishing village was essentially destroyed.

Captain-General de Corcuera collapsed his spyglass. "Captain de Bolaza, have the first company assemble on deck. And summon Father Blanco here."

De Bolaza, the captain of seamen and infantry for the *San Raimundo,* saluted. His detachment of twenty-five marines was not part of the invasion force, unless matters became desperate, but they were in charge of traffic control.

By the time the soldiers were assembled, shoulder to shoulder, on the main deck, Father Blanco had joined de Corcuera on the poop deck.

"What is your pleasure, sir?"

"A suitably martial prayer."

"Of course." Father Blanco went to the railing looking down at the troops and motioned for silence. Then he began reciting from King David's Psalm: "Blessed be the Lord, my rock, who trains my hands for battle, my fingers for war . . ."

Chapter 41

The *San Raimundo* dropped its anchor about a quarter-mile offshore of the mouth of the San Lorenzo. Diego de Aro had the ship's boats lowered into the gently rippling water, and Captain de Bolaza made sure that the first company of infantry boarded the boats in an orderly manner.

The gunners remained at their station and, up in the tops, sailors watched the shore for any sign of Japanese troops. There were none, but smoke signals could be seen rising from both the palisaded farming village and the high fortress.

On the lead boat, the helmsman shouted, "Out oars!" and then, "Make way!" The men on board started rowing, the soldiers doing their best to match the movements of the sailors.

The lead boat cut through the surf and a wave took it onto the beach. "Ship oars!"

The sergeant on the lead boat ordered the soldiers, a mix of pikemen and arquebusiers, to disembark and take up a defensive position. The rest of the boats, and their soldiers, followed suit.

The boats then returned to *San Raimundo* to pick up more soldiers. It took several trips just to move a single company of a hundred men, and the *San Raimundo* had four on board.

Captain-General de Corcuera and Father Blanco transferred to shore with the fourth company.

De Corcuera and a small party of guards went to look for a suitable vantage point. The fishing village had been situated on a low ridge, perhaps sixty feet high. The San Lorenzo River, coming down from the north, was turned east by this ridge, resuming a southward course where the ridge ended, about half a mile to the east of where the river swerved.

A broad, arrowhead-shaped plateau pointed toward the San Lorenzo, the tip terminating very close to the river and a mile from de Corcuera's observation point. The near face of this plateau ran in a northeasterly direction up to that tip. To de Corcuera's west, there was what appeared to be a large lagoon. Any troop advance would need to be along the west bank of the San Lorenzo, as far from the marshy ground as possible.

There was, as expected from the reports made the preceding year, a palisaded settlement at the tip of the plateau. This, according to the captured fishermen, was a farming village. Some farming was done in the region between the plateau and the coast, but it was subject to flooding in the winter rainy season. Most farming was therefore done up on the plateau. De Corcuera estimated that the plateau was eighty or so feet high.

A second, narrower plateau was stacked on top of the first one and de Corcuera could see the High Fortress at the tip of this second tier. Unlike the farming village, this was protected, according to the captured fishermen, by stone walls. And its tier rose at least a hundred feet, perhaps two hundred, above the first one.

"Should we start bringing up the artillery, sir?" asked his adjutant.

"First, let's get troops into position to block anyone in the farming village from escaping to the High Fortress."

De Corcuera left one company to hold the beachhead and advanced with the other five companies. These were pikemen, arquebusiers, and musketeers, but no cavalry.

At about a hundred yards, they came under arrow and musket fire from the stockade. De Corcuera ordered the troops to deploy into an open formation and four companies returned fire.

The fifth stayed back, out of arrow range, and looked for an easy route up onto the plateau. It found a ravine about five hundred yards to the southwest and ascended. It then worked its way through a wooded area and finally onto the edge of the cultivated fields west of the farming village.

The High Fortress, Upper Kodachi Machi, lay north of those fields. Any Japanese still in the farming village who sought refuge in the High

Fortress would now have to pass the gauntlet of fire from this advance Spanish company.

Heishiro and his son were out on the bay, line fishing for kingfish. The kingfish was not found in Japanese waters, but it somewhat resembled the *guchi*, the croaker. At Kodachi Machi, it was mostly used to make *kamaboko*, a fish paste.

The kingfish was adept at stealing bait and Heishiro had baited his hooks with shrimp. It was a bit of a nuisance, but once hooked, the kingfish didn't put up much of a fight.

Heishiro was hauling in a line when his son, who was at the tiller, called out, "Father, what's that sound?"

Heishiro lifted one hand to his ear, and cupped it to better funnel the sound. "It's no sound of the ocean. That's gunfire," he yelled back, alarmed. When Heishiro had been on the *Ieyasu Maru*, Captain Haruno had occasionally ordered gunnery drills. This sound was fainter, but unmistakable.

"Is the High Fortress drilling its gunners, you think?" the son asked.

"The sound is from that direction... But I don't think so. And it is too prolonged to be a salute. I think Kodachi Machi is under attack from the sea."

"What should we do?"

"Cut the lines and flee south, as fast as we can."

"To Andoryu?"

"To Maruya, if we can make it, so we are out of sight of warships on the bay. And perhaps further south than that, to Chumash territory."

Captain de Bolaza's marines and the *San Raimundo*'s sailors began the arduous task of transporting artillery pieces to the shore. These were strictly naval artillery pieces. While there were reportedly some heavier cannon in the Veracruz Arsenal, de Corcuera had been unable to even get the responsible officials to admit to their existence, let alone agree to have them transported to Acapulco for use in California.

Insofar as the naval artillery was concerned, the general backwardness of Spanish naval artillery practice worked somewhat to de Corcuera's advantage. Among the Dutch or English, warship guns were mounted on four-wheeled sea carriages. In contrast, many Spanish naval guns were still mounted on two-wheeled field carriages.

These had large wheels and a trace, although in some cases the trace had been cut down so as to better fit on a crowded deck.

Since the *San Raimundo* was not a war-galleon, the available artillery did not include any heavy pieces. However, it did carry long-range *culebrinas*, firing sixteen-pound shot, and twelve-pounder *cuartos canones*, which were more or less equivalent to the Spanish army's field artillery. Even if the Armada ships had carried true siege guns, it would have been difficult to transport them to a point close to the High Fortress, given the nature of the terrain.

De Bolaza's teams lifted the cannon barrels off the carriages, and partially disassembled the latter. The parts were hoisted into the ship's boats, brought to shore, and reassembled. Most of the company left to hold the beachhead, and many sailors were recruited to escort the cannon northward and to man them once the siege of the High Fortress began.

The only guns remaining on board the *San Raimundo* were lighter pieces: *sacres*, *medio sacres*, and swivel guns. It was assumed that if the Japanese were able to muster enough junks to transport a significant force, then this light armament would be sufficient to fend off or sink the unarmed junks. And as a further precaution, a guard boat was stationed nearby, to give warning of such an attack.

Not that de Corcuera thought that there was much chance such an attack would take place. No junks had been seen heading toward Kodachi Machi.

Chapter 42

The wooden stockade of Middle Kodachi Machi was no match for the Spanish artillery. Several sections were breached within the first hour of bombardment.

"Have the first and second companies advance into the breaches," said de Corcuera to his aide. "No quarter."

Father Blanco, standing beside him, pleaded with him to revoke the last order. "Captain-General, we believe these Japanese to be adherents to our most Catholic faith. You should offer them surrender terms."

"Didn't the Japanese catapult heads into Fort Santiago until the fort surrendered? Didn't they threaten to crucify every Spanish man, woman and child in Manila? Weren't some Spanish civilians killed after the fort surrendered?"

"What you say is true, but those Japanese were not Christians. Surely, Japanese of the True Faith who do not bear arms against us should be spared."

"I will give you the opportunity to request their immediate surrender, Father Blanco. If they do, then all may be spared. If not—" De Corcuera shrugged. "They pay the same price that any town does that chooses to resist."

The Spanish stopped firing as Father Blanco advanced, holding an improvised white flag. He hoped that the Japanese understood the significance of the flag.

He was not fired upon, but wasn't sure whether this was because they accepted him as a herald, or out of respect for the bravery of a lone Spaniard openly approaching their position.

He called out in Japanese, and after a few minutes a lone samurai came out to meet him.

"Your town cannot withstand the cannon fire. You should surrender the town so the people inside are spared. Otherwise, all will be put to the sword, men, women and children."

"Samurai cannot surrender," the Japanese emissary said. "It is ludicrous to even suggest it. Will you allow the civilians to leave before you make your assault? They are of your own faith."

"I cannot make that decision. I will have to ask our commander." He paused. "Do you know whether they have had a priest to minister to their needs? To give the sacraments of Holy Communion, Confession, Marriage and Anointing of the Sick?"

"There's no priest here," said the samurai. "But that is certainly not their immediate concern, neh?"

"Agreed," said Father Blanco.

They bowed to each other.

As Father Blanco walked back to the Spanish lines, he thought about the plight of the *kirishitan*. The Japanese fishermen captured by the San Raimundo had said that they lacked a priest, but they lived in the village of Andoryu, across the bay from the capital of the colony. But this village was close to the High Fortress. If they, too, lacked a priest, then it meant that there was probably no priest anywhere in this *kirishitan* colony.

It was bad enough that these *kirishitan* were in peril of their lives, but worse that they were in spiritual peril. Without marriage, they must either be chaste, or live in sin. Without confession, they could not be forgiven for their sins. Without anointment, their souls were not strengthened against the temptations of the Devil when facing death. And without communion, they could not properly experience the presence of Christ. How Father Blanco wished he could help them, and their fellows!

Well, once the Spanish humbled their samurai overlords, they would bring the Japanese here under Spanish rule, and the True Faith.

Father Blanco made his report. After quoting the samurai's words, he added, "If you spare the civilians, you can put them to work moving the artillery into position for bombarding the High Fortress."

"True," said de Corcuera, "but then we must feed them."

"Then have them move the artillery and let them escape to the High Fortress, to draw down its supplies."

De Corcuera thought about this. "Go back and tell the Japanese that the women and children may leave with what they may carry. No beasts of burden, no carts. They have an hour to leave, and they are to cross the San Lorenzo and remain on that side."

"And the male civilians?"

"If there is no surrender, they must take their chances."

"Then I will ride with the women and children to ensure their safety."

"I am surprised you care," said de Corcuera. "Didn't the Inquisition judge the captured fishermen to be heretics?"

"It found them to be in error, but innocently."

"Well, be quick about it."

The samurai emissary allowed him to enter the farming village and, a half-hour later, Father Blanco emerged leaving a procession of Japanese women, some carrying or holding the hands of children. They left by the south gate, turned east, and forded the San Lorenzo River. The women had requested that he escort them to the Indian village of Sokue, about five miles to the east, and he agreed. He could intercede if they encountered a Spanish patrol.

As the Spanish companies advanced on Middle Kodachi Machi, some Japanese men tried to escape north to the High Fortress. However, they were pinned down by Spanish fire from the west.

In the High Fortress, their plight was noticed by the Japanese leadership.

David Date, Date Masamune's baptized son, pointed down at the farming village. "Father, there are villagers trying to escape. Let me take down a troop to drive the Spanish off so the villagers can make it here."

"We don't know how many Spanish are in those fields. And if they retreat into the woods, cavalry is less effective against infantry."

"We don't have to kill the Spanish, just drive them deep enough into the woods so they can't stop the escape."

Date Masamune considered the matter. In one sense, it was foolish to risk the samurai to protect civilians who at best would be more mouths to feed. But a sortie, if it weren't a complete disaster, would improve the morale of the High Fortress' defenders, and would also help his son, who was too young to fight in the last war in Japan, develop a martial reputation.

"Take twenty horse-archers. You are not to enter the woods, you are not to escort the villagers. You are just to disrupt the Spanish to give our people a chance to cross the killing ground."

It was, David Date mused, very old-fashioned. While it had been common a couple of centuries ago for samurai to fight as horse-archers, nowadays horse-archery was more a sport than anything else. In the wars of the Sengoku, samurai relied on spears and later arquebuses, and often fought as dragoons rather than on horseback.

Still, there was no difficulty finding twenty samurai who could shoot fast and accurately, and even from horseback if need be.

They rode out of the main gate and trotted toward the Spanish position. When they came within range they commenced firing. The range of their composite bows was easily three times that of the Spanish muskets, so they were able to force the Spanish to retreat into the woods, from which they could not effectively harass the escapees.

The boldest civilians were the ones who had tried to escape to the High Fortress before David Date's troop came to their aid, and most of them had been cut down. So there was a few moments' hesitation before more decided to run for it. But run for it they did.

David Date's troop fired a final volley and galloped back to the High Fortress, where they were cheered by the defenders on the battlements.

Chapter 43

Middle Kodachi Machi was successfully assaulted, and its small samurai detachment died to the last man, disdaining to flee to the High Fortress when David Date's troop sallied. The vicious fighting inside the village, in which the samurai took full advantage of their knowledge of the layout, took its toll on the Spanish, and de Corcuera audibly regretted having given Father Blanco the chance to save the women and children.

The Spanish took possession of the supplies and tools left behind by the Japanese villagers. It was a much-appreciated augmentation of their own supplies, which were running short after the long voyage.

From the northwest corner of the village palisade it was only two hundred yards to the northeast corner of the High Fortress, and the Spanish placed a battery there.

They placed a second battery near the northwest corner of the village, as it had a direct sight line to the High Fortress' barbican. Unfortunately for the Spanish, the range to the barbican was more like five hundred yards. Moreover, the barbican was at the top of a ravine, and so if there was a small error in the traversal of the Spanish artillery, the shot would bang harmlessly into a hillside.

The cannon, being naval artillery, could only be elevated about fifteen degrees, which limited their range. Since the High Fortress was a good hundred feet higher than the Spanish batteries, the elevation of the guns had to be just right, too.

A Spanish company was sent to climb the hills to the west of the

High Fortress. They were unable to find a path by which the artillery could be brought up without months of tree cutting and excavation. However, their presence on the hills was essential, lest the Japanese be able to obtain fresh supplies there.

There was no serious risk of resupply from the north, as there was a sheer drop from the walls of the High Fortress on that side. The Spanish did send occasional patrols into that region, however.

The Spanish began the bombardment of the High Fortress. There was little in the way of counterfire. Either the Japanese didn't have artillery, or they were saving their ammunition for fending off a direct assault.

With the artillery in position, de Corcuera determined that it was high time that the other Japanese settlements on Monterey Bay be dealt with. The *San Diego*, with a company of soldiers on board, sailed east to attack Niji Masu, and the *Loreto* south, to assault Andoryu. Both were directed to fly Dutch flags until they began their bombardment. Given the size of Monterey Bay, there was a small but finite chance that the other settlements were still unaware of the attack on Kodachi Machi.

The *Galgo* and *San Bartolome* were given leave to hunt down any Japanese junks still in the bay.

On the lookout tower of Pine Point, west of Andoryu, two watchers were posted. One was telling the other a joke he had heard the night before. "So the fox said to the peasant . . ."

"Hush!"

"What's wrong, I'm almost at the punch line. . . ."

"Look, you idiot!" The second watcher was pointing north.

The joke teller turned. He could see the approaching *Loreto*.

"Is it ours? Or the Dutch? Or the Spanish!"

"Not for us to decide." He started sending the smoke signals indicating that a large ship of western design was approaching, and the joke teller grabbed his red flags and started waving them.

In Andoryu, the signals were spotted and the battery commander, Sakai Kuroemon, was awakened. It was a few minutes before his eyes were focusing well enough to make out details in his spyglass.

What he saw made him uneasy. The approaching ship was

larger than the Dutch ships that the Japanese had copied for the "exile" fleet. It could be one of the Portuguese *galetas* that the Japanese had seized in Nagasaki harbor in 1633, or the Spanish galleon that the Japanese had captured at the Cavite shipyard in 1634, but . . .

"Ready the signal cannon," he commanded. "Three firings." It was the signal for hostile ships approaching.

As the signal was fired off, Kuroemon studied the progress of the presumed-enemy galleon. Ideally, the villagers would take refuge at Kodachi Machi, the most fortified settlement. But the galleon was coming from the direction of Kodachi Machi and in any event, Kodachi Machi was twenty-five miles away by sea, and thirty-five along the coast.

His pair of ancient Dutch three-pounders wouldn't have any discernible effect on the hull of a galleon. It could flatten Andoryu with its broadside, and pay no more attention to Kuroemon's cannon than an elephant would to a gnat.

Was it better to wait and hope that the enemy launched boats that he could hope to sink? Or to lead the villagers to a place of greater safety?

While his samurai spirit urged him to stay by the cannon and cause some harm to the enemy, his sense of duty prevailed.

"Assemble the villagers!" he ordered.

Once this was done, he told them. "A large enemy warship is approaching. The village is lost. Pack food and water quickly. I will blow my whistle two times. On the second blow, I will lead those who are ready into the hills. If Maruya is safe, we will go there. If not, we will stay in the hills."

Perhaps two-thirds of the villagers were ready to follow him on the second blow of the whistle. Others were hiding or packing their goods. Some had decided to flee by sea in their fishing boats or by land, drawing carts, to Kawamachi, the next settlement east.

Kuroemon was tempted to slap them into line, but that would take time, and would penalize the villagers who had followed orders.

"All right, follow me!"

The captured junk, the *De Anzuelo*, was burned, being of no further use to the Spanish. A patache, the *Galgo,* was sent back to Acapulco, carrying a triumphant (and somewhat premature) communique from de Corcuera:

> *"In the service of His Most Catholic Majesty, I have destroyed two of the Japanese settlements in California, and have laid siege to their main fortress. I expect it to fall within a month or two. Manila has been avenged."*

Chapter 44

The *San Diego* had sailed east from Kodachi Machi harbor, anchoring near the mouth of the Pajaro River. It found no target worthy of its cannon. This was not a complete surprise to Don Bernardino. The previous year, the *De Anzuelo* had reported that the town Niji Masu was several miles upriver, out of range of the Spanish naval guns.

The town could be seen from the *San Diego*'s maintop. The lookout reported that it had a wooden palisade and towers, and that there were boats by the riverbank near the town. He also described the terrain flanking the river, as best he could.

The *San Diego*'s longboat entered the Pajaro River and took soundings, then explored the nearby coast, and finally returned to the *San Diego* to report.

"There is a sandbar at the mouth," said the boatswain. "Even at high tide, I doubt the *San Diego* can cross it. And if it could, about three-quarters of a mile upriver from the mouth, to follow the channel, it would need to turn to face east-northeast. The wind would make it quite difficult to proceed further. Moreover, the channel quickly narrows to perhaps one hundred eighty feet across. The *San Diego* is over a hundred feet long, so it would not be able to turn around easily, if it needed to return to the bay."

"What is the terrain like?" asked Don Bernardino.

The boatswain snorted. "The terrain? On what passes for a coast, more water than land. On either side of the river, for perhaps a mile inland, there is marsh. Beyond that, there is forest."

It was plain to Don Bernardino that assaulting Niji Masu would not be easy. The soldiers would need to travel in the ship's boats. "How many soldiers can be carried at once if we use all our boats?"

"Perhaps forty," said the boatswain.

The boats would have to be rowed upriver, or across the marsh, at least to the forest line, then leave the soldiers behind and fetch the second wave. The first wave would have to hold their position for a good hour before reinforcements could arrive.

Well, they didn't have to sail right up to the walls of Niji Masu. He turned to an ensign. "Summon Captain Avila."

"Yes, sir!"

The captain was close at hand and saluted Don Bernardino. "What is your pleasure, sir?"

"You will take your company and assault Niji Masu, upriver. Assign soldiers to the four ship's boats. The boatswain will tell you how many can fit in each. Your lieutenant is to take them upriver, to the first good landing spot on the east side of the river, provided it is a least a mile from the river mouth. He is to take up high ground commanding the river, if that is possible, and then send the boats back for the second half of your company.

"You will come with the second half and then, once you come abreast of your lieutenant's position, you will both proceed upriver, you in the boats and your lieutenant on the riverbank. Attempt to capture the enemy shipping as it will help you assault the town."

The captain saluted. "Yes, sir. Will I have any artillery?"

"Send the longboat back and we will give you a pair of falcons." Those fired three-pound shot. "That should be adequate for breaching a wooden fort."

Niji Masu was west of the Pajaro, and almost four miles from the coast. Besides its wooden palisade, it was partially protected by sloughs.

While the authorities at Niji Masu were still unaware of the attack on Kodachi Machi, a fishing boat had reported the approach of the *San Diego* and Moniwa Motonori, the *daikan*, was ready for trouble. Scouts had been posted to warn of the approach of the Spanish, and the Indian allies of the Japanese were also asked to be watchful.

The scouts used birdcalls to send messages back to Niji Masu. The Spanish didn't know the local birds at all, and therefore wouldn't be realize that the "bird" that was singing was one found only in Japan. Each scout had his own assigned territory and an identifying birdcall.

"The tit has seen a snake," one of the samurai reported to Motonori.

He smiled thinly. "So the Spanish have come up river." The Japanese tit had a snake-specific alarm call that the river scout had appropriated. It sounded like a rattle.

"How many?"

"About forty, so far."

"Then let us give them a warm welcome," he replied.

Don Bernardino did not know that the "shipping" that had been spotted were not merely defenseless fishing boats, but also the *Unagi Maru*. It had remained on the Pajaro after delivering Isamu, Yells-at-Bears and Bluebird to Niji Masu. Its sails were furled and Don Bernardino's lookout had taken no particular notice of it.

It was no match, of course, for the *San Diego*. But given that it was armed with eight three-pounders and four swivel guns, it was quite capable of sinking the *San Diego*'s boats, if it could get close enough to them.

The *Unagi Maru* hoisted its sails and started moving downstream. The draft of the *Unagi Maru* was less than half that of the *San Diego*, so it had had no difficulty coming up the rainy season Pajaro as far as Niji Masu. And it was doing fine now, even though it was heavily loaded with full crews for all of its cannon, courtesy of Moniwa Motonori.

The first Spanish detachment, in the ship's boats, advanced without incident as instructed by Don Bernardino, and the boats were sent back. They waited, senses keyed up, for any sign that the Japanese were creeping up on them, but all they heard was the gurgle of the river and the tweets of the birds.

The second detachment arrived and the captain, hearing that there had been no contact with the enemy, ordered the advance.

They followed the river northward. About three miles from the river mouth, the river turned eastward and here they could see, poking above the trees, the tops of the masts of a boat coming down river.

Out for an afternoon fishing? thought Captain Avila. *Won't they be surprised!*

The Spanish flotilla rounded the turn, and it was they who were surprised. The masts belonged to the *Unagi Maru*, and its broadside was facing them.

Captain Avila's jaw dropped.

So did the arm of the master gunner of the *Unagi Maru*. "Fire!"

A moment later, shots struck two of the four Spanish boats, sinking them almost immediately. That included Captain Avila's longboat, which after all was the largest target. The rowers on the other two boats raised their oars, uncertain whether to press on, hold position, or retreat.

While the gunners on the *Unagi Maru* reloaded, some of the samurai on board fired matchlocks at the remaining Spanish boat crews. The Spanish soldiers fired back, but the boats were not very good gun platforms. They were able to fire a second round while the Japanese reloaded their matchlocks—the Spanish *miquelet* muskets offered a higher rate of fire—but that was their last hurrah. The *Unagi Maru*'s three pounders spoke again, sinking a third boat. The fourth one turned tail and fled.

In the meantime, the advancing Spanish land force, under Avila's lieutenant, had come under fire from samurai in the forest. In response, the Spanish soldiers took cover and returned fire.

Some of the Japanese were armed with composite bows, rather than matchlocks, and those had a rate of fire greater than that of the *miquelets*. On the other hand, an arrow was more likely than a bullet to be deflected by foliage. Still, the Japanese brought the Spanish to a halt.

And then the impasse was resolved. The *Unagi Maru*, having disposed of the Spanish flotilla, turned its attention to the Spanish on land. It enfiladed the Spanish position, first with round shot, and then with hailshot.

The Spanish lieutenant was killed, and the Spanish routed. The samurai drew their swords, and pursued, cutting down all who did not surrender. Those who did were taken back to Niji Masu for interrogation.

"Boat ahoy!" cried the lookout on the *San Diego*.

"Captain Avila must have already won," said Don Bernardino to the shipmaster.

"There are hardly any men rowing on that boat," said the master, his eye to his spyglass. "And I see a lot of dead bodies on board."

It was not long before the survivors told Don Bernardino what had happened, though they claimed to have been sent back to fetch the three pounders, rather than to have fled. Don Bernardino ordered them confined in the brig for cowardice.

The *San Diego* waited at anchor until the following morning, hoping that the survivors of the land force would reach the shore and wave for rescue. But none appeared. Don Bernardino ordered the master to sail for Kawamachi. While the *Loreto* should have gone there after bombarding Andoryu, hopefully there was something Japanese still standing there that he could shoot at. And then he could creep back to Kodachi Machi.

In the meantime, he started writing a report to de Corcuera on the Niji Masu debacle. "Thanks to the incompetence of Captain Avila . . ."

Chapter 45

Sausuendo

Iroha-hime and Yells-at-Bears were picnicking under an oak tree when the messenger from Niji Masu rode into Sausuendo. He slid off his horse and shook himself, sending dust flying.

"Lady Iroha, I bear bad news."

She looked up sharply. "Is there something the matter with my father?" Date Masamune was almost seventy years old.

"The Spanish have attacked Monterey Bay. Andoryu and Kawamachi have been practically destroyed. Kodachi Machi is under siege and Niji Masu just repelled an attack."

"I should go to Niji Masu and rally the troops."

"Moniwa Motonori, our *daikan*, begs that you remain here for now. But he asks, on your father's behalf, that you request assistance from the Dutch."

She agreed to do this, and ran back to the "government house" of Sausuendo to make the necessary arrangements. Fortunately, the *Miyagi Maru* was in port. Isamu, Yells-at-Bears and Bluebird were sent to the *Miyagi Maru* to alert Captain Shiroishi, and they would sail with her and Matsuoka to the Dutch Fort Maurice. Iroha-hime was aware that the size of her entourage would affect the Dutch perception of her importance.

She summoned Matsuoka Nagatoki and brought him up to speed. In the meantime, Iroha's maid was packing her necessities for the trip.

✣ ✣ ✣

"Matsuoka-san, I will be ready to board the *Miyagi Maru* in an hour," ordered Iroha-hime. "Isamu, Yells-at-Bears and Bluebird should already be on board."

"Are you sure you don't want to first send him to fetch Lord Shigehisa?" asked Matsuoka.

"Quite sure," said Iroha. "Kodachi Machi has never been under siege before. My father's samurai are well-trained, but their numbers were reduced by the shogunal commissioners, and few of them have been in combat. The last large-scale fighting in Japan was the siege of Osaka, which ended in 1615! The Spanish certainly have more artillery than we do. We need to persuade the Dutch to send their warships to Monterey Bay. To wait is painful."

"Indeed. But Lord Shigehisa is one of the few samurai in New Nippon who has been on the battlefield."

Iroha-hime shrugged. "And you are another. We'll be fine. You'll need to leave someone in charge here, of course, in our absence."

"I suggest Sanada Jiro."

"That is fine with me."

Fort Maurice (Dutch San Francisco)

Commander van Galen stared curiously at Iroha-hime. At first the Dutch had assumed that she was present merely as an interpreter for Matsuoka Nagatoki. She looked a good thirty years younger than the old samurai warrior, and, of course, she was a woman.

Her first words dispelled that notion. "I am the Lady Iroha, daughter of the grand governor of New Nippon, Date Masamune, and appointed by him as the magistrate of Sausuendo, what the up-timers would call Alviso. My late husband, Matsudaira Tadateru, was the uncle of the present shogun, Tokugawa Iemitsu."

Very well, then, van Galen thought, *a well-connected woman. No doubt sent to plead for payment of the tithe promised to the shogun.*

He was proved mistaken on that account, too. "The Japanese aided the Dutch people against your enemy, Spain, taking Manila in 1634. The Spanish have now counterattacked—against our settlements on Monterey Bay."

Van Galen's eyes widened. If the Spanish had come as far north of

New Spain as Monterey Bay, they could be expected to soon turn their attention to San Francisco Bay. Spanish scholars were certainly aware of the California Gold Rush, and the Spanish appetite for gold was insatiable.

"How long ago did this happen?"

"A Spanish squadron entered Monterey Bay earlier this month. They bombarded several villages, and lay siege to the main fortress, at Kodachi Machi—the up-timers' Santa Cruz. They bombarded Kawamachi—Castroville. And they made an unsuccessful attack on Niji Masu—Watsonville."

"How recent is your information on the situation?"

"A courier left Niji Masu about a week ago." She gestured toward the young man standing behind Nagatoki. "That one, but he does not speak Dutch."

"How many ships in this squadron?"

"Five ships, originally. Three large ones and two small ones. According to the prisoners interrogated by the *daikan* of Niji Masu, the large ones are the Manila galleon *San Raimundo*, and the war-galleons *Nuestra Señora de Loreto* and *San Diego del Milagro*. The small ones are pataches, the *Galgo* and the *San Bartolome*. However, the two pataches have not been seen recently."

"Unfortunately, I do not know any of those ships by name. What is their armament?"

Iroha-hime conversed in Japanese with the courier. "We cannot say exactly. The prisoners, unfortunately, were soldiers, not sailors."

Van Galen fought back a sigh. *Landlubbers!* "How many cannon on each ship?"

"On each of the big ships, at least thirty. But they took all, or most, of the cannon off the *San Raimundo*, to deploy against the High Fortress."

"My flagship, the *Meermin*, carries twenty-eight guns. I have three war-yachts: twenty-two, eighteen and sixteen guns. And two small yachts for scouting. What is the armament on the ship you came on?"

"The *Miyagi Maru* carries twenty guns."

"Of what weight?"

"I don't know how heavy they are."

"I mean, what weight is the shot they fire?"

Iroha-hime quickly conferred with Matsuoka Nagatoki. "They are what you would call six-pounders."

Van Galen frowned. Shot that light could kill sailors on deck, and carry away sails, but they wouldn't do much damage to the hull of a war-galleon. The heaviest guns on the *Meermin* were 20-pounders.

"Where were the Spanish ships? And how recent is your information?"

"According to the messenger, they were initially concentrated by Kodachi Machi. They off-loaded artillery and several companies of infantry, and those laid siege to the High Fortress of Kodachi Machi. Later, the two war-galleons moved off. One of them bombarded Kawamachi and then left, its subsequent whereabouts are unknown. The other landed a company to attack Niji Masu, but it was rebuffed. The High Fortress remains under siege. And our forces at Kawamachi retreated inland."

"The messenger, you said, is from Niji Masu. How does he know what was happening at Kodachi Machi and Kawamachi?"

"There is—was—a guard tower about a mile east of Kodachi Machi. It is supposed to warn Kodachi Machi of hostiles approaching from the east but Kodachi Machi sent it a semaphore message about the attack, and it sent a mounted messenger to Niji Masu. He arrived soon after Niji Masu repelled the attack by the *San Diego*. As for Kawamachi, a few of the survivors escaped to Niji Masu."

"And is Niji Masu still in communication with Kodachi Machi?"

"Intermittently. The Spanish noticed and destroyed the guard tower about a week after they first landed. So it depends on a scout being able to get in position to see a semaphore signal from the High Fortress."

"So you don't know whether Kodachi Machi is still resisting?"

"It is, according to the latest scout report. Besides, if Kodachi Machi had fallen, the Spanish would have moved all their forces against Niji Masu. As of a week ago, when the messenger left Niji Masu, they hadn't done that yet."

Van Galen pondered this intelligence. If the Spanish naval forces remained scattered, and the first galleon was taken by surprise, there was a good chance of defeating them at sea, even if the Dutch were nominally out-gunned. Why, in 1615, van Spilbergen with five ships had engaged an eight-ship Spanish squadron off the coast of Peru. The

Spanish had lost two ships and the Dutch none. And the Spanish lost four hundred fifty men to the Dutch forty.

"How many Spanish troops are involved in the siege?"

"According to my father's last semaphore report, about seven hundred men."

"And how many soldiers defend your High Fortress?"

"About two hundred. There are another hundred at Niji Masu, and there are, or were, small squads at the other settlements."

That was promising, thought van Galen. The Japanese had a good reputation throughout Asia for their martial skills, and they were behind walls of some kind. Even with three-to-one odds and an overwhelming artillery advantage, this High Fortress would be a hard nut to crack. The Spanish commander would be better off leaving a covering force by the High Fortress and annihilating the company at Niji Masu.

But even if their naval support were destroyed, seven hundred Spanish would be a bit of a problem. The crews of his ships totaled four hundred men, but he would want to hold back half of them to sail the ships and man their cannon. Even if he could unite the Spanish and Japanese troops, the Spanish would still outnumber them on land.

"And what troops do you have on board the *Miyagi Maru*?"

"Not many," said Iroha. "Just half a dozen. Plus the three samurai warriors in this room." She was referring to Nagatoki, the messenger from Niji Masu, and Isamu.

"A drop in the bucket then," said Commander van Galen. He proceeded to first explain the military uncertainties of engaging the Spanish, first at sea and then on land. And then he turned to the heart of the matter.

"I recognize that the Spanish are a common enemy. And it is possible my superiors would agree that it is worth risking the survival of this Dutch colony in order to aid you against the Spanish. But if I took the risk without their approval, they could court-martial me, imprison me, take away my property. They could even order my execution. And it would take a year to get approval."

Iroha-hime bristled. "So you intend to do nothing? Surely you see that your colony will be their next target? Even if they did not know already that you are here, they will find it out if they take Kodachi Machi!"

"You could sweeten the pot," said van Galen. "Give us a concession in return for the aid. A concession valuable enough so my superiors would agree that it was worth the risk of helping you."

"What did you have in mind?"

"You could waive the tithe. . . ."

Iroha crossed her arms. "That is beyond my authority. Beyond even my father's authority. The tithe was part of your agreement with the shogun. And the shogun, too, has been known to order the execution of those subjects who overstep their bounds."

"It appears we are at an impasse."

"How long do you think it will take you to find the gold fields? Months? Years?"

"We have the up-timers' maps and histories," said van Galen.

"So did we," said Iroha-hime. "Did you know that we sought the gold fields, too?"

Van Galen's gaze sharpened. "That was not mentioned to me. Did you find them?"

"My late husband led the expedition up the Sacramento River. Our ship was wrecked off the Golden Gate—"

"We saw the wreckage," admitted van Galen.

"But he continued on, with two longboats. "The up-time maps misled them, but eventually they found gold. Alas, most of them perished when the river flooded, but a gold nugget was brought back to me."

"I see," said van Galen.

"Lord Shigehisa, who is now at Suiden, knows where it was found."

"Suiden?"

"It is our colony on the Carquinez Strait."

"And you would have Lord Shigehisa lead my miners to the gold?"

"Lord Shigehisa, or one of the other survivors. And at Suiden and Daikoku, there are another three score samurai. That would increase our strength. Assuming they can be spared from the defense of the colony."

"Very well," said Commander van Galen. "Send the *Miyagi Maru* to collect them, and Lord Shigehisa. In the meantime, I will prepare my squadron for war."

Chapter 46

Suiden

The samurai bowed. "Lord Shigehisa, the *Miyagi Maru* has been sighted. And it is flying the *jirushi* of Iroha-hime." A *jirushi* was a battle standard, and one had been designed and adopted by Iroha-hime when she was appointed *daikan* of Sausuendo. It was not, of course, expected that she would ever be on a battlefield, but she had argued that she should have one, to show that she was in residence in Sausuendo.

The only reason for the *Miyagi Maru* to be flying that standard was that Iroha-hime was on board. But why would she be sailing to Suiden? A ceremonial visit by the grand governor's daughter would, no doubt, be appropriate once the Suiden settlement was better established, but Iroha-hime certainly had the good sense to wait for an invitation from Lord Shigehisa before coming.

The only reason Shigehisa could come up with, as he made his way to the shore, was that Sausuendo had been attacked and she had been forced to flee. By the local Indians? The Dutch? The Spanish? None of those seemed likely, but what other explanation could there be?

Or perhaps something had happened to the grand governor . . . He was, after all, almost seventy. But then wouldn't she go to Kodachi Machi, not here?

Well, the *Miyagi Maru* had already lowered a longboat. Soon he would have an answer.

✣ ✣ ✣

Iroha-hime was guided to Lord Shigehisa's command hut. "Lord Shigehisa," said Iroha-hime, "the Spanish have discovered and attacked our settlements on Monterey Bay. The High Fortress of Kodachi Machi is under siege."

"That is grim news," said Shigehisa.

"In my father's last semaphore message, as conveyed to me by the *daikan* of Niji Masu, I was to seek an alliance with the Dutch of Fort Maurice. I did so. They ask that if you can do so expeditiously, you collect samurai from here and Daikoku so the *Miyagi Maru* will be well-manned for boarding operations, and join them at Fort Maurice."

"How long ago did the attack take place?"

She gave him the details.

"How many soldiers do you have on board the *Miyagi Maru*?"

"Nine, including Matsuoka Nagatoki."

"I will take all but one samurai from each of Suiden and Daikoku. Daikoku is virtually on the way back to Fort Maurice. But I do not think that it is worth the time it would take to collect more samurai from Sausuendo, at the south end of San Francisco Bay.

"My apologies, but you will need to commandeer a fishing junk at Daikoku in order to return to Sausuendo."

"That's not a problem," said Iroha-hime. "But this colony is very new. Do we know whether the natives are friendly or hostile? Have you had time to train the villagers to defend themselves?"

"The Karkin have not been hostile so far. But they do collect shellfish from the mudflats at low tide, and we will be sowing rice there soon. We are not sure if this will lead to any conflict. As for a militia, since we arrived in December, outside of planting season, we have tried to train the villagers to handle spears, at least." He paused. "I have not been impressed with their progress, to date."

"Then should we evacuate Suiden and take them to Daikoku for the time being?"

"I would have to check with Captain Shiroishi, but I think it is feasible. It is a short trip. But if we do that, we will not have a rice crop, unless we returned very soon. And it is likely that the natives will ransack the settlement once they see it is abandoned, and we will lose most of the goods and the collected food and drinking water. The *Miyagi Maru* can't hold all the colonists and their goods. I think we must leave the colonists here and hope for the best. They do have a palisade to protect them, save when they are tending the rice crop on the mudflats, or out fishing in the Strait."

"Well, you are the daimyo of San Francisco Bay *han*. It is ultimately your decision, not mine."

"Excuse me," said Lord Shigehisa, "but if we are to take advantage of the outgoing tide, I need to start giving orders."

An hour later, Lord Shigehisa declared, "We can leave now."

"Wait," said Iroha-hime. "We need to tell the *kirishitan* why we are leaving."

"The samurai officer I am leaving behind can do that."

"It will be better received if it comes from us," said Iroha-hime. "And it serves an important political purpose. Why have the *kirishitan* been persecuted, killed, and now sent into exile in the first place? It is because of the *San Felipe* incident, neh?" In 1596, the pilot of the *San Felipe*, when asked why the Spanish came to Japan, had shown the Japanese a map of the Spanish empire and claimed that it gained its colonies by first sending in missionaries to convert the natives to Christianity and then invading with conquistadors.

"The shogunate has given New Nippon only lukewarm support because it feared that when the Spanish came there, the *kirishitan* would rebel. This is an opportunity to divorce the *kirishitan* from the Spanish."

"I see your point," said Lord Shigehisa. "You go ahead. You are the daughter of the grand governor after all. I will get things in order on the *Miyagi Maru*."

Lord Shigehisa's appointee summoned the headmen, who in turn summoned all of the villagers. They assembled in the open field surrounded by the circle of huts they had constructed. Young and old, male and female, they stared curiously at Iroha-hime.

"I am Date Iroha-hime, daughter of the grand governor, Date Masamune, and *daikan* of Sausuendo. You came here seeking a better life for you in your family, one in which you can practice your religion without fear.

"Other *kirishitan*, like you, were settled in the south, at Monterey Bay. There they have been attacked, slaughtered, by those you may have thought your friends . . . Spaniards. The Spanish don't care that you pray to the same God. No, they only care that you are occupying land they covet. They will kill many of you, and treat the survivors as they do the *indios* of New Spain . . . little better than slaves.

"We must stop them at Monterey Bay, teach them the peril of warring on *Nihonjin*. You know by now that we are taking most of the samurai from this place and Daikoku. We are sailing with our Dutch allies to avenge the slaughter and relieve the siege of Kodachi Machi.

"We know that this weakens Suiden and Daikoku, which we truly regret. But so far, the natives nearby have not been hostile. Treat them fairly, maintain a watch at your walls and gates, have your militia practice . . . and know that we will return in triumph!"

Fort Maurice

Lord Shigehisa was ushered into Commander van Galen's office at Fort Maurice.

The commander got right to the point. "So you found gold in the north."

"I did," said Lord Shigehisa. "Or, more precisely, the miners that accompanied me did."

"And you recall where they found the gold? Well enough to return there?"

"I do."

"And where would that be, roughly?"

Lord Shigehisa just smiled.

"I merely ask to determine whether it is in the area where our maps suggest that gold is to be found."

Lord Shigehisa kept smiling.

Van Galen sighed. "Well, I think we have a deal. Although I am a little worried that you will get yourself killed."

"There are other survivors of our prospecting expedition in the San Francisco Bay area," said Lord Shigehisa. "If it is my karma to perish, then Iroha-hime will make one of them available as a guide."

"Well, then, I welcome you and your fellow warriors to my command." Van Galen emphasized the final word.

✣ ✣ ✣

When the Dutch squadron was ready to depart, Lord Shigehisa ensured that at least one samurai who spoke Dutch or Portuguese was placed on board each of the Dutch ships, to improve communications between the allied forces.

Sausuendo

By the time Iroha-hime, Yells-at-Bears and Bluebird returned to Sausuendo, it was common knowledge there that the Monterey Bay colony had been attacked. The headmen approached Iroha-hime when she returned, asking whether there was any possibility of sending more samurai to Sausuendo, in case it, too, was attacked by the Spanish.

"Certainly not!" she said. "They are needed where the fighting is! And Sausuendo is in no immediate danger from the Spanish. They probably don't even know it exists! And if they did, they'd either have to make their way through the fog banks of the Golden Gate, and then come all the way south, or cross the mountains from Niji Masu and come up the valley."

The headmen continued to grumble and Iroha-hime said, "Enough! If you are still worried, your young men can volunteer for militia training. Sanada Jiro and Sanada Saburo will be happy to teach them the way of the spear. Perhaps even how to shoot."

When the headmen complained that this was too difficult, Iroha-hime summoned Yells-at-Bears, and gestured in her general direction.

"This native woman from the northern islands has had militia training! Are you saying your young men can't do it and she can? Perhaps I should call up the women of the village and have them form a militia!"

That silenced the protests.

In the *daikan*'s office that was now hers by right, Iroha-hime sat on a *zabuton* cushion, and motioned for Yells-at-Bears to do the same. Iroha's cushion, of course, was slightly higher than that of her guest's.

"Thank you for seeing me, Lady Iroha."

"It is always a pleasure to have you in my company, Yells-at-Bears. What can I do for you?"

"I think it is time for me to leave your company, my lady. We are so distant from the conflict here, and I worry about what is happening to Isamu."

"I understand. But you should not be in the war zone just because he is."

"I wish to go to Niji Masu. It fought off the Spanish assault so it is reasonably safe. And if it is attacked again, I can retreat overland. All the way here, if need be. But in Niji Masu, I can find out whether the *Miyagi Maru* has come to Monterey Bay. And how it has fared."

"I will have Sanada Saburo guide you there. And may the Christian God, and all the buddhas and kamis, protect you both."

Chapter 47

Año Nuevo Peninsula, North of Monterey Bay
March 1637

"Ship ahoy!" shouted the lookout at the bow of the *Jager*. The small *jacht* was the lead ship of the Dutch-Japanese relief squadron.

"What kind of ship?" Captain Albertszoon bellowed back.

"One of those Japanese fishing boats."

"What's it doing?"

"I think . . . I think it's heading toward us."

Had the *Jager* been alone, Captain Albertszoon would have feared that this was some sort of Spanish trick, that Spanish soldiers were hiding below the deck of the boat. But whoever skippered the fishing boat could surely see that the *Jager* had powerful companions. Any hidden Spaniards who stormed the deck of the *Jager* would soon be under the guns of the *Meermin*, right behind it.

The fishing boat came closer and they were hailed in Japanese. Fortunately, there was a samurai on board the *Jager* who spoke Dutch, and could translate for Captain Albertszoon.

The information the Japanese fishing boat had brought to Captain Albertszoon was important enough to warrant signaling a request for an "all-captains" meeting.

Commodore van Galen studied the faces of the assembled captains. "So, the fishing boat that approached us brought important news. It was out in the bay when the Spanish squadron arrived. It headed out to the open sea to evade capture and then made its way here, where the fishermen on board had friendly relations with the local Indians. With their help, they were able to hide their boat from the Spanish pataches that scouted the coast shortly after the invasion.

"The Spanish have mostly ignored the Indians. They allow them to fish, paddling their *tule* boats, quite close to the Spanish beachhead. And they trade for fish from them, to supplement their own provisions.

"At least as of last week, the Spanish had failed to take the High Fortress of Kodachi Machi."

"What of the other settlements?" asked Lord Shigehisa.

"That is not known. These Indians don't venture more than a few miles from their village. They have not gone further than where the up-timers' Aptos is located."

"And what do they say about the disposition of the Spanish forces?"

Commodore van Galen frowned. "I fear they are not knowledgeable enough about military matters to tell us much. We do know that many ship's guns were unloaded and brought inland to bombard the High Fortress."

"How often do the Spanish scout up where we are now?"

"It has been weeks since they last did so. The winds are often unfavorable to coming west from Kodachi Machi, and then north along the coast."

"Then I propose that we have an Indian take one of our people in a *tule* boat to study what the Spanish are up to."

The Ohlone boats were about ten feet long and three feet wide. They could hold as many as four people. Two natives therefore took one of the Dutch and one of the Japanese.

There was, however, a problem.

"What the fuck? You say I have to be naked?" sputtered the Dutch lieutenant.

"Yes," said the samurai, who was already shucking clothing. "The Indians are naked, and if we are close enough to shore to make good observations, we are close enough for a Spaniard with a spyglass to see if we're dressed. They may not be expecting a Dutch naval force, but they are certainly worried that the Japanese forces outside Kodachi Machi might try to sneak ashore and hit them from behind."

✣ ✣ ✣

"At ease," said Commodore van Galen.

The lieutenant (now back in uniform) relaxed, and van Galen indicated he should sit down.

"What is your report?"

"Sir, there are three Spanish ships in harbor. One appears to be a large galleon of the sort said to be used in the Manila-Acapulco trade, and the other two are war-galleons."

Van Galen grimaced. He had hoped that the Spanish galleons would still be scattered around the Bay, as was first reported. Then they could have been defeated one by one.

"Are they patrolling the coast?"

"No, sir, they are all moored about five cable lengths from the shore. Their sails are all furled or taken down altogether, so they aren't going anywhere quickly. Their bows all face east. The great galleon is the one closest to us."

Van Galen relaxed fractionally. The Spanish galleons would take time to come into action. He could take advantage of that.

"Are they armed?"

"Their gunports were closed, sir, so I do not know what they have below deck. The great galleon had guns on the fore- and sterncastles, but none in the waist. The war-galleons did have guns in the waist."

"Do they have boarding nets up?"

"No, sir."

"And are they guarded?"

"There were three guard boats in the water, each with a swivel gun in the bow, and there were lookouts on deck and in the crow's nest on the mainmast of each galleon. There were also some soldiers on the shore."

"Were the gun-crews on deck?"

"No, sir."

"Any artillery on shore?"

"None that I could see, sir."

"The Spanish are said to have a couple of pataches. Did you see them?"

"No, sir."

The Dutch attacked before sunrise, propelled by a wind from the west. The *Meermin* had raised black sails, to best take advantage of attacking from the dark side of the horizon. It surged past the great galleon. Its target was the first war-galleon, the *Loreto*.

The *Meermin* turned to port when it was equidistant from the *San Raimundo* and the *Loreto*. The *Meermin*'s guns fired as they came to bear, first those of the port bow, then the chase guns, and finally the full starboard broadside, one gun after another. The *Meermin* heaved-to, so as to keep its broadside oriented toward the *Loreto*'s stern, the weakest part of the ship.

The Dutch warship also had marksmen in the tops, and they were under orders to keep the *Loreto* from raising sails. They couldn't see the helmsman at the whipstaff, which was indoors, but moving the rudder wouldn't do the *Loreto* any good if it didn't have any sails up to give it headway. They did their best to force the *Loreto*'s crew below decks.

In the meantime, like a pack of wolves, the three *war-jachts* following the *Meermin* swarmed the great galleon, the *San Raimundo*. Their cannon were loaded with chain shot—two balls connected by a chain. The chain shot tumbled after leaving the muzzle, and the balls moved apart, stretching the six-foot chain taut. Even at close range, some projectiles missed, but others struck home, bringing down first the mizzenmast, and then the mainmast. The *San Raimundo* was immobilized.

Most of the *San Raimundo*'s crew was ashore, manning the cannon, and the musket and cannon fire from the three *war-jachts* had forced those on board to take shelter below deck. This left them effectively toothless, since the cannon assigned to the enclosed gun decks were on shore. The Spanish could poke a musket out of a gunport, and that was about it.

One of the *war-jachts* laid itself alongside the *San Raimundo*, and boarders leaped onto the *San Raimundo*.

The *Miyagi Maru*, in the meantime, bore down on the guard boats. It sank two and then destroyed the third after it was beached on the shore.

Captain Shiroishi then ordered his helmsman, "Make for the *Loreto*." He was grimly determined to make the Spanish pay a heavy price for their assault on New Nippon.

Chapter 48

On board the *Meermin*, a sailor saluted van Galen. "Your pardon, sir, but the maintop says that the third target is raising sail."

Van Galen cursed, and ordered, "Wear ship!" The turn was sluggish at first, as the *Meermin* needed to build up headway. But the *Meermin* continued to pound the *Loreto* as it came around. It sailed east, past the *Loreto*, giving the *Loreto*'s starboard flank a single broadside from the *Meermin*'s port battery as it did so. Hopefully, the *Loreto* was softened up enough for the *Miyagi Maru* and the *war-jachts* to keep it contained.

The *Miyagi Maru* came up behind the *Loreto*. The way was thus clear for the *Miyagi Maru* to send its longboat forward. It cautiously approached the *Loreto*'s stern, but the *Loreto*'s stern guns had been disabled. Coming up close, the longboat men hammered wedges between the rudder and the rudder post, disabling the helm of the *Loreto*.

The Dutch had told Lord Shigehisa that it was not a good idea to board at the stern of an enemy ship since it was likely to be higher than the waist or forecastle of the attacker. But the *Meermin*'s fire had shredded the rear of the *Loreto*, killing the officers on the quarterdeck, shattering the stern and quarter galleys, and exposing the interior of the great cabin.

The *Miyagi Maru* came up and laid its starboard bow against the *Loreto*'s stern. Grappling hooks were thrown and secured.

The samurai from San Francisco Bay had been divided into three detachments of twenty men each. The first was led by Matsuoka

Nagatoki. His samurai leaped across the gap and into the great cabin. Beyond it lay the small cabin where the helmsman operated, or tried to operate, the whipstaff. They cut him down and then broke the whipstaff for good measure.

There was a ladder here, leading up to the quarterdeck, and they posted a couple of guards at the base of the ladder and the rest cautiously ascended. The quarterdeck was damaged but negotiable. They knew that the tops of the *Loreto* had been cleared by sharpshooters on the *Miyagi Maru*, so the concern was that there might be some Spanish on the main deck, in places hidden from view from the *Miyagi Maru* by the bulk of the sterncastle.

They crawled to the front of the sterncastle. Keeping out of sight as best they could, they spotted a few Spaniards on the forecastle, but none so far on the main deck. There were a couple of swivel guns on the fore side of the sterncastle. Matsuoka Nagatoki divided his men into two fire teams. He whispered them that if they saw the Spanish making a deliberate advance on the sterncastle, one team was to respond with musket fire, and the other was take control of the swivel guns and fire upon the enemy.

Then Isamu led the second detachment across. They relieved the guards Nagatoki had placed by the ladder, and continued on to the next compartment forward, which contained the upper half of the main capstan.

The Dutch ensign accompanying the Japanese spoke up. "Ware! The next door should lead to the main deck."

On Isamu's orders, one of the Japanese took the crossbar lying in one corner of the compartment, and laid it in position across the door. It wouldn't stop a determined attack, but it would slow it down. There were loopholes on either side of the door, and the Japanese looked through one of them. "There are Spanish coming up on deck, just a few of them. They are looking all around, not just at the sterncastle." Presumably, they had seen the *Meermin* pass them and they had come up, once they were sure the *Meermin* wasn't going to cross their bow, to assess the damage.

Isamu shrugged and pointed to the cannon in their present compartment. "Aim them forward." The Japanese repositioned the cannon to point toward the bow of the ship, charged them with powder, and loaded them with hailshot. Both were conveniently at hand, presumably for defense against small boat attack. While the Spanish had not left any slow matches in the compartment, the Japanese carried matchlocks, and so they had their own means of ignition.

Isamu assigned a gun crew and told its sergeant, "Keep watch. Fire if they try to break through the door, or if they mass enough on deck to make it worth revealing ourselves to them."

Van Galen had told the Japanese leaders that the typical crew for a galleon the size of the *Loreto* or the *San Diego* was fifty or sixty men. While a war-galleon might carry one or two companies of soldiers, it seemed unlikely that they were on board at the time of the Dutch-Japanese attack. If they had been, there would have been more resistance to the boarding . . . and more bodies littering the deck.

Perhaps, Isamu mused, they had been sent off to lay siege to Kodachi Machi. And if that was correct, and half the crew had been killed or incapacitated by the *Meermin*, then once Lord Shigehisa's detachment came across, the Japanese would outnumber the defenders by two-to-one.

Isamu pointed at a hatch in the floor, and asked the Dutchman, "Where does that lead?"

"To the lower capstan compartment, so more men can be put to work hauling up the anchor. I doubt anyone's there, since they didn't man the upper compartment."

"Anything else of value down there?"

"The gun deck is forward. That would be where most of the Spanish are, I would think. Those that aren't hiding in the forecastle, at least. Aft, you would have the officers' store and the gunners' store."

"Gunners' store? Powder?"

"No. Shot, slow match, quoins, handspikes, and so forth. The powder is in the magazine, the compartment below the lower capstan compartment. It's on the orlop deck."

"Is there a hatch in the lower capstan compartment, down to the magazine?"

"No, sir. The magazine has a single door, facing forward. The powder monkeys fetch the powder and bring it up to the gun deck as needed. There's a companionway by the mainmast. That is, the part of the mainmast that is at that deck level."

"You know the layout very well," said Isamu, "considering this is an enemy ship."

"We Dutch have captured our fair share of Spanish galleons. We know their layout."

"Unfortunate that we cannot reach the magazine. If we could, we might threaten to blow up the ship if the Spanish did not surrender."

"Yes, but you'd be hard pressed to blow up the ship without blowing us up," the Dutchman protested.

Isamu shrugged.

The Dutchman apparently understood Isamu's unspoken message—*the exchange would be worth it*—as he swallowed nervously.

Chapter 49

The *San Diego del Milagro* slowly turned, presenting its starboard broadside to the *Meermin.* Commander van Galen ordered the *Meermin* to turn as well, bringing its port broadside to bear. In theory, the *San Diego*, having the heavier broadside, would have the advantage, but the Dutch gun crews were better trained.

In the exchange, the *Meermin*'s foretop sail was shredded. The *San Diego* was hulled at the waterline, but its carpenter and caulker did their best to plug the holes, and they pulled several sailors below deck to work the pumps. On both vessels, guns were overturned, and men killed or maimed by shot or splinters.

The junior officer left in command of the immobile, undermanned *San Raimundo* recognized the futility of further resistance. The Spanish thrust improvised white flags out of the main hatch and one of the gunports.

A prize crew was placed aboard the *San Raimundo*, and the surviving Spaniards were confined deep within the hold. Two of the *war-jachts* went to reinforce the *Meermin*, and the third moved to aid the *Miyagi Maru*.

Lord Shigehisa came on board the *Loreto* with the third Japanese detachment, and came forward to confer with Isamu and the Dutchman.

"Isamu, go ahead and fire on the forecastle. Otherwise, if the Spanish realize we hold the *tolda*, they may turn the forecastle guns on us!

"Also they may try to ambush us from below. Send some men down to that deck, and barricade the lower capstan compartment. And have a care. There are cannon they can turn around on that deck, too."

The command was prescient. Shortly after Isamu's men had rolled some barrels over to block the door to lower capstan compartment, they heard a thud as the Spanish rushed it. There was a temporary lull in the assault on the door, and then Isamu could hear the Spanish hacking at it with their hatchets.

When the Spanish had succeeded in creating a foot-wide opening at shoulder level, one of the samurai tossed a grenade through it. These had been provided by the Dutch. They were hollow iron balls filled with gunpowder and bearing a burning fuse the samurai had lit a moment earlier.

The grenade exploded, and the attack on the door halted abruptly, and the screaming began. A samurai moved up as close to the door as the barrels permitted, and tried to look out, but was shot in the face and dropped to the ground. Plainly, the Spanish were still out there, although it was possible that they were now thinking of preventing the Japanese from breaking out of the compartment, rather than of regaining it themselves.

"Keep to the sides of the cabin," Isamu had warned the men sent below. If the Spanish decided to fire a cannon blindly into the cabin, they most likely would aim for the center. However, they did not try, possibly out of concern for damaging the main capstan, or the whipstaff and tiller behind it.

After Isamu's men had fired several rounds into the forecastle, Shigehisa led his detachment forward, with covering fire from Nagatoki's men on the quarter deck. They took the forecastle and the main deck guns below it. However, they were unable to work their way down further, to the actual gun deck, as the hatch was secured from below.

They tried prying up the floorboards around the jeer capstan, between the mainmast and the foremast, but the Spanish fired up through the main deck to discourage this. It was not a risk-free tactic, as the splinters flew down as well as up, and holes were created through which a grenade, firepot or stinkball could be dropped.

Shigehisa ordered that a smoky fire be kindled on the main deck, near the main hatch. His purpose was to trick the Spaniards into believing that the main deck and superstructure were on fire, causing them to surrender or abandon ship. Starting a fire was easy enough, given the plentitude of wood, cordage and linen at hand, some of it laden with tar or linseed oil. Controlling the fire was trickier.

But the Japanese succeeded in evoking the desired response. Suddenly the gunport hatches opened, and the Spanish jumped out, regardless of whether they could swim or not. Some of the latter had the forethought to jump while holding a piece of wood.

Shigehisa did not know, of course, whether all the Spanish had abandoned ship. He ordered a simultaneous attack from the sterncastle, the forecastle, and on the main hatch.

There was a risk, of course, that the boarders would mistake each other for the enemy. Fortunately, while there were some tense moments, no one was killed by friendly fire. The only Spanish found to still be on board were the injured men in the lazaretto, and the surgeon caring for them. These were left where they were found, but guards were posted at the door to the lazaretto.

By this point, a Spanish infantry company had detached itself from the siege and attempted to fire on the *Miyagi Maru*. However, it was outside accurate musket range from the shore, and there were no intact boats remaining on the beach or at anchor that they could take advantage of, so they had no way to close the distance.

The Japanese restored the guns that were turned, and still operable, to their proper positions, and returned fire. This caused the infantry company to retreat.

Shigehisa and his detachment returned to the *Miyagi Maru*, while Isamu and Nagatoki remained on board the *Loreto*. Shigehisa told Captain Shiroishi that they couldn't remain where they were; it was only a matter of time before the Spanish decided to withdraw artillery from the siege and fire upon the *Miyagi Maru* and the *Loreto*.

Captain Shiroishi sent his first mate over to the *Loreto* to inspect its condition, and he returned with a grim expression on his face.

"The ship is no longer seaworthy," said the first mate. "And it would probably take a real shipyard to fix it."

"Can we at least sail it to Carmel Bay?" asked Captain Shiroishi. "There it would have some protection from the winds."

"Doubtful," said the first mate. "Sink it so the Spanish don't get its cannon back."

"But then we don't get the cannon either," complained Lord Shigehisa. "What if we sailed it along the coast a bit, to someplace where the Spanish won't see it, perhaps to Aptos?"

"It's possible if the wind doesn't strengthen too much," said the first mate. "And if the *Meermin* has driven away, sunk or captured the *San Diego*."

Sailors from *Miyagi Maru* removed the wedges, freeing the rudder of the *Loreto*, and splinted the whipstaff, so the *Loreto* could be steered. The prize crew on the *San Raimundo* got that ship jury-rigged and moving, then it and the *Miyagi Maru* attached tow lines to the *Loreto*, and hauled it out of the harbor. The little flotilla cleared the point that lay about two miles east of the mouth of the San Lorenzo River, then eased in toward the beach a few more miles along the coast. With some sails up, the *Loreto* was released and allowed to ground itself on the beach. They were now five miles from Kodachi Machi harbor. While that was no great distance, the Spanish would not have seen where they went once they passed Pleasure Point, and there were no roads, just hills, forests and streams, between Kodachi Machi and this landing site.

The beach was just a thin strip of land, overlooked by hundred-foot cliffs. While the Spanish infantry could in theory fire down from the cliff tops, reaching the beach would be an ordeal, and it was unlikely that they could descend the cliffs without making themselves quite vulnerable to the Japanese and Dutch musketeers and the captured artillery.

Chapter 50

Seeing two *war-jachts* racing to join the fight, the master of the *San Diego* decided that discretion was the better part of valor. He did not have to obtain Don Bernardino's approval for this decision, as that general was with the Peruvian companies at the siege of the High Fortress.

The problem was obtaining enough sea room to escape. His best bet was to head southwest but the *war-jachts* cut him off.

The third *war-jacht* left the *Miyagi Maru* and the two captured vessels at this point, joining the game of cat-and-mouse against the *San Diego del Milagro*.

The new odds of four-to-one proved too much for the shipmaster; he surrendered. Its crew, under orders from the Japanese, were carried, a few at a time, to the shore near the ruins of Kawamachi, where they were searched for weapons and placed under guard.

Commander van Galen and Lord Shigehisa met with Moniwa Motonori in Niji Masu to decide how to proceed. Prisoner interrogations had revealed that they didn't have to worry about the two pataches; one had been sent to Acapulco with dispatches, and the other had been lost to a sudden squall.

"It is excellent that you have neutralized the Spanish naval forces, but there is still the problem that their land forces lie between us and Kodachi Machi, and, even if we could join the soldiers in Kodachi Machi with those under my command, the Spanish would still outnumber us," said Motonori.

"Their supplies must be limited," said van Galen. "They were at sea for three months, according to the prisoners, and then they were maintaining a siege."

"True, but they would have captured some supplies when they took Middle Kodachi Machi. And they could commandeer food from nearby Indian villages, or even send out foraging parties to collect berries and acorns, hunt deer, or fish."

"How limited are the supplies in the High Fortress?" asked Lord Shigehisa.

"They've had a couple of years to stock up," said Motonori, "and there are fewer samurai there now than there were in 1634. My guess is that they could survive a year's siege."

Isamu was pleasantly surprised to find Yells-at-Bears at Niji Masu. She and Iroha-hime had found passage from Daikoku to Sausuendo. Then Yells-at-Bears had requested permission to go to Niji Masu, so she would be reunited with Isamu sooner. There was no reason for Isamu to return to Sausuendo.

At Niji Masu, Yells-at-Bears had anxiously awaited news of the naval battle. Even when it was known that the Dutch and Japanese had been victorious, it did not guarantee that Isamu had survived.

But while his superiors plotted the next move, Isamu enjoyed a reunion with Yells-at-Bears. Once they were lying relaxed in bed, Yells-at-Bears turned to Isamu and said, "I have some interesting developments to report."

He raised his eyebrows.

"While you were heading off to war, I was with Iroha-hime at Sausuendo. And after we got to know each other better, she had a confession to make."

"Yes?"

"Her father told her to study me and decide whether I was a fit wife for you."

Isamu sat up suddenly. "And did she also confide in you what she reported?"

"Of course. She wasn't going to tell me the one thing and not the other. She recommended that we be allowed to marry!"

Isamu hugged her. "That's wonderful news... But... has the grand governor received her report?"

Yells-at-Bears grimaced. "Probably not. She sent the message scroll to Niji Masu."

"So . . . it's probably still sitting there, given that the High Fortress is under siege."

"I am afraid so."

But despite this encouraging development, there were still two obvious impediments to their marriage: Date Masamune, whose approval was needed, sat in a castle under siege, and Isamu could expect to be back on the front lines shortly.

When the scope of the disaster at sea became clear, the Spanish pulled two companies and some of the artillery back from the siege line, into the ruins of Middle Kodachi Machi. They repaired its defenses.

Middle Kodachi Machi was at long range for the Dutch naval ordnance, and on elevated ground to boot. So the Dutch did not waste precious shot bombarding it. Neither did they try disembarking some of their cannon and moving them to a closer position. But they did prevent the Spanish from making any use of the coast, including fishing and shellfish gathering.

Moniwa Motonori sent about eighty samurai to harass the Spanish. These joined the sixty, including Isamu, commanded by Lord Shigehisa. They did not make any direct assault on Middle Kodachi Machi, but they attacked Spanish foraging parties.

The Japanese also sent emissaries to the Indian villages in the region. These were already hostile to the Spanish because they had killed Indians living in Lower Kodachi Machi. Now they were given some captured Spanish weapons, and they, too, reduced the ability of the Spanish to resupply.

Motonori's men restored semaphore communications with the High Fortress. The Spanish did not dare venture out to interfere, not knowing for sure how many men Motonori might have lying in ambush.

Motonori's men found Father Blanco in Sokue. They were about to send him off to the prisoner-of-war camp at Kawamachi, when they were stopped by the Japanese survivors of Middle Kodachi Machi, the village near the High Fortress.

The eldest of the survivors bowed to the officer commanding the detachment.

"Most illustrious samurai," she said, "this man protected us from slaughter by the Spanish and led us to safety here. And he is the first priest any of us have seen since we left Japan. For many of us, since 1616, when the priests were expelled. Since we came here, he has been hearing our confessions, lifting a great weight from our souls."

The officer hurriedly conferred with the other samurai. As far as he knew, there were no priests in the Monterey Bay colony, and that, it was rumored, had been a matter of deliberate, albeit unstated, policy, lest they encourage rebellion against the colony's still mostly pagan rulers. Indeed, a Franciscan brother, Francisco Tanaka, who had managed to get passage to Kodachi Machi with the "Second Fleet," had caused a religious squabble—with fellow *kirishitan*, no less—and was sent to the cinnabar mine as punishment.

To leave Father Blanco here in Sokue would be in contravention of that implicit policy. As the Chinese proverb had it, "spilt water never returns to its tray."

On the other hand, it seemed ungracious, even dishonorable, to reward his good behavior by sending him to the prisoner-of-war camp. And likely to result in these confounded women petitioning the grand governor. It was not how he wanted to come to that personage's notice.

What to do? What to do?

Ah. An elegant solution.

"Plainly, this gentleman speaks both Japanese and Spanish, neh? We need him to be our emissary to the Spanish, to call upon them to surrender before they starve to death."

And after that, thought the officer, *he will be my superior's problem.*

In due course, Father Blanco was sent, with a white flag, to Middle Kodachi Machi to convey Motonori's proposed terms.

De Corcuera refused to leave unless the Japanese returned to him the three captured ships, and allowed him to leave with all arms and armor. And that was unacceptable to the Japanese and Dutch. So there was an impasse.

De Corcuera invited Father Blanco to remain; de Corcuera could send someone else in his place to bring de Corcuera's answer back to the Japanese. But Father Blanco declined.

"I gave my word that I would return with your response," said

Father Blanco. "Also, there is work for me to be done among the Japanese."

"Work?"

"Yes, pastoral work. Some of them are Christian, but they have no priests, and thus no lawful marriages have been celebrated among them since the True Church was forced out of Japan, save for those lucky enough to find a priest in hiding. Until I came among them, they didn't even have the opportunity to confess their sins and reconcile with Our Savior."

De Corcuera gave him a disdainful look, which Father Blanco chose to ignore. He had no doubt that he was doing the right thing.

Chapter 51

Near Kodachi Machi (Santa Cruz)
May 1637

In May, the strategic situation changed: the Fourth Fleet arrived. Back in the fall of 1634, the grand governor had asked the shogunate to send the exile fleets earlier, so the new colonists could help with spring plantings. But the wheels of the shogunate bureaucracy turned slowly. Fortunately, the commissioners who had come with the Third Fleet in 1636 had seen reason.

With the Fourth Fleet came six hundred samurai. While most of them were present just to keep the *kirishitan* in line during the voyage, Lord Shigehisa was quick to realize that they shifted the numbers against the Spanish.

He had gone out in the *Miyagi Maru* to meet the Fourth Fleet and explain the situation. He made sure that the Fourth Fleet ships passed close enough to be seen by the Spanish from their vantage point in Middle Kodachi Machi. The ships were then directed to Niji Masu, Kawamachi, Andoryu and Maruya. The latter had not been attacked by the Spanish; possibly they thought to deal with it when they were on their way back to Acapulco.

After shelters were constructed for the new colonists—and the survivors among the old ones—the ships sailed back to Kodachi Machi, carrying most of the samurai. Some of the old colonists went there, too, and were given spears to carry, whether they had militia training or not. The point was to make the numerical disparity seem even greater than it really was.

A herald was sent to the Spanish camp under flag of truce.

The herald, a Dutchman who spoke fluent Spanish, cleared his throat. "By order of the grand governor of New Nippon, you are offered the following terms of surrender:

"Officers will be permitted to keep their swords. All other arms and armor will be surrendered. All cannon, shot and powder, whether on land or on board, will be surrendered.

"Your soldiers and sailors will be permitted to volunteer for service to the United Dutch East India Company, or to the province of New Nippon. Those who do not volunteer, or whose petition to volunteer is refused, will be permitted to return to Acapulco in the *San Raimundo*. The other ships will be kept as prizes."

"These are strong demands, considering we are still a viable fighting force," said de Corcuera. "And we even outnumber you."

"If that were still true, that would just mean you would starve to death sooner," said the herald. "You destroyed the fields by the coast in your rampage, and the Japanese taught you the folly of venturing inland, away from your ship's guns. Many of which are now our guns.

"And we now have the advantage of numbers. You no doubt saw the fleet that entered the Bay a week ago. Just the soldiers on that fleet outnumber your own. We can drive you up against the walls of the High Fortress, like a hammer striking an anvil.

"And we now have more cannon to array against you, and fresh supplies of shot and powder."

He paused. "You are fortunate that the grand governor has not demanded that your soldiers be put to hard labor, rebuilding the settlements they destroyed, before they are allowed to leave. He had advisors that thought that would be just. For that matter, some thought you should be given no terms and no quarter.

"Oh, there is one more thing. All maps and logbooks will be surrendered."

"How will we find our way home?" asked de Corcuera.

"Follow the coast," said the herald. "The winds and currents will take you to Acapulco, where you belong."

"With these terms, I am not sure that it is wise for me to return."

The herald shrugged.

✣ ✣ ✣

De Corcuera called a council to discuss the terms. It was understood by all attending that there was really no alternative to accepting the terms. Rather, the purpose of the council was to diffuse the responsibility for the decision. After some posturing by members of the council—along the lines of, "it wasn't my fault"—the council unanimously authorized de Corcuera to surrender.

About a third of the sailors of the Armada were foreigners—Portuguese, Italians, Greeks, Flemings, Germans, Irish and even French and English. A good number of these decided that they were better off enlisting with the Japanese than returning to Acapulco.

Father Blanco also decided that it was his duty to remain. Despite the general and understandable hostility of the Japanese colonists toward the Spanish, the women of Middle Kodachi Machi spoke once again in his favor.

So, too, did the *kirishitan* religious leaders, who were all lay catechists or baptizers. As they told David Date, "We can baptize infants if no priest is available, but we can't give communion, grant penance, anoint the sick, or solemnize a marriage."

Back in Japan, after the persecutions began, whenever a missionary reached a secret community of Christians, he would perfect the marriages that were not yet sacramentally valid, and give communion. Of course, the number of missionaries in Japan had steadily dwindled since 1614, when the priests were officially expelled, so there was plenty of work for Father Blanco to do in New Nippon.

David Date gave permission for Father Blanco to stay, but assigned an escort to him. Officially, the escort's purpose was to protect Father Blanco from injury from colonists who had been harmed by the Spanish. But the escort was also expected to make sure that Father Blanco did not conspire against the Japanese authorities.

The rest of the Spanish were transferred to the stripped-down *San Raimundo*. It limped off to sea the following day.

Chapter 52

Isamu led his detachment into the High Fortress. He received a summons to meet with David Date in the audience chamber.

"It has been kept a secret, for the sake of morale," said David, "but my father is in poor health. He is old, and he spent many days and nights out on the battlements, even in the rain, to encourage his men. His physician is not sure how much longer he will live."

"I am sorry to hear that," said Isamu. "I will pray to Yakushi Nyorai for his recovery."

"Thank you," said David. "While you have not mentioned it, I know you are concerned about the status of your petition for approval of marriage. It has been granted, and he thanks you for your service."

Isamu gave him the full ninety-degree bow, and stammered, "From the temple to the village." It was the custom for villagers to bring gifts to their local temple twice a year. If the temple gave gifts to the villagers, that would be very unusual. Isamu's meaning was that the gift given by the grand governor was far greater in value than what Isamu had provided.

Commander van Galen also received an invitation to the audience chamber.

"On my father's behalf," said David Date, "I thank you once again for your aid to New Nippon."

Commander van Galen bowed slightly. "We are allies against a common enemy, let us never forget that."

"I understand that Lord Shigehisa and my sister Iroha-hime made a promise to you. Lord Shigehisa is prepared to sail back with you to Fort Maurice as soon as you are finished with repairing battle damage and reprovisioning."

"That is good of him," said Commander van Galen. "But I know that he is needed here, too. It would be fine if he were to come to Fort Maurice in, say, August. But I do have a favor to ask."

"What would that be?"

"The loan of the *San Diego del Milagro*!"

"Of course! The warships of the Fourth Fleet can protect Monterey Bay until you bring it back. But what do you intend to do with the *San Diego*?"

Van Galen smiled. "The *Armada del Mar del Sur* is now destroyed. That means that the viceroy of Peru has no warships to carry silver to Panama. And if we leave now, there is a good chance we will reach Panama before this year's silver does."

It was David Date's turn to smile. "I see. So that is why you did not want to linger for the celebration I—I mean my father—has ordered for next week." While several of the Monterey Bay settlements had suffered destruction of homes, crops and fishing boats, much had been brought over by the Fourth Fleet, and David Date had thought the celebration of the victory to be good for morale.

"I wish you a most profitable voyage south!" added David.

Yells-at-Bears and Bluebird arrived at the High Fortress a week later, and Isamu brought his fiancée up-to-date.

"So just how do we get married? Do we need to go before a Shinto priest? The only one on Texada is Tanaka, but he is a priest of Kanayago-kami, who doesn't even like women! Is there a Shinto priest here, or do we call upon Father Blanco?"

"Don't worry about a priest," said Isamu. "Back in Japan, marriage is a household affair. The family members lead the ritual; priests are not involved."

"Well, isn't that a problem? You have no relatives on Texada."

"The letter David Date gave me, from the grand governor, acknowledged that. It authorizes Haru to act on their behalf."

"So Haru will represent both our families?"

"Yes, but of course you can invite your sister and brother-and-law to come."

Yells-at-Bears thought about this. "Of course they should. And my friends Arinobu and Umako from the smithy, and Jusuke, Dembei, Saichi and Fudenojo from the *Ieyasu Maru*, and—" She broke off. "I will make a list. . . ."

Isamu's and Yells-at-Bears' belongings, under Bluebird's anxious supervision, were taken down to the *Unagi Maru*. It would leave in consort with the *Miyagi Maru*, which was returning, with Lord Shigehisa, to San Francisco Bay. But the *Unagi Maru* would make the longer journey to Texada.

Before Isamu and Yells-at-Bears left Kodachi Machi, they had final meetings with both Chiyo-hime and David Date. Chiyo-hime gave Yells-at-Bears a small self-portrait. "Display it at your wedding ceremony, and that way I will be there, in spirit, to witness it!" She also gave Yells-at-Bears some clothing for her trousseau.

Isamu's meeting with David Date was less emotional. "Enjoy your wedding, but be ready to come back to work soon after," said David Date.

"Am I confirmed as *daikan* of Texada?" asked Isamu hopefully.

"I think there are bigger things in store for you," said David. "The commissioners were talking about replacing the *kirishitan* on Texada with Buddhists. I don't know whether my brother Tadamune was able to change their mind. If not, then you will have to lead the *kirishitan* somewhere else. And with all the damage to the Monterey Bay settlements, we want to send some of the new colonists up north, to lessen the economic strain here.

"My father is thinking of having you found and lead a new colony at what the up-time maps call Vancouver."

"What's there?" asked Isamu.

"If the up-time sources are to be relied on, zinc, copper, something called 'nickel,' and, up the Fraser River, gold."

"Have you spoken to Yells-at-Bears about the tribes in that area?"

"Chiyo-hime did. They are the Sto:lo, and they speak a language similar to her native Halkomelem."

✣ ✣ ✣

Captain Araki had given Isamu and Yells-at-Bears the privilege of the quarterdeck, and they stood by the taffrail as Captain Araki, his back to them, shouted down to his sailors, "Cast off!"

Bluebird was at the bow, watching dolphins leaping in front of the *Unagi Maru*. Isamu put his arm around Yells-at-Bears, and squeezed her for an instant, while the sailors were preoccupied with the departure. "Time to go home," he said.

Cast of Characters

fi d-t, Fictional Down-Timer
hi d-t, Historical Down-timer
OTL, old timeline
Only named characters are listed.

Characters from the **Ieyasu Maru**

Deguchi Masaru (fi d-t), samurai, and a recent Date hire

Dembei (fi d-t), Japanese castaway on Vancouver Island rescued in *1636: Seas of Fortune* by the *Ieyasu Maru*; originally from Osaka

Fudenojo (fi d-t), second mate, and commander of the sailors assigned to the exploration party under Isamu

Goemon (fi d-t), translator of Kwak'wala to Japanese (another rescued Japanese castaway)

Hosoya Yoritaki (fi d-t), samurai marine commander

Jusuke (fi d-t), Japanese castaway on Vancouver island, rescued in *1636: Seas of Fortune* by the *Ieyasu Maru*; originally from Osaka

Morimoto (fi d-t), the carpenter's mate

Oyamada Isamu (fi d-t), samurai from an old Date retainer family

Saichi (fi d-t), assistant mining engineer and prospector, and foreman of the miners assigned to the exploration party under Isamu

Speaker-to-Strangers (fi d-t), Indian, translator (ex-slave purchased by Japanese in *1636: Seas of Fortune*)

"Tenjiku" ("India") Tokubei (hi d-t), first mate and supercargo

Yamada Haruno (fi d-t), captain of the *Ieyasu Maru*

Yells-at-Bears (fi d-t), Snuneymuxw (Nanaimo) Indian woman, translator for the party (ex-slave purchased by Japanese in *1636: Seas of Fortune*)

Zensuke (fi d-t), Fudenojo's lieutenant

Characters from the **Iemitsu Maru**

Arinobu (fi d-t), smith contracted to go to Texada Island

Daichi (fi d-t), smelter "fireman"

Fukuzawa (fi d-t), captain

Fukuhei (fi d-t), headman of the fishermen

Harunobu (fi d-t), son of Arinobu and Umako

Hidezo (fi d-t), headman of the farmers

Imoji (fi d-t), iron caster

Jiro (fi d-t), son of Naoki and Moriko

Kaito (fi d-t), a teenager

Moriko (fi d-t), Naoki's wife

Naoki (fi d-t), *yamako* (chief charcoal burner)

Tanaka (fi d-t), junior priest of Kanayago-kami

Taro (fi d-t), son of Naoki and Moriko

Terasaka Haru (fi d-t), samurai in Date Masamune's service, previously assigned to the samurai guard of the *Ieyasu Maru*, but later the escort for the ironworkers

Tetsue (fi d-t), *murage* (smelter supervisor)

Umako (fi d-t), Arinobu's wife

Wataru (fi d-t), farmer, friend of Hidezo

Characters from the Unagi Maru, Tohoku Maru, *and* Miyagi Maru

Araki (fi d-t), captain of the *Unagi Maru*

Miyoshi (fi d-t), captain of the *Tohoku Maru*

Shiroishi (fi d-t), captain of the *Miyagi Maru*

Torakichi (fi d-t), first mate of the *Unagi Maru*, formerly third mate on the *Ieyasu Maru*

Other Japanese in the Monterey Bay and San Francisco Bay Regions

Daidoji Shigehisa (hi d-t), former commander of the guard of Lord Matsudaira, Iroha-hime's now deceased husband; later appointed daimyo, San Francisco Bay *han*

Date Chiyo-hime (fi d-t), Date Masamune's daughter, born after 1613, possibly to a favored concubine

Date Iroha-hime (hi d-t, 1594–OTL 1661), eldest daughter of Date Masamune

Date Masamune (hi d-t, 1567–OTL 1636), grand governor of New Nippon

Date Munesane (hi d-t, 1613–OTL 1665), baptized "David Date" in NTL 1634, Masamune's sixth son

Heishiro (fi d-t), former captain of Japanese fishing vessel that was carried across the Pacific and wrecked on Vancouver Island; he was rescued by the *Ieyasu Maru* and brought to the Monterey Bay area

Iwakushu (fi d-t), "Singer to Rocks," pseudonym of mining engineer on *Ieyasu Maru* during its first trip across the Pacific, subsequently residing in Monterey Bay colony

Katakura Shigetsuna (hi d-t, 1585–OTL 1659), chief counsellor to Date Masamune

Koya (fi d-t), Iroha-hime's maid

Matsuoka Nagatoki (hi d-t, 1564–OTL 1644), senior guardsman

Moniwa Motonori (fi d-t), *daikan* of Niji Masu

Sanada Jiro (fi d-t), guardsman

Sakai Kuroemon (fi d-t), samurai commander of battery defending Andoryu

Sanada Saburo (fi d-t), guardsman

Yamaguchi Takuma (fi d-t), Japanese Christian from Nagasaki; formerly a merchant; given administrative duties in New Nippon

Japanese in the Philippines

Kimura, Francisco (fi d-t), a Japanese-Christian living in Manila

Kimura, Juan (fi d-t), his son

Tla'amin (Sliammon) Indians

Calm-Water (fi d-t), the chief of Wide-River-Bed

Fast-Drummer (fi d-t)

Red-Feet (fi d-t)

Splitter-of-Waves (fi d-t)

Standing-Bear (fi d-t), an elder of Wide-River-Bed and rival to Calm-Water

Shishalh (Sechelt) Indians

Chickadee (fi d-t), Yells-at-Bear's sister (formerly known as Salmon-Berry)

Holds-a-Bundle (fi d-t), the chief at Kalpilin

Little-Raccoon (fi d-t), his grandnephew

Tall-Post (fi d-t), Chickadee's husband

Snuneymuxw (Nanaimo) Indians

Bluebird (fi d-t), a slave

Four-Fingers (fi d-t), Yells-at-Bears' father

Rain (fi d-t), a chiefly class woman

Spaniards

Arquin, Francisco Baptista (fi d-t), boatswain, *San Raimundo*

Atondo (fi d-t), captain of the galleon *Concepción* (*almirante*)

Avila (fi d-t), captain of marines on the *San Diego*

Blanco, Father Pedro (fi d-t), Jesuit, chaplain, *San Raimundo*

Castellete, Geronimo (hi d-t), *calificador* (Mexico City)

de Arce, Pedro (hi d-t), bishop of Cebu

de Aro, Diego (fi d-t), quartermaster's mate, later boatswain, *San Raimundo*

de Bolaza, Antonio (fi d-t), captain of seamen and infantry, *San Raimundo*

de Cabrera Bobadilla Cerda y Mendoza, Luis Jerónimo Fernández (hi d-t), count of Chinchón, viceroy of Peru

de Corcuera y Gaviria, Sebastián Hurtado (hi d-t), captain-general of the *Armada de Retribución* (1636)

de Mendoza y Larrea, Don Bernardino Hurtado (hi d-t), general of the *Armada del Mar del Sur*

de Molina, Juan (fi d-t), water constable, *San Raimundo*

de Molina, Juan Andres (fi d-t), shipmaster, *San Raimundo*

de Morillo, Gabriel (hi d-t), Franciscan, *calificador* (Mexico City)

de Noval, Juan (hi d-t), Dominican, master *calificador* (Mexico City)

de Polduian, Gerardo (fi d-t), steward, *San Raimundo*

de Sotomayor, Enrique Enriquez (hi d-t), the president of the Audiencia de Panama and governor of the Province of Tierra Firme, the Spanish Main

del Agulla, Guillermo (fi d-t), pilot major, *San Raimundo*

Díez de Aux de Armendáriz, Lope (hi d-t), marquess of Cadareyta, viceroy of New Spain (Mexico)

Enrique, common sailor, *San Raimundo*

Ernesto, common sailor, *San Raimundo*

Escalante (fi d-t), merchant passenger on the *San Raimundo*

de Garcia, Antonio (fi d-t), ensign, *San Raimundo*

Jose, common sailor, *San Raimundo*

Mendoza (fi d-t), captain-general of the galleon *San Raimundo*

Philip IV (hi d-t), king

Soltero, Doctor Bartolomé González (hi d-t), Inquisitor (Mexico City)

> **Note:** The commander of a Spanish flotilla is the "general" (or sometimes captain-general) and his flagship is the *capitana*. The second-in-command is the "admiral" and his flagship is the *almirante*. Typically, both have military rather than nautical backgrounds.
>
> Also, on an early seventeenth-century Spanish merchant galleon like the *San Raimundo*, the shipmaster is merely the economic administrator, and indeed may be a part-owner, and the pilot is responsible for navigation. In contrast, in period English naval practice, the master ("sailing master") sailed the ship.
>
> The author has deliberately used the modern term "port" for the left side of the ship, rather than the contemporary (but unfamiliar and confusing) "larboard" or "backboard."

Dutch in San Francisco Bay

Albertszoon (fi d-t), captain of the *jacht Jager*

van Galen, Commodore Cornelis (fi d-t), of the *Meermin* (28 guns)

Notes on Personal Names

North American Indians

We do not have any documentation as to names used by any of the Indian groups in the early seventeenth century. In addition, in Pacific Northwest culture, formal names were considered inheritable "property." And finally, I had enough readers complain about having trouble remembering the Japanese names that I thought it imprudent to compound the problem several-fold by introducing Indian names.

Hence, unless otherwise stated, all of the Indian names given in this novel are English epithets (such as "Yells-at-Bears"). Thus, they should be construed to be English translations of nicknames for the Indians in question. I assume the nicknames are based on a significant incident in the person's life, or some noteworthy attribute. While it is not unusual for nicknames to poke fun at the person—the Romans had Brutus (stupid), Dentatus (toothy), Bibulus (drunk), Rufus (red haired—unlucky) and Naso (big nose)—I have avoided these as the Indians have had enough grief. . . .

Japanese

The Japanese put the surname before the given name. Strictly speaking, only those of the samurai class should have surnames, with very few exceptions (e.g. swordsmiths), but it wasn't unheard of for a commoner to informally adopt one.

Vancouver Island and Vicinity First Nations and Linguistic Groups

The boldfaced names are the ones used in this novel. The names generally define groups (and subgroups) of peoples with a common language and culture. Subgroups are indicated with a • symbol in the first column. The groups and subgroups are not political entities; there is no paramount chief. Hence, while they may be referred to in some sources as "nations" or "tribes" that does not imply common leadership.

The "principal geographic area" for each group and subgroup is stated, but bear in mind that tribal territories were fluid, often overlapping, and not well documented even post-contact. For the early seventeenth century, they are completely speculative.

Prior Academic Name	Indigenous Name	Principal Geographic Area
Kwakiutl	**Kwakwaka'wakw** means "speakers of Kwak'wala")	northern and northeastern Vancouver
•Kwakiutl	K'wagu'l	around modern Fort Rupert, northeast coast of Vancouver Island
•Quatsino	Gwat'sinux	around modern Winter Harbour, northwest coast of Vancouver Island
•Nakomgilisala		Cape Scott, northern Vancouver Island
•Lekwiltok (a.k.a. Southern Kwakiutl; Euclataw)	**Laich-kwil-tach** Ligwilda'xw	somewhere on the shores of the Johnstone Strait; they moved into the Campbell River area in the early nineteenth century

Prior Academic Name	Indigenous Name	Principal Geographic Area
Nootka	**Nuu-chah-nulth** ("along the mountains and the sea"). Also known as the "Westcoast People."	west coast of Vancouver Island, but not the northern or southern ends
•	**Mowachaht**	live primarily adjacent to waterways communicating with Nootka Sound
Coast Salish		southeastern Vancouver Island and on the mainland opposite it
•Nanaimo	**Snuneymuxw** (language is Halkomelem)	primarily on southeast Vancouver Island, from Parksville to Chemainus
•Island Comox	K'omoks	primarily on east coast of Vancouver island, from Salmon River to Parksville
•Pentlatch (Puntledge)	Pentl'ets (extinct language)	centered on lower Puntledge River and Courtenay; absorbed by Island Comox
•Sliammon	**Tla'amin**	primarily on mainland, from Bliss Landing to Saltery Bay; centered on Powell River
•Homalco	Xwémalhkwu	primarily on the mainland, around Bute Inlet and nearby islands

Prior Academic Name	Indigenous Name	Principal Geographic Area
•**Klahoose**		primarily on the mainland, around Toba Inlet and nearby islands
•Sechelt	**Shishalh**	primarily on mainland between Jervis and Sechelt Inlets
Haida	**Haida**	Queen Charlotte Islands

Coastal Central California Native Americans

In this novel, the Native American cultural group living in the San Francisco Bay and Monterey Bay areas is called, generically, the "Ohlone." Scholars further divide them into language groups, including the Karkin (Carquinez Strait area), Chochenyo (East San Francisco Bay), Ramaytush (the San Francisco peninsula), Tamyen (Santa Clara valley), Awaswas (Santa Cruz Mountains and adjacent coast), Mutsun (northeast Monterey Bay), and Rumsen (southeast Monterey Bay). The Uqpi speak the Awaswas language.

As with their Canadian counterparts, these aren't "nations" in the European sense of the term.

Notes on Geographic Names

The Japanese colonists have given names to their various settlements and discoveries, and some of these also have modern equivalents or native names.

Texada Island

Iron Landing (near but east of Welcome Bay)

Quarry #1 (near the Prescott Mine)

Camp Double Six (just west of the Paxton Mine)

Rattling Bird Lake (Paxton Lake)

Marsh Berry Lake (Cranby Lake, once known as Cranberry Lake)

Marsh Berry Creek (leads from Cranby Lake to Gillies Bay)

Sandy Bottom Bay (Gillies Bay; Tla'amin **ʔi:səm** "Ee sum," "Clear-Sandy-Bottom")

Burnt Village (Shelter Point archaeological site; the burning was artistic license)

Creek discovered by Masaru (this is the creek leading into Davis Bay)

Angry Geese Lake (Myrtle Lake)

Gosling Lake (modern name not known, north of Myrtle Lake. A topographic map suggests that it is intermittent and in the dry season is just Myrtle Creek)

Gosling Creek (see above. Modern maps consider it a tributary of Rumbottle Creek, which it joins north of Myrtle Lake)

Sentinel Island (the island off Shelter Point; Tla'amin **k^{W}θaysqɛn** "Kwoo thays qen," meaning "small island)

Welcome House and Iron Haven (south of the Lake Mine)

Sea Hawk Village (near the modern Retreat Motel, on Gillies Bay Road)

Bucktooth Dam Creek (modern name not known; parallels but a little south of School Road, runs into Marsh Berry Creek)

Big Fern Run (modern name not known; last tributary of Bucktooth Dam Creek)

Bucktooth Dam Village (at confluence of Big Fern Run and Bucktooth Dam Creek)

West Dragon Bay (Limekiln Bay; Tla'amin **ʔayajuθəm**, meaning unknown)

East Dragon Bay (Blubber Bay; Tla'amin **t̓atlaχ^{W}nač**, TatlaXw nach, meaning "Water-Swirls-Around")

Vancouver Island & Vicinity

Kahkaykay (modern Grace Harbor; "Kahkaykay" on a 1916 Royal Commission map; Tla'amin **q̓aq̓ɛyq̓ay**, "Qah Qeh qay" meaning "Camp-Overnight)

Kalpilin (modern Pender Harbour; Sichalh village)

Kwalsarwahl (Snuneymuxw summer village near mouth of Nanaimo River)

Pointed-Nose (Harwood Island; Tla'amin **ʔagayqsən**, "Ah gyk sun," meaning "Pointed-Nose")

Sah Yah Yin (Texada Island; Tla'amin **sayayın** meaning "the end of something")

Wide-River-Bed (Tla'amin **tískw'et**, Wide-River-Bed. The village was on the southeast side of the mouth of the Powell River.)

Yuquot (Friendly Cove; "where the winds blow from many directions"; summer village of Mowachaht on Nootka Island, off west coast of Vancouver Island)

San Francisco and Monterey Bays

Andoryu (Monterey)

Daikoku (Leona Heights)

Fort Maurice (Fort Mason, San Francisco)

Kawamachi (near Castroville)

Kodachi Machi (Santa Cruz)

Maruya (Carmel)

Niji Masu (near Watsonville)

Sausendo (Alviso)

Suiden (Glencove)